LAT

Kampung Boy

Dedicated to my mum, Cik Norazian, and dad, Mohd. Khalid.

I cannot truly recall, of course, what happened in the first few years of my life. It was not until I had learned to speak and been able to conduct conversation with my mother that I found out about my early days.

I was born in a kampung in the heart of the world's largest tin-mining district—the Kinta Valley in Perak.

According to my mother, I was born at about ten o'clock on a Monday morning in our house. The task of delivering me into this world fell to my own grandmother. She had been the official midwife in the kampung for many years. I was Mum's first child. My father's memory of this day was also quite clear. According to him, he was under the house waiting anxiously when my grandmother called:
"Come and cradle your son!"

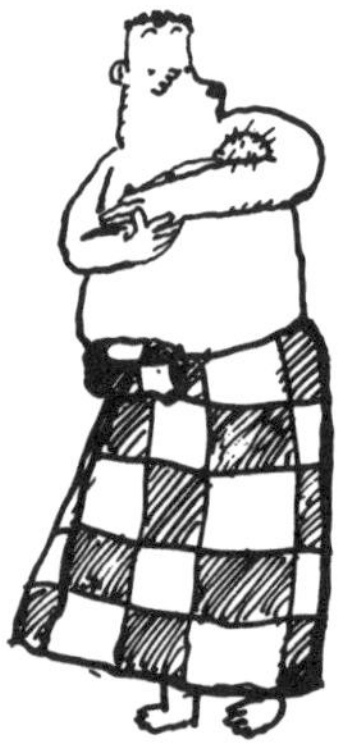

Minutes later dad was standing in the anjung (lounge) with me in his arms. Then he whispered the muezzin's call softly in my ears just as any good Muslim father would do to his newly born child.

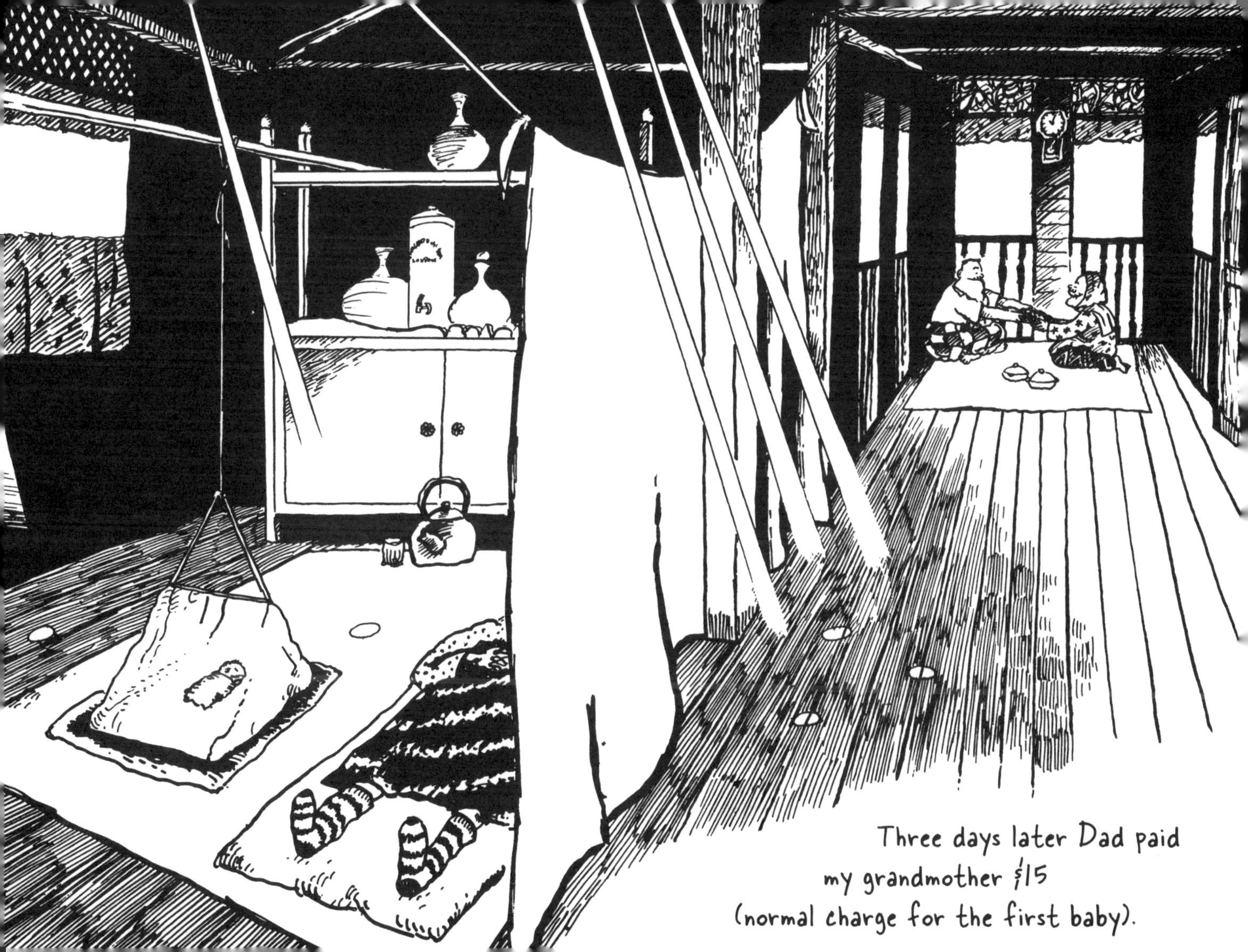
Three days later Dad paid
my grandmother $15
(normal charge for the first baby).

Dad also presented my grandmother
with the following items:

A roast chicken
A plate of yellow rice
A batik sarong.

These gifts were just a formality.
On the 45th day, the day of my mother's
complete recovery from her "pantang" (taboo)
period, I underwent some formalities myself.
It was the "adat cukur kepala" (my hair-
shaving ceremony). Quite an affair, I must
say. Dad invited neighbors and relatives. It
was on this day that, just as the sun was
rising, I was brought out of the house for the
first time to feel the air outside.

The first part of this ceremony was of
course the shaving. Grandma (who else?) did
it. Then, bald and naked, I was carried to the
front yard where, witnessed by more than a
dozen well-wishers, she gave me a bath.

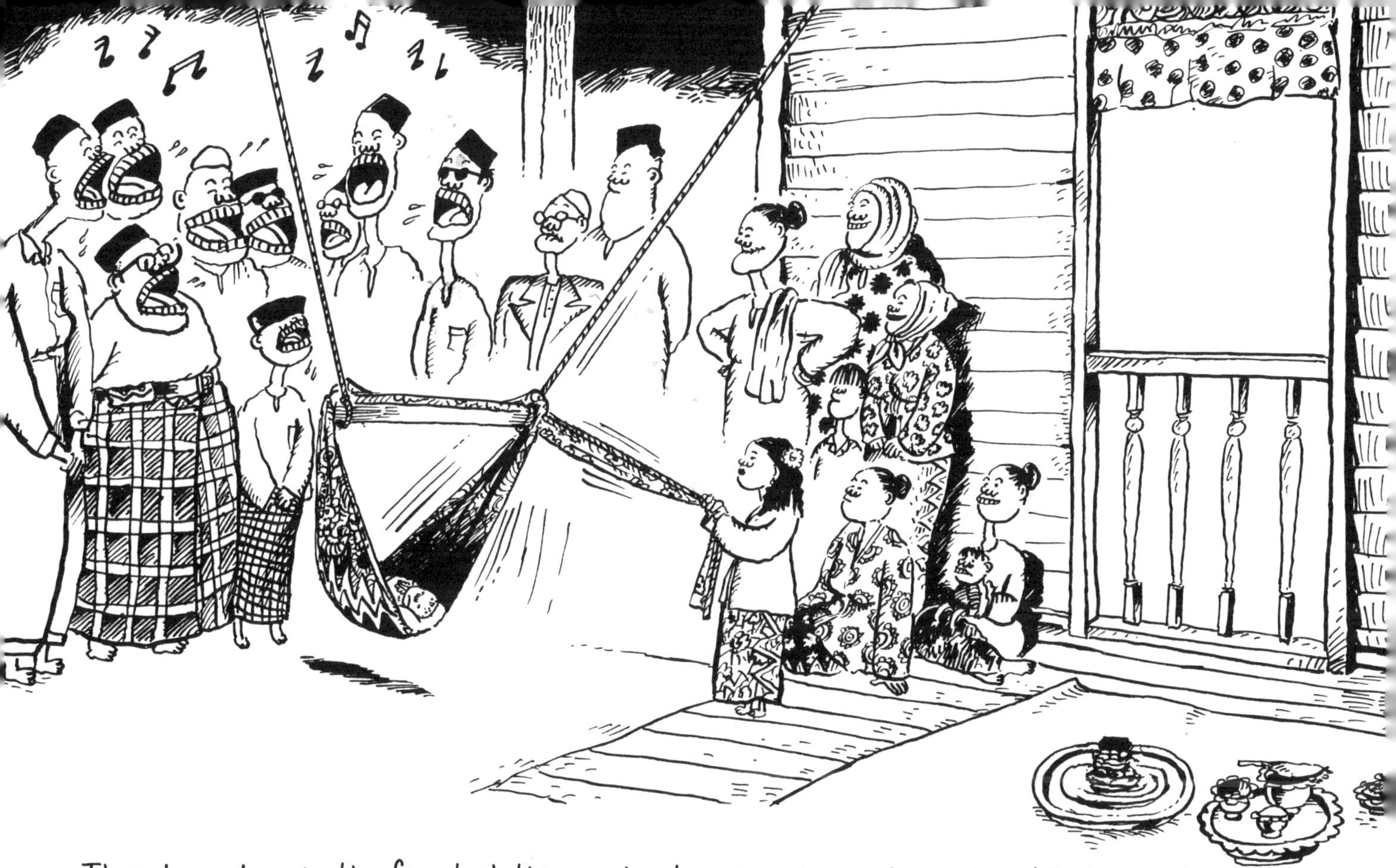

They dressed me in the finest clothing and put me in a hammock, in which I had never been before. I must have felt very comfortable. Just as the hammock was swaying slowly, a group of the guests began chanting the sacred lyrics of the "Marhaban" (a song about the Prophet).

Before long I dozed off. Then the gathering adjourned for some refreshments my folks had for them.

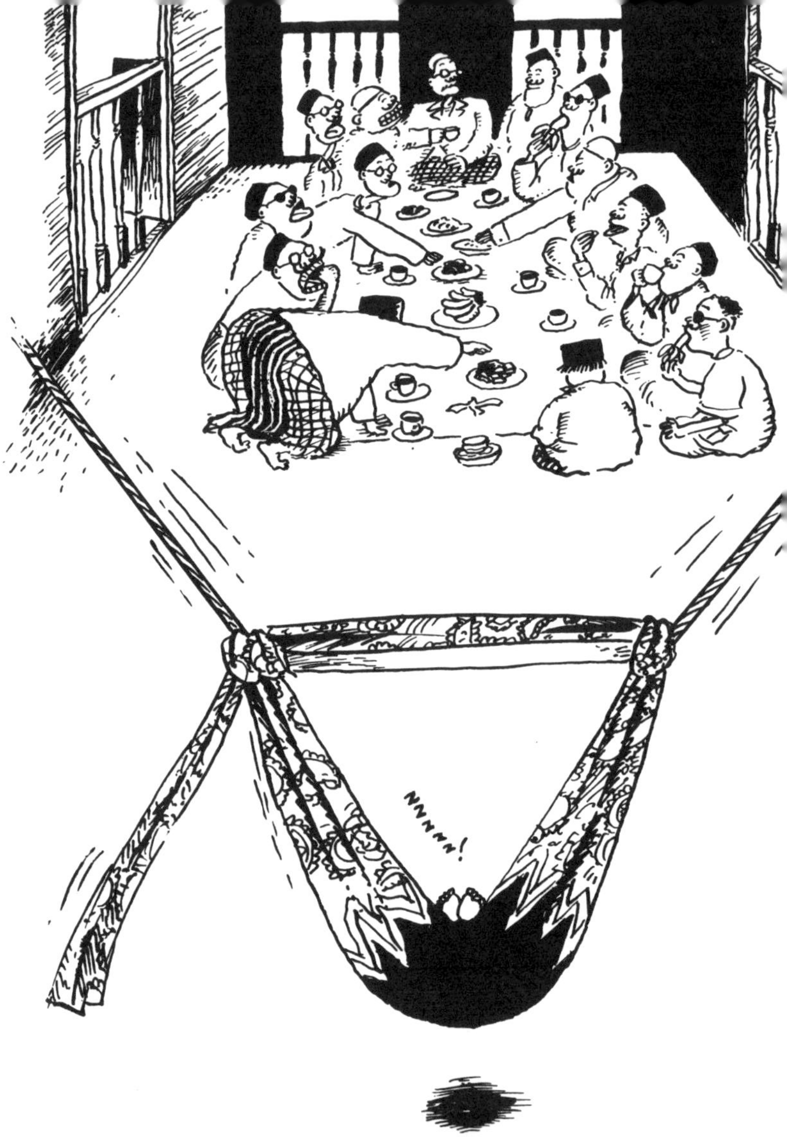
ZZZZZ!

And so life began with
a mother's love...

Oh! How affectionately and tenderly Mum
cared for me. Everyday she would wrap up
my whole body in the swaddling clothes...

ptooi!

Then she'd stuff
me with porridge.

As I grew bigger, I learned to crawl. By this time I had already started showing my own physical features as an individual. I had a full, round face and although the bridge of my nose was quite low I had no complaints because, as I discovered later, none of my ancestors had a high nose bridge.

However, Mum's description of my looks was rather vague and unsatisfying. She said I looked sweet whenever I smiled but on the whole I was by no means a beauty.

I would crawl all around the house all day long. Sometimes I'd play with the spots of sunlight that fell on the floor.

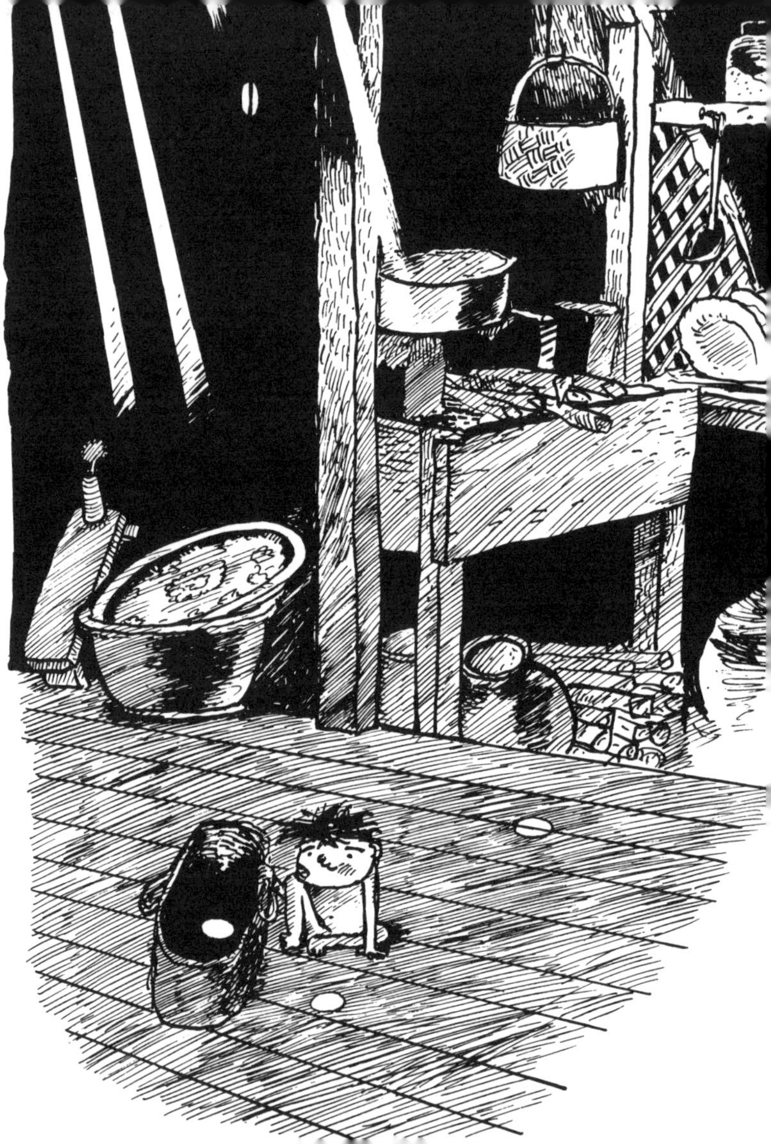

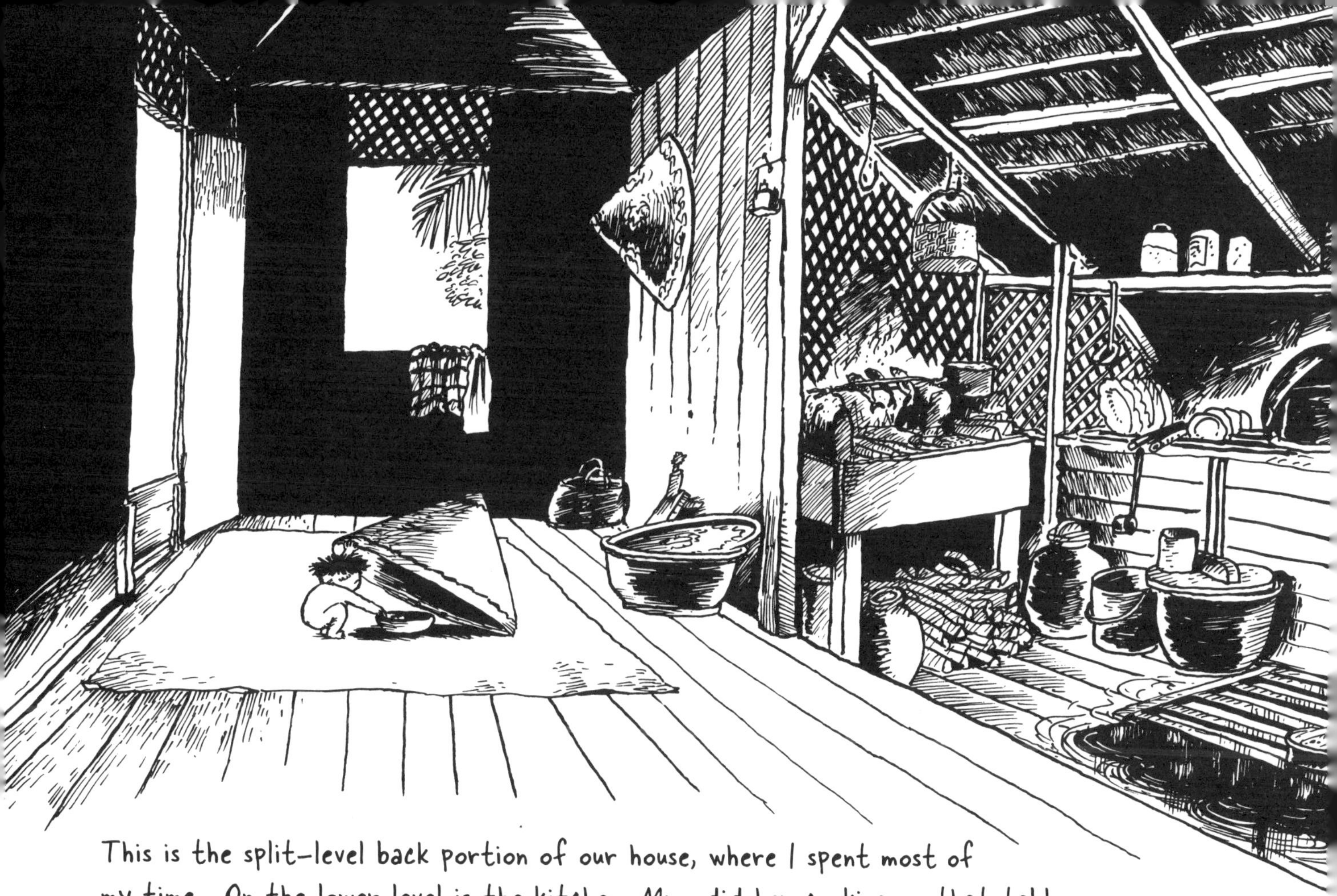

This is the split-level back portion of our house, where I spent most of my time. On the lower level is the kitchen. Mum did her cooking on that table.

It was also in the kitchen that Mum bathed me, since I was too young to go to the river.

From the window in the front part of the house I could see a rubber estate.

It was from the direction of this estate that a distant roaring sound came and never seemed to stop. It was the sound of a tin dredge, about which I shall tell you more later in this book.

I loved to look out of the window because that was the closest I could get to the surroundings outside the house. I was not allowed to go outside yet.

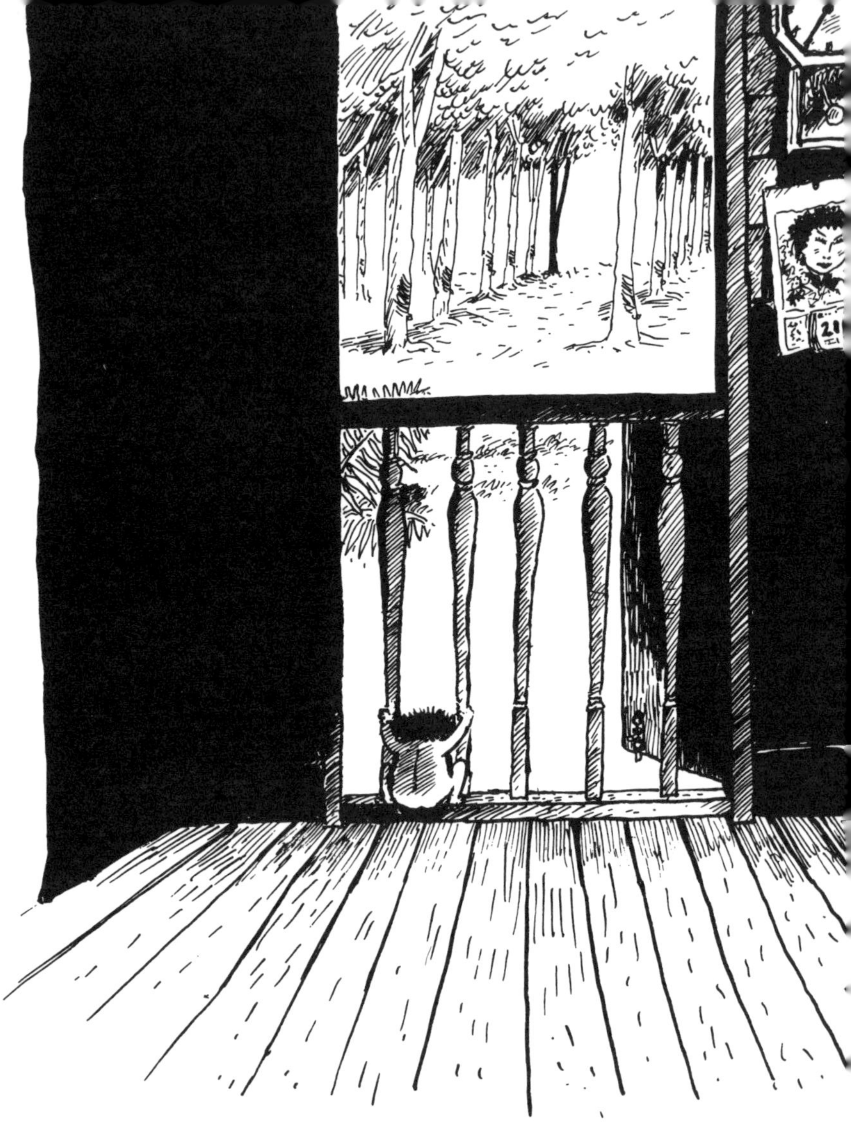

Sometimes I stuck my head out too far...

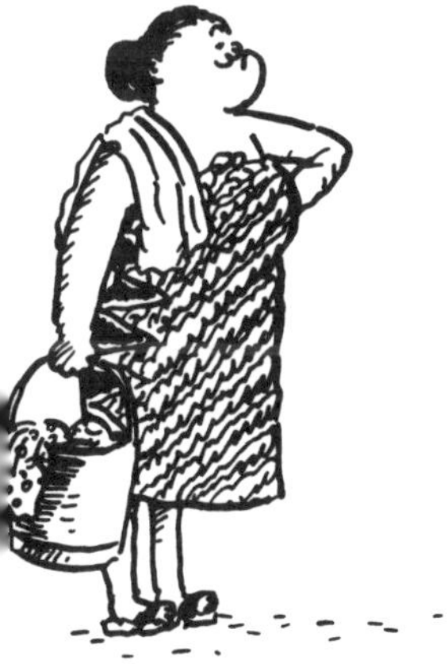

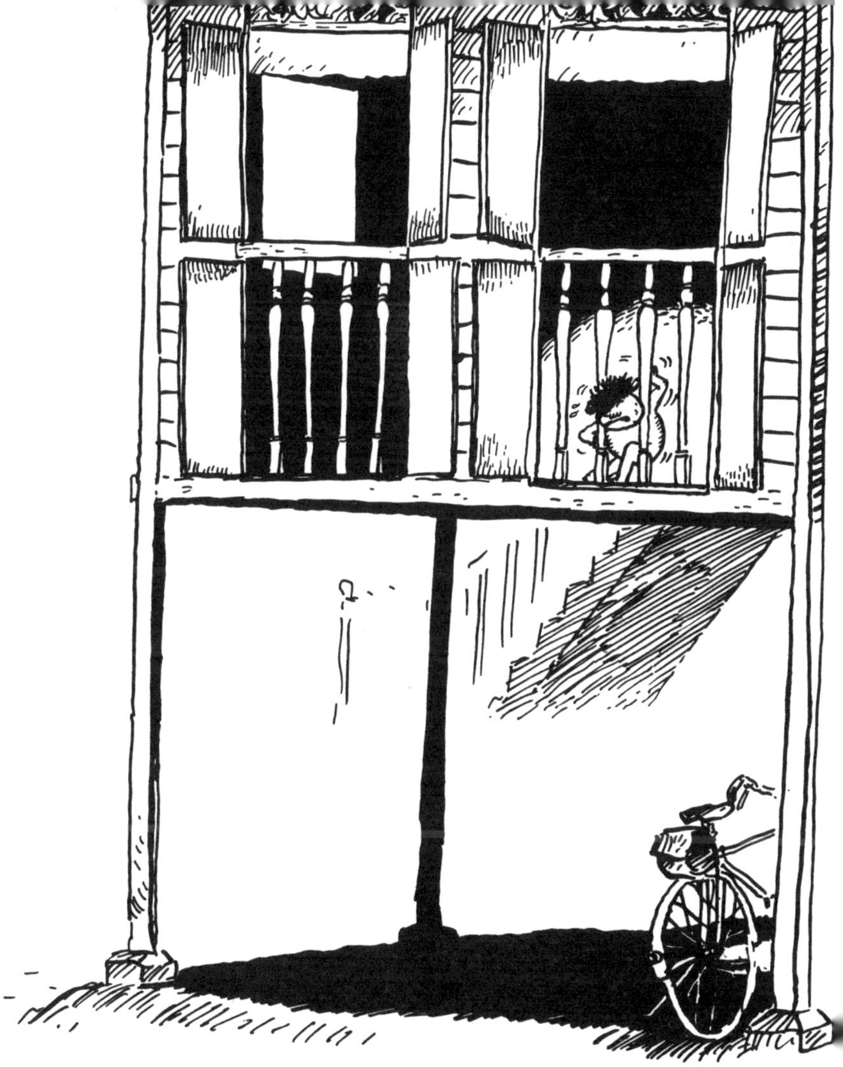

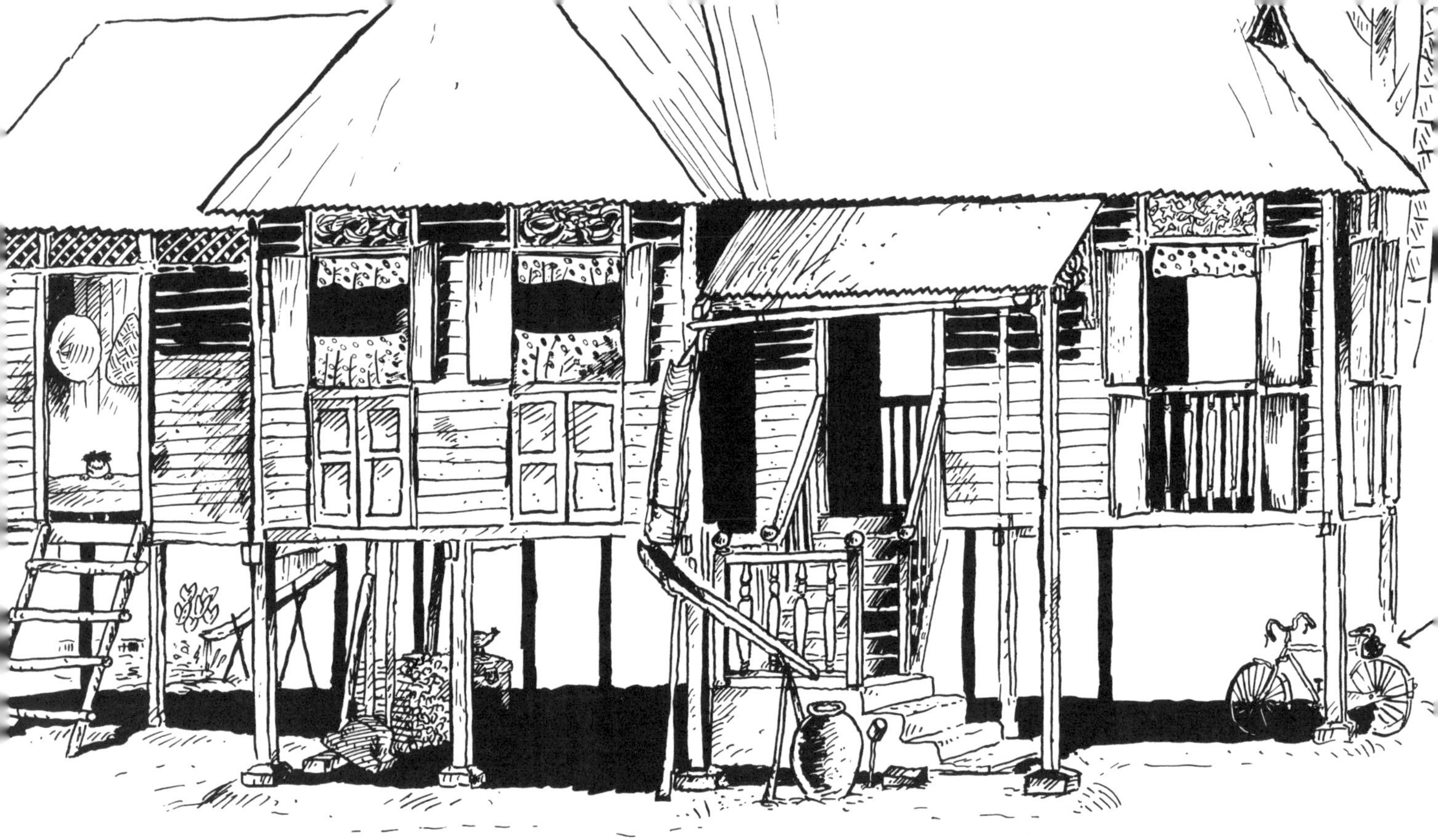

Our house was made of "chengai" wood.
The chengai tree gives very handsome timber that really lasts a long time.

At the age of four...happiness was seeing Aunt Khatijah, a rubber small-holder, coming back from her daily tapping late in the morning.

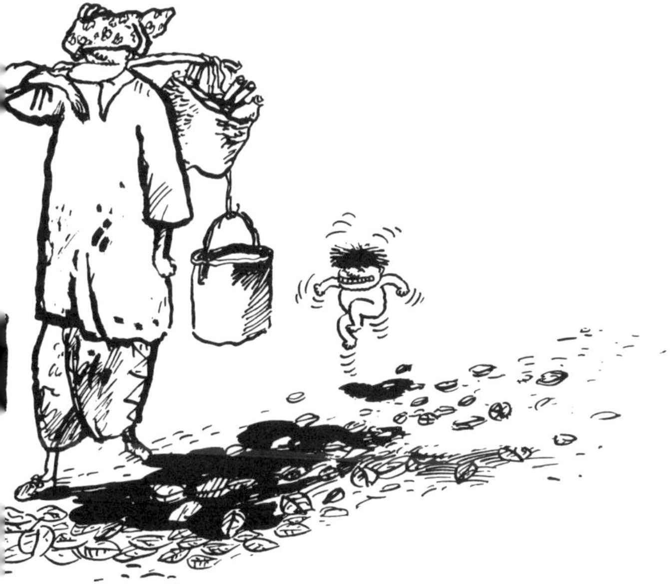

I always offered her a helping hand in processing the "milk of the rubber tree." First, she'd add some liquid (later I discovered it was formic acid) to the latex and we'd stir it.

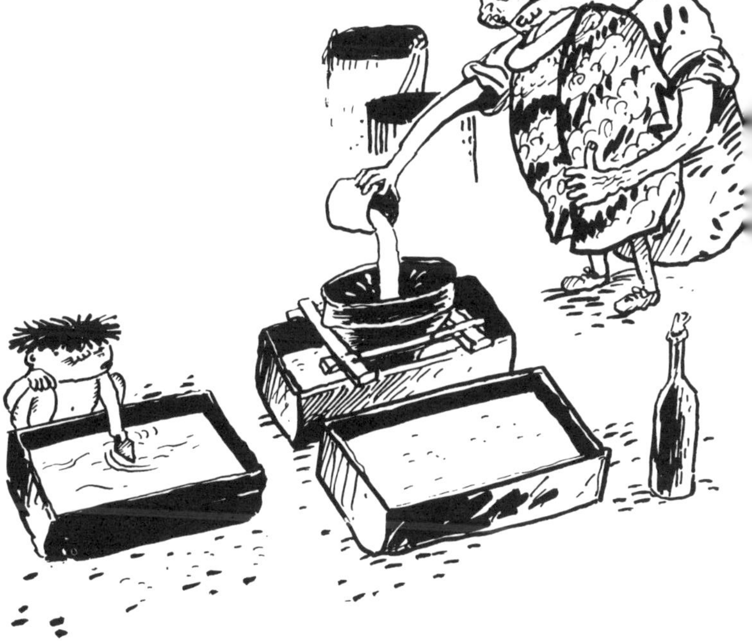

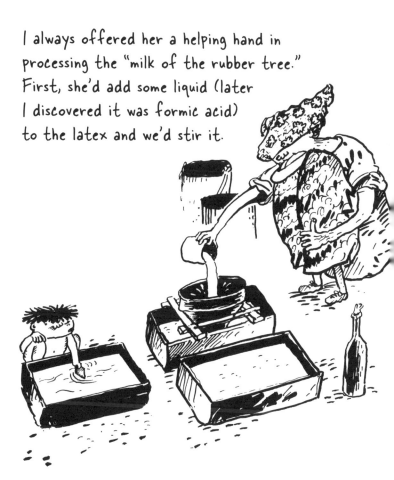

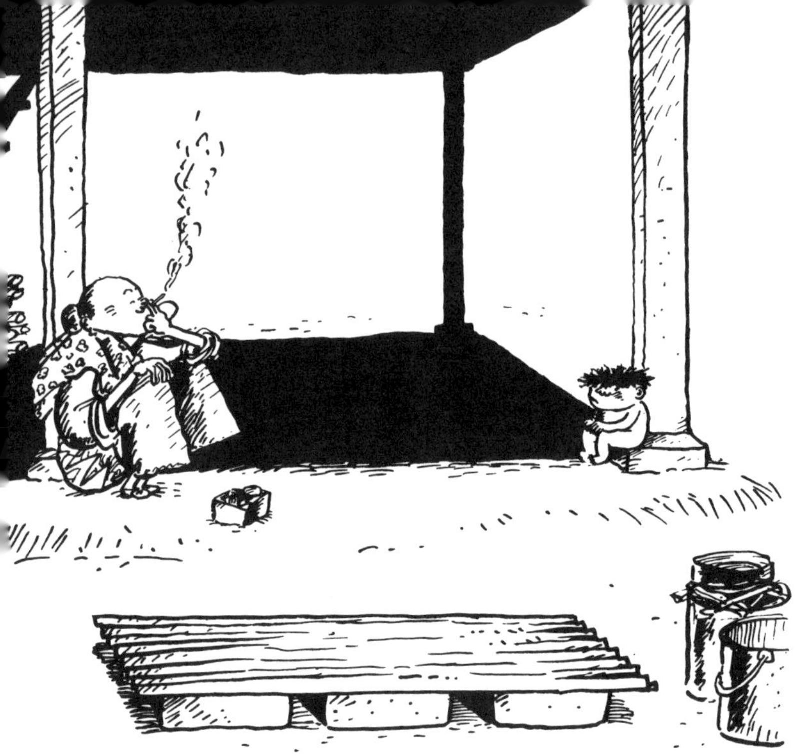

Then we'd wait for about 15 minutes or so for the latex to harden.

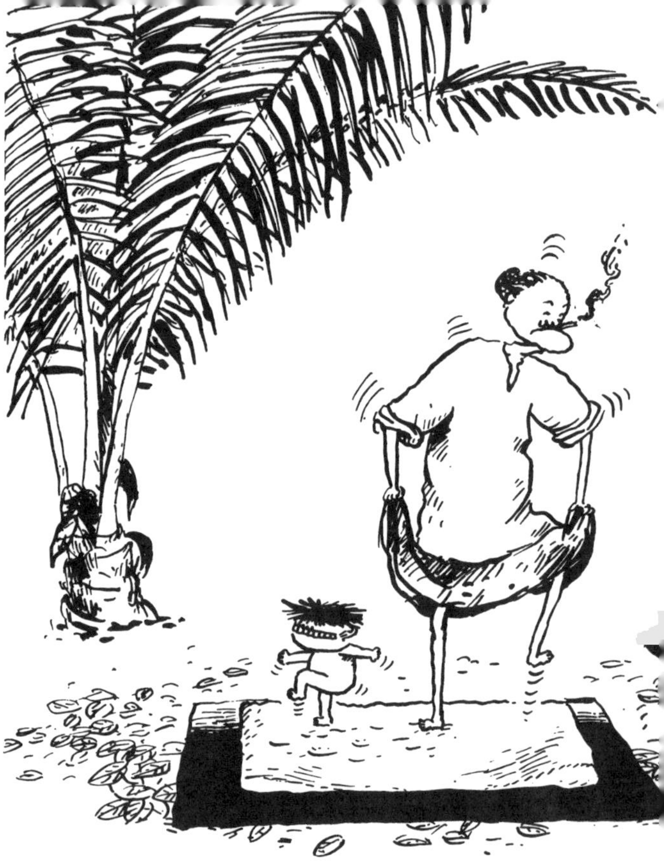

After that I'd help her flatten the coagulated rubber...

Then it went to the rollers to be turned into sheets. Usually by this time I had to leave because Mum would be calling me back.

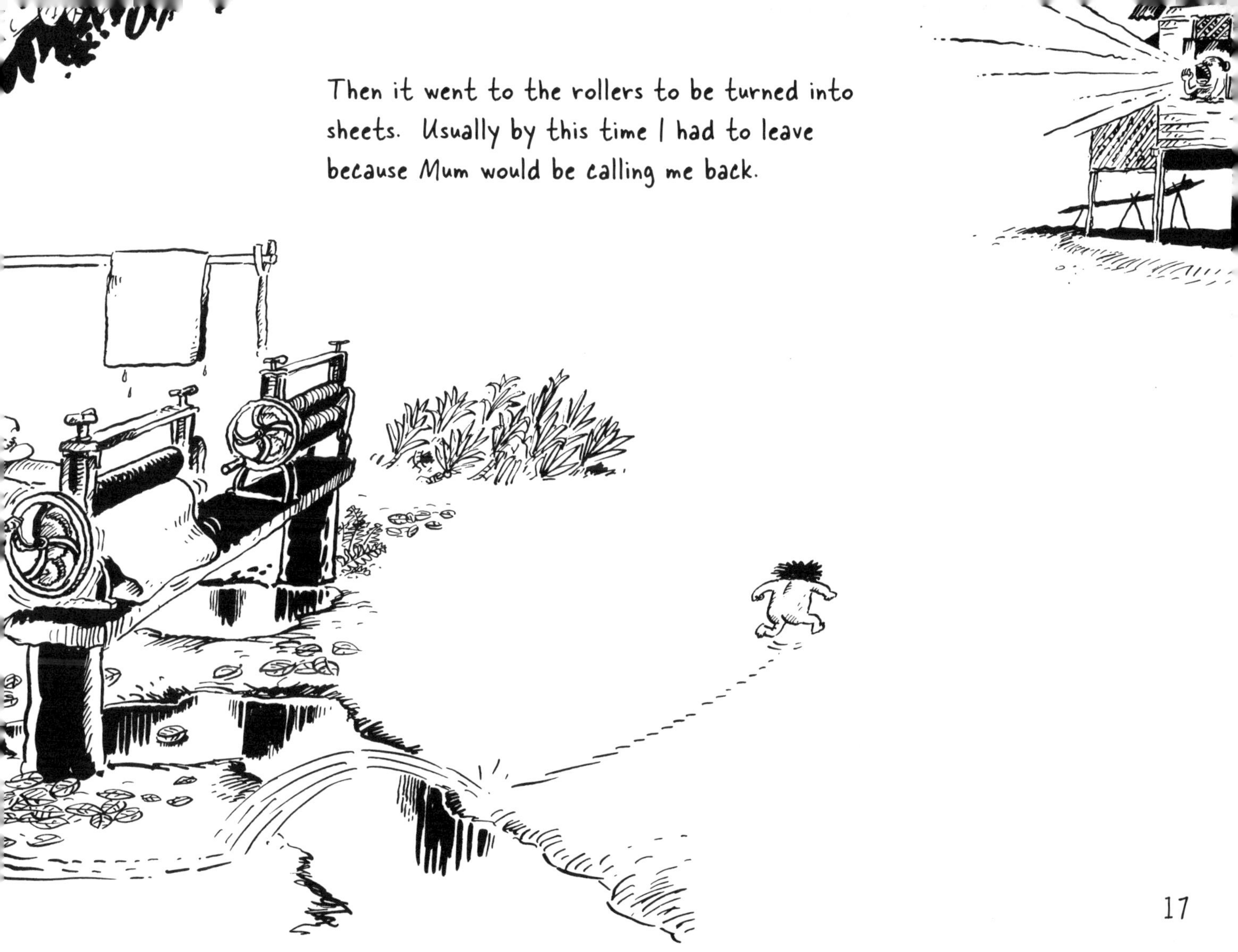

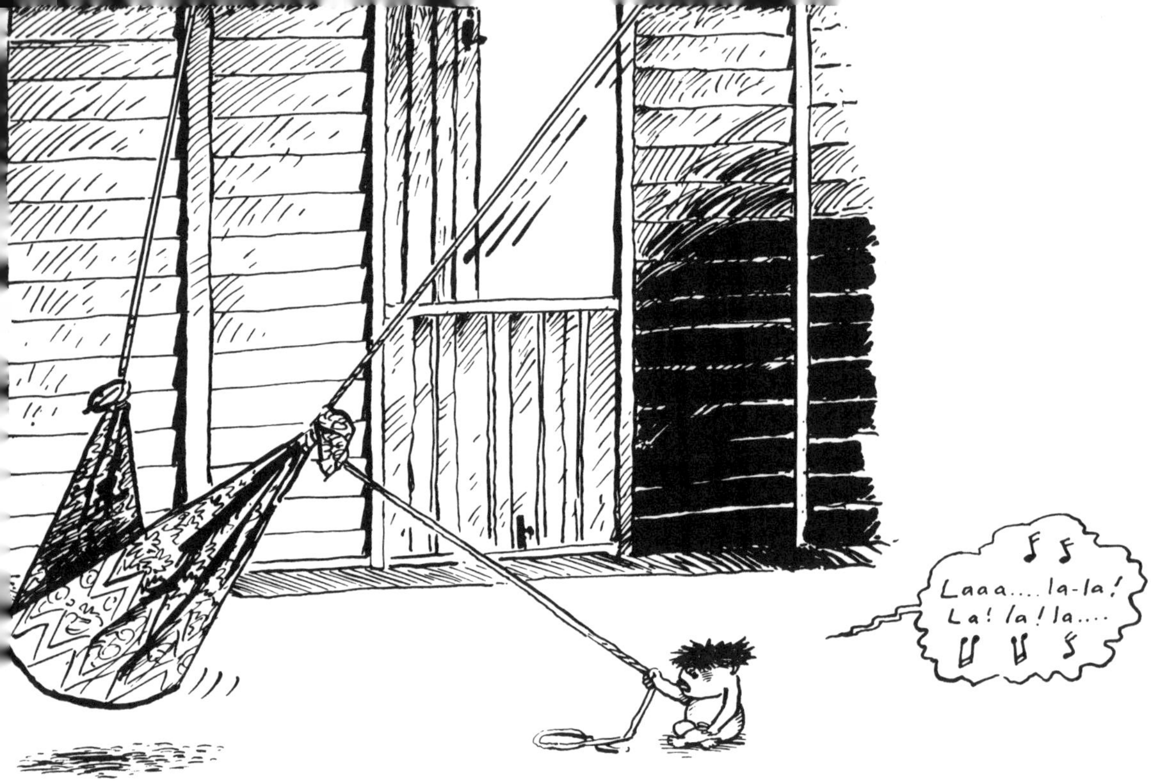
Laaa.... la-la!
La! la! la....

The reason Mum called was for me either to eat or to take care of my sister. Oh yes! Our family had already been blessed with another member then—my sister, Maimunah.

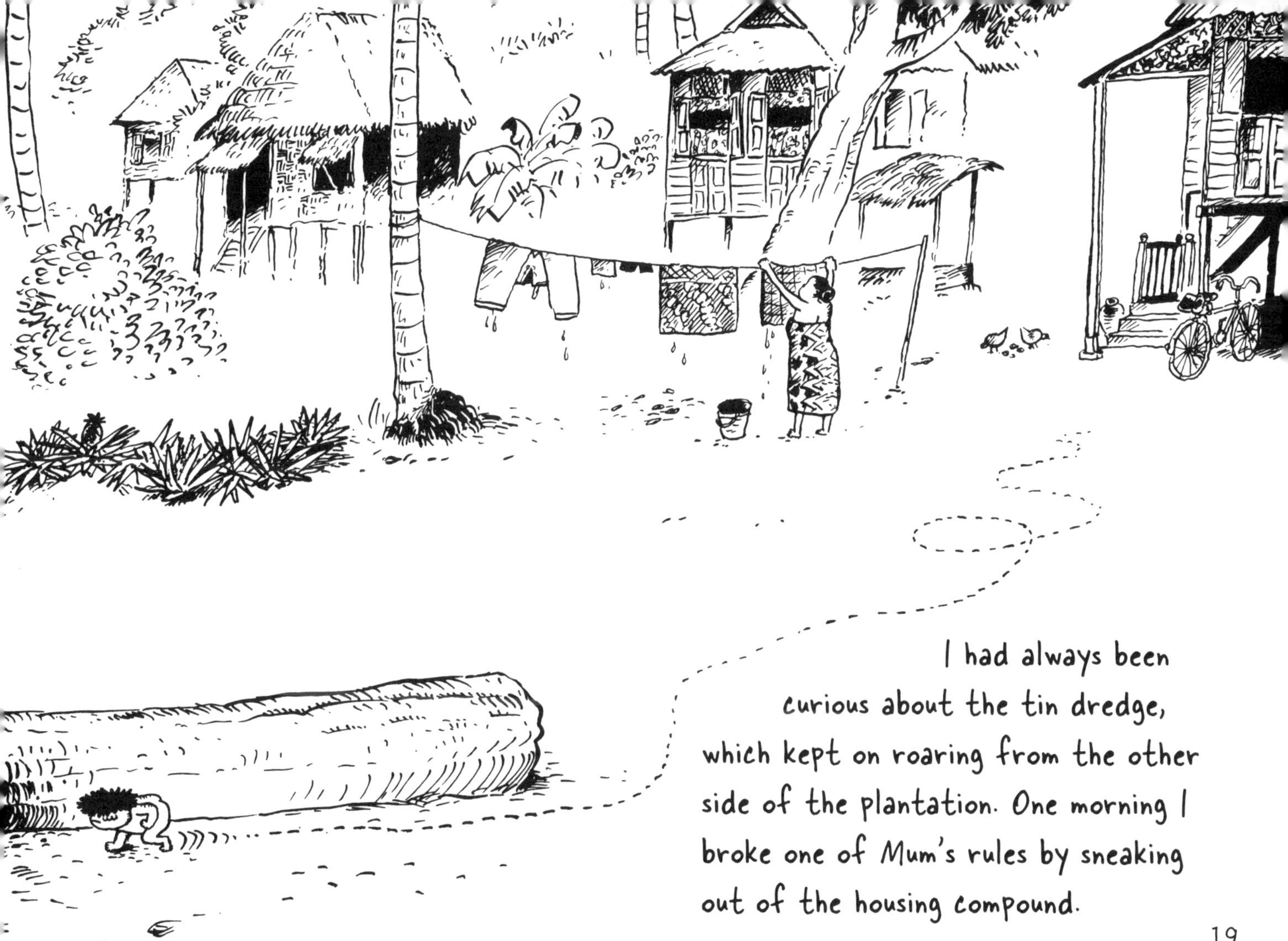

I had always been curious about the tin dredge, which kept on roaring from the other side of the plantation. One morning I broke one of Mum's rules by sneaking out of the housing compound.

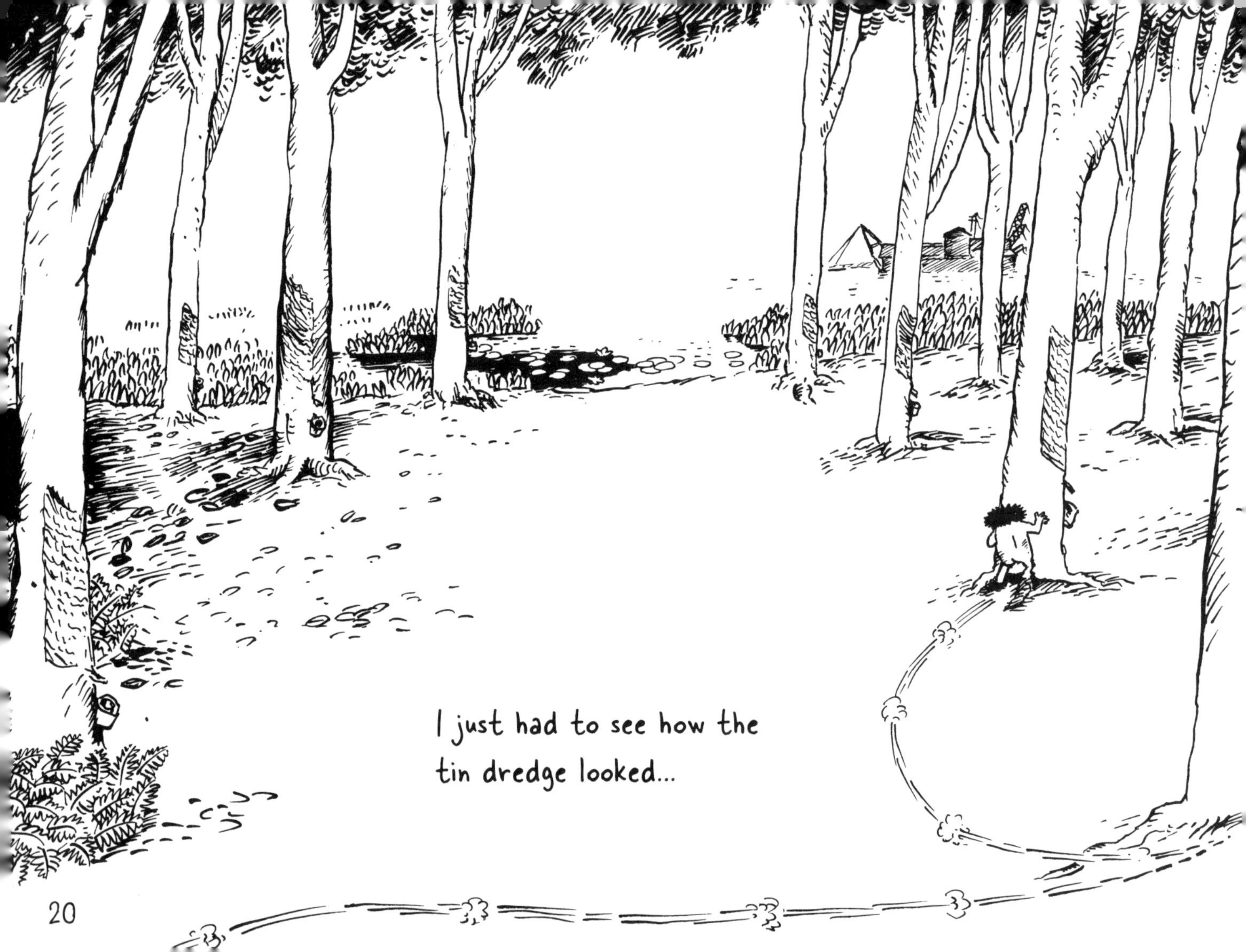

I just had to see how the tin dredge looked...

What I saw was a huge
thing floating in the big pool of
mud. It had to be huge, for even
at a distance it looked very big.
No wonder it sounded so loud. It
would roar and once in a while groan
frighteningly...
like a monster!

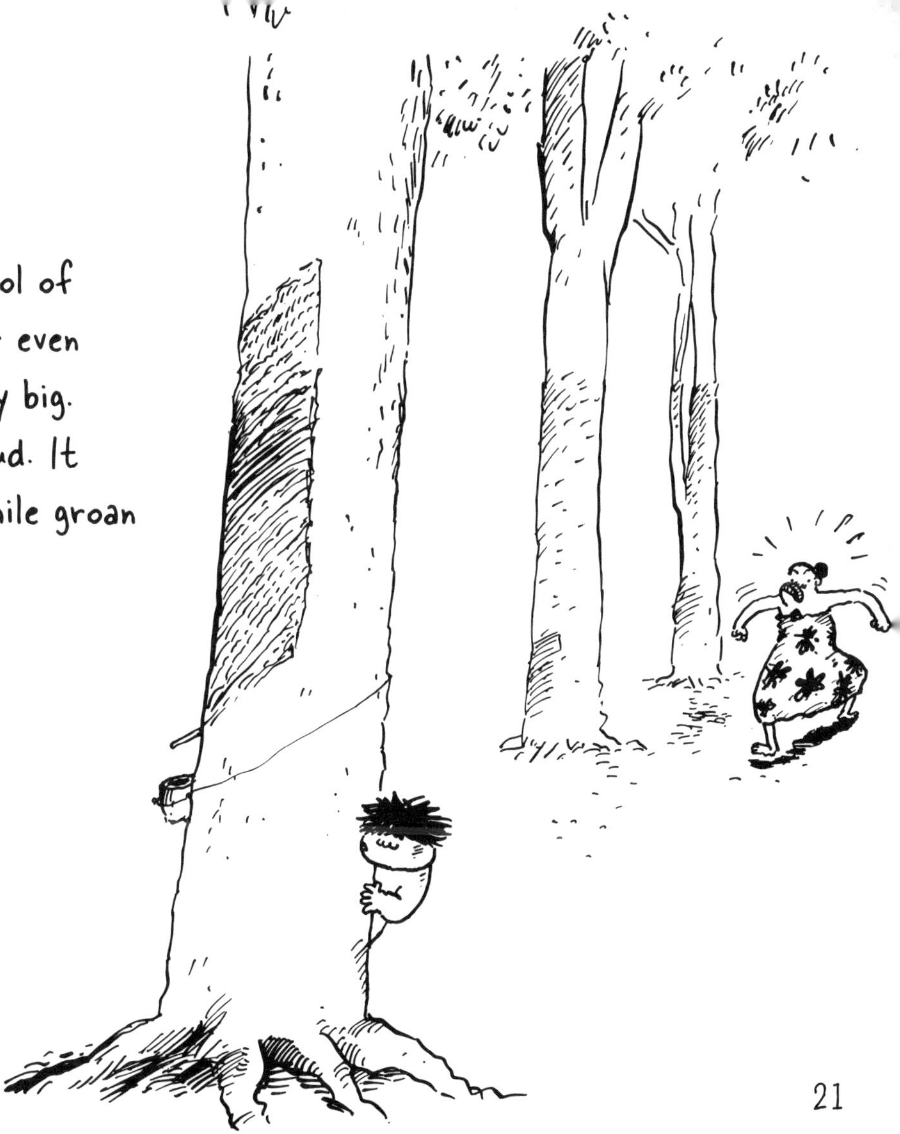

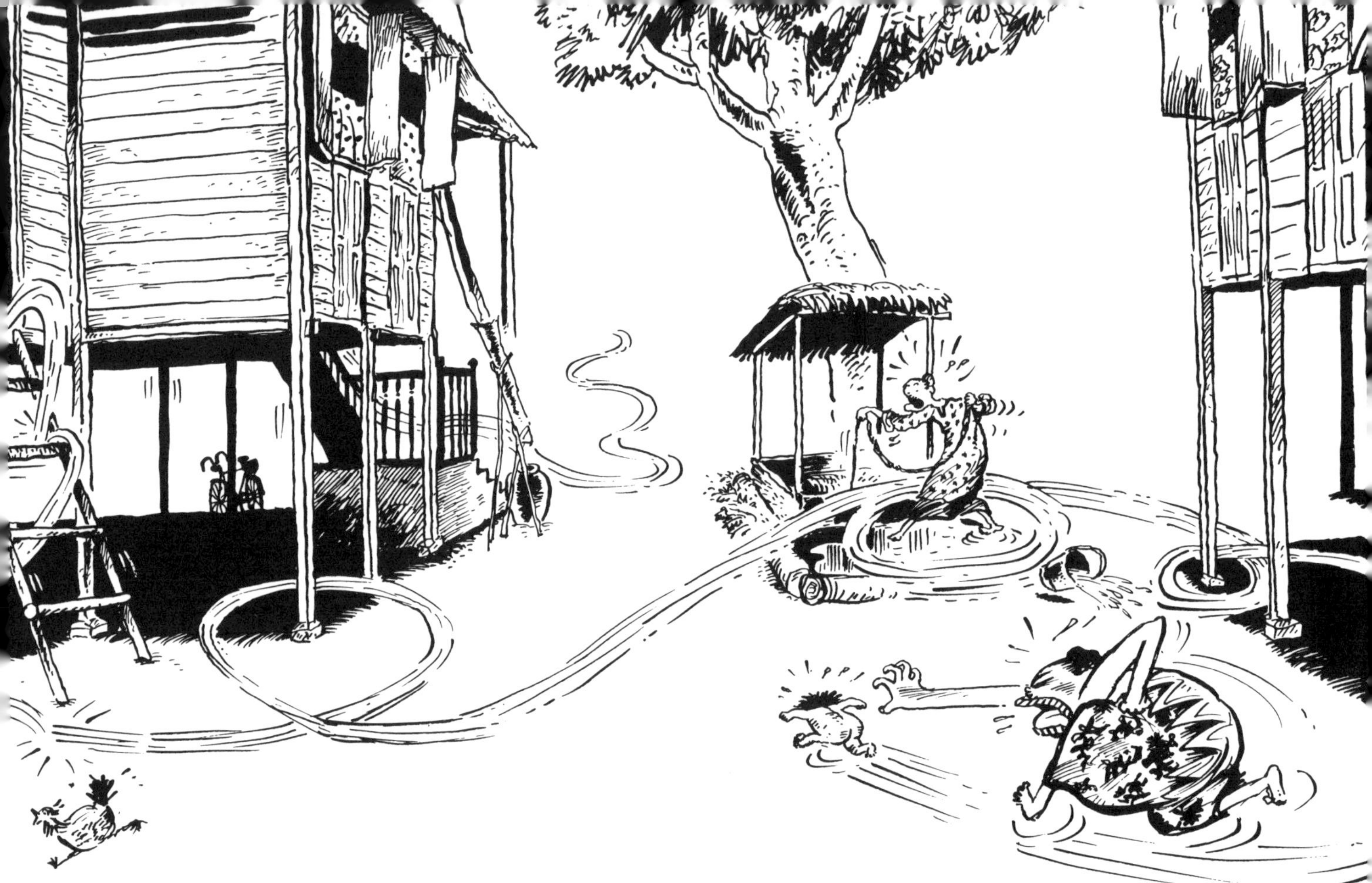

Well...that was also the day I
discovered how angry Mum could get.

I was so afraid of what Mum would do to me that I was running like a barking deer! She lost me near Pak Alang's house when the man, who knew me by sight, showed sympathy for me...

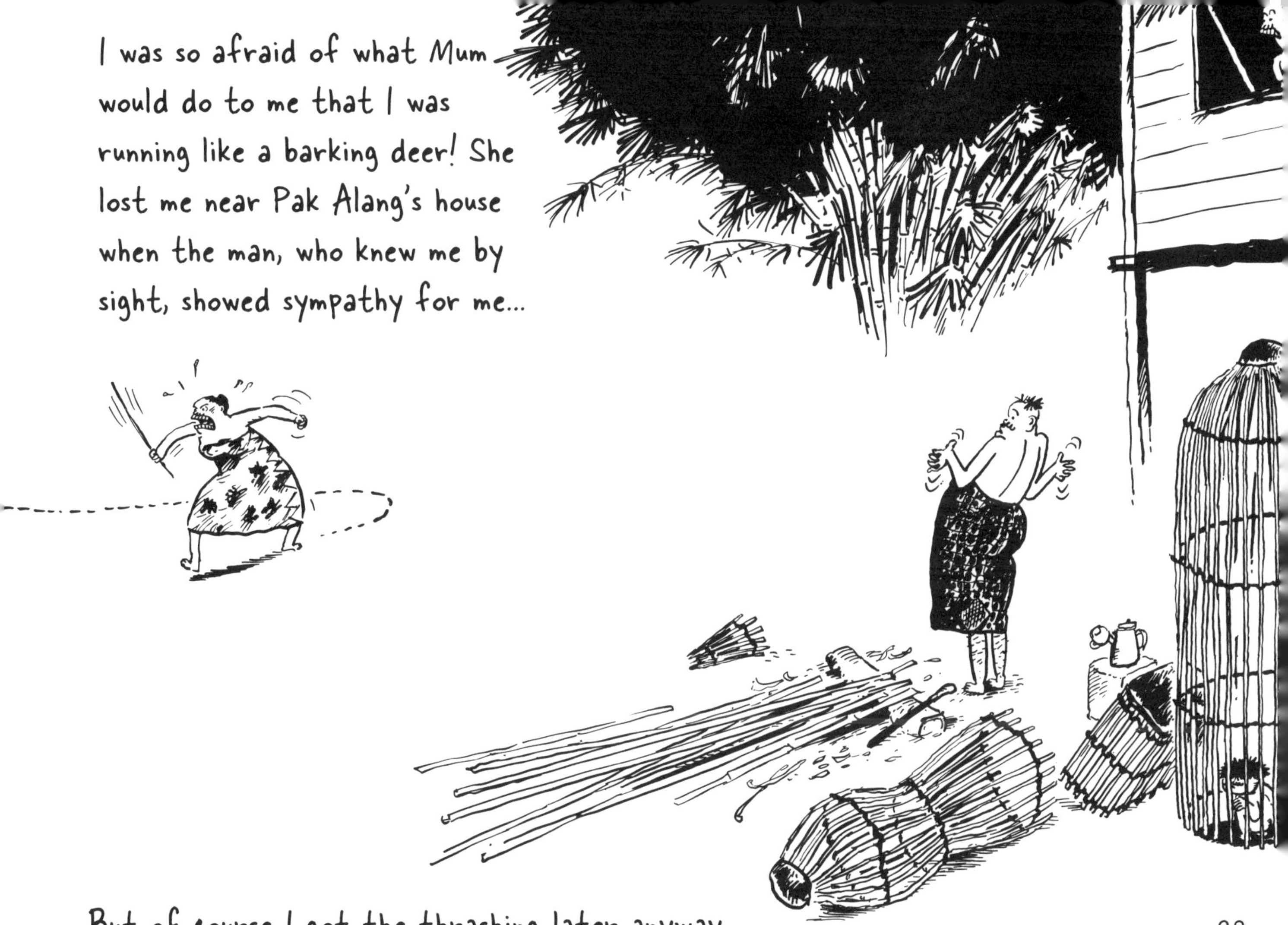

But of course I got the thrashing later anyway.

My father was different. He was a funny fellow. My sister and I would look forward to seeing him coming back from work in the afternoon. He was a government clerk in Batu Gajah.

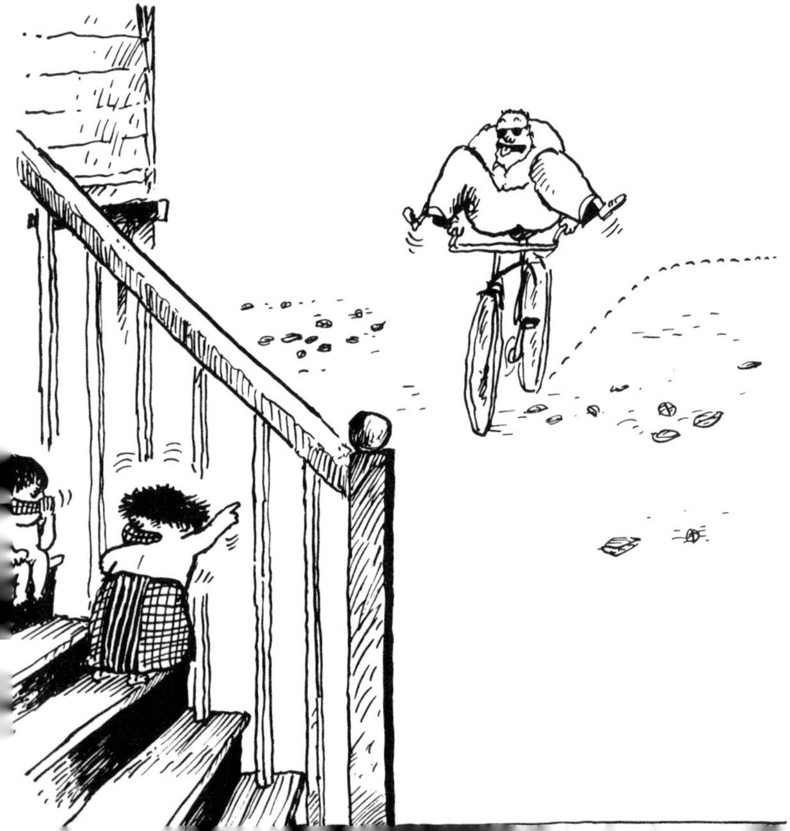

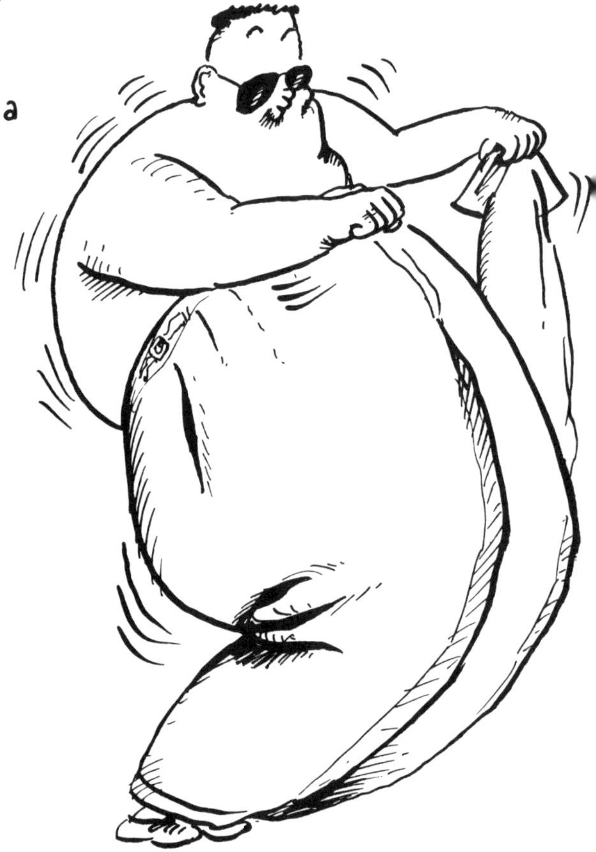

He was a big man. This was what he'd do first...

Then it was tea time for us. Usually we'd have either fried bananas or fried tapioca. Or boiled bananas...or...boiled tapioca. But occasionally Mum would bake our favorite cake—kueh bengkang.

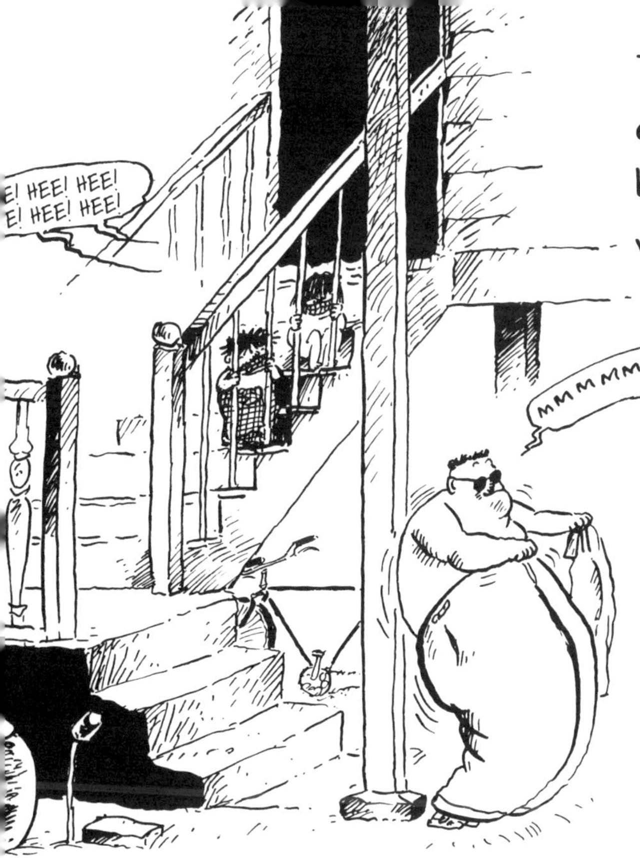

E! HEE! HEE!
E! HEE! HEE!
MMMMMM...

...scratch his back.

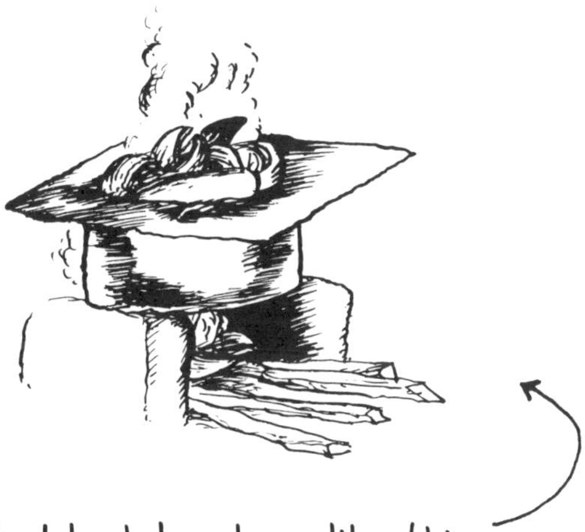

Mum baked kueh bengkang like this with a fire on top and below because we didn't have an oven. The cake is cylindrical in shape and made of rice flour, coconut milk, egg, and palm sugar.
Very tasty.

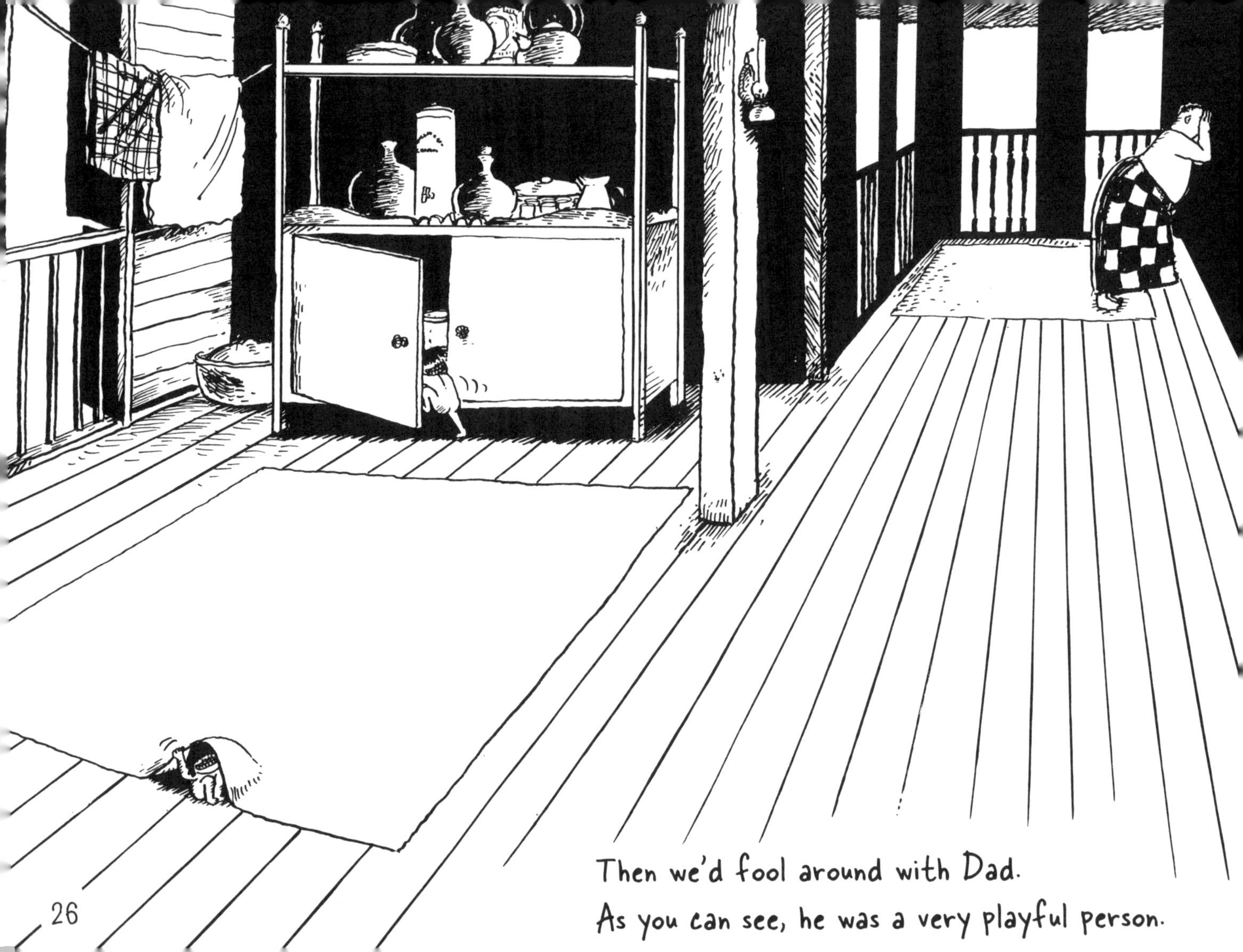

Then we'd fool around with Dad.

As you can see, he was a very playful person.

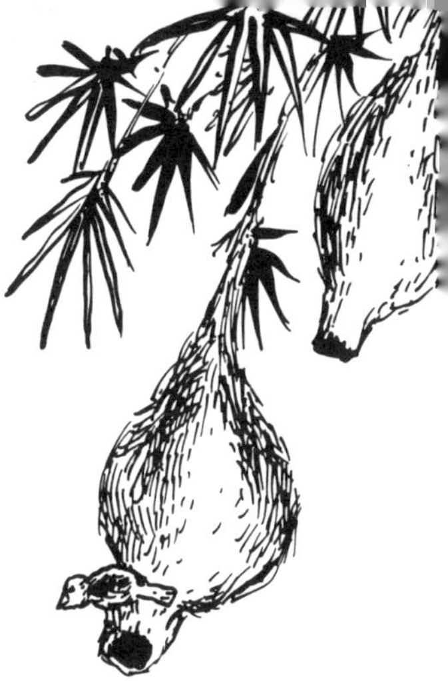

Just before sundown it was bath time. This was another time we looked forward to: when Dad would take us to the river not far behind the house.

On the way, we often stopped to look at the weaverbirds' nests that hung high on top of the bamboo trees.

I remember Dad telling us an astonishing fact about the weavers.

"These birds are very clever," he said. "When the time comes for mama weaver to lay eggs, papa weaver will do anything to make her comfortable.

"He will catch a firefly at night and take it back to light up their home."

Dad knew a lot about such things.

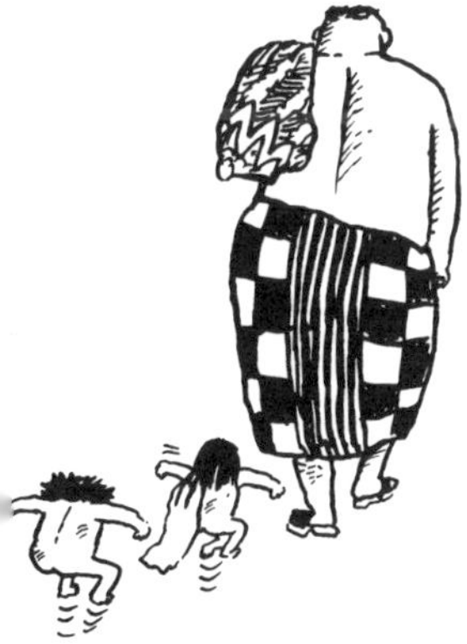

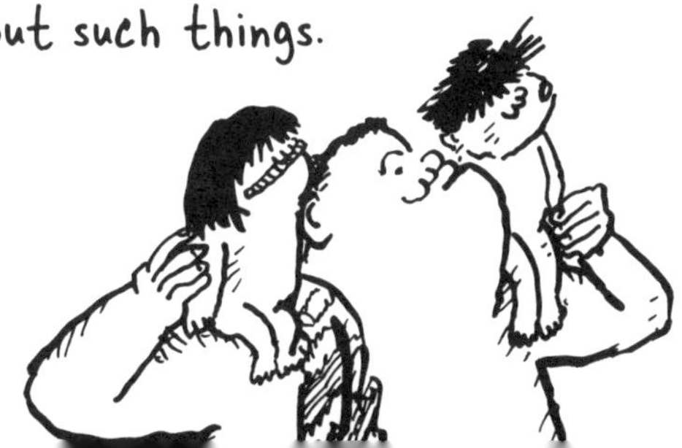

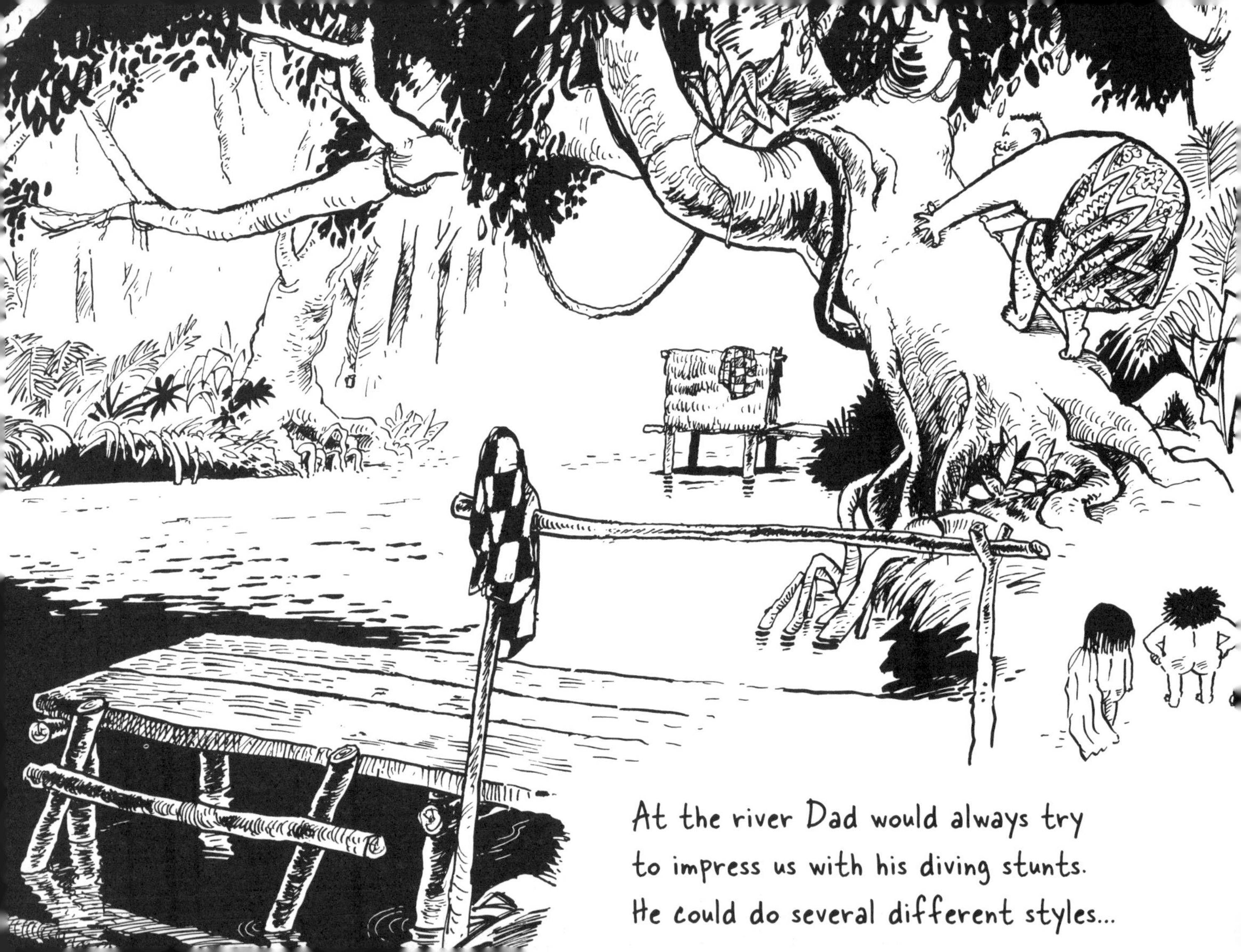
At the river Dad would always try
to impress us with his diving stunts.
He could do several different styles...

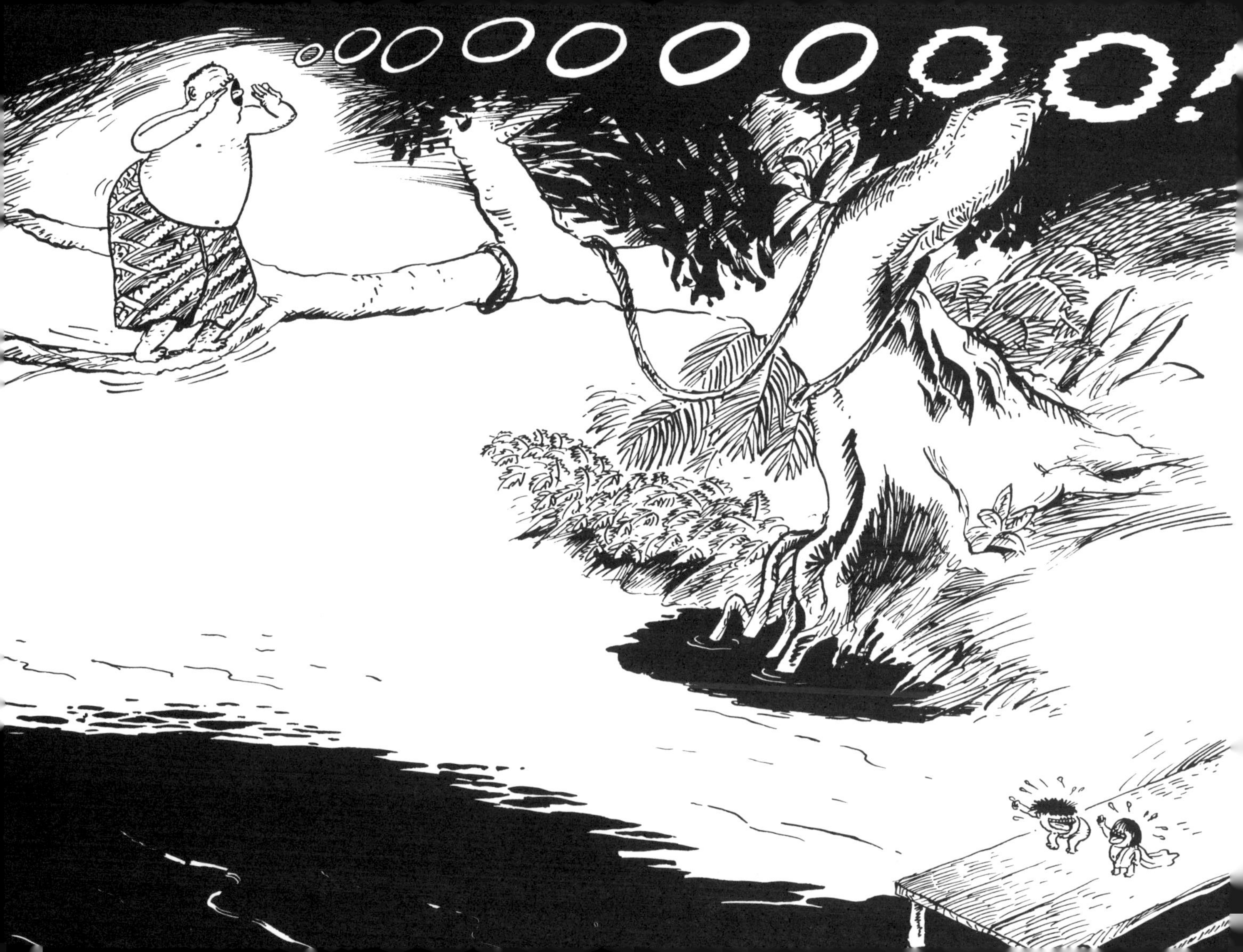
OOOOOOOOO!

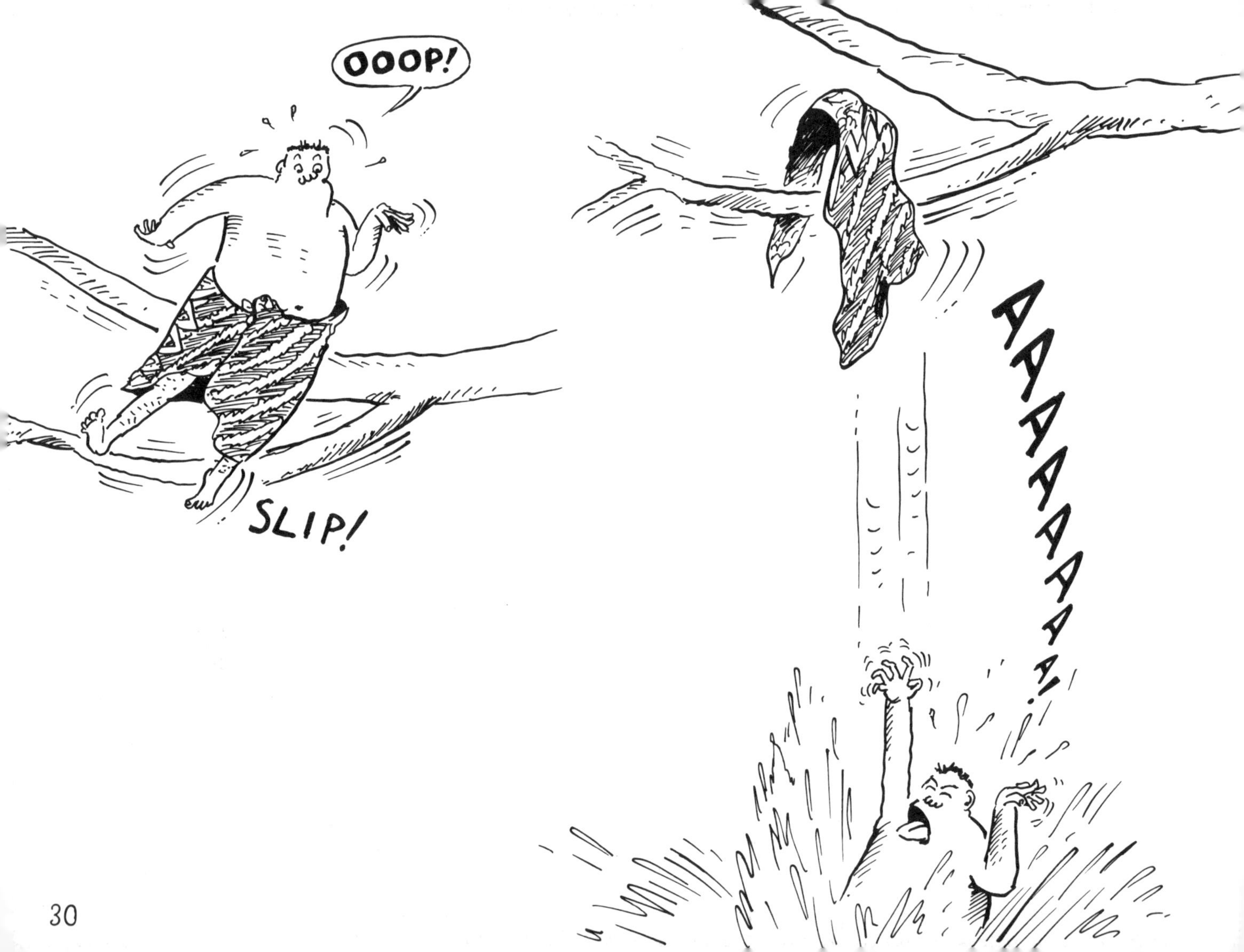
OOOP!
SLIP!
AAAAAAAA...!

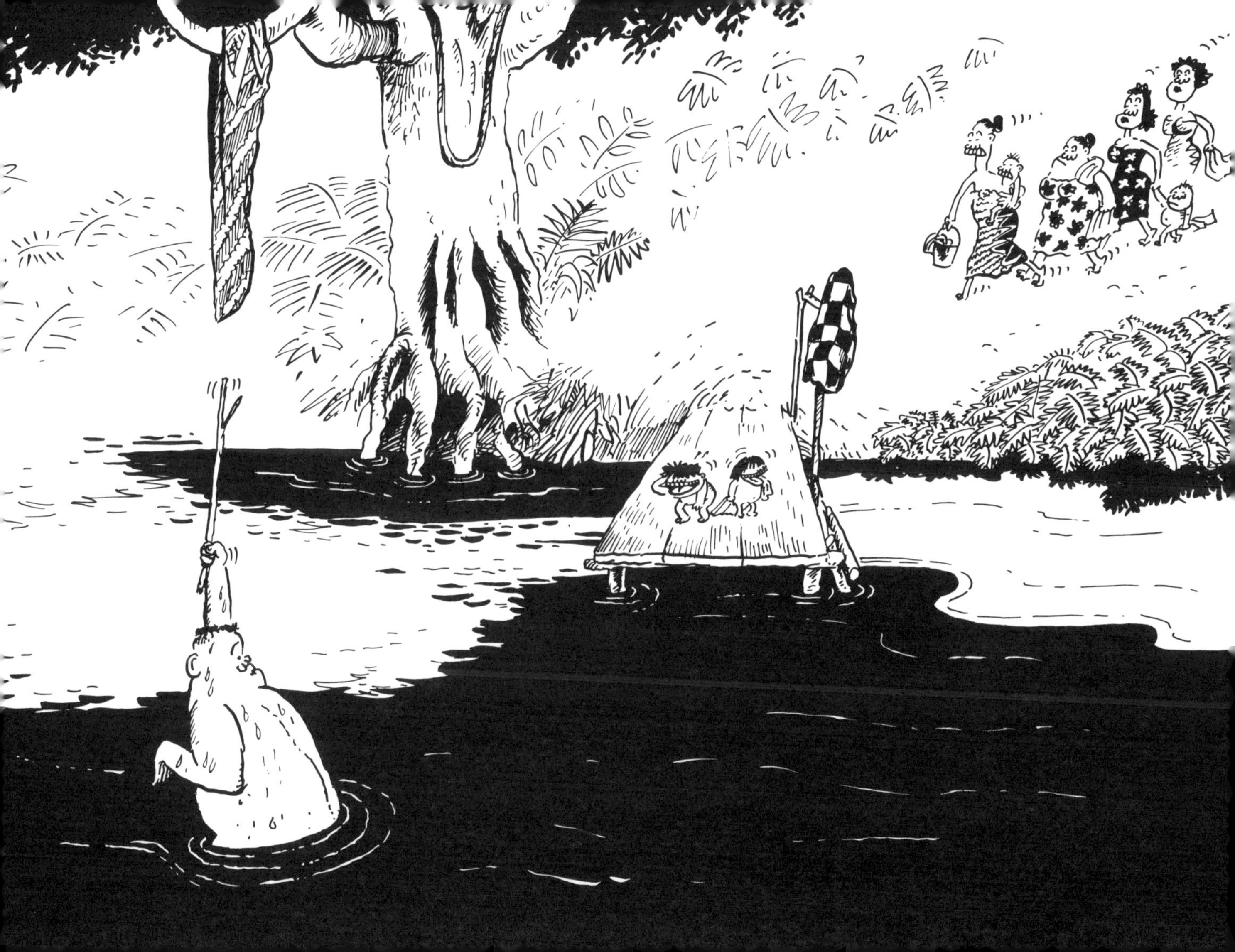

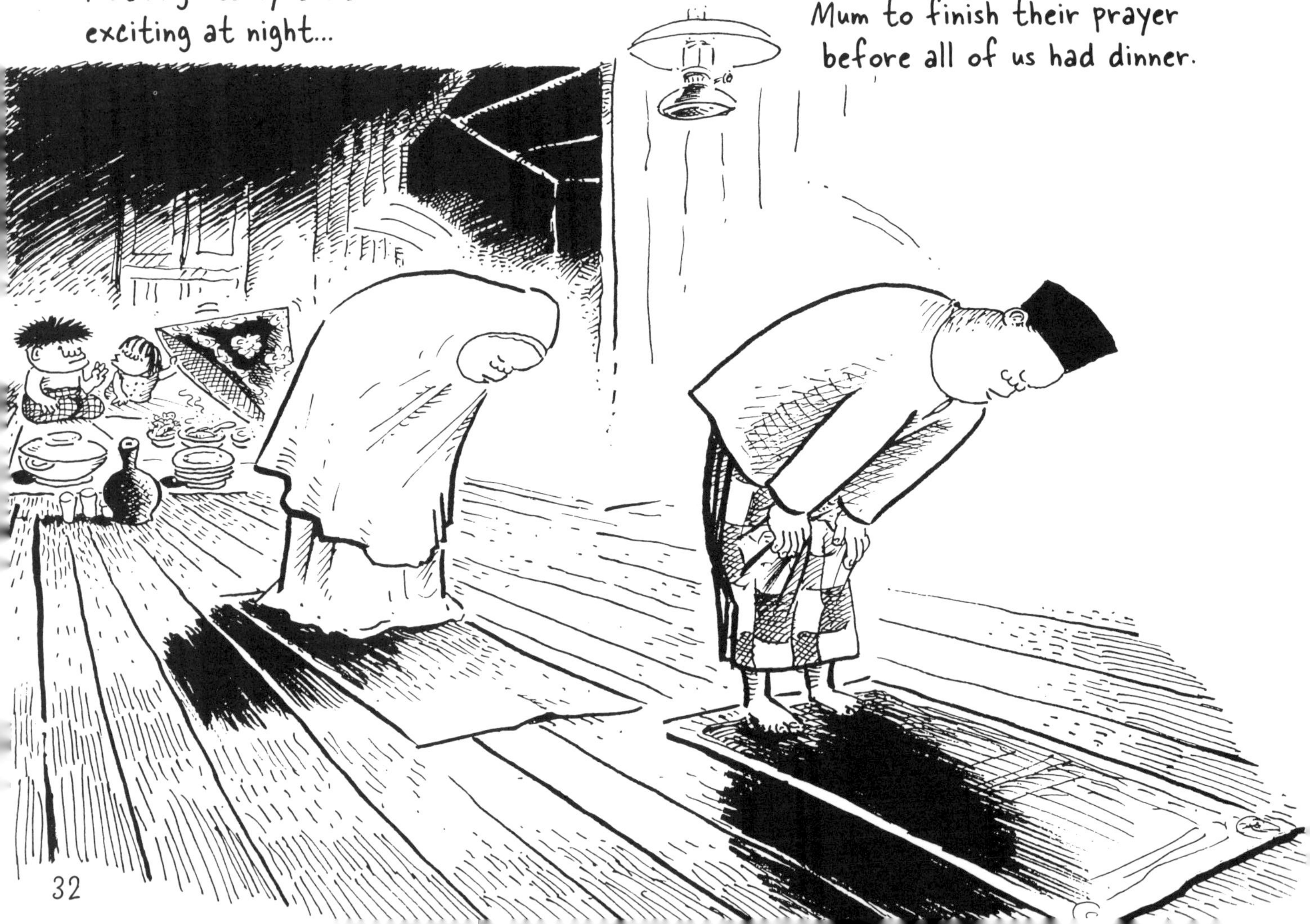
Nothing nearly that exciting at night...
Maimunah and I would wait for Dad and Mum to finish their prayer before all of us had dinner.

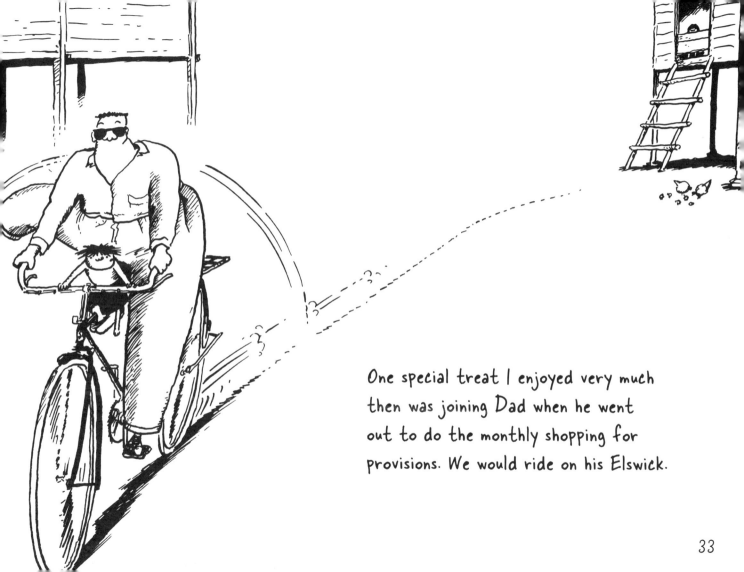

One special treat I enjoyed very much then was joining Dad when he went out to do the monthly shopping for provisions. We would ride on his Elswick.

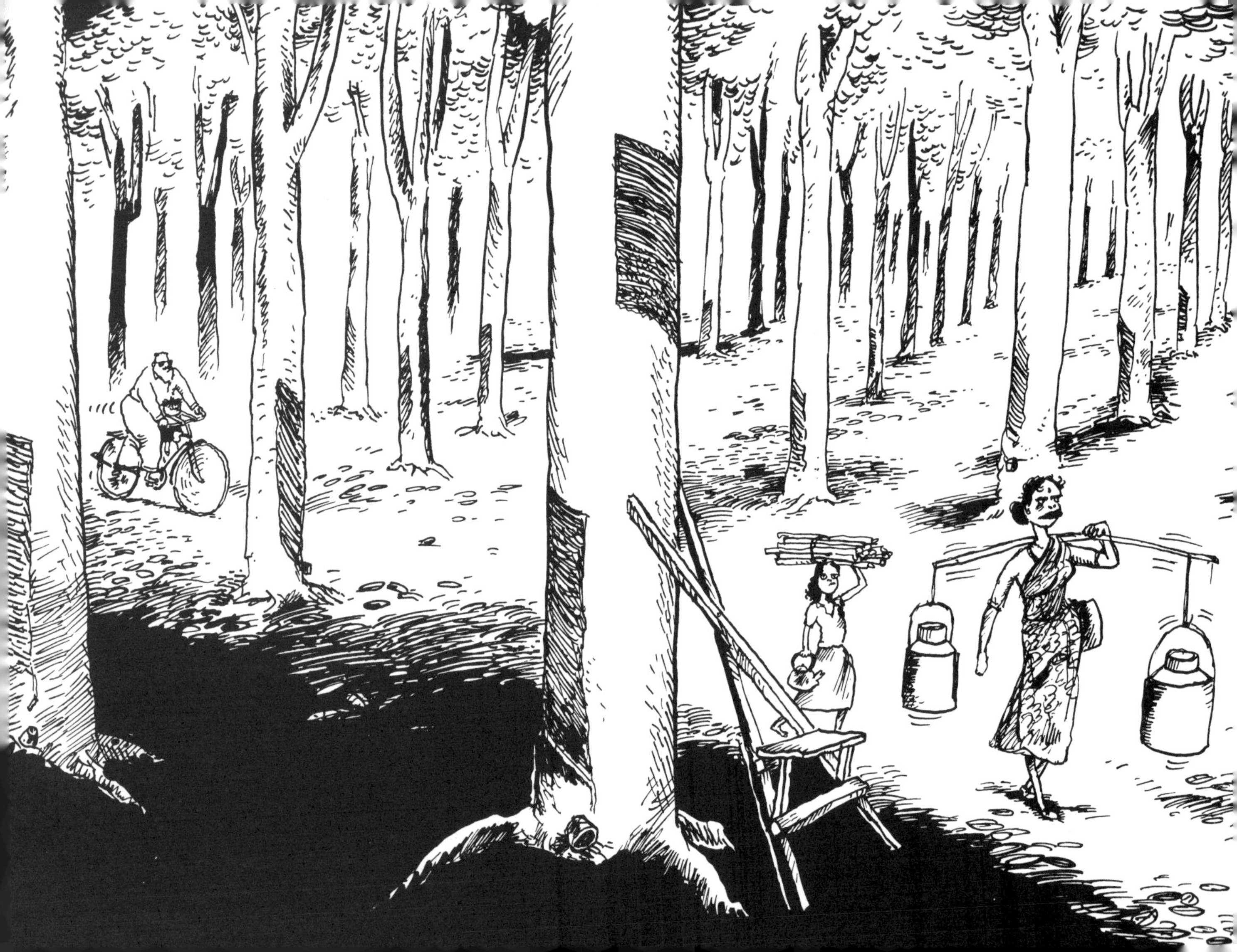

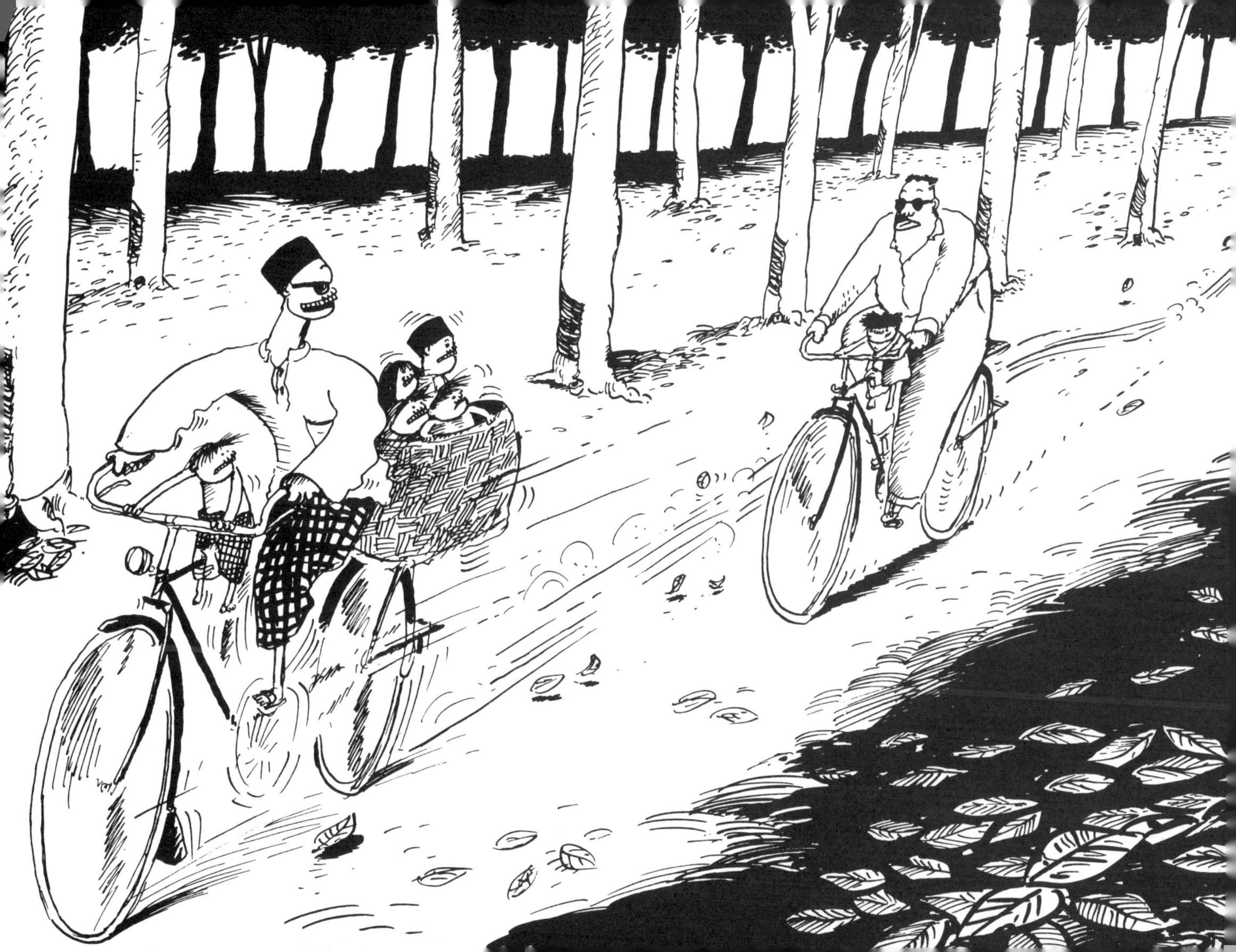

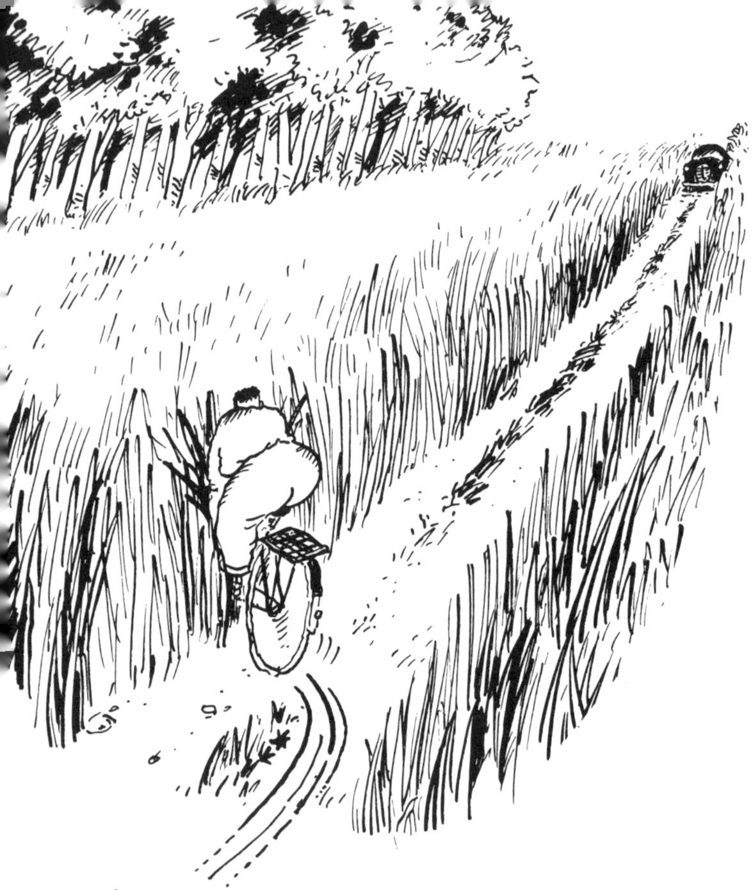

As you can see, our kampung lane was very narrow. Very rarely would we see a motorcar passing by. But when we saw one...

...we had to give way.

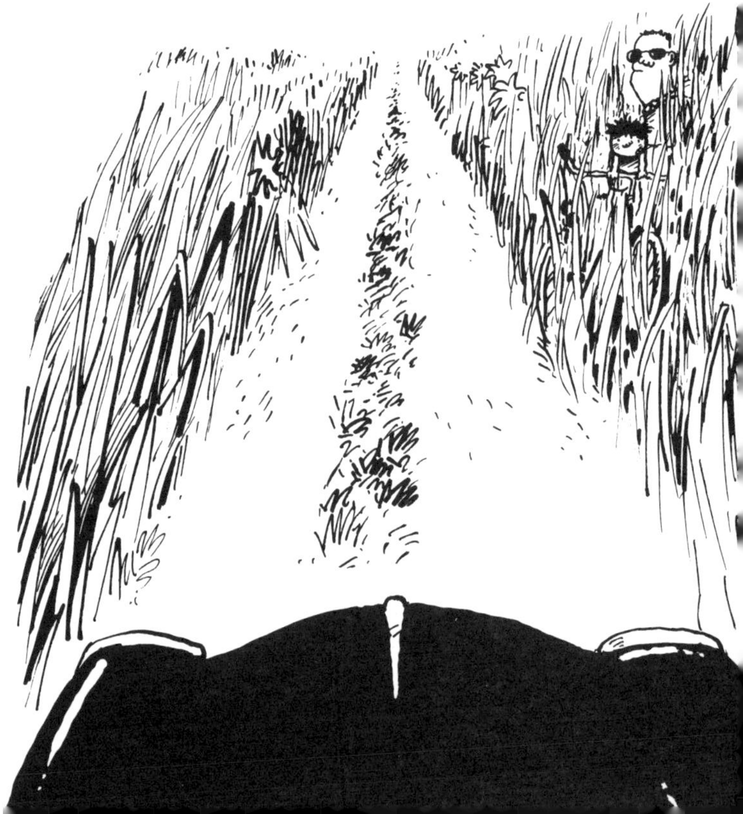

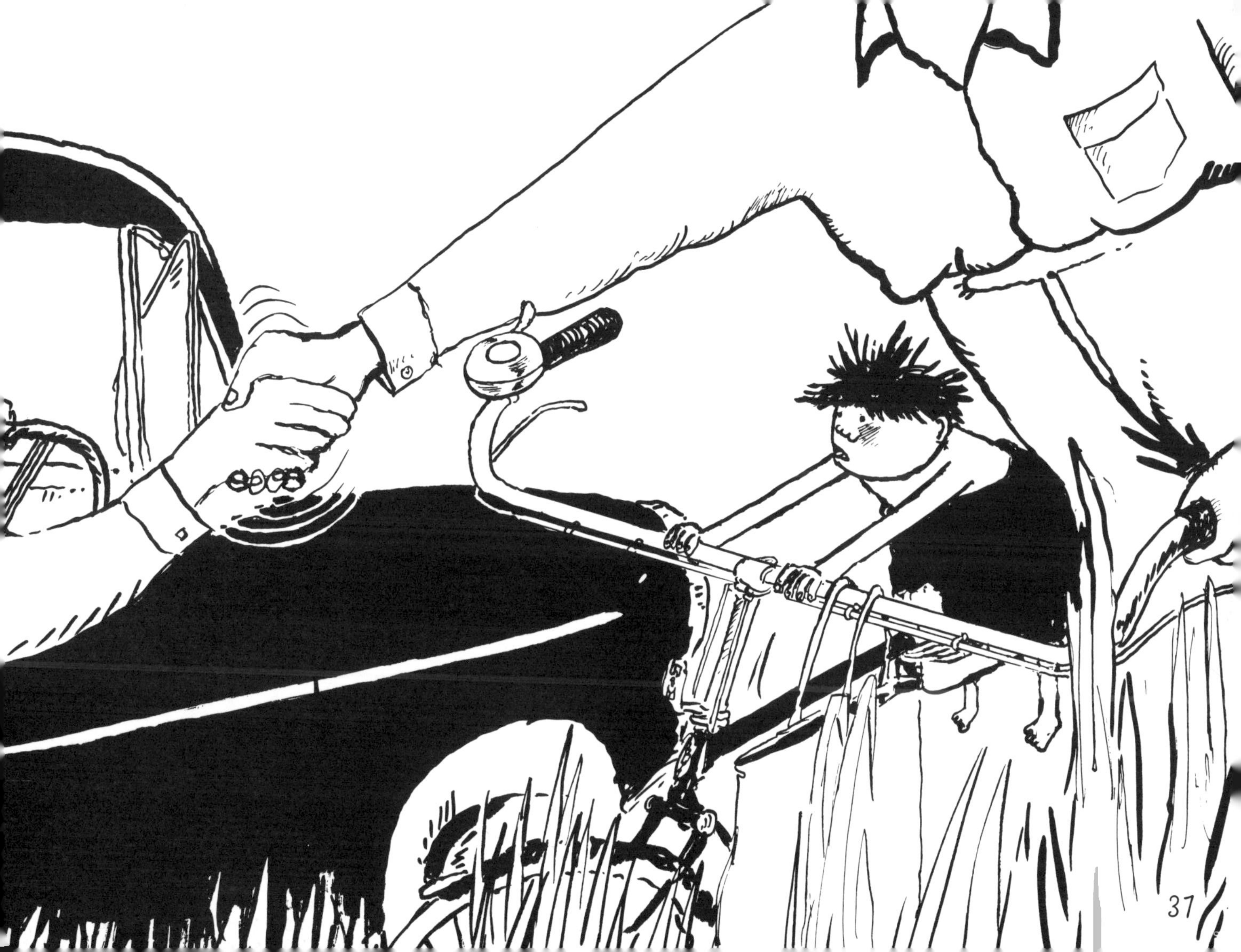

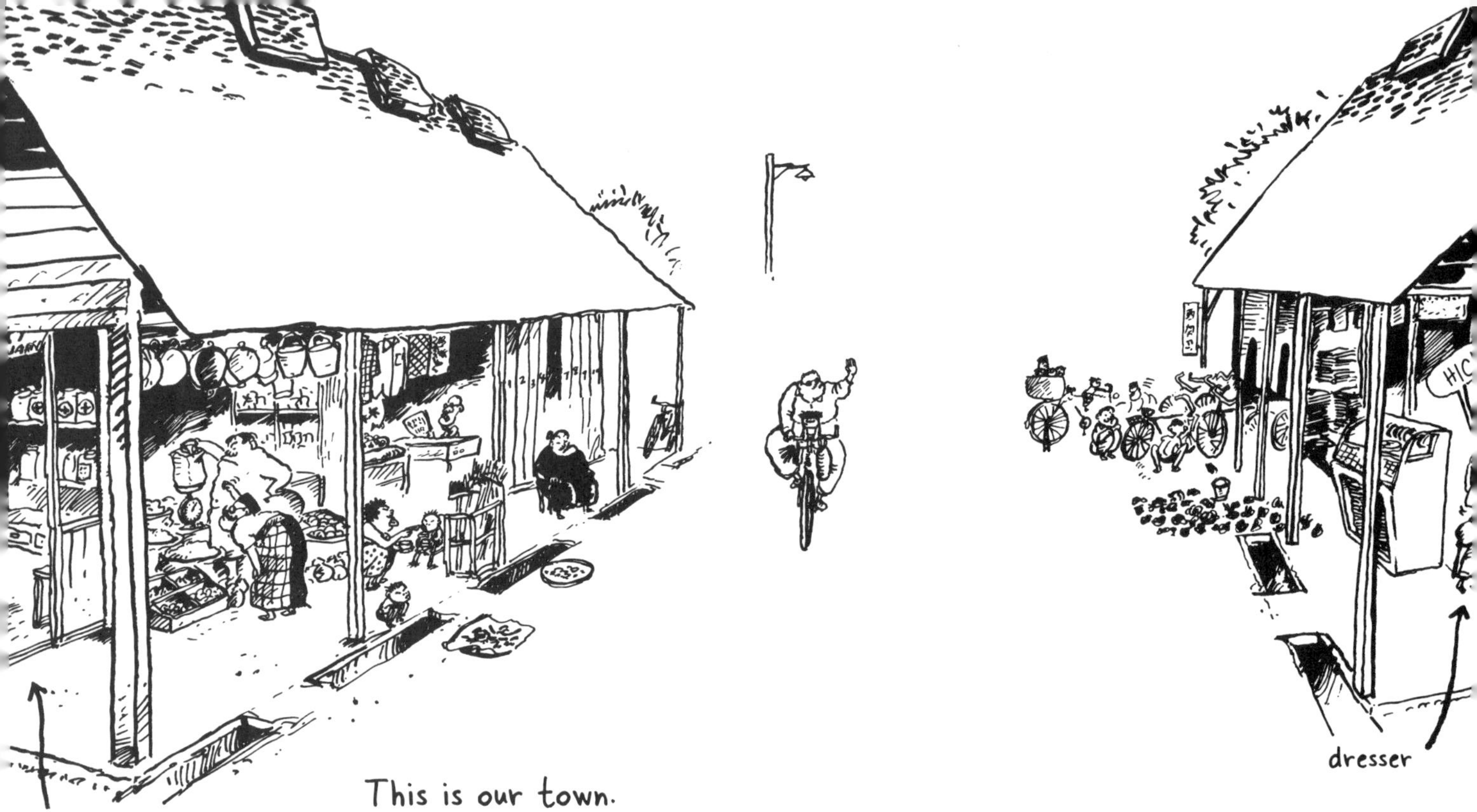
government
dispensary
dresser

This is our town.

Next to the dispensary on the left is Ah Yew's shop, where we do our shopping, and next door is a cloth dealer who is also a small-time goldsmith. On the right is an Indian eating shop; followed by a book shop, a rubber dealer, and a bicycle shop.

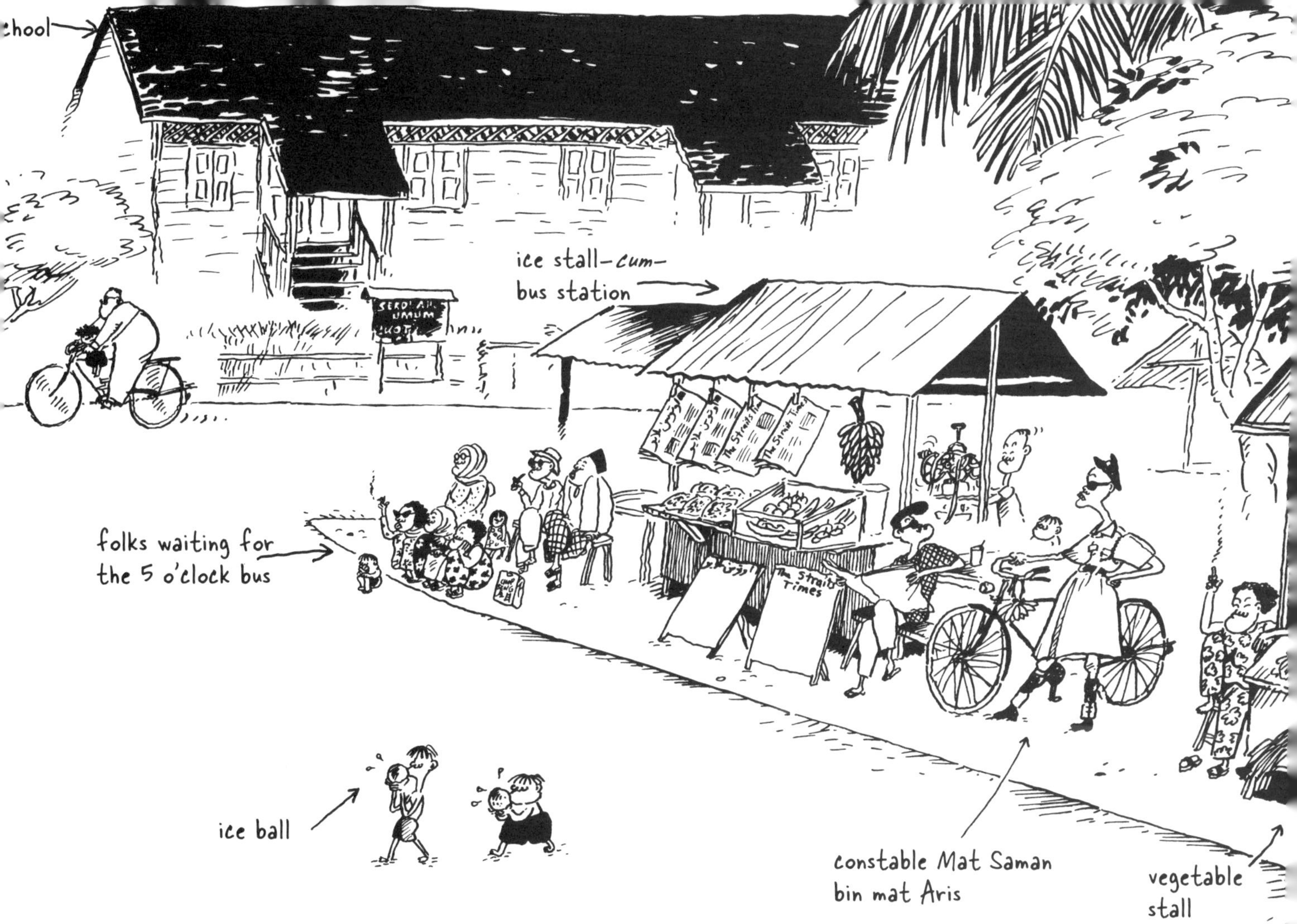

school
ice stall-cum-
bus station
SEKOLAH
UMUM
LOT
The Straits Times
The Straits Times
folks waiting for
the 5 o'clock bus
The Straits Times
ice ball
constable Mat Saman
bin mat Aris
vegetable
stall

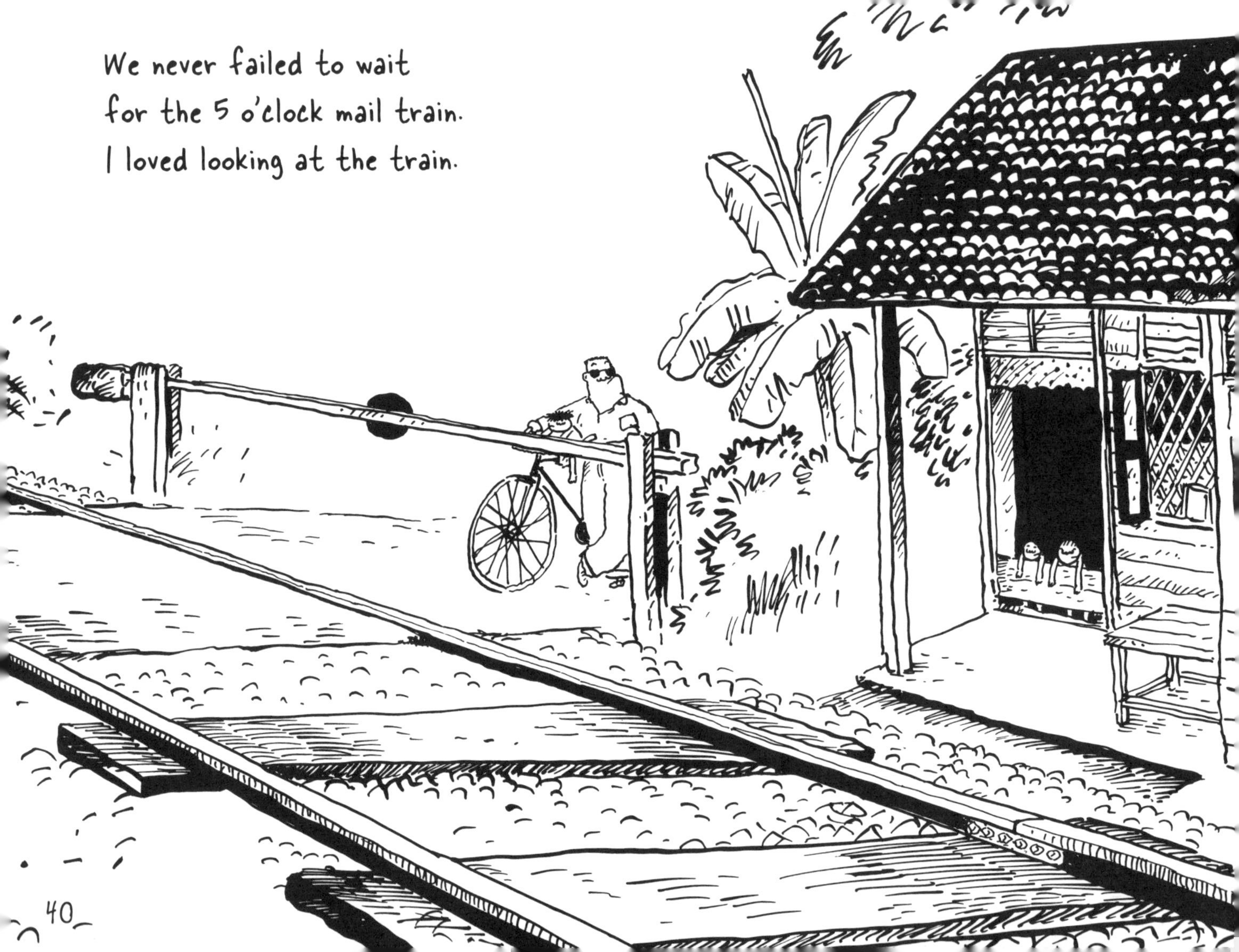
We never failed to wait
for the 5 o'clock mail train.
I loved looking at the train.

But of course it never stopped at our kampung.

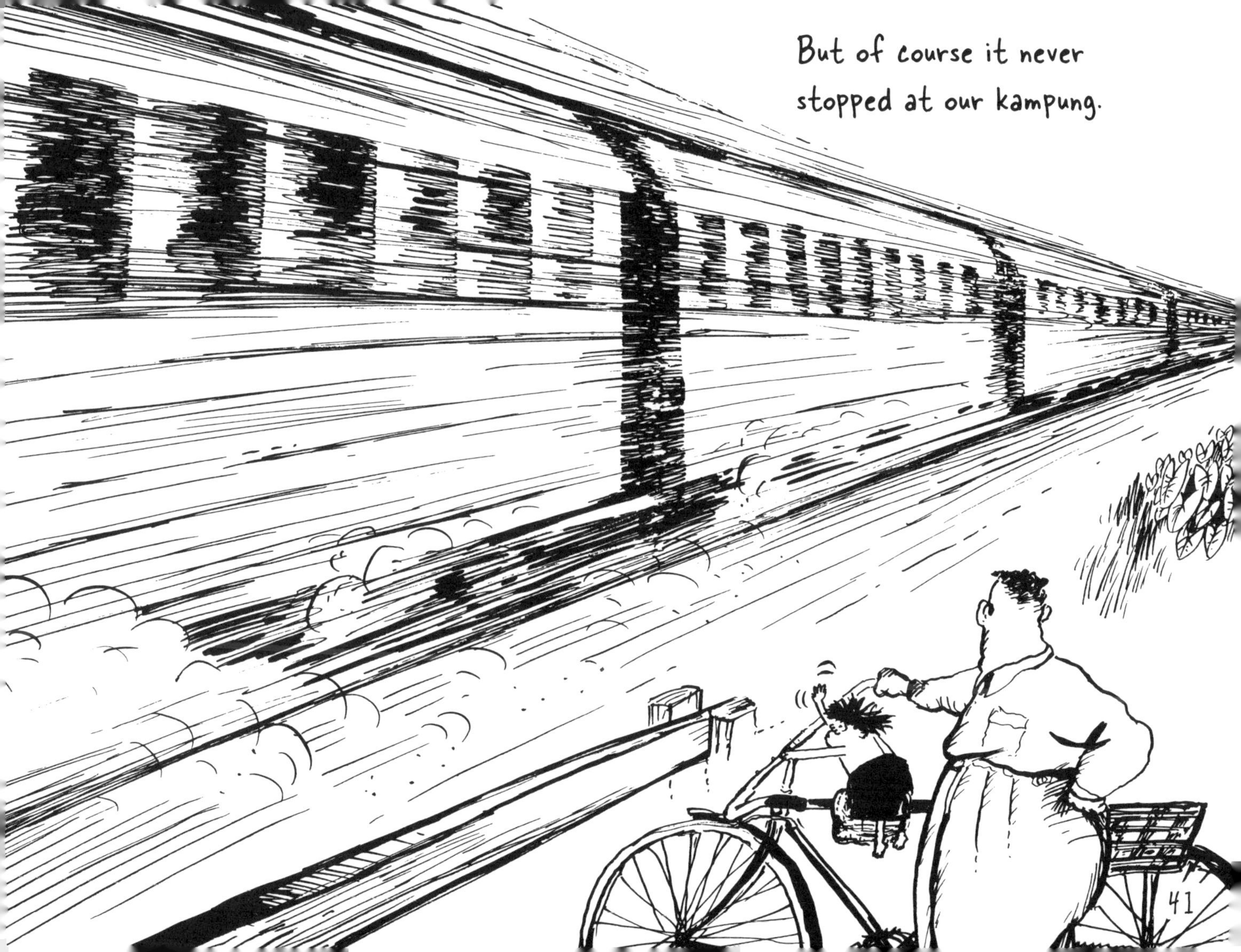

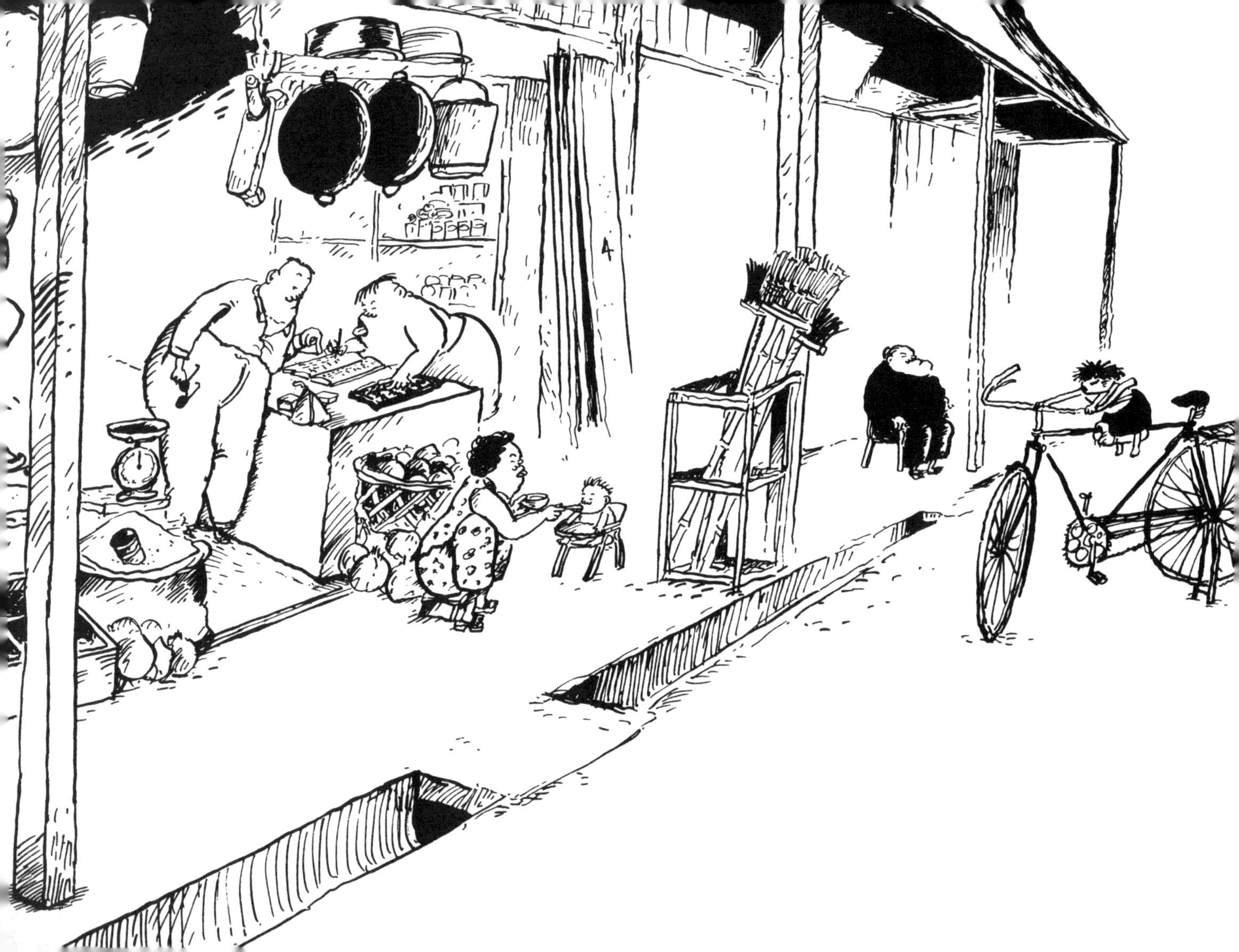
4

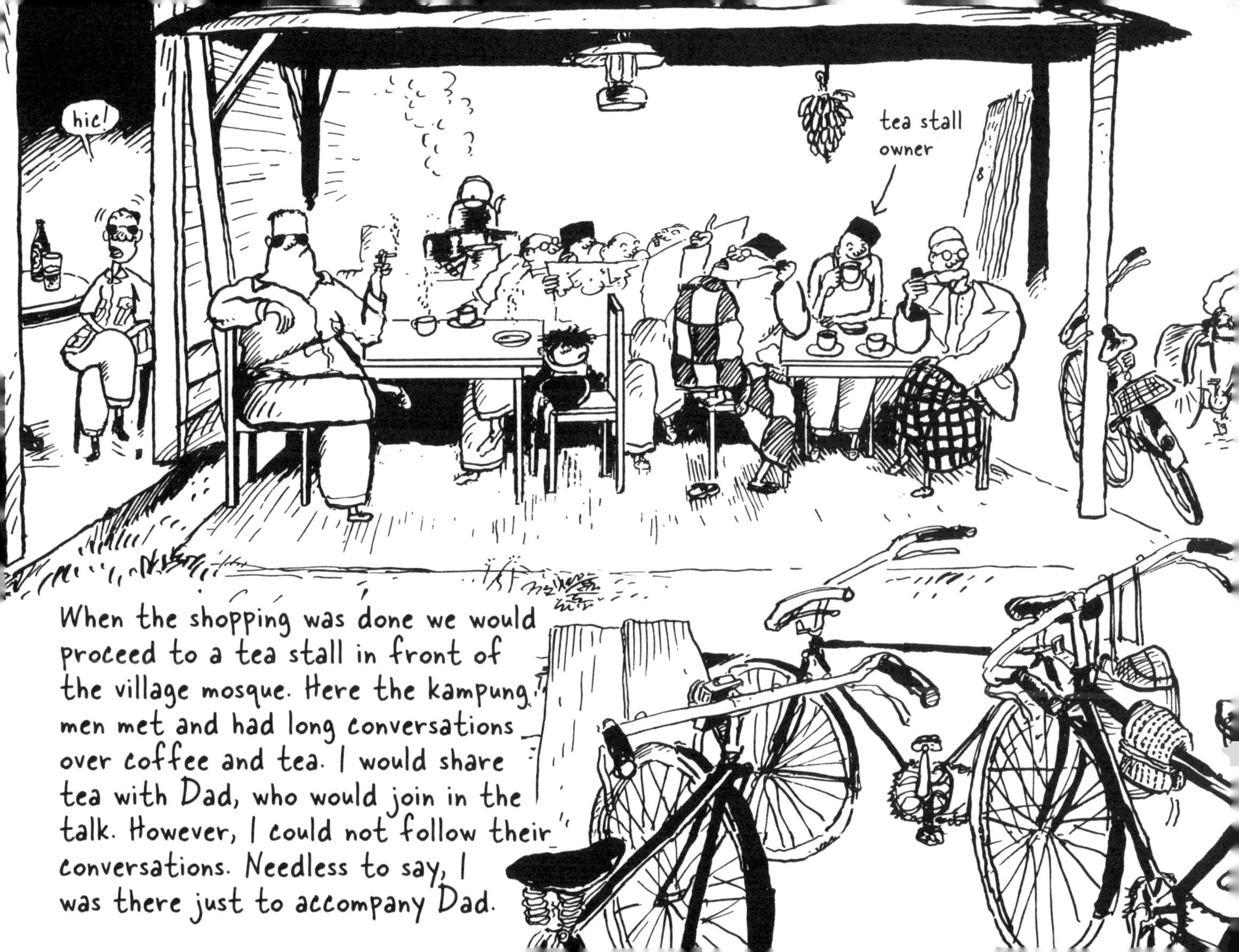
hic!
tea stall owner
When the shopping was done we would proceed to a tea stall in front of the village mosque. Here the kampung men met and had long conversations over coffee and tea. I would share tea with Dad, who would join in the talk. However, I could not follow their conversations. Needless to say, I was there just to accompany Dad.

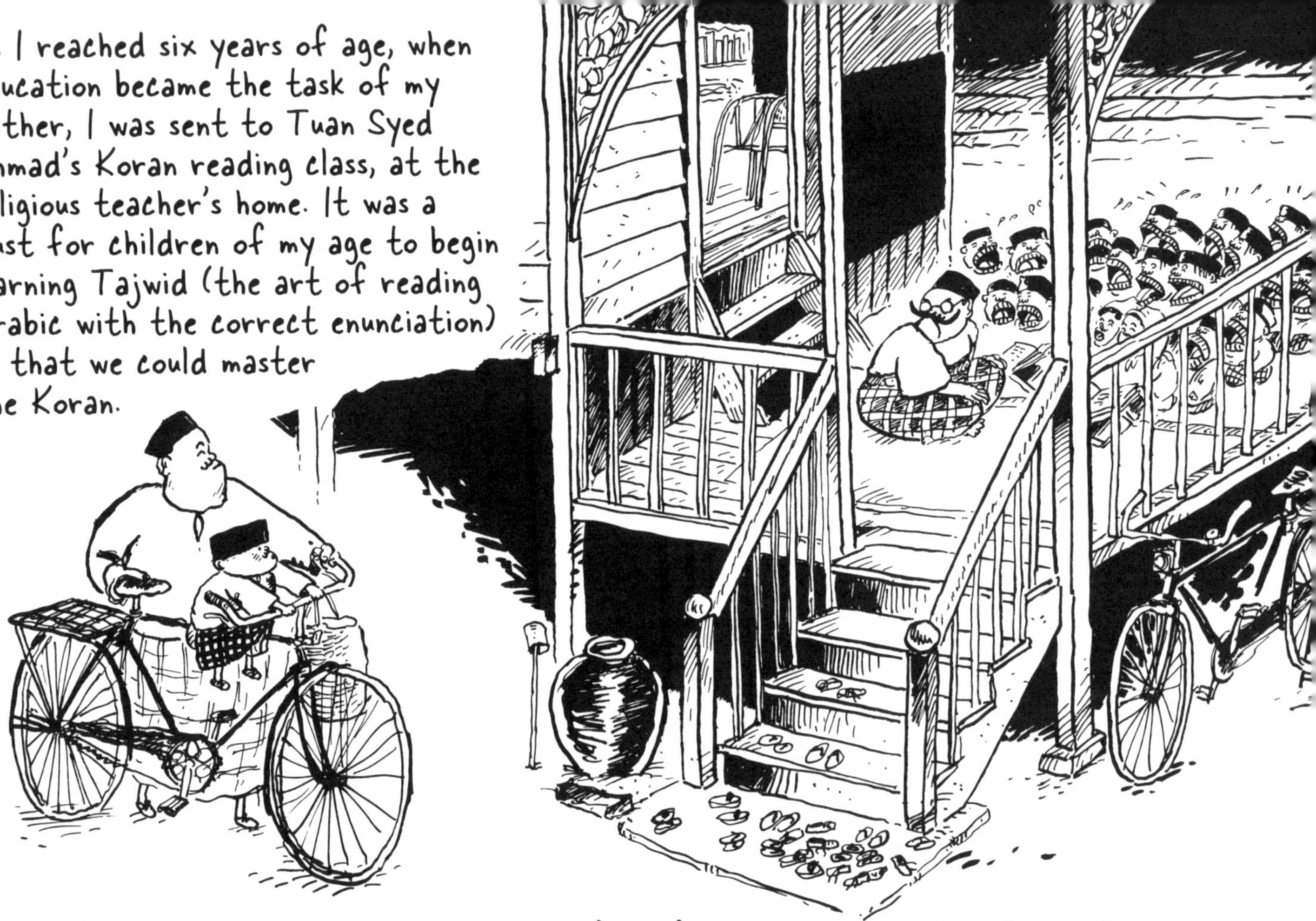
As I reached six years of age, when education became the task of my father, I was sent to Tuan Syed Ahmad's Koran reading class, at the religious teacher's home. It was a must for children of my age to begin learning Tajwid (the art of reading Arabic with the correct enunciation) so that we could master the Koran.
Although it was the earliest stage of my formal education, I must admit that I was not very happy to see Tuan Syed for the first time that afternoon.

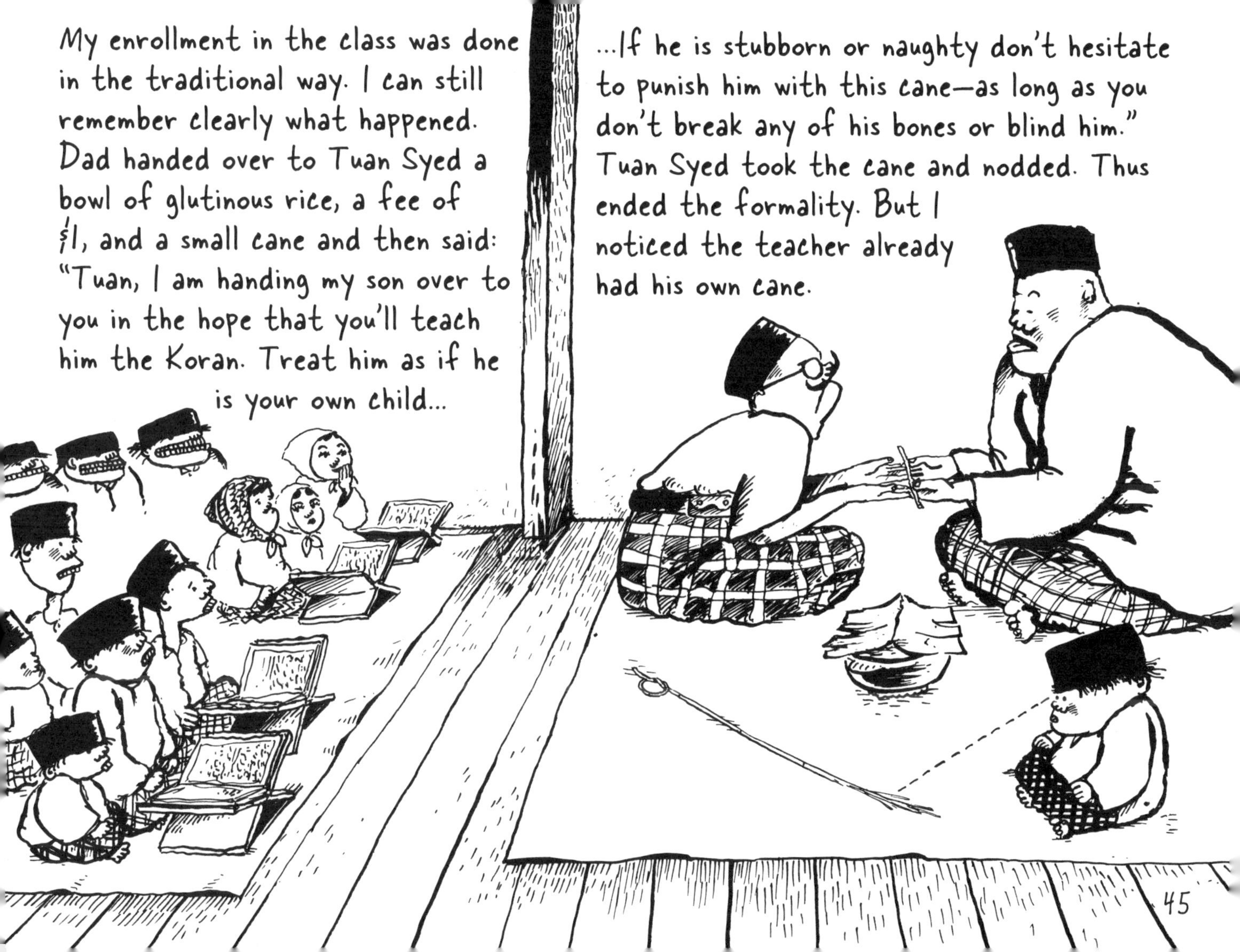
My enrollment in the class was done in the traditional way. I can still remember clearly what happened. Dad handed over to Tuan Syed a bowl of glutinous rice, a fee of $1, and a small cane and then said: "Tuan, I am handing my son over to you in the hope that you'll teach him the Koran. Treat him as if he is your own child...
...If he is stubborn or naughty don't hesitate to punish him with this cane—as long as you don't break any of his bones or blind him."
Tuan Syed took the cane and nodded. Thus ended the formality. But I noticed the teacher already had his own cane.

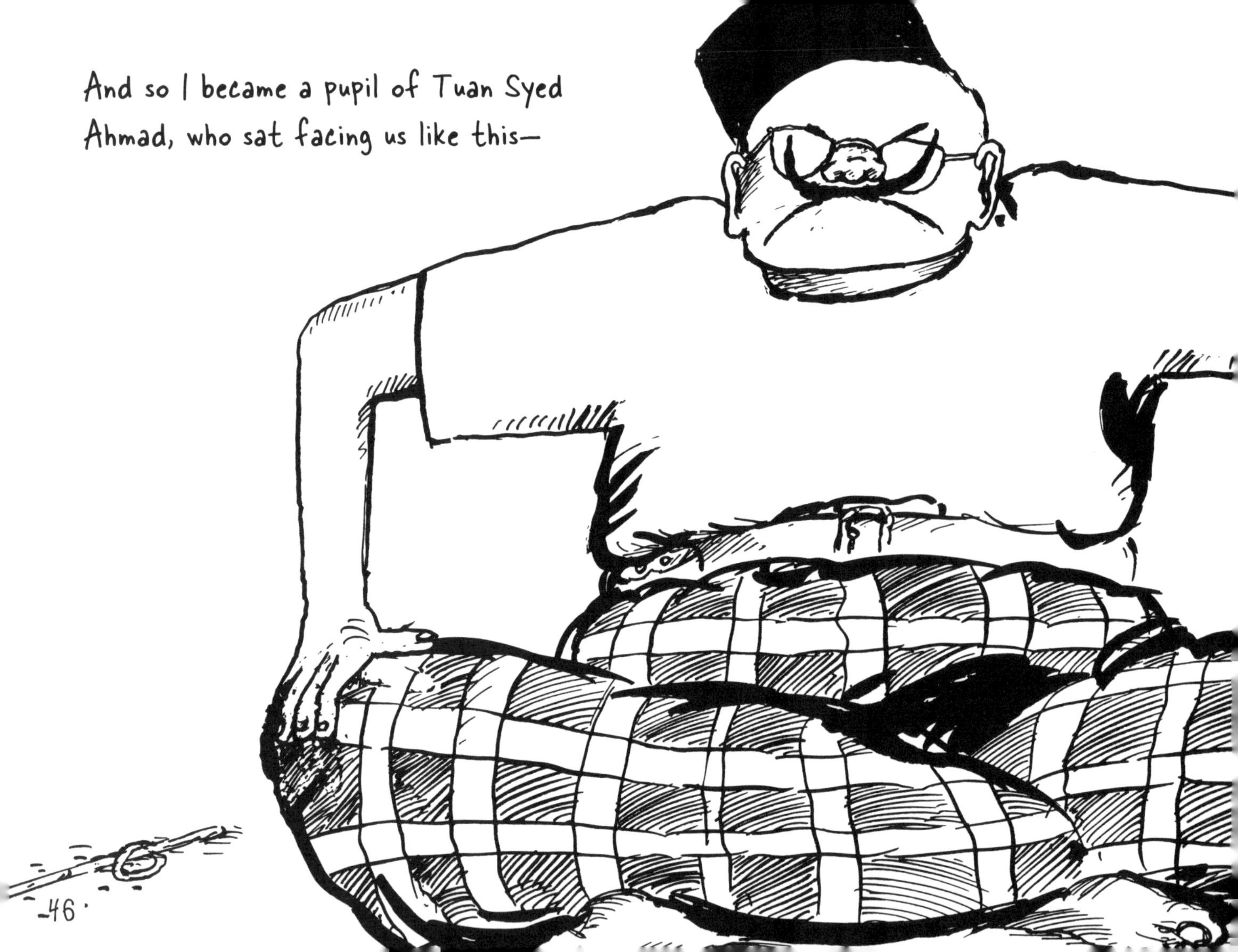
And so I became a pupil of Tuan Syed Ahmad, who sat facing us like this—

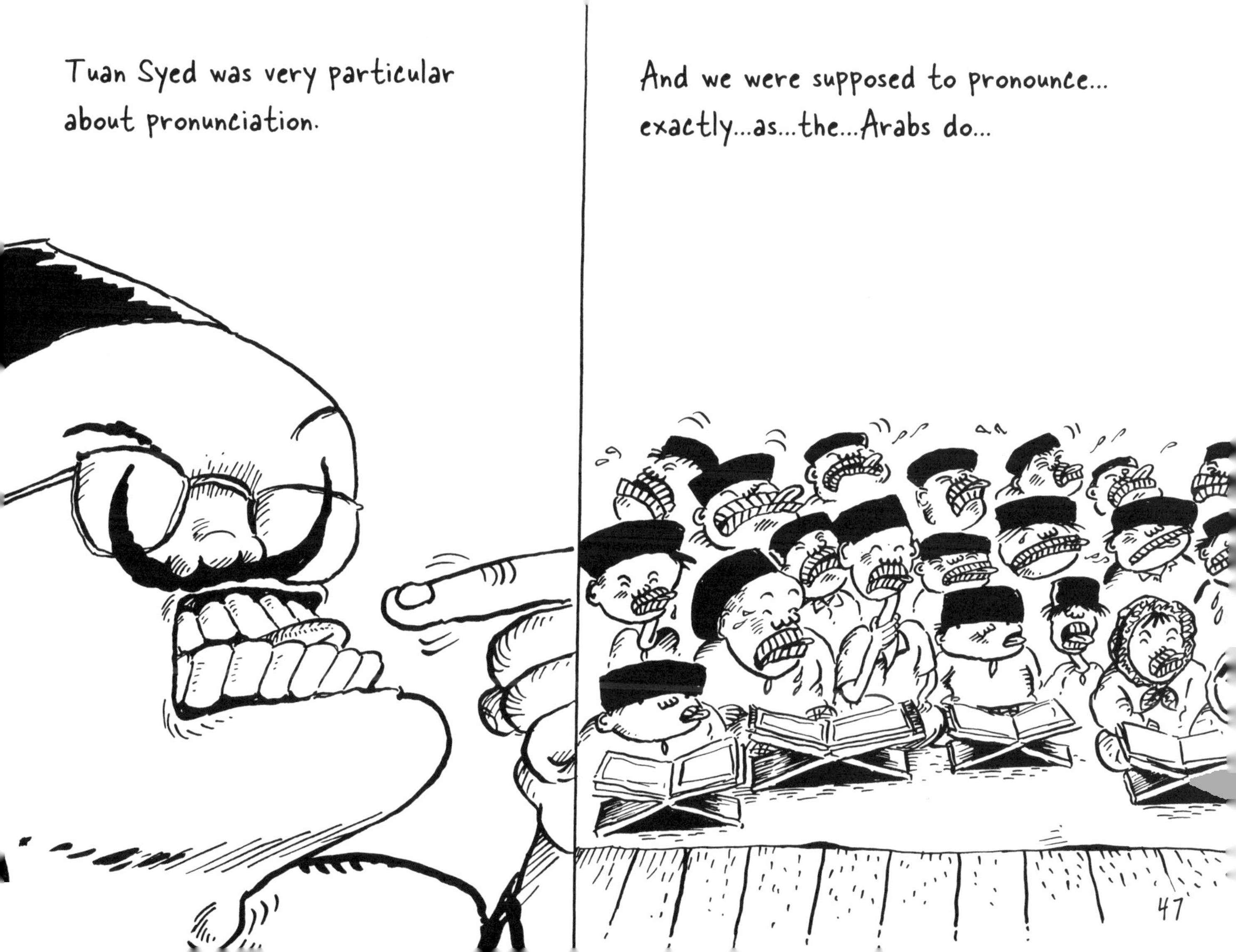
Tuan Syed was very particular about pronunciation.
And we were supposed to pronounce... exactly...as...the...Arabs do...

One thing I discovered about an afternoon class was you tend to get sleepy...

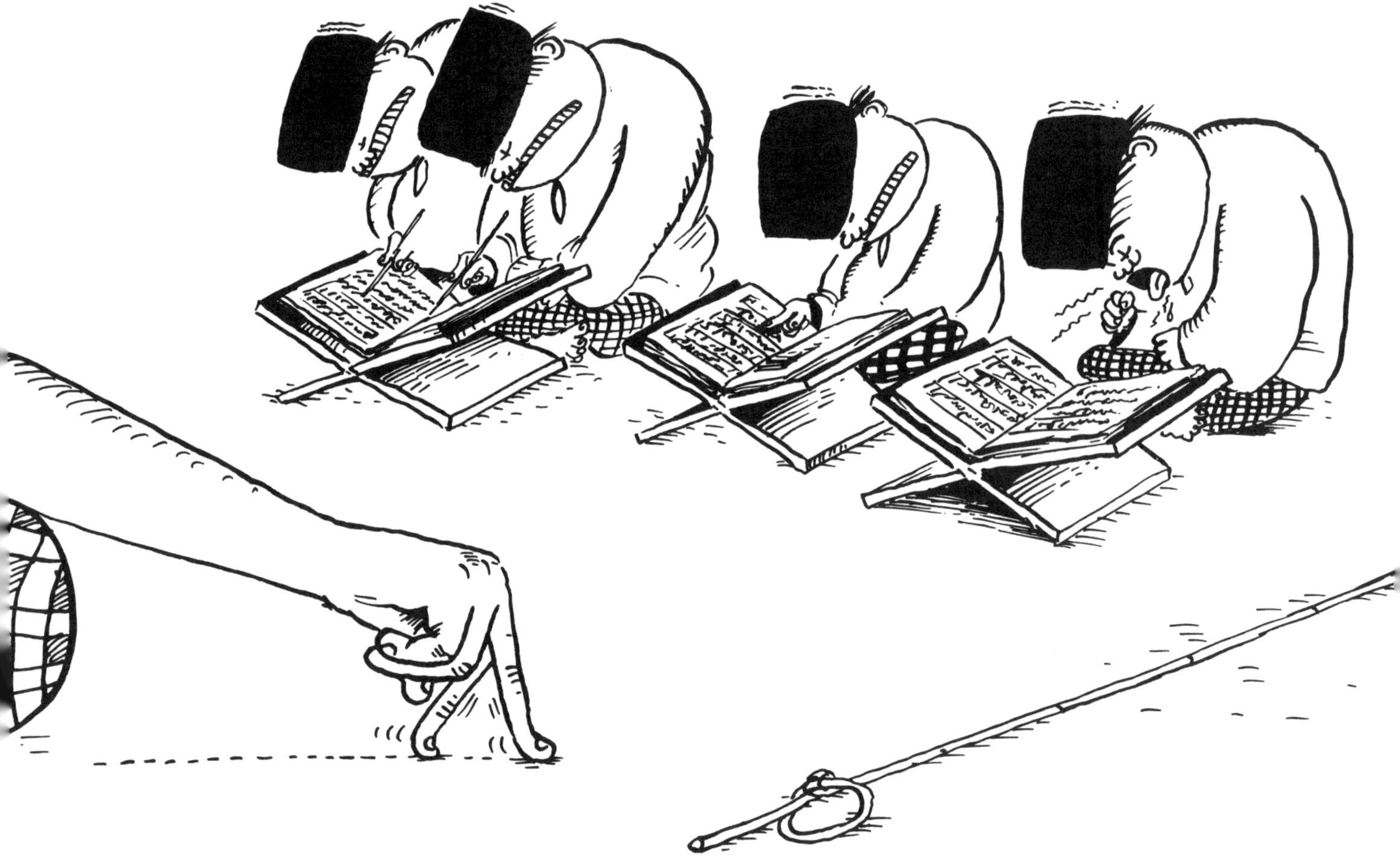

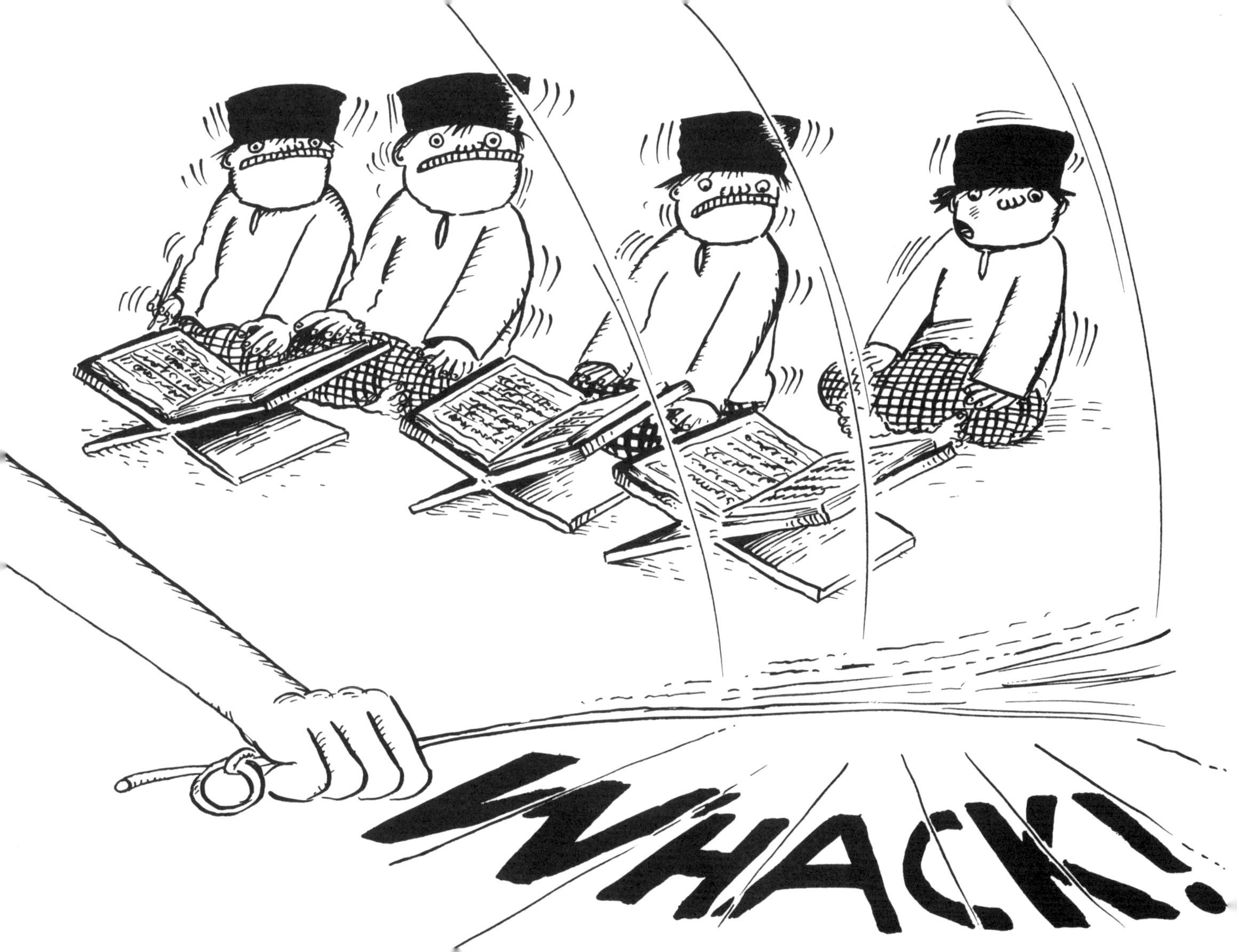
WHACK!

Before long I became used to the scene and had befriended some of the fellows. At the end of each month we'd pay the teacher for his service. Tuan Syed accepted any form of payment. Some of us would give him $1, some gave 50 cents, others gave him a plate of rice or sugar.

Or we could be like these three brothers here (the children of Meor Yusoff), who gave teacher firewood they picked on their way to class.

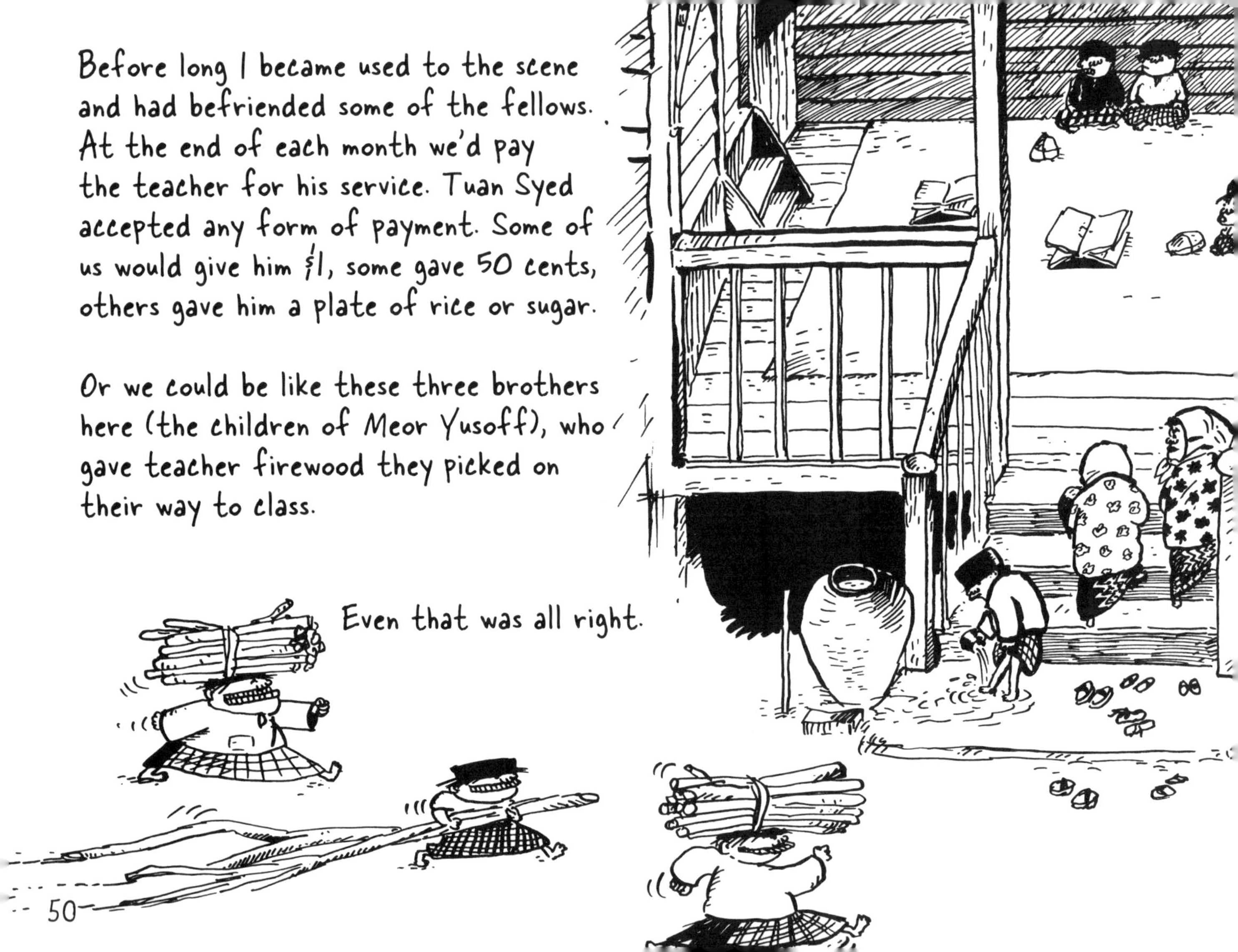

Even that was all right.

These children of Meor Yusoff were in fact the first friends that I made. I was rather afraid of them at first because the way they talked and moved around led me to think they were rough. But I admired them for their knowledge of fishing, which seemed to be the most important thing in their lives.
They always had interesting things to tell about the river and fishing and many a time they invited me to come along and watch them inspect their fish traps. But I would turn down their invitation because I was not sure whether I was brave enough to go to the faraway and remote parts of the river.

But Meor Din, the eldest of the Meor brothers, would say to me each time before we parted: "If you want to know the best spots for swimming and if you want to learn fishing, follow us."

One day I just couldn't resist.

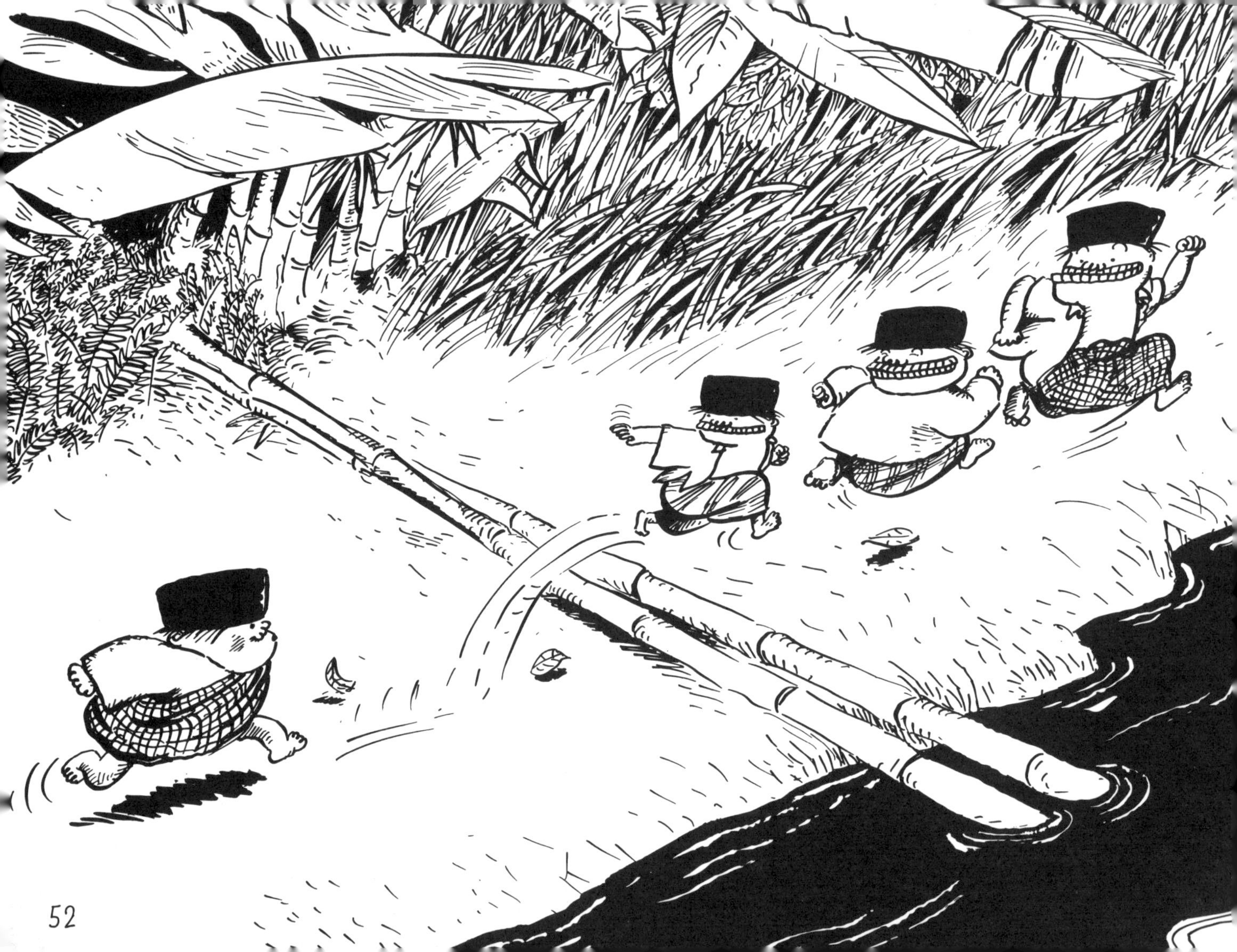

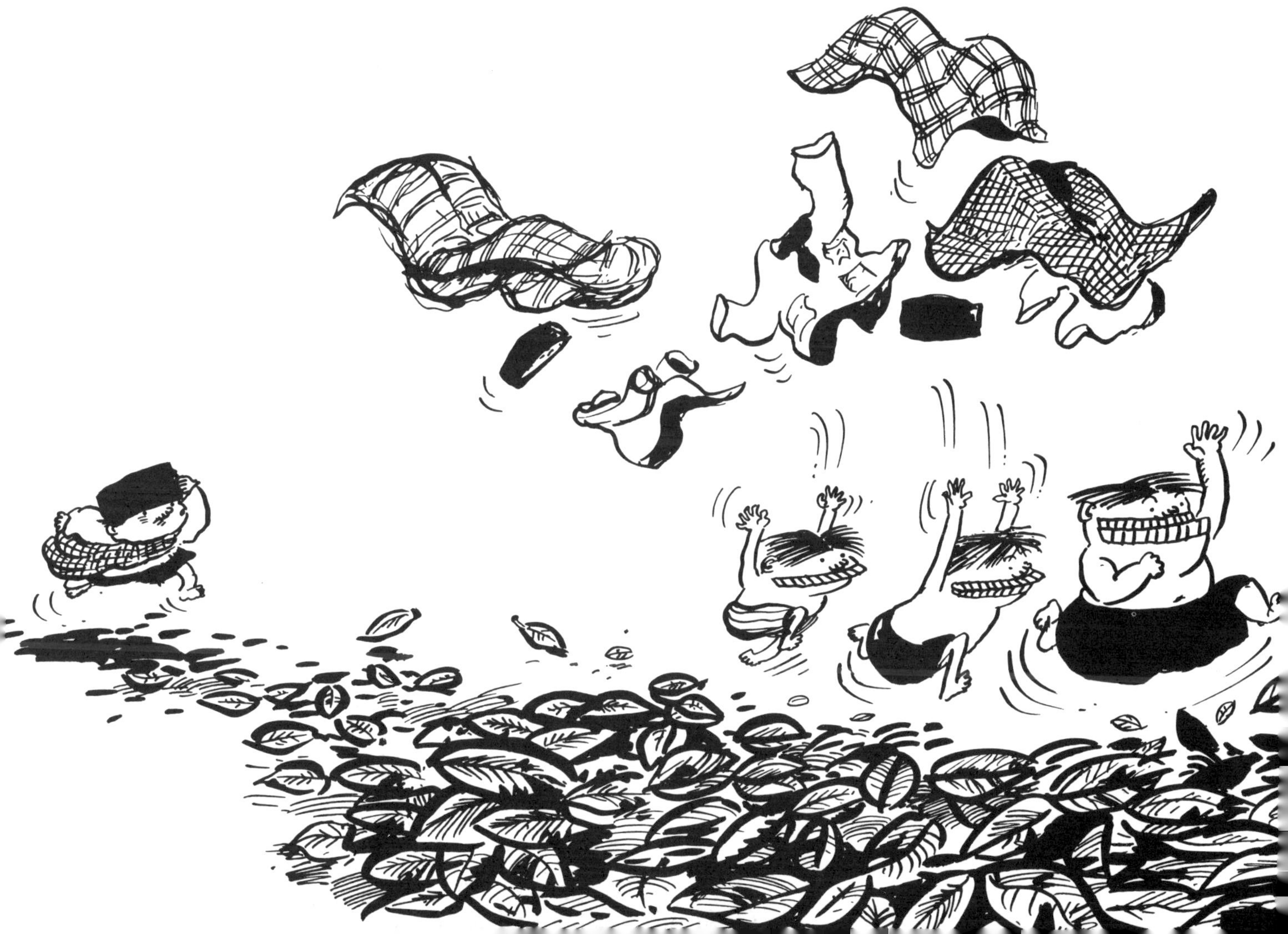

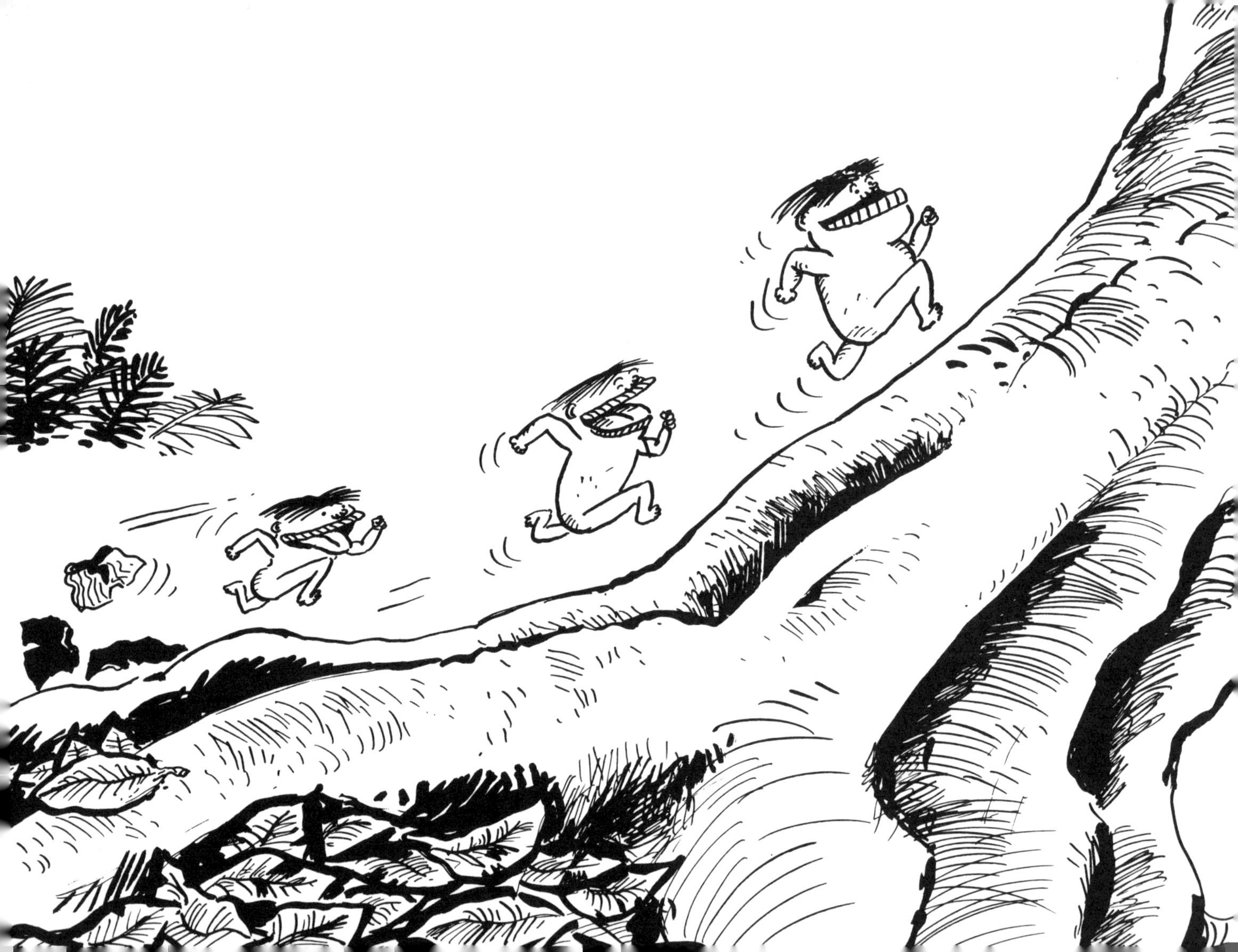

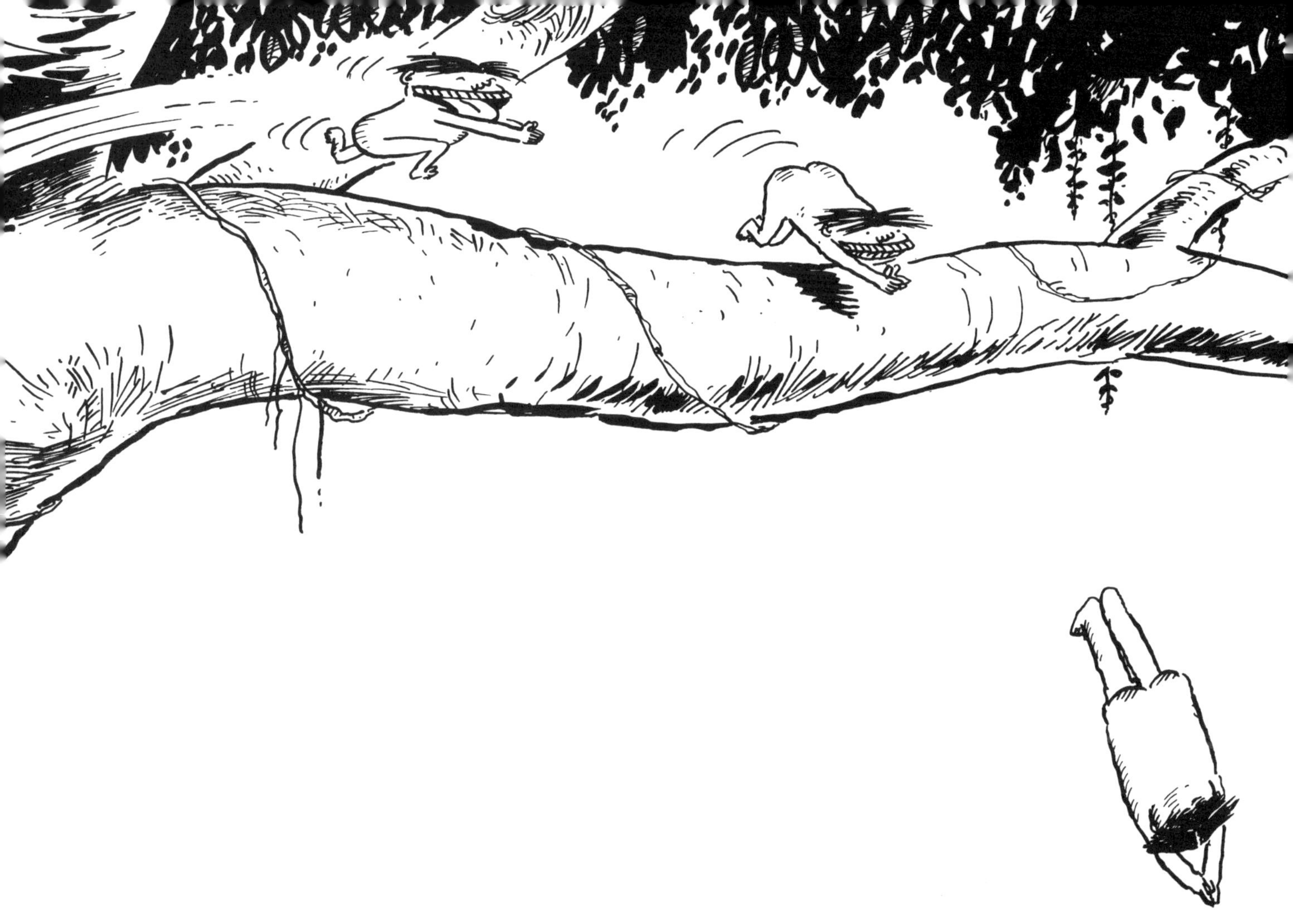

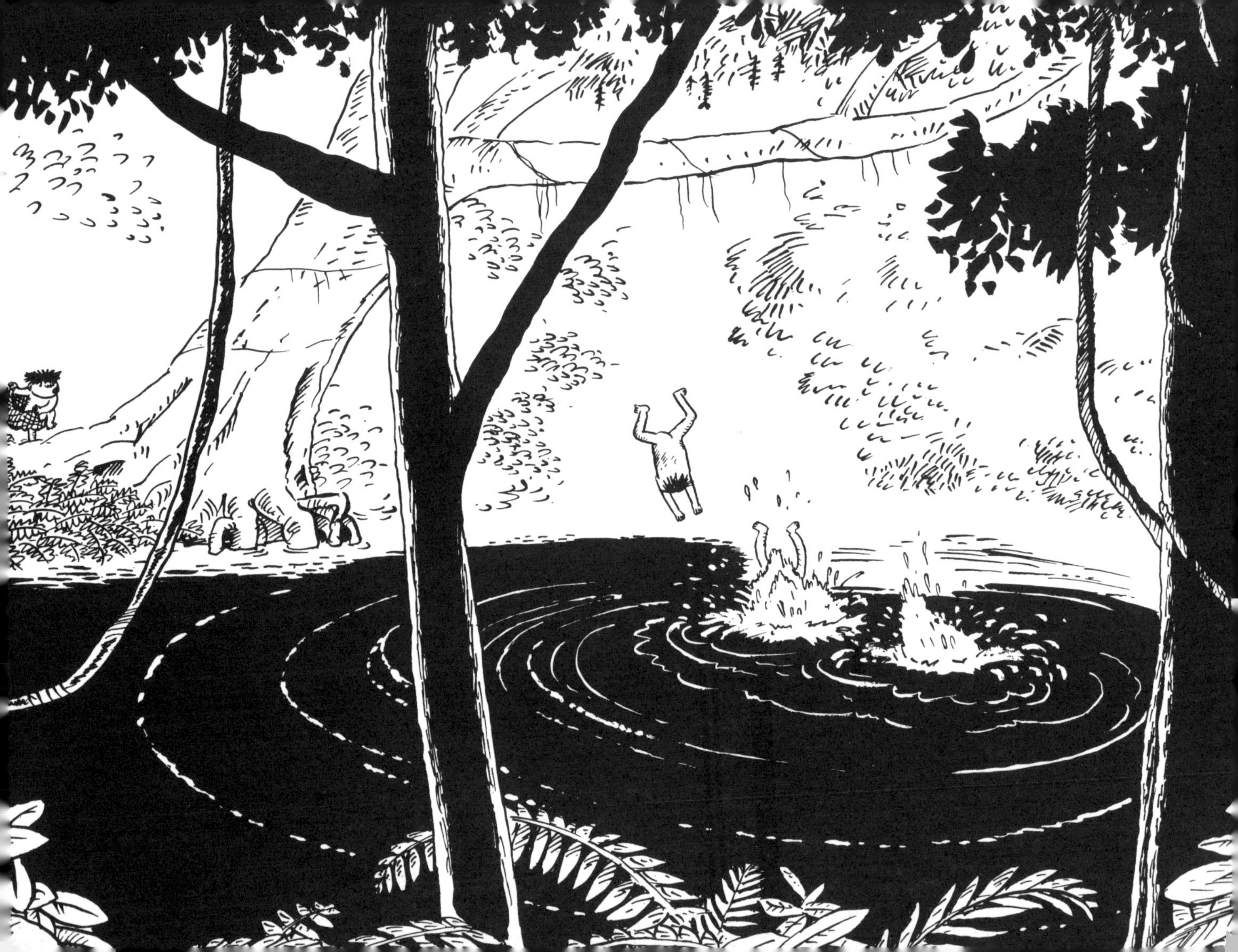

Those fellows really knew know to dive...
and how long they could stay underwater!

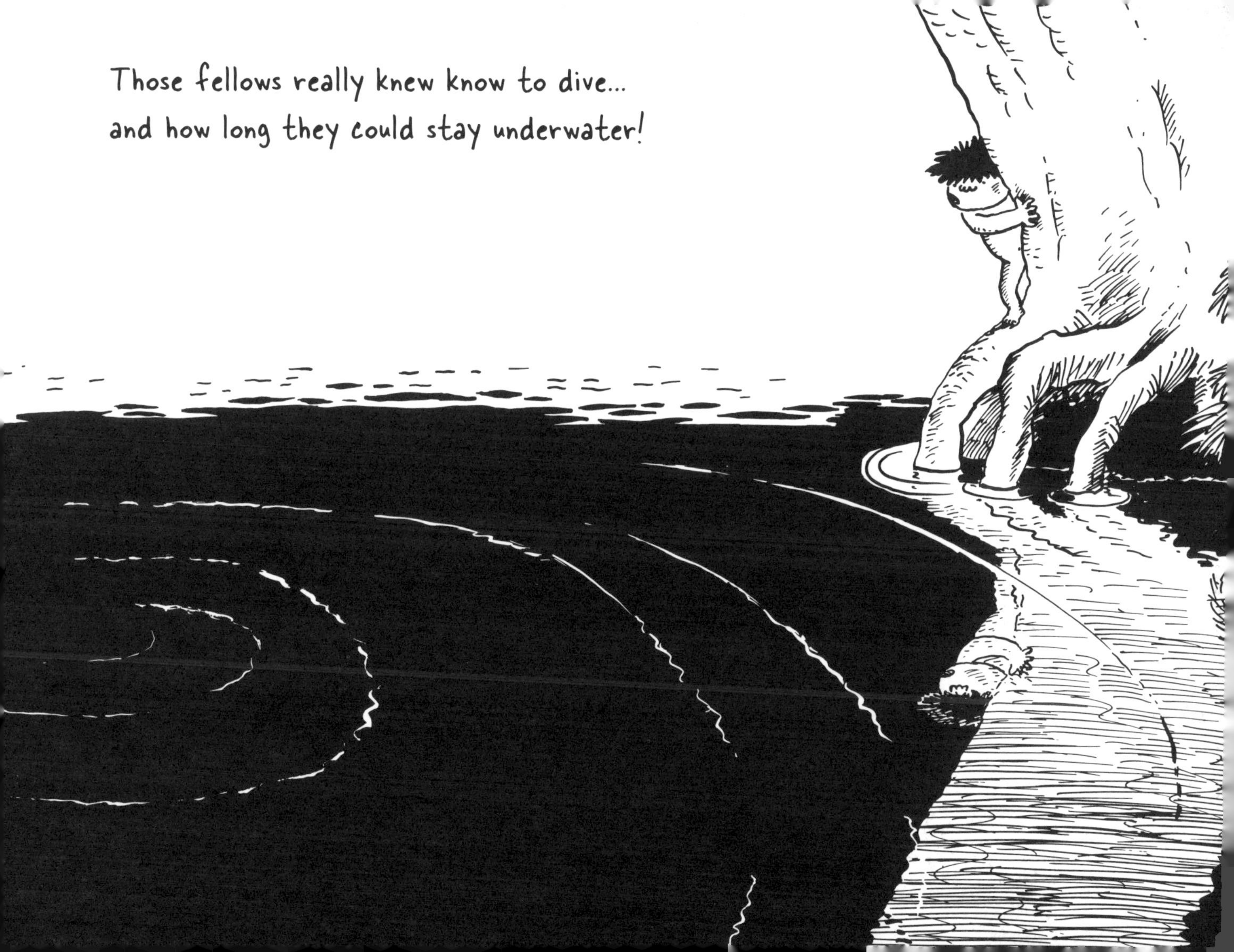

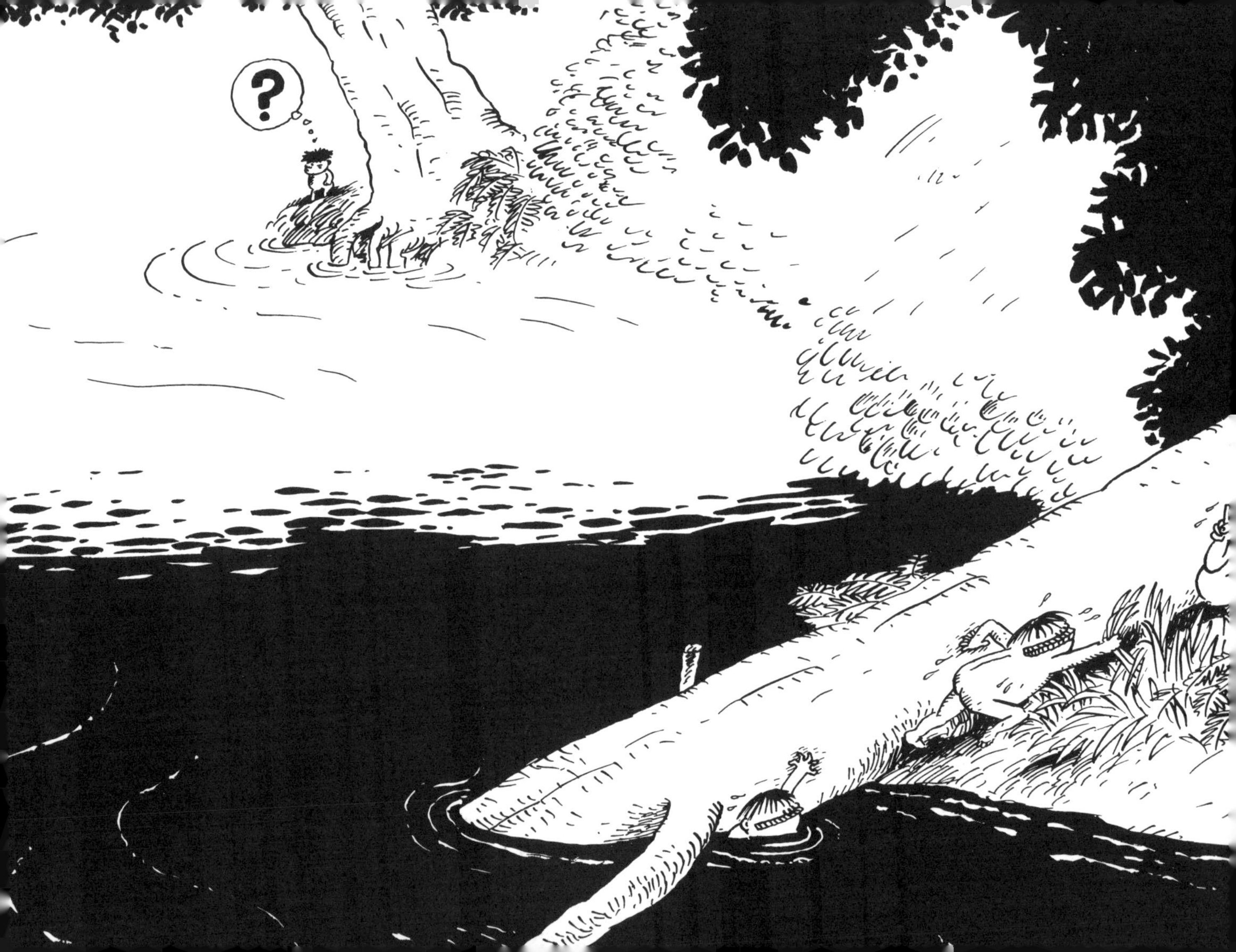
?

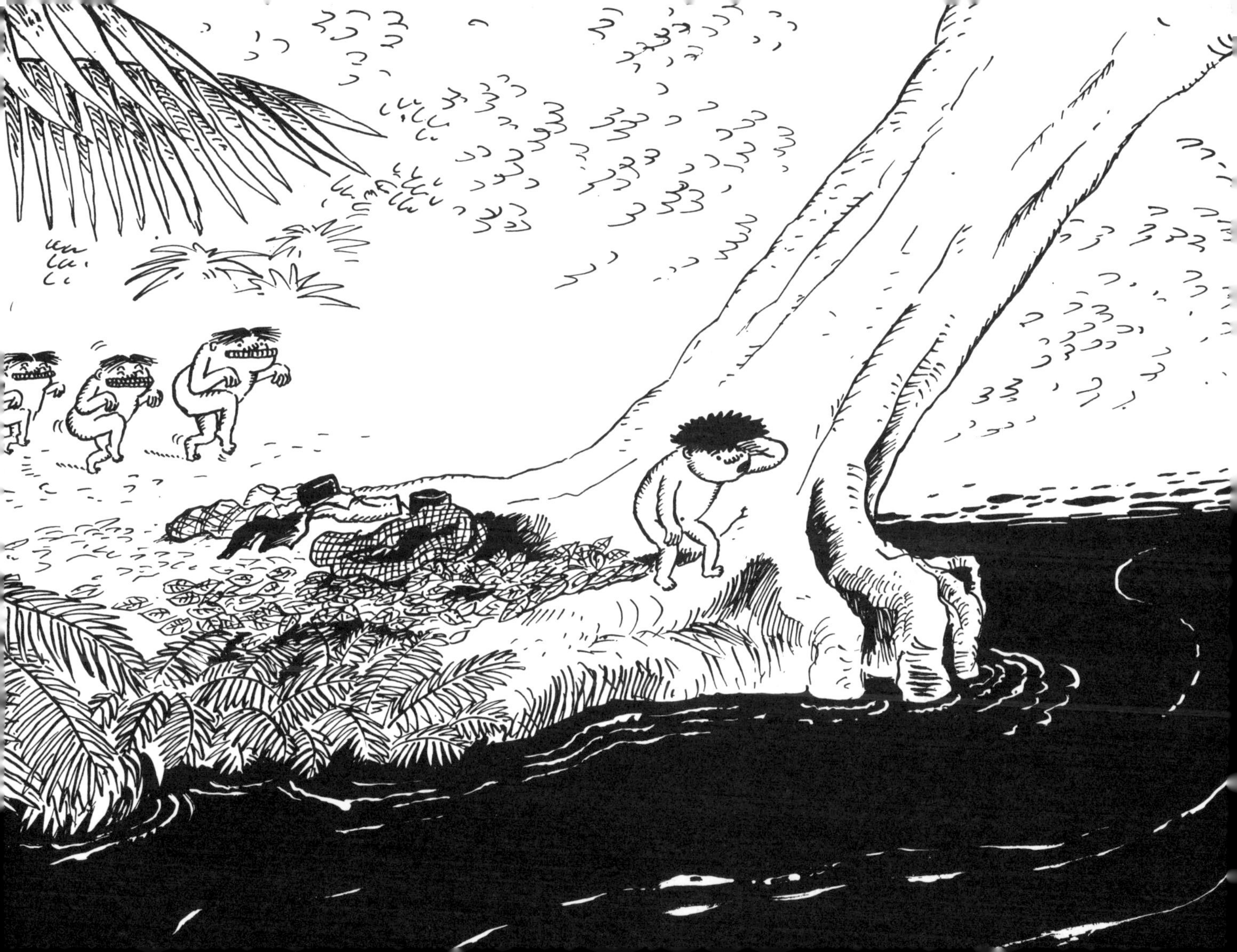

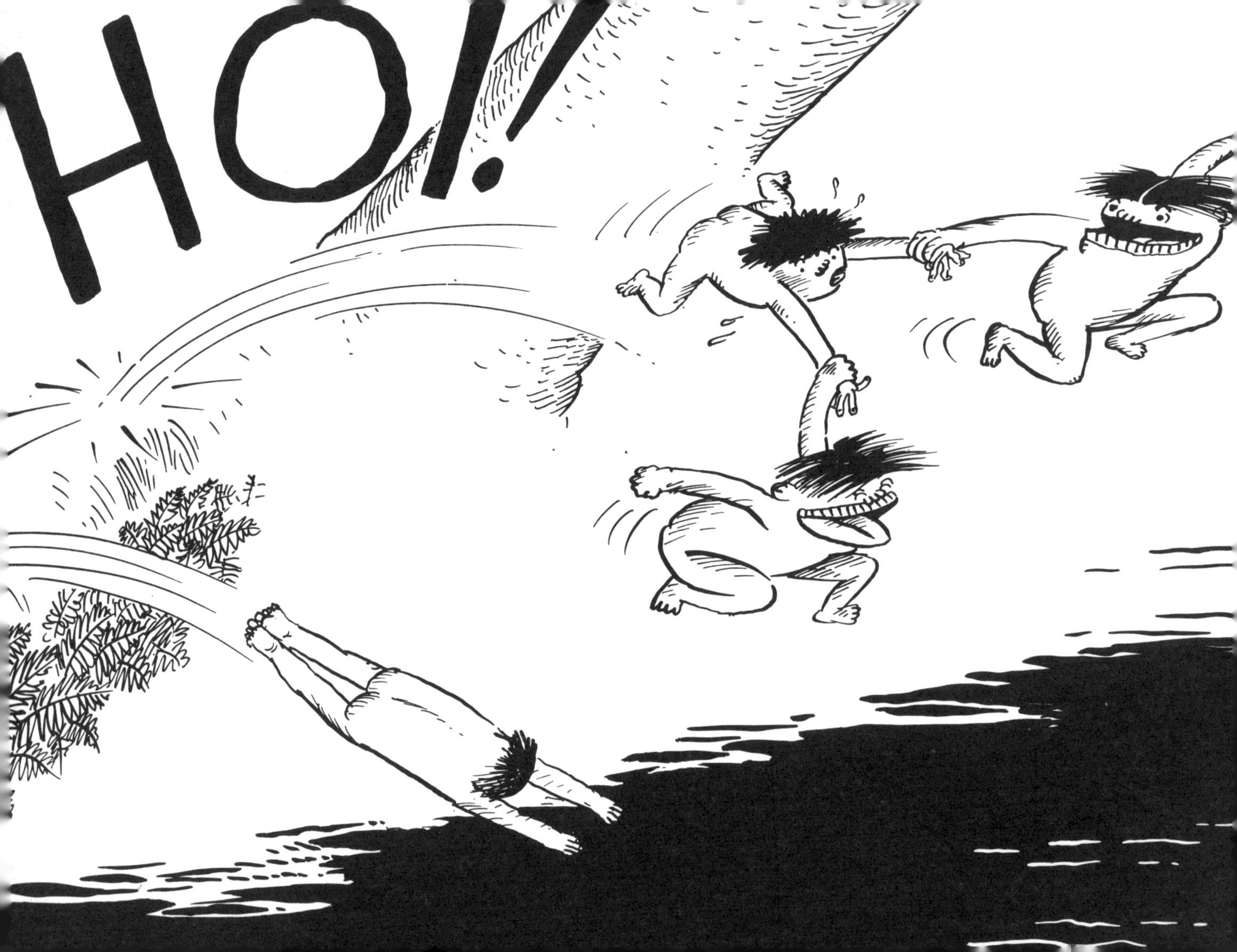
HO!!

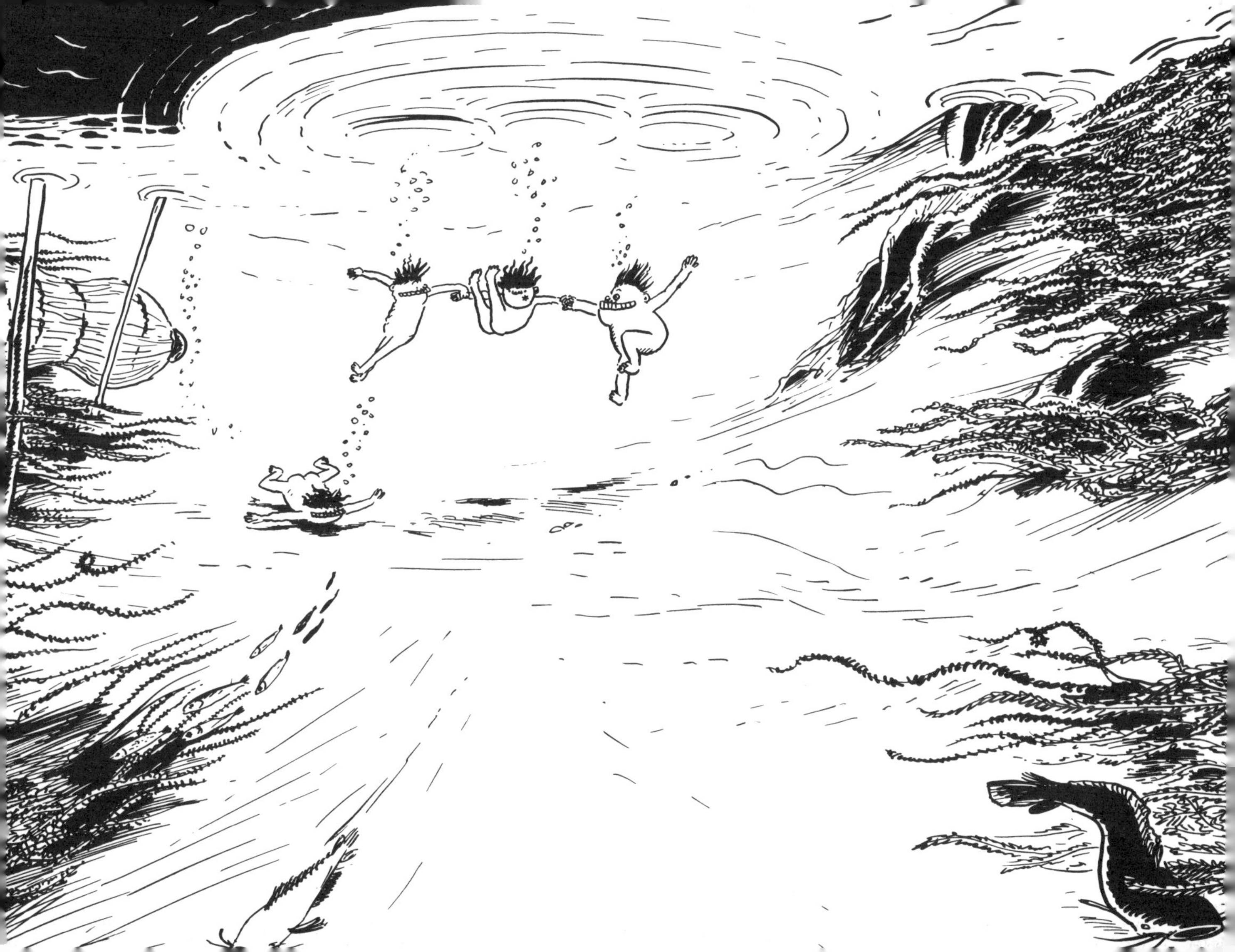

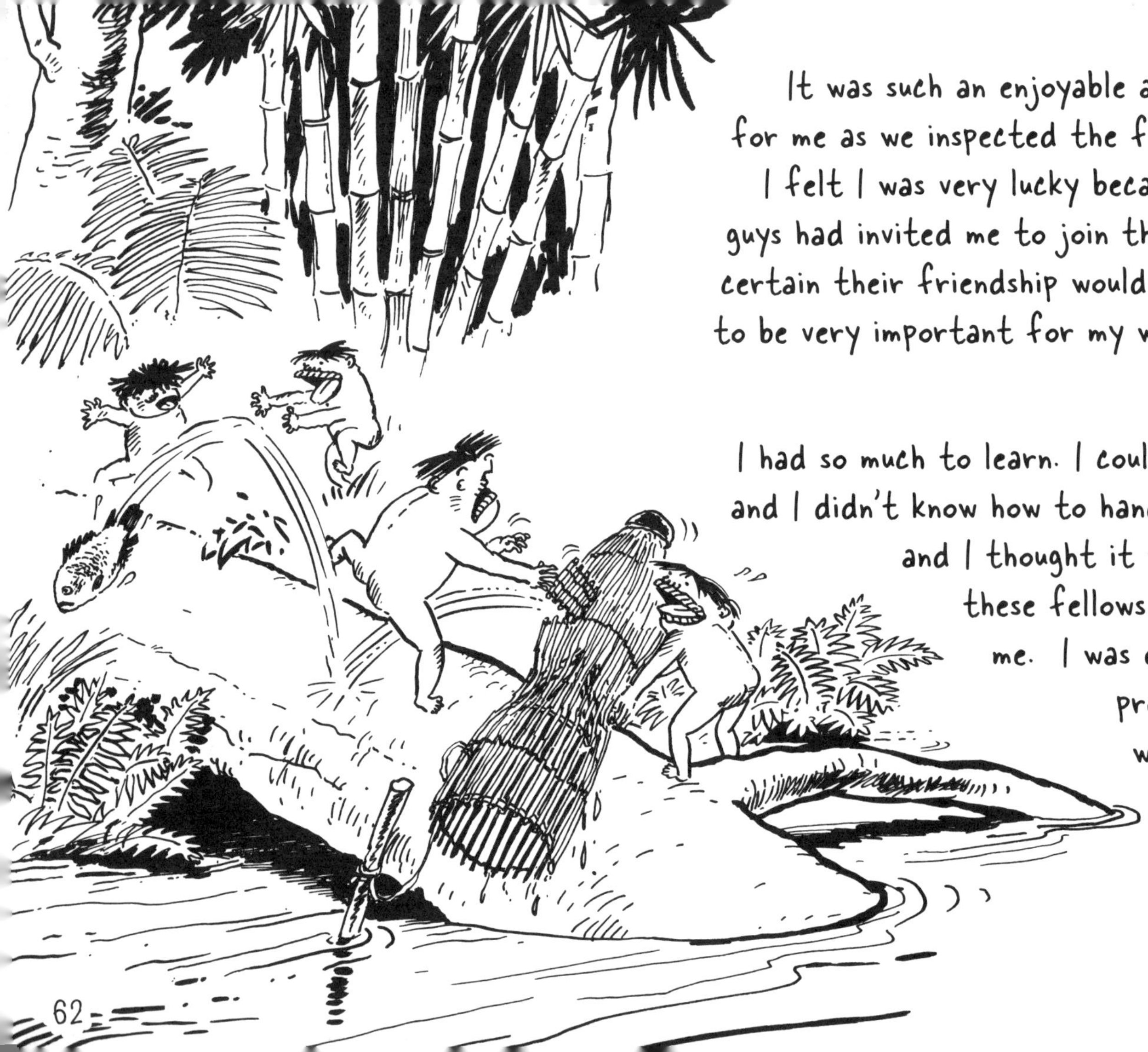

It was such an enjoyable afternoon for me as we inspected the fish traps. I felt I was very lucky because these guys had invited me to join them. I was certain their friendship would turn out to be very important for my whole life.

I had so much to learn. I couldn't swim and I didn't know how to handle a fish and I thought it was up to these fellows to teach me. I was extremely proud to be with them.

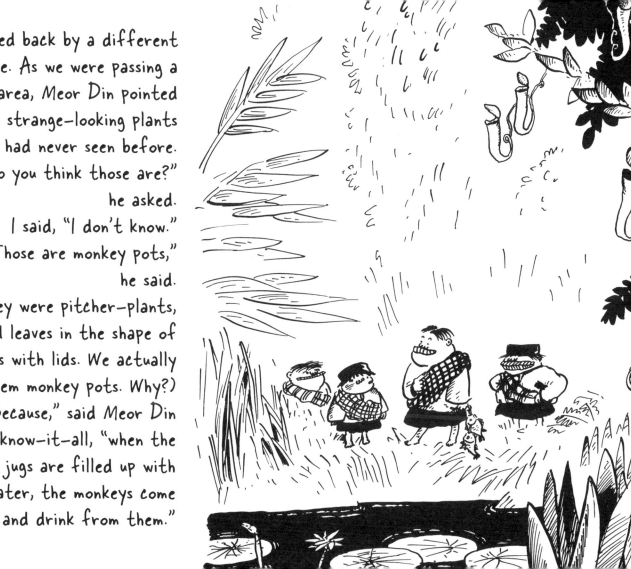

We walked back by a different route. As we were passing a swampy area, Meor Din pointed at some strange-looking plants I had never seen before.

"What do you think those are?" he asked.

I said, "I don't know."

"Those are monkey pots," he said.

(They were pitcher-plants, which had leaves in the shape of little jugs with lids. We actually call them monkey pots. Why?)

"Because," said Meor Din the know-it-all, "when the little jugs are filled up with rainwater, the monkeys come and drink from them."

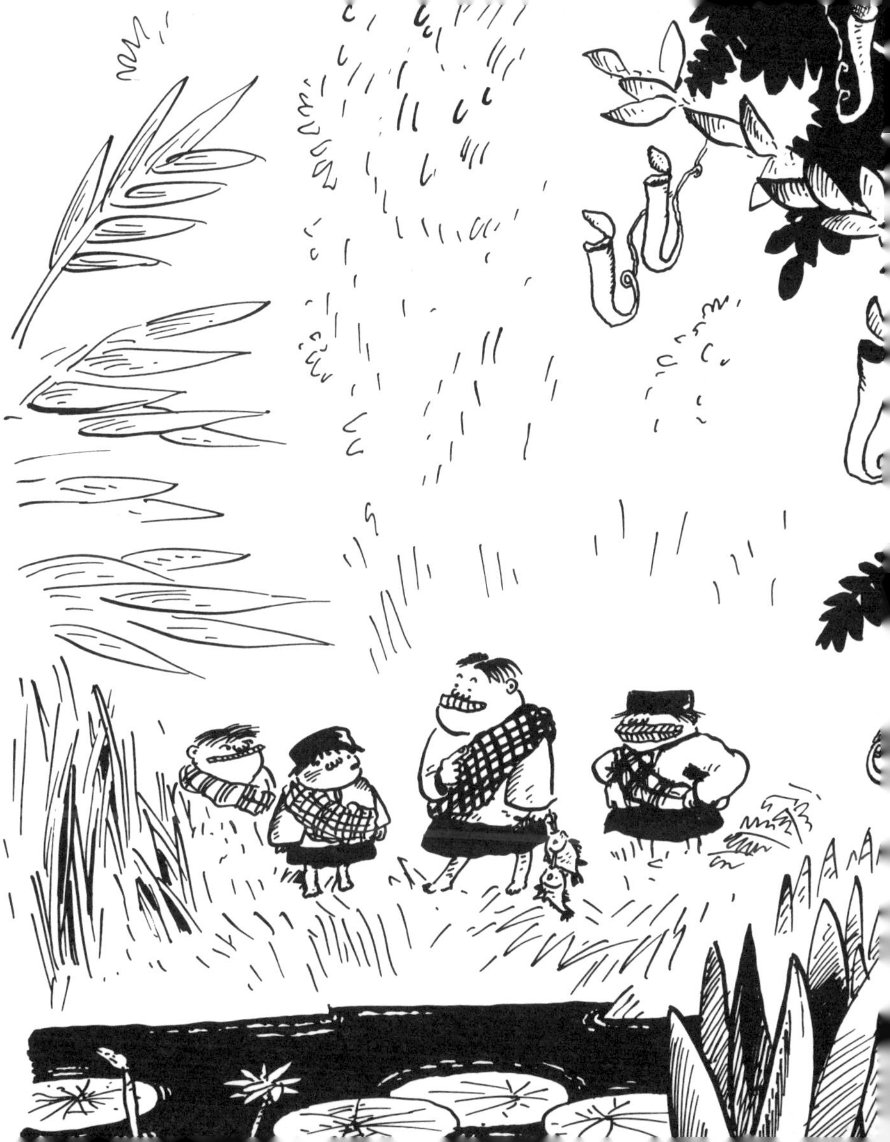

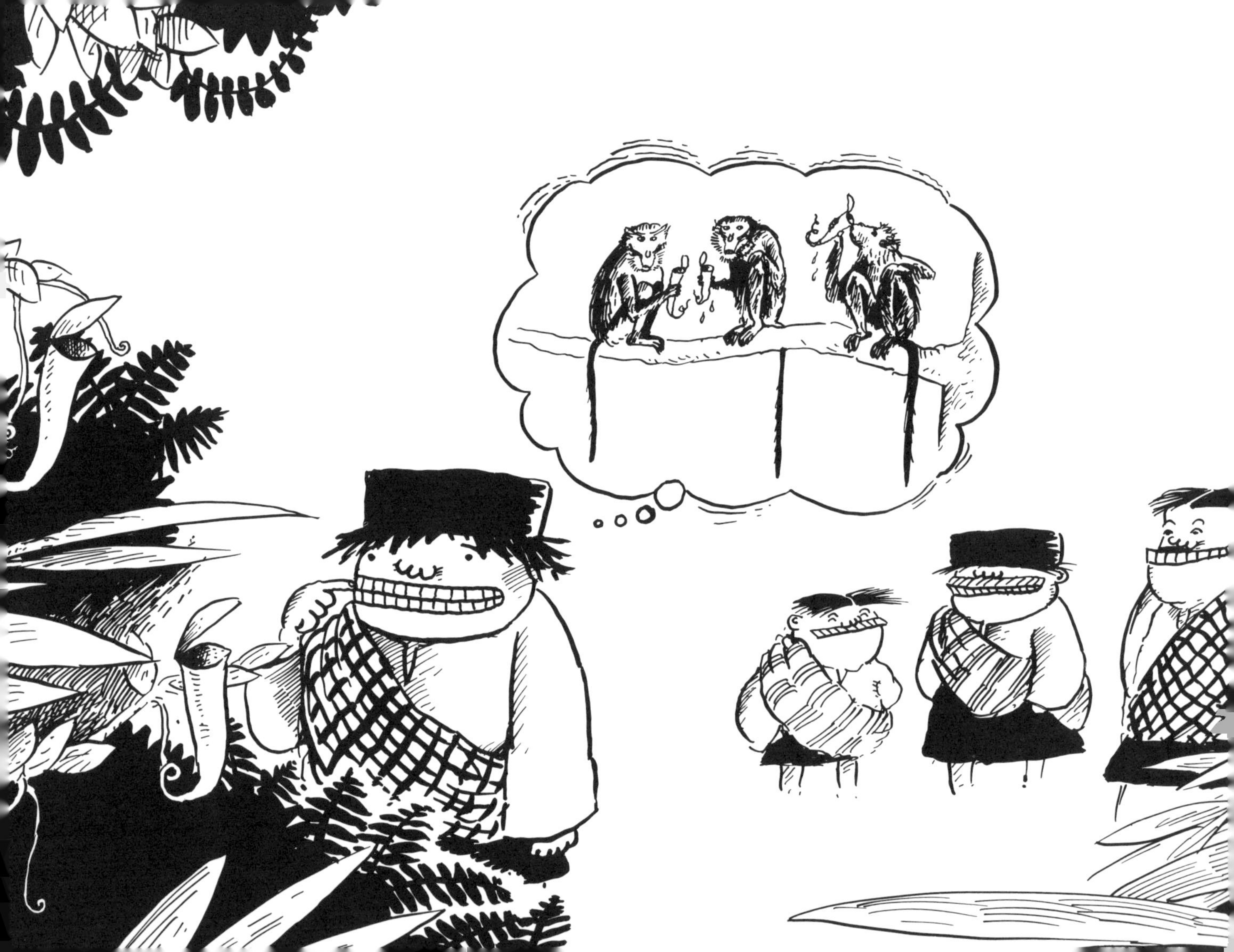

Then we passed through a dredging area. It was the first time I saw a tin dredge up close. I told the boys that when I was younger I was scared of the dredge because I thought it was a monster.

The fellows laughed.

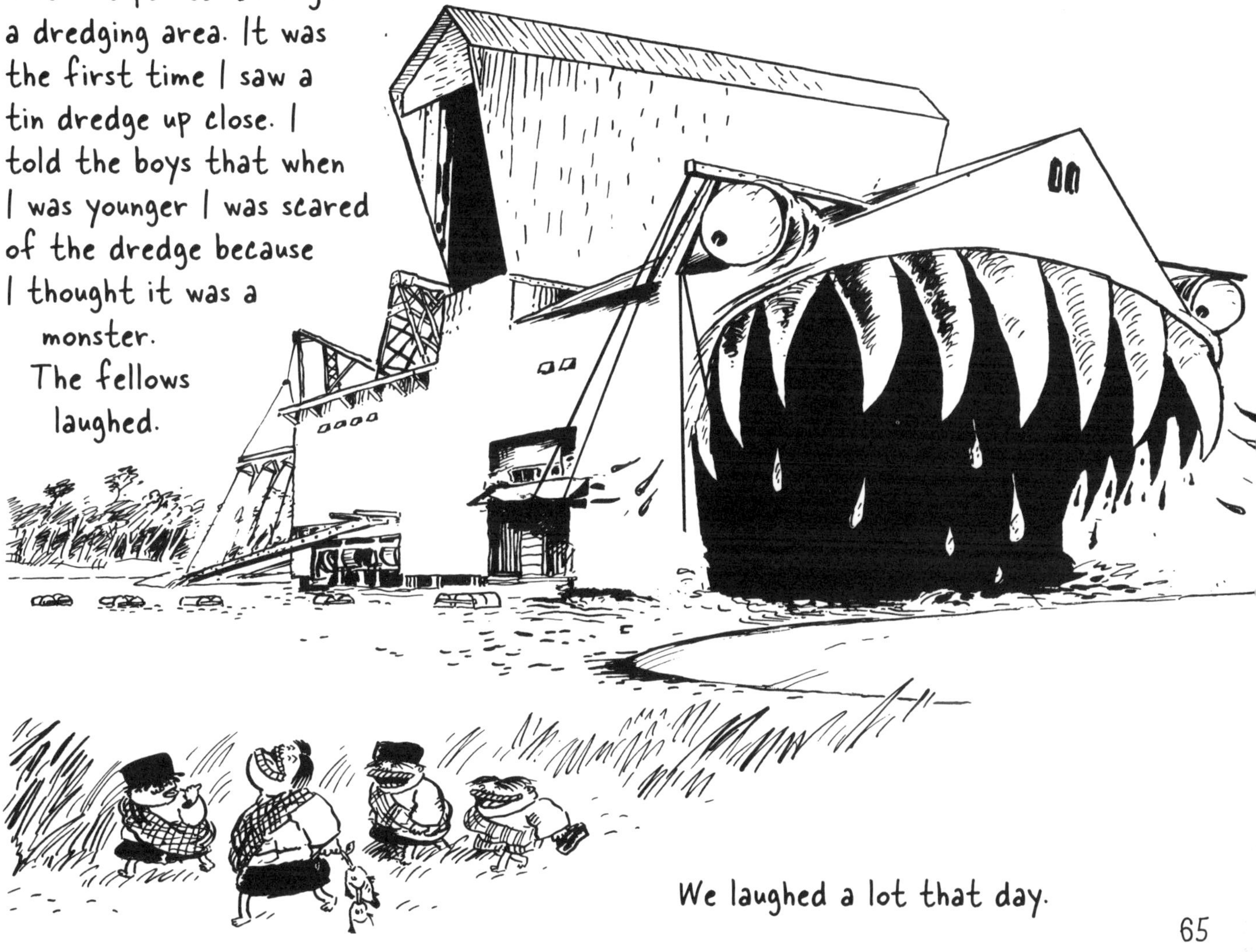

We laughed a lot that day.

As far as I can remember, the first time I ever stepped out of the kampung was to attend the wedding of a male relative of ours in a nearby village. My family and I were in the party that accompanied the groom to the Akad Nikah ceremony at the bride's house.

We went in two cars. The groom was driven in a new Morris Minor belonging to a teacher and we followed in the dresser's Austin.

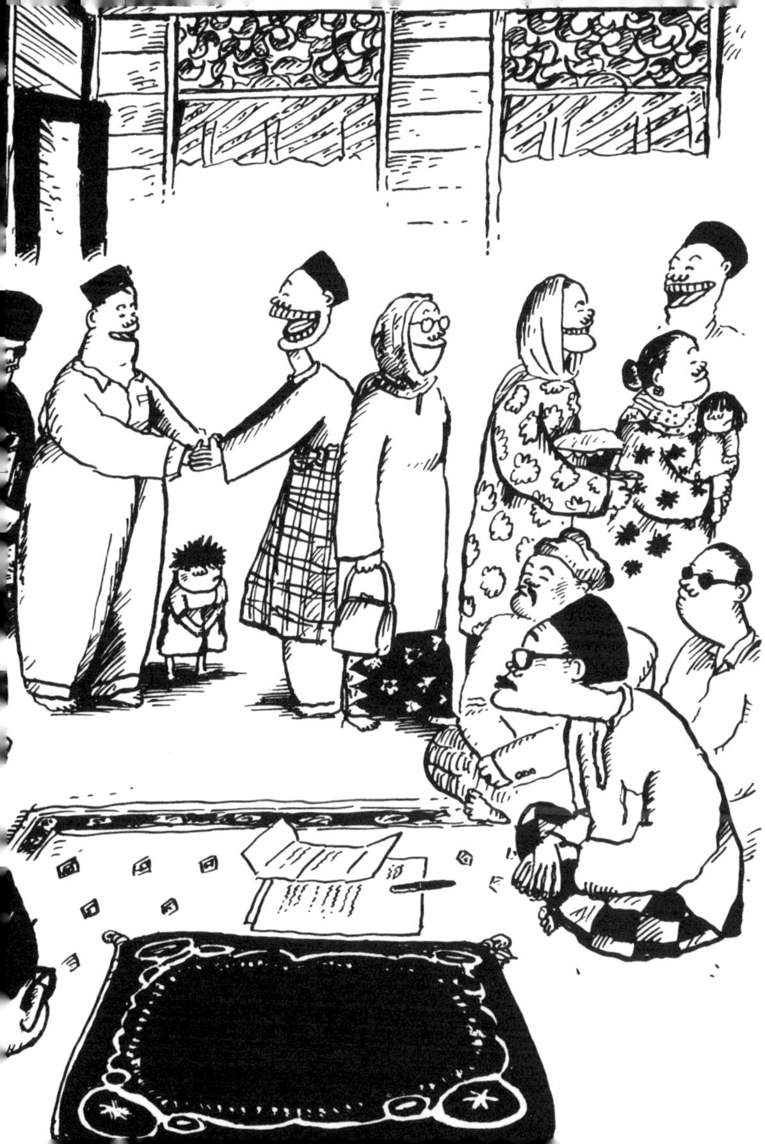

Our party was very well received by the people at the bride's house although we arrived an hour late. Bridegrooms never arrive on time, as I discovered in later years.

It was truly a big occasion and there was a huge crowd outside the house. As I entered I could tell, by the look of the handsomely built house and its furniture, that the girl was from a well-to-do family.

Waiting inside were the Kathi (judge), other guests, and witnesses.

There was no sign of the bride because in this Akad Nikah ceremony only the groom was needed by the Kathi to sign the marriage papers.

Then came the tricky part. Watched by witnesses, the groom was asked to recite after the Kathi the holy words of matrimony in one breath. In my cousin's case, he had to do it three times because the witnesses weren't satisfied until the third time...

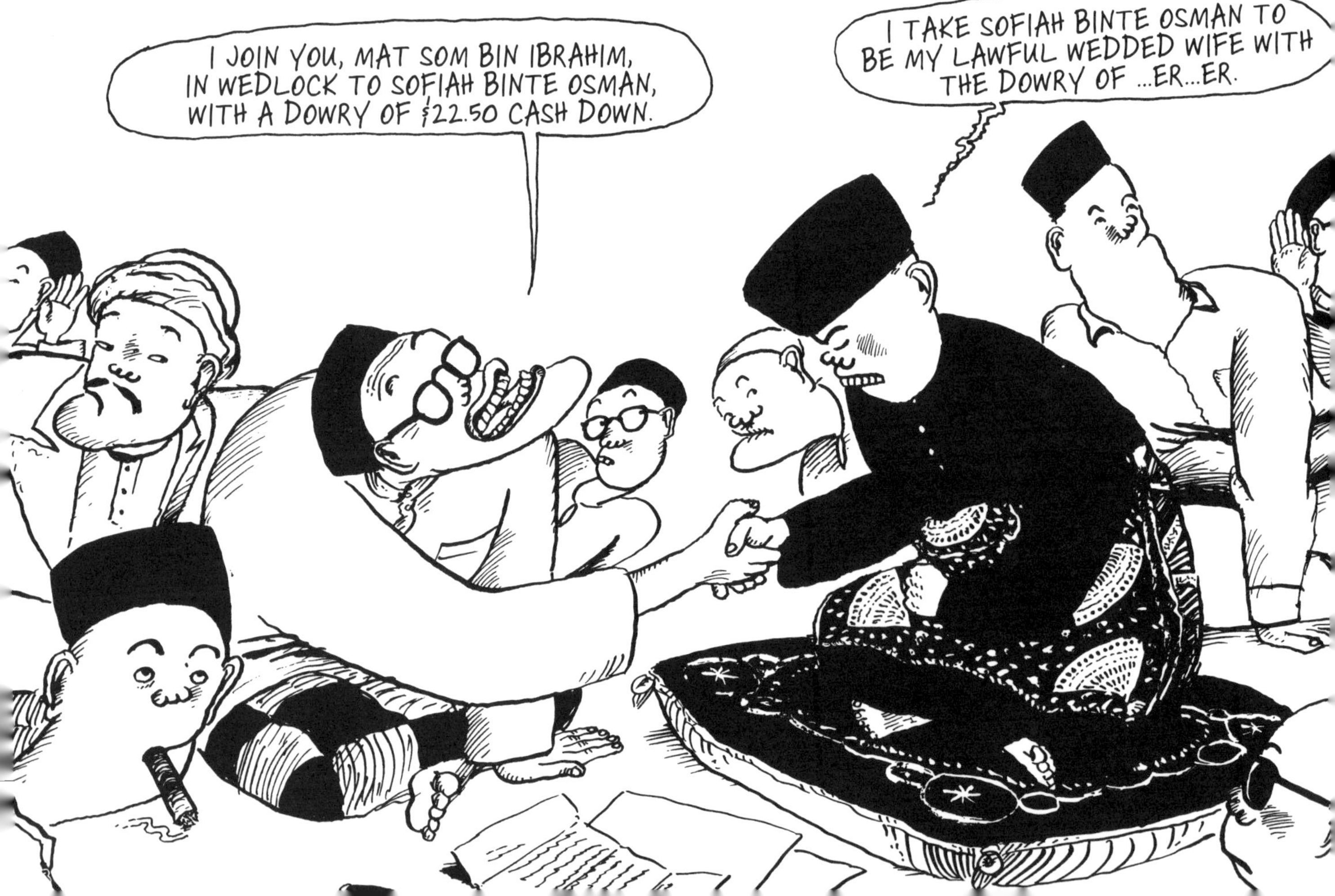
I JOIN YOU, MAT SOM BIN IBRAHIM, IN WEDLOCK TO SOFIAH BINTE OSMAN, WITH A DOWRY OF $22.50 CASH DOWN.
I TAKE SOFIAH BINTE OSMAN TO BE MY LAWFUL WEDDED WIFE WITH THE DOWRY OF ...ER...ER.

After that our party left with the groom to go to another house to rest. Everything had been arranged earlier for this temporary stay at the house.

At about 2 o'clock we returned to the bride's place for a big feast, and most important of all, for the Bersanding ceremony, in which the bride and groom sit on a platform.

Although this ceremony did not take long, they had to do it again that night, when we were served more food. But that was the last time we saw them, for after the second Bersanding at about 8 p.m., the bride and the groom were ushered into their bedroom and left alone.

Suddenly things outside began to swing! There was a loud happy tune with the Joget beat. We rushed out. There was a band and a group of dancing girls!

This was really something. I had never seen anything like this before. Probably those girls were hired from a cabaret in Ipoh, a big town 30 miles away.

And they were ready! The band was playing. All they needed now was for men folks to come up to the stage (built temporarily for this wedding) and dance with them! Anybody could go up!

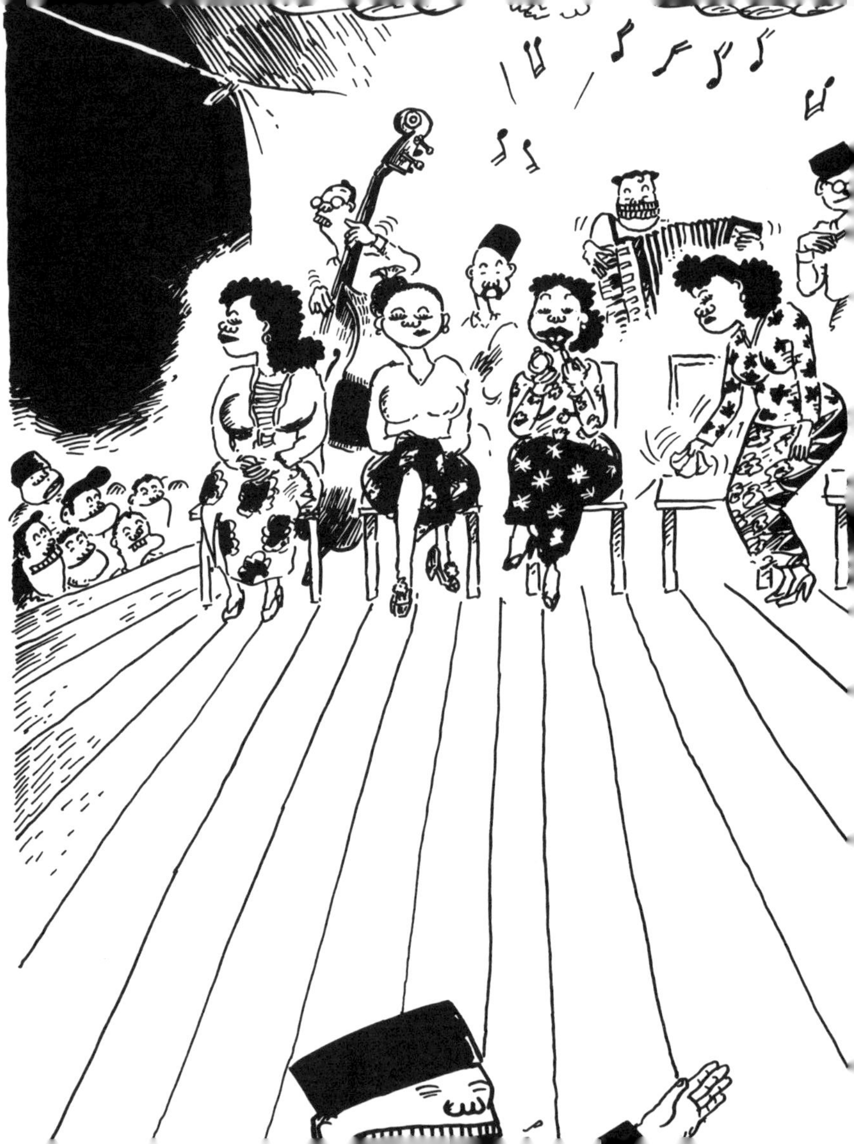

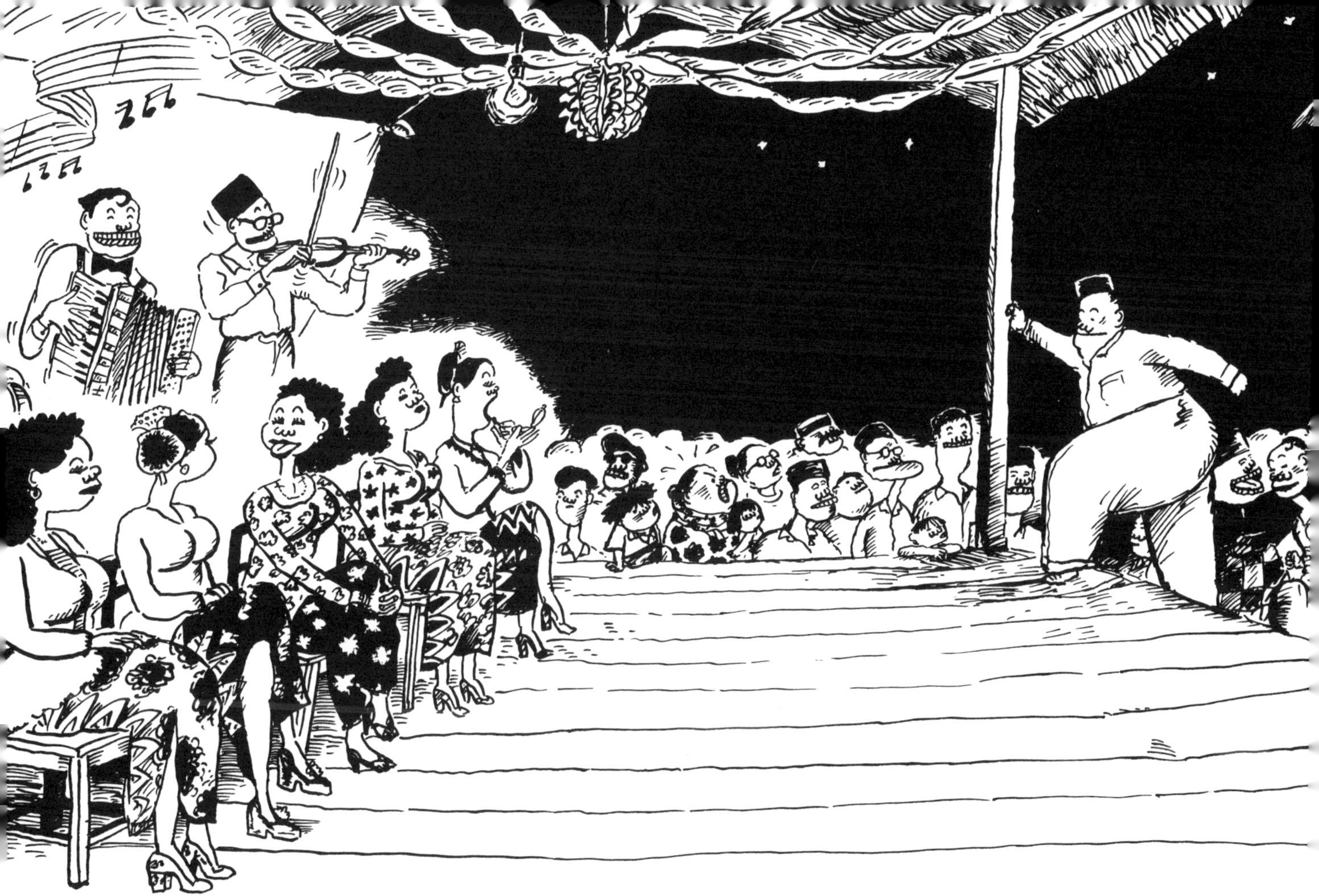

To my surprise, it was Dad who went up first!

The beat went on and in no time the stage was crowded with sporting men and their jovial partners doing the Joget. It's not difficult to do. Just move your feet and flap your wings.

They danced the night away. Dad was on the stage most of the time. On the whole it was a very happy occasion.

But later at home...the atmosphere was not good. Mum was in a bad mood because she didn't like Dad dancing with the girls.

From inside my kelambu I could hear her whispering in anger: "A father of two doesn't dance with cabaret girls, you know! That is meant for bachelors! Next time you do that I'll go on stage and pull you by the ears!"

Dad kept quiet.

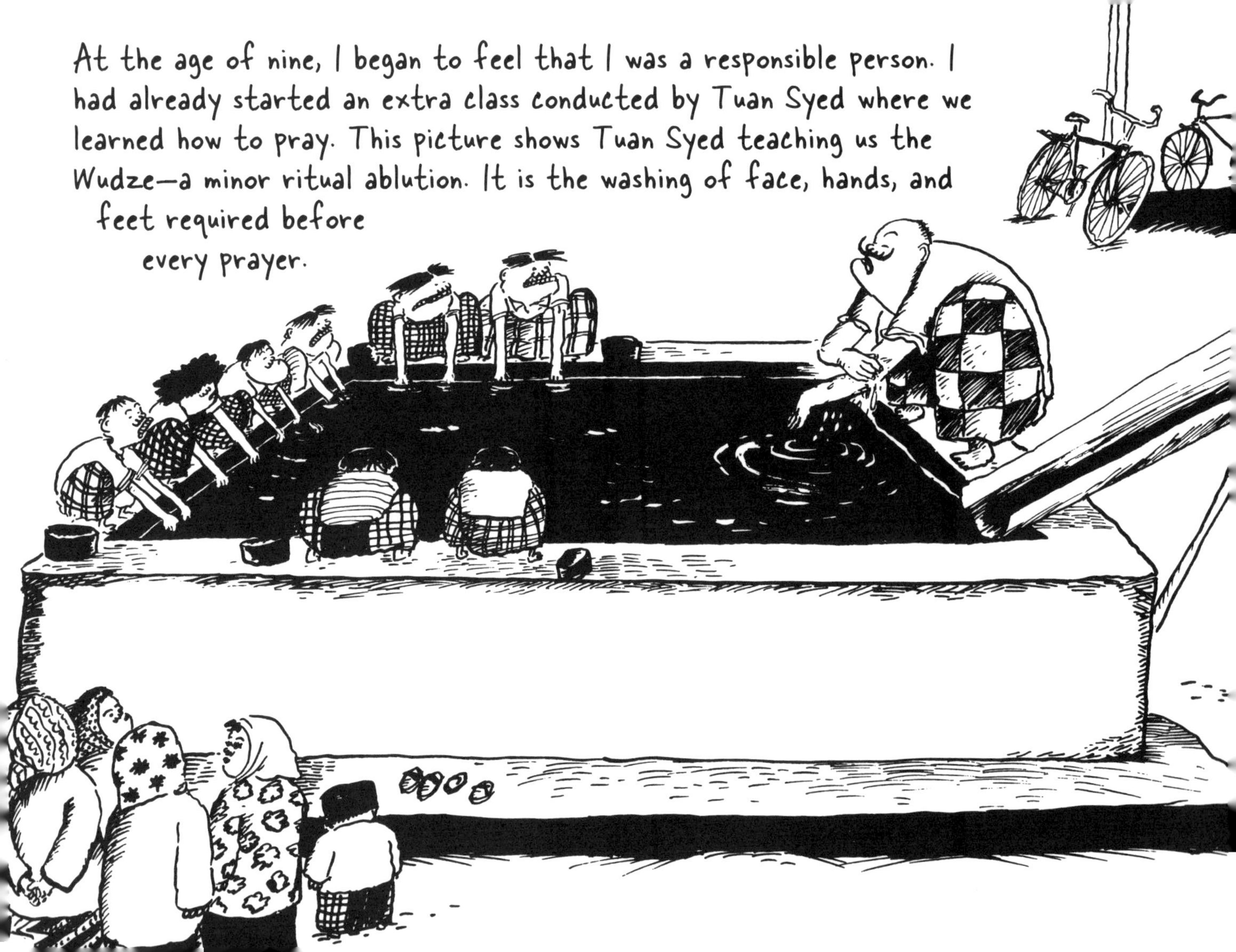
At the age of nine, I began to feel that I was a responsible person. I had already started an extra class conducted by Tuan Syed where we learned how to pray. This picture shows Tuan Syed teaching us the Wudze—a minor ritual ablution. It is the washing of face, hands, and feet required before every prayer.

Oh, yes! By this time we already had another fellow in the family. My brother, Abdul Rahman. As you can see, he enjoyed being taken for a ride on the spathe of the Pinang tree.

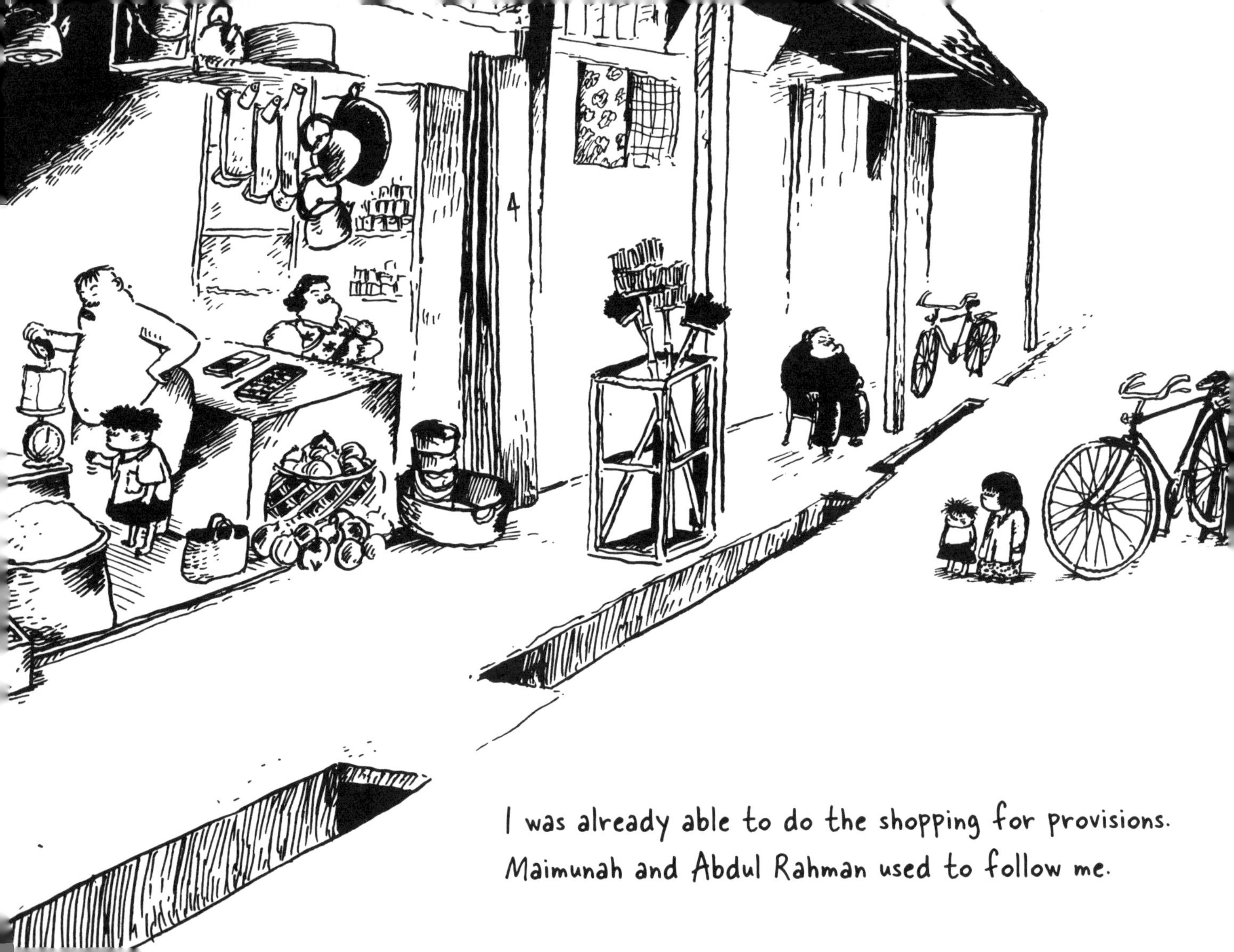
4
I was already able to do the shopping for provisions.
Maimunah and Abdul Rahman used to follow me.

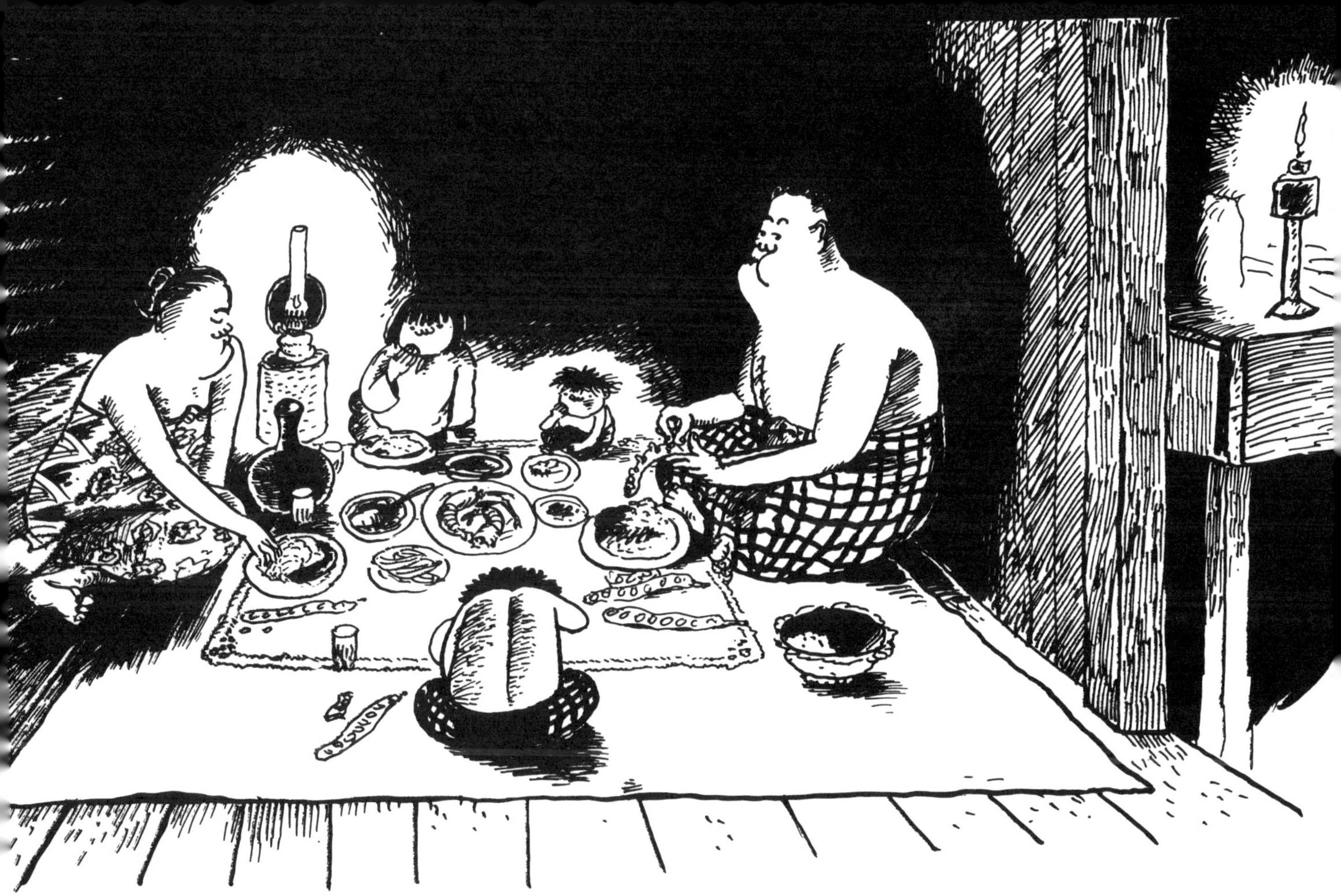

But most of the time I was missing from home because I would spend the whole day with the Meor brothers. My family would only see me at dinner time.

Dad and Mum were not in favor of this at all. And many a night I became the subject of their discussions.

Dad said I only seemed to enjoy going out fishing and playing around with the boys and this would eventually affect my studies.

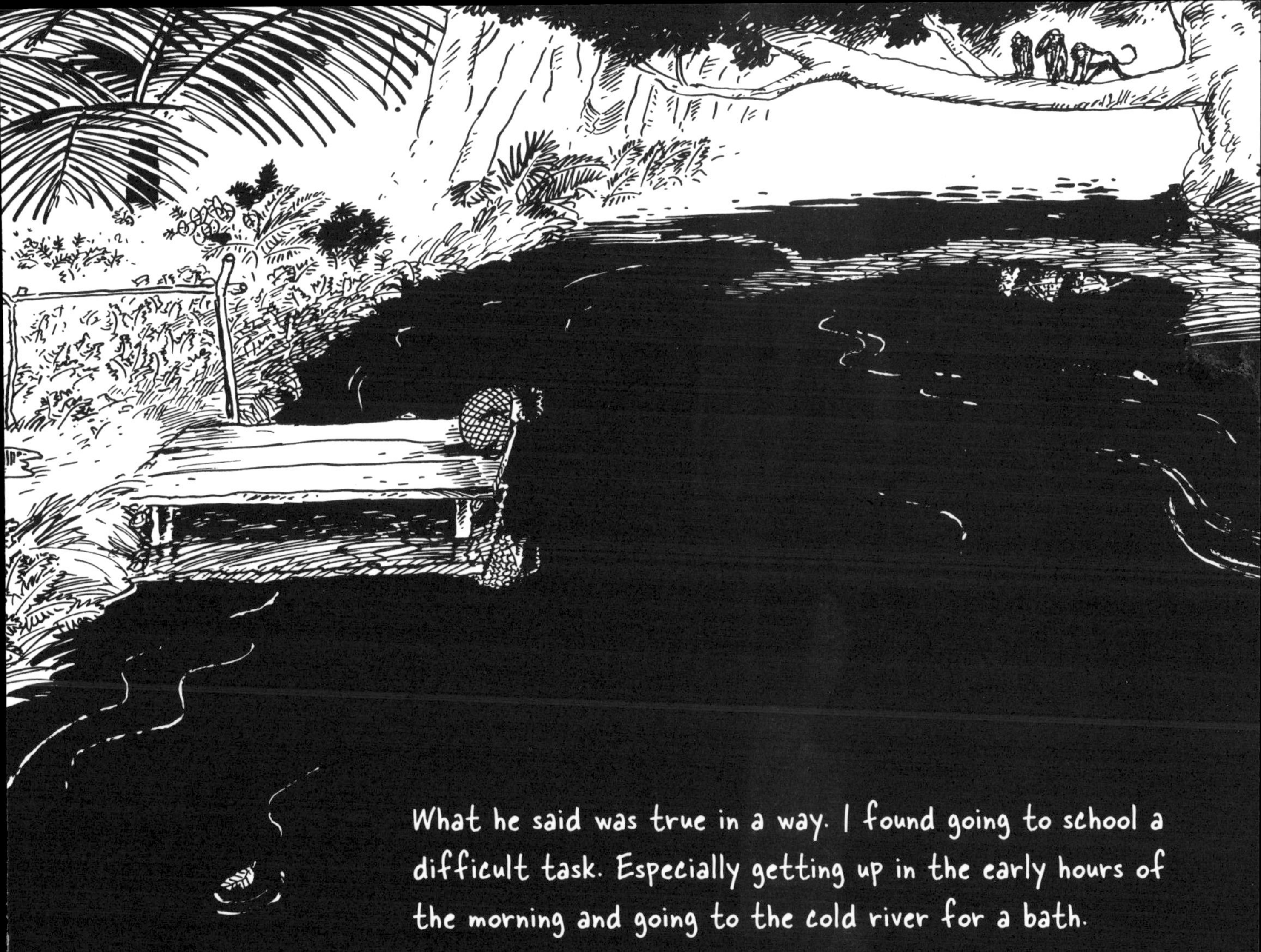
What he said was true in a way. I found going to school a difficult task. Especially getting up in the early hours of the morning and going to the cold river for a bath.

Before going on my way to school it was very important for me to look at my fish trap.

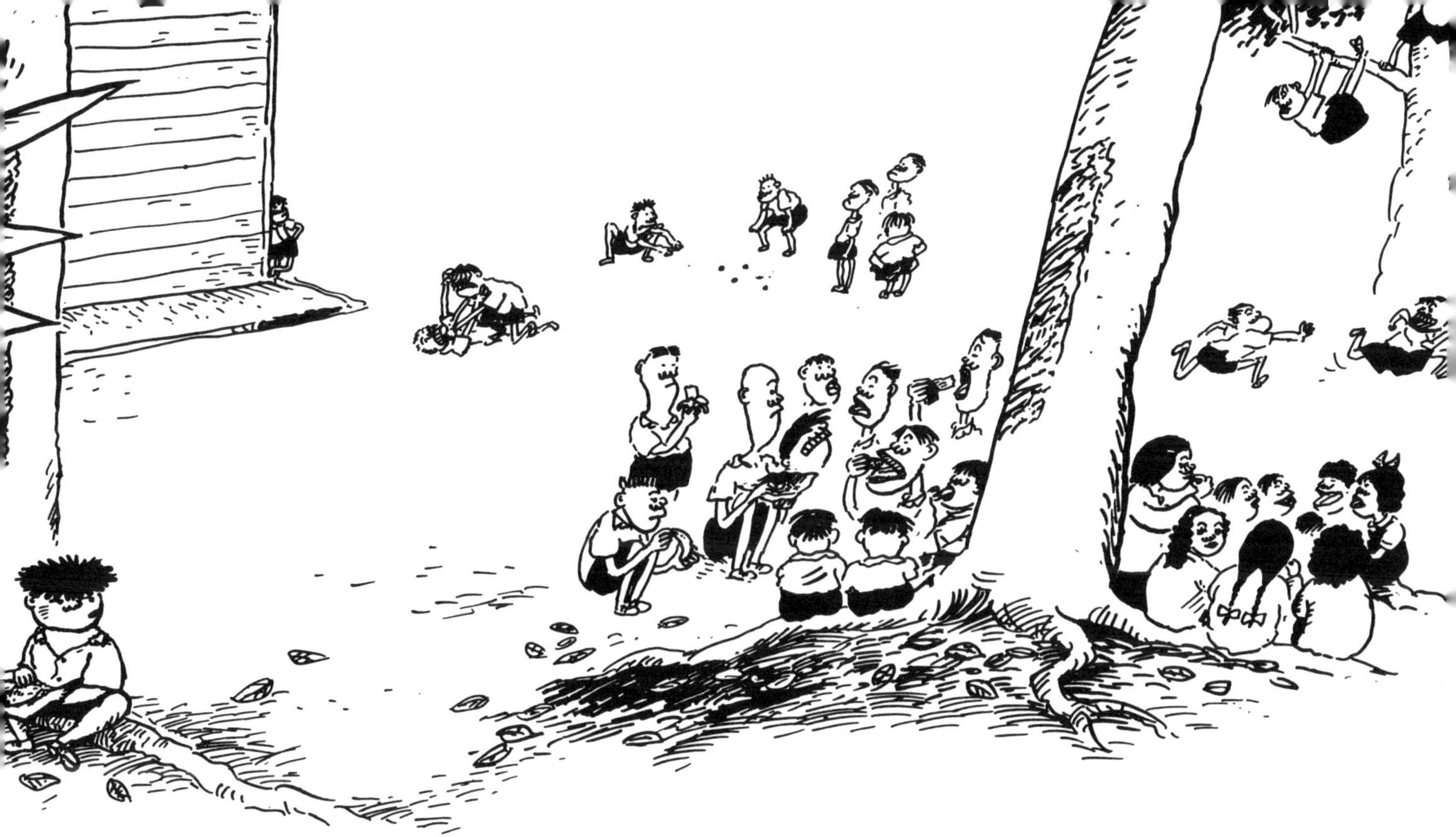

In school I was a quiet person. I'd rather be by myself. Even during school recess I'd eat alone. Some boys called me a dreamer.

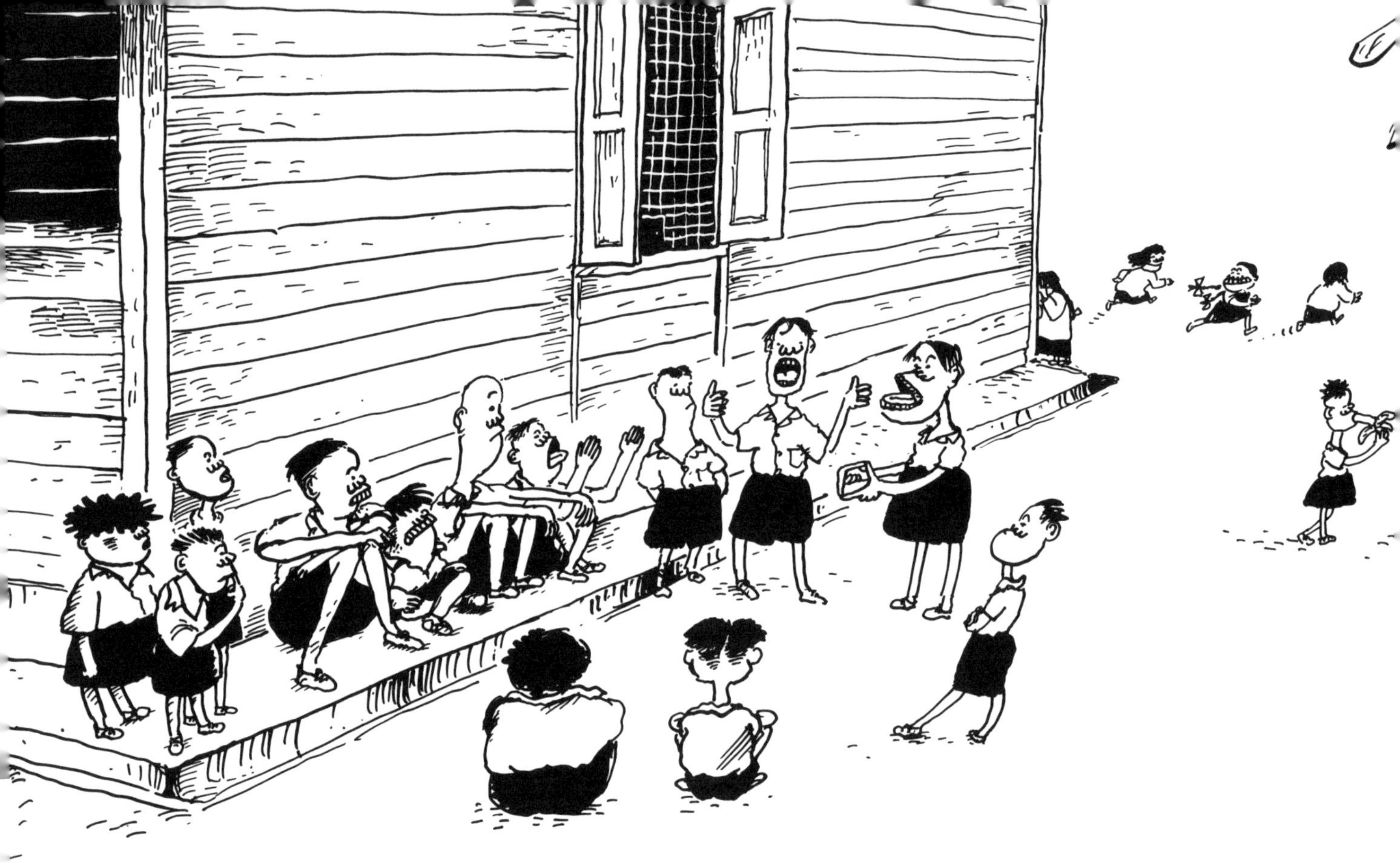

When the boys gathered to talk about fishing I'd only listen from the back. I never participated.

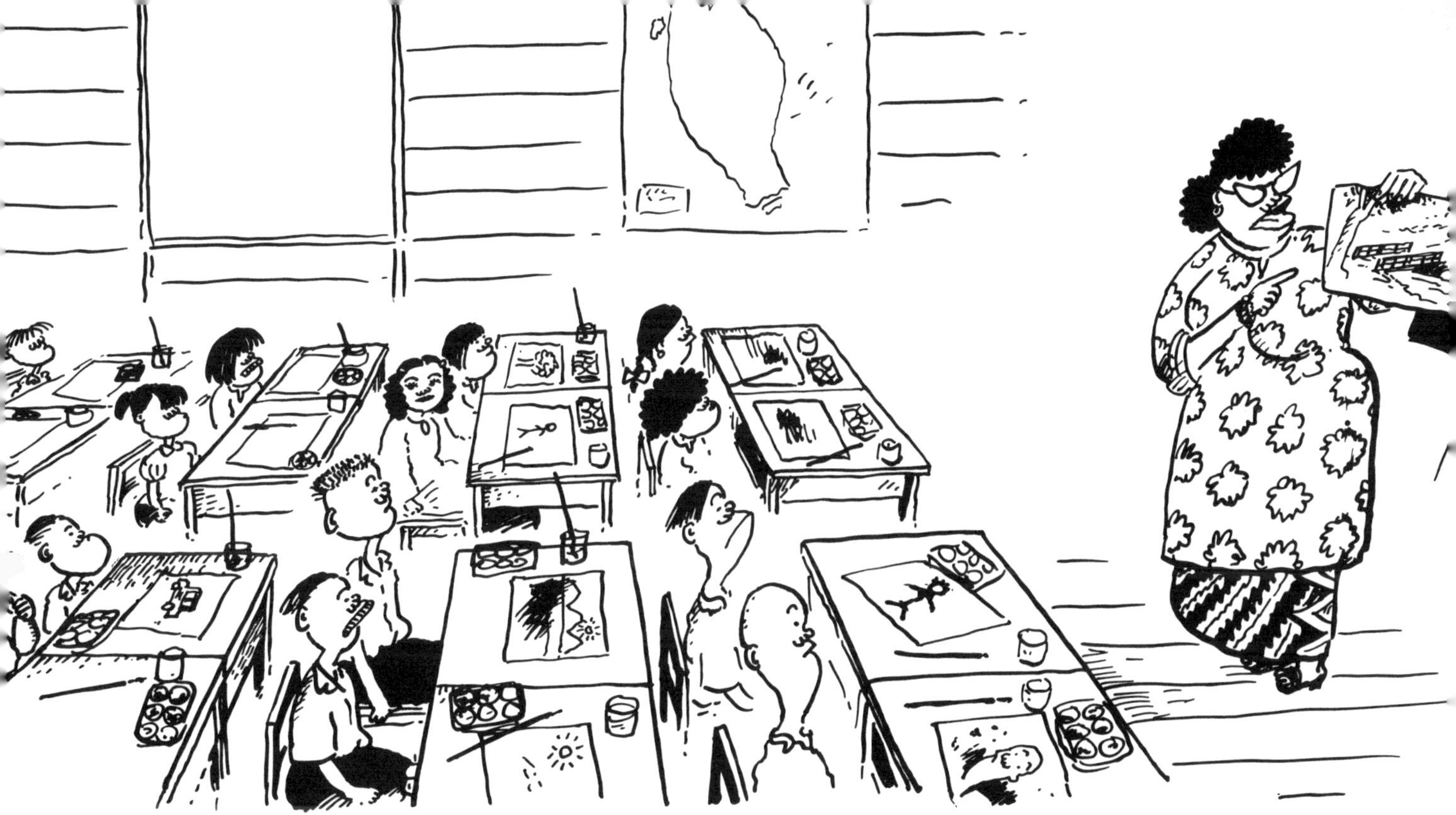

However, I was good at drawing. And I knew I was good because our teacher always picked my work to show the class as a good example.

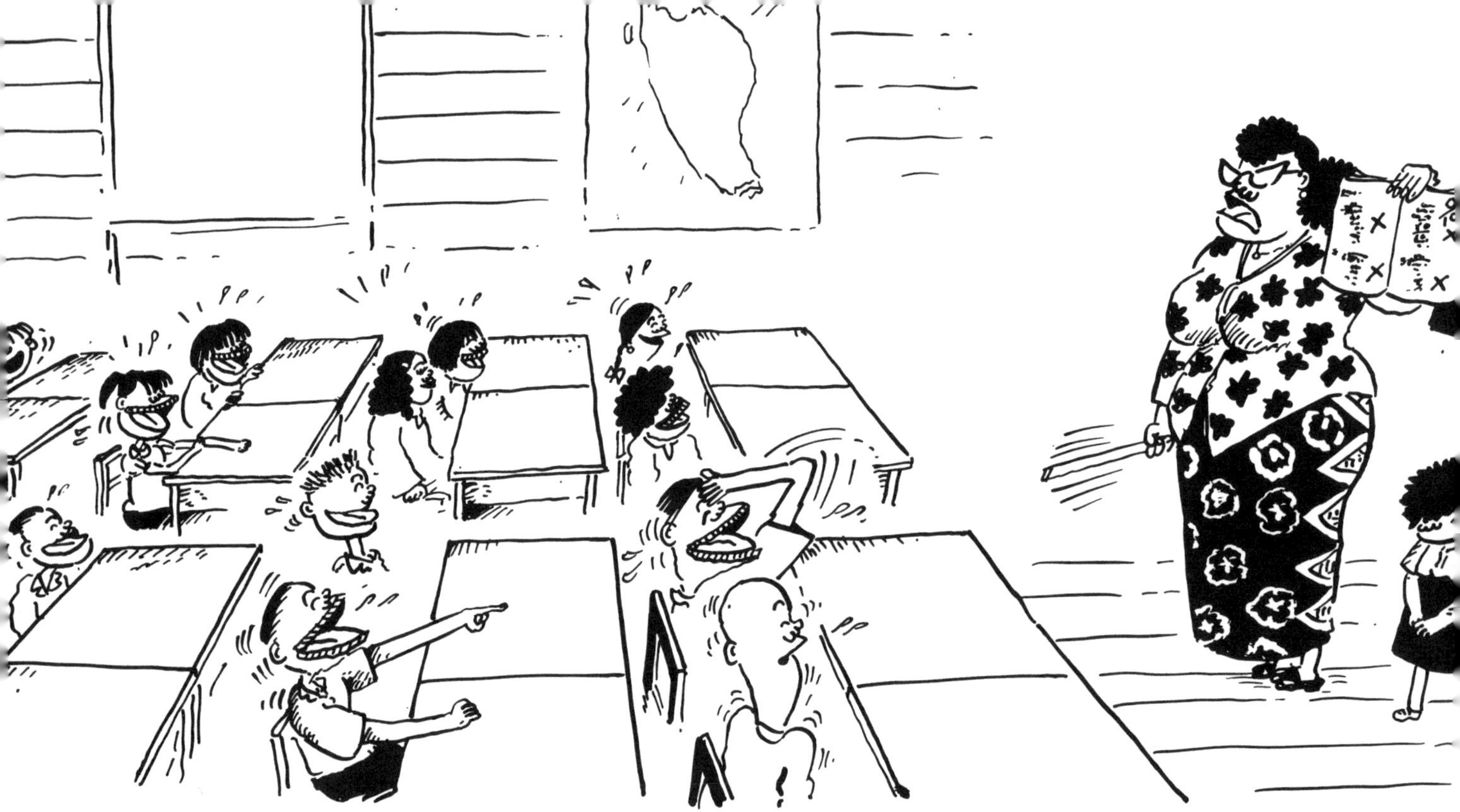

But I was rather poor in arithmetic and my work was often shown as a bad example.

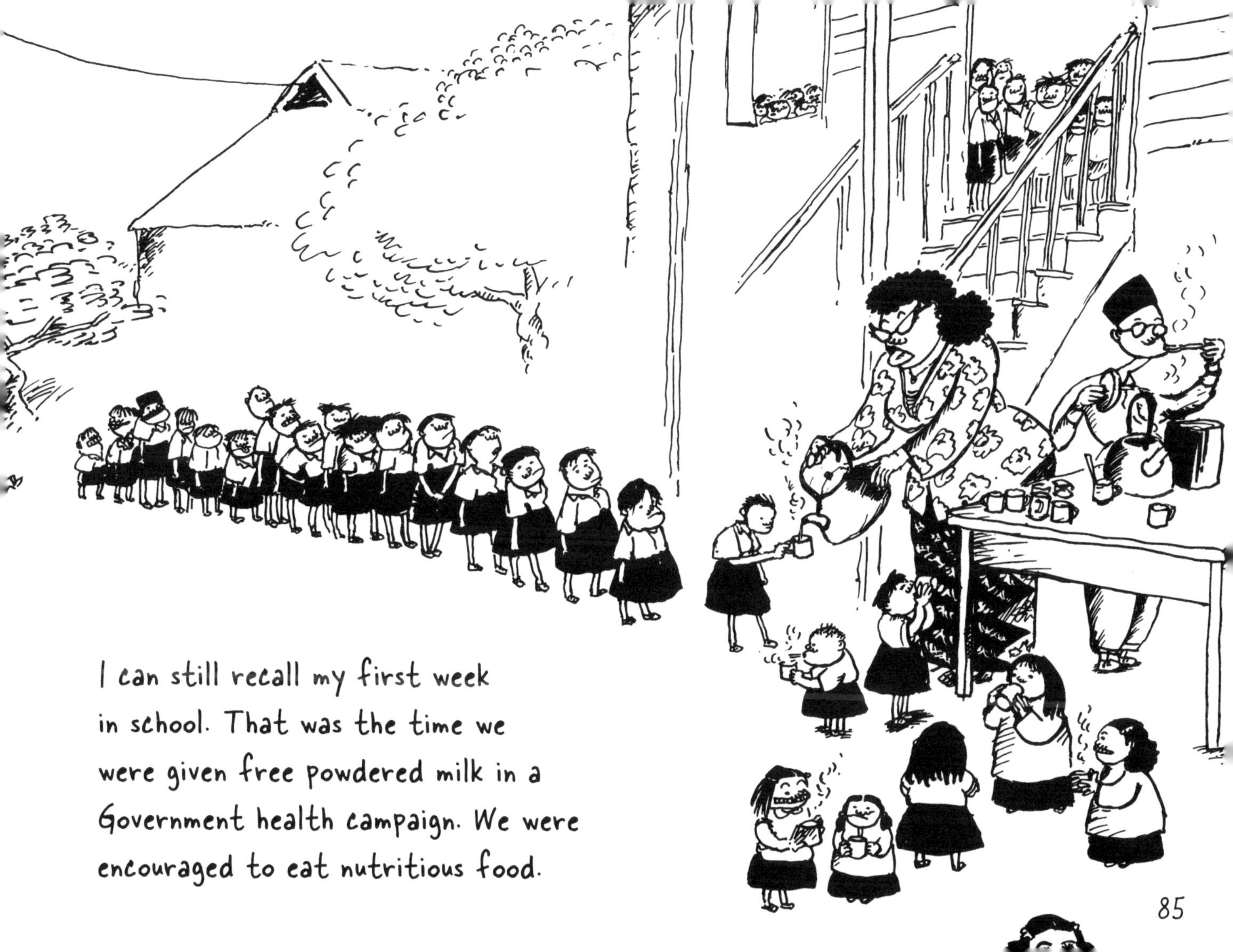

I can still recall my first week in school. That was the time we were given free powdered milk in a Government health campaign. We were encouraged to eat nutritious food.

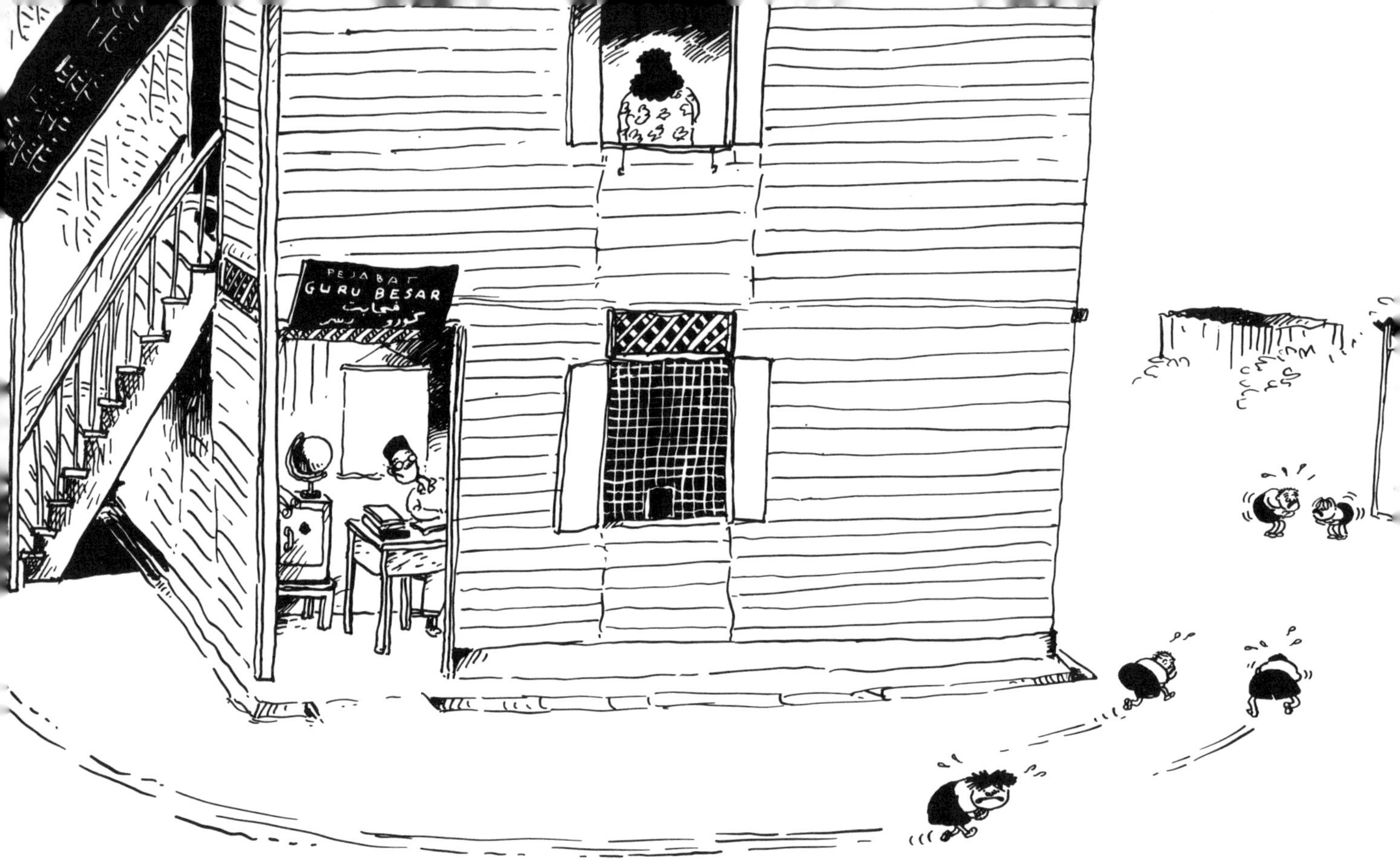
PEJABAT
GURU BESAR

For some of us, it was the first time we tasted powdered milk.
And we had a bit of stomach trouble.

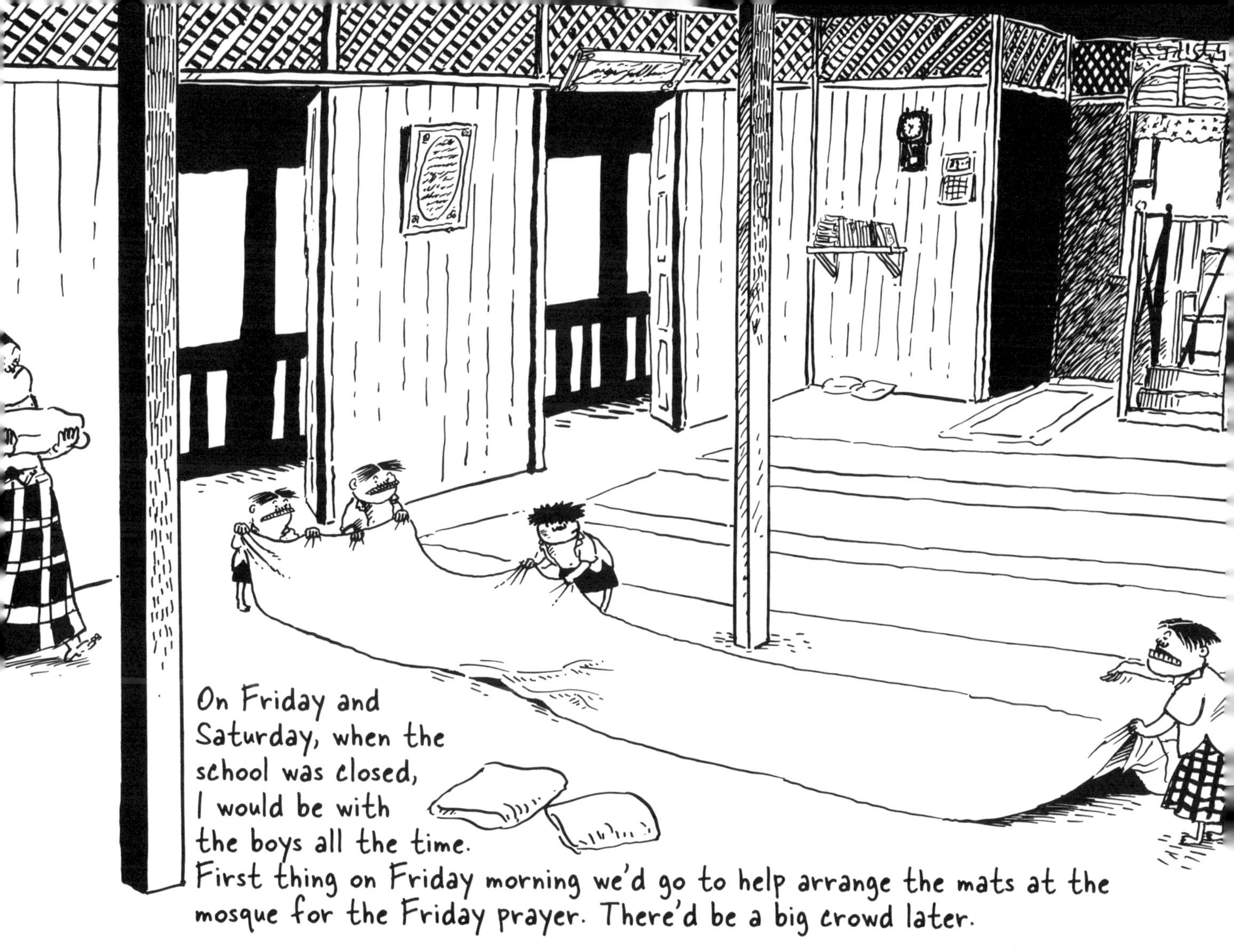
On Friday and Saturday, when the school was closed, I would be with the boys all the time.
First thing on Friday morning we'd go to help arrange the mats at the mosque for the Friday prayer. There'd be a big crowd later.

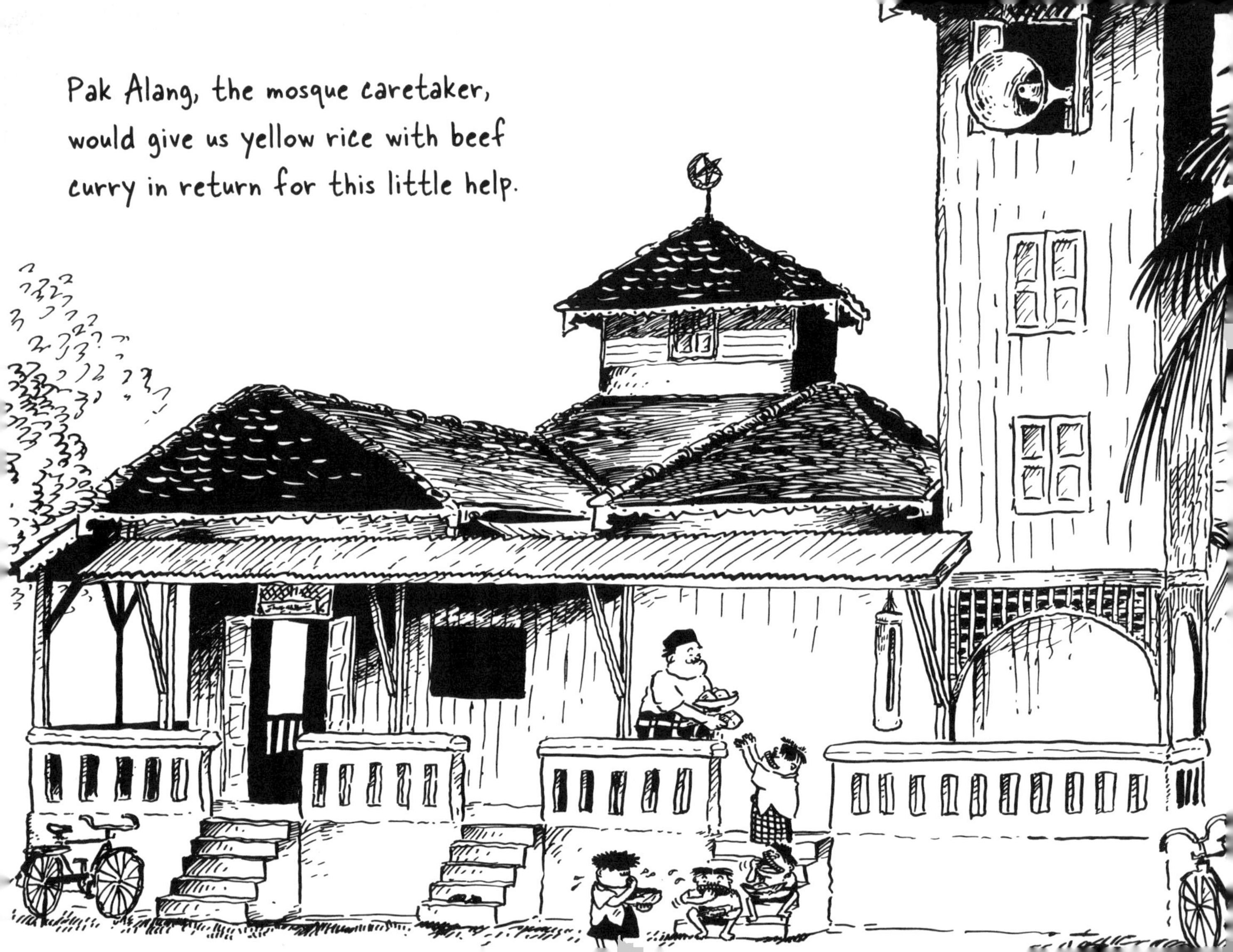
Pak Alang, the mosque caretaker, would give us yellow rice with beef curry in return for this little help.

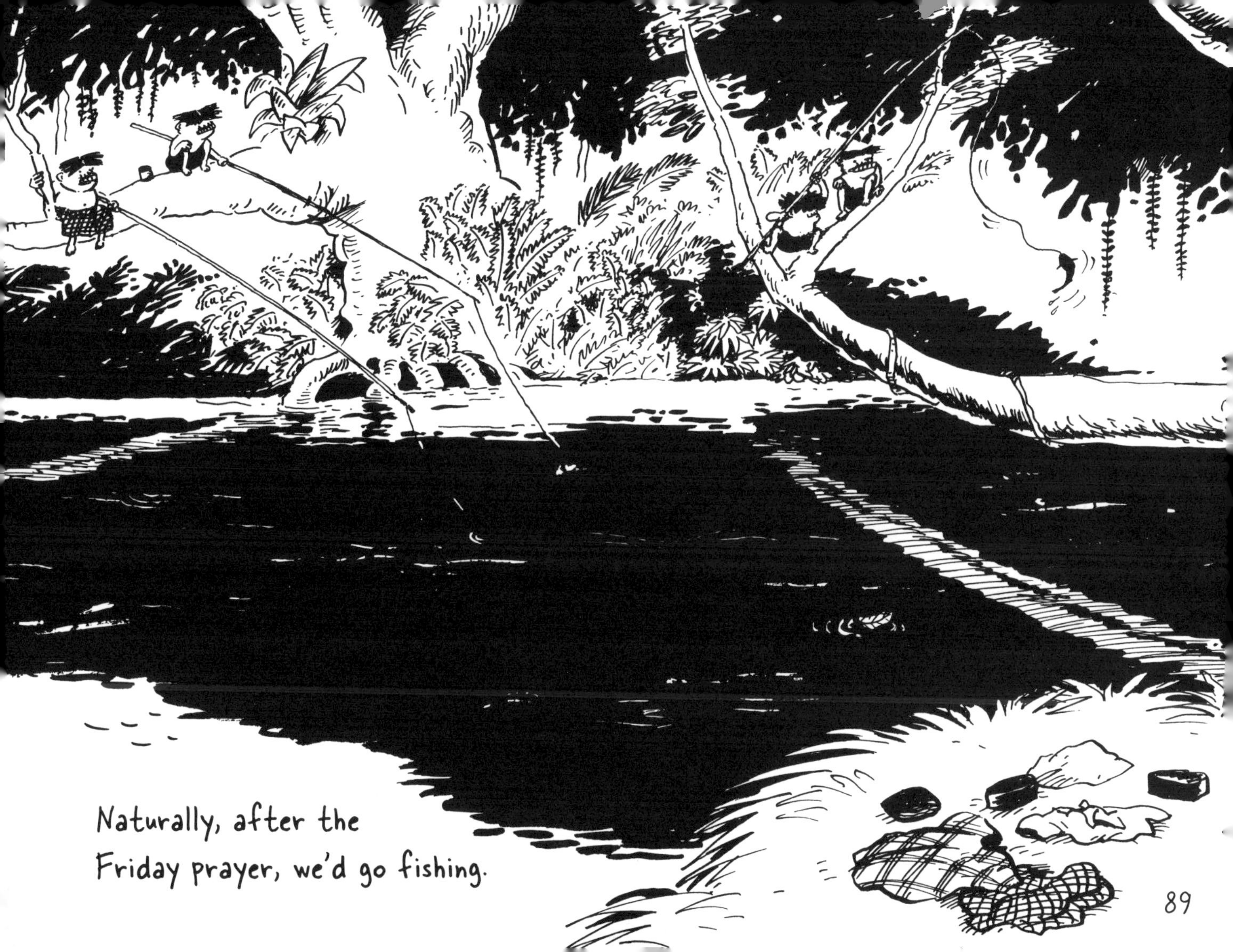
Naturally, after the
Friday prayer, we'd go fishing.

By this time I was already quite good at it. I knew how to handle a catfish without giving it a chance to sting my fingers.

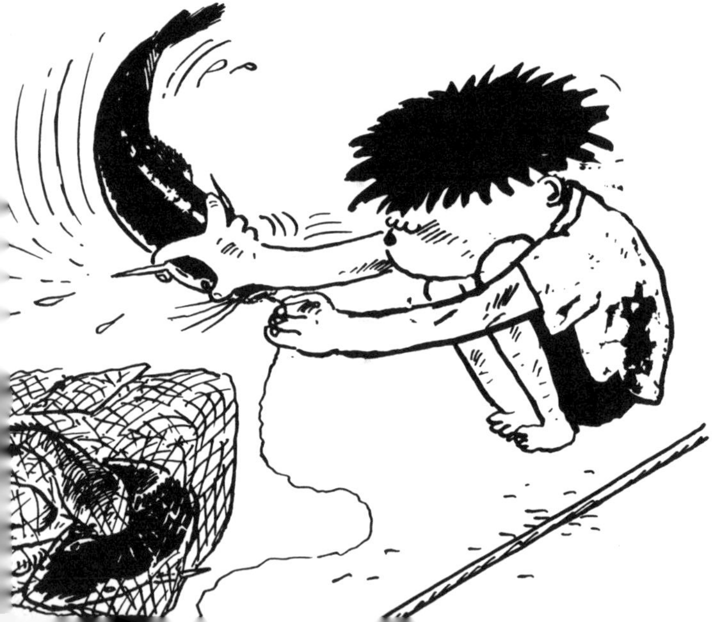

And sometimes we would go hand-fishing in the water. This was, of course, more daring.

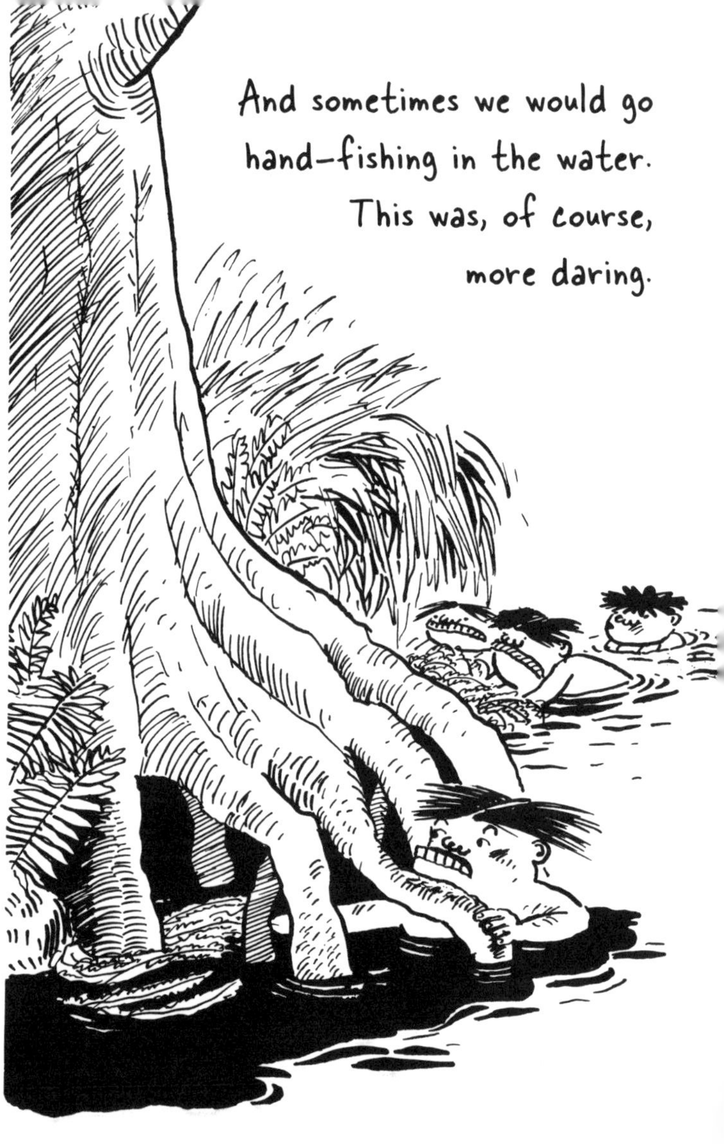

But this could be dangerous, too, because some fish—like the haruan—could be very aggressive when cornered.

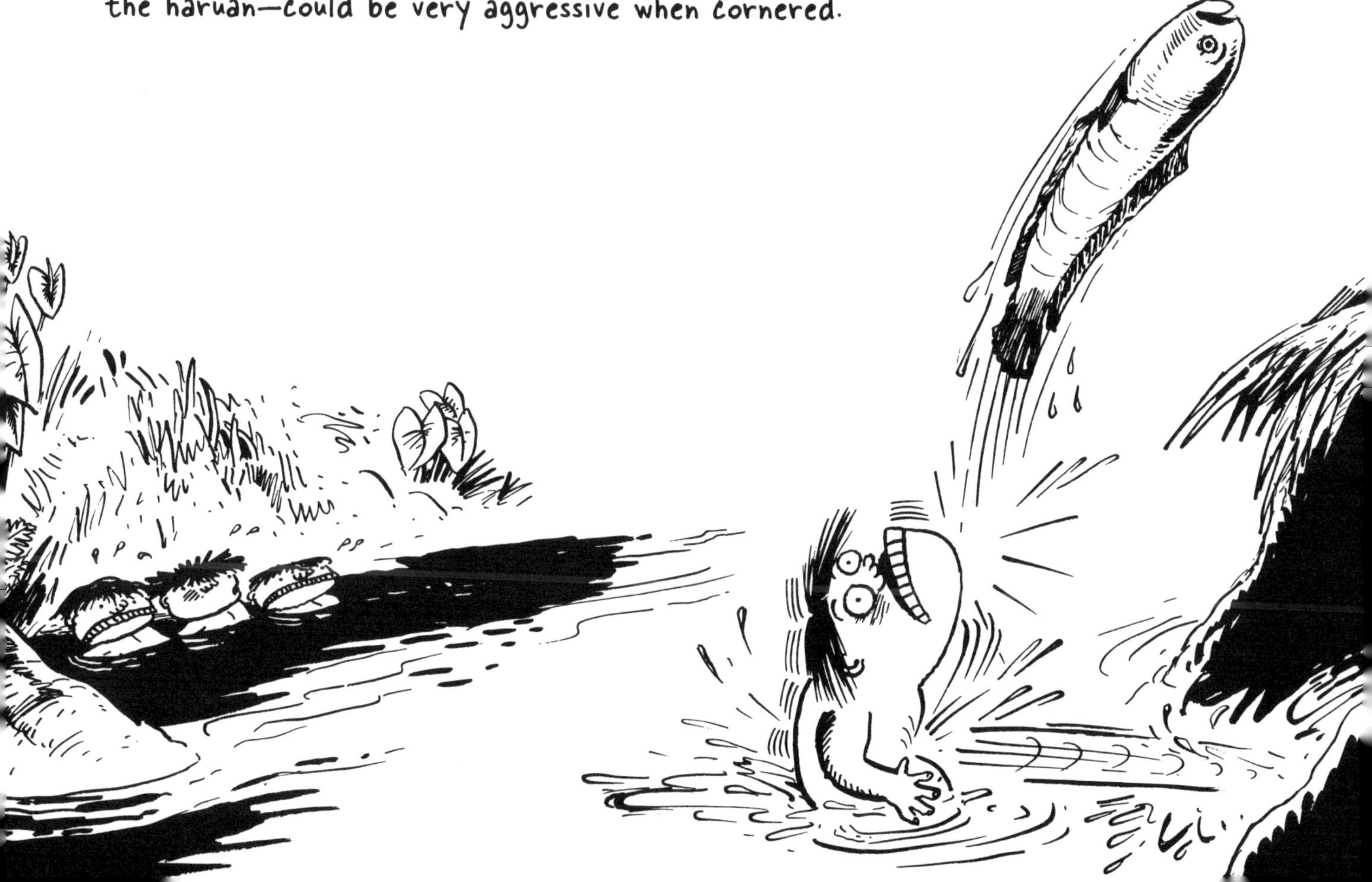

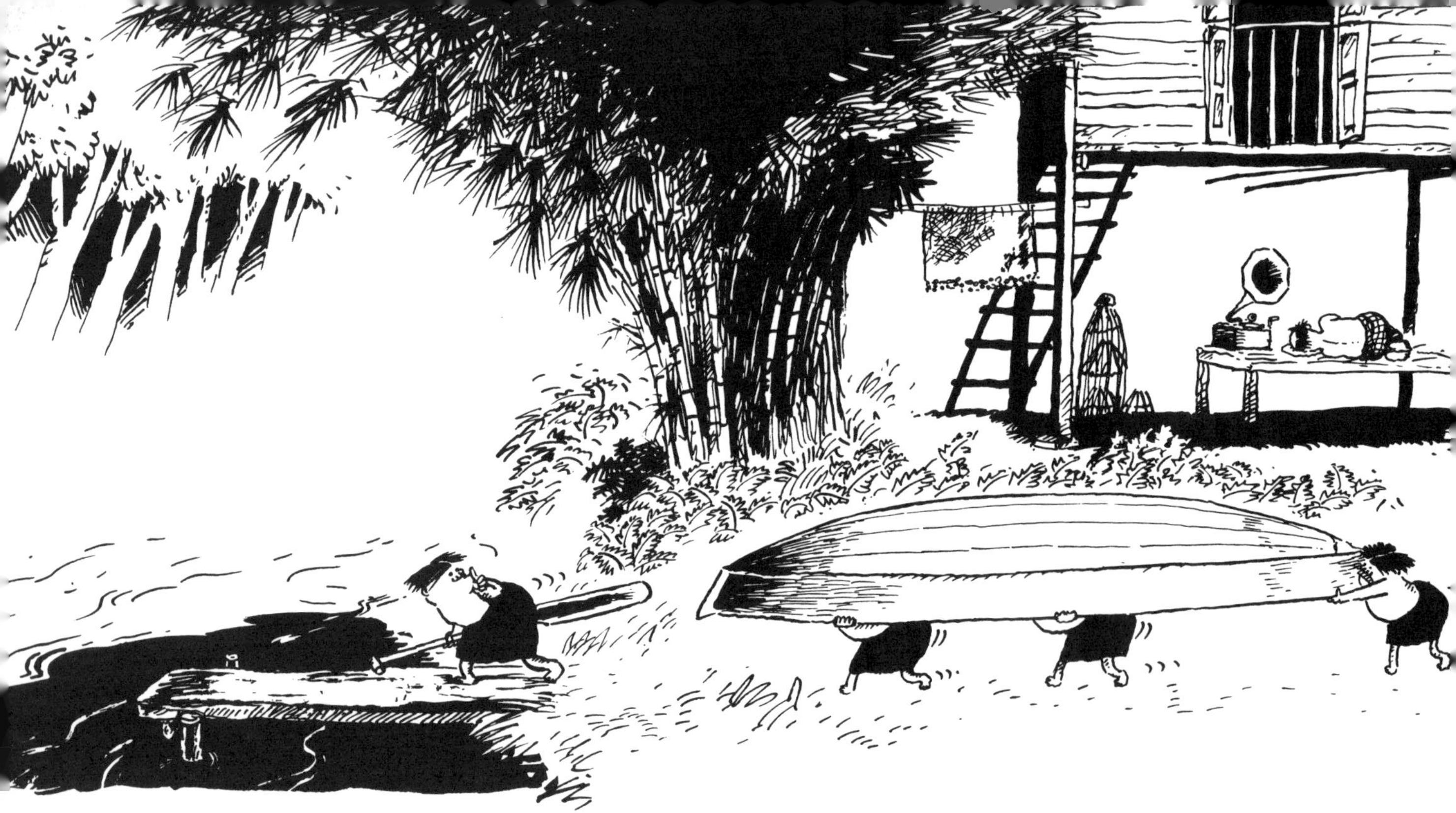

Sometimes we'd borrow Pak Alang's sampan to go fishing with a net.

We used to catch lobsters with the net. And we were not bad at manning the sampan too...even the one with a big hole could be put into use—with the proper know-how.

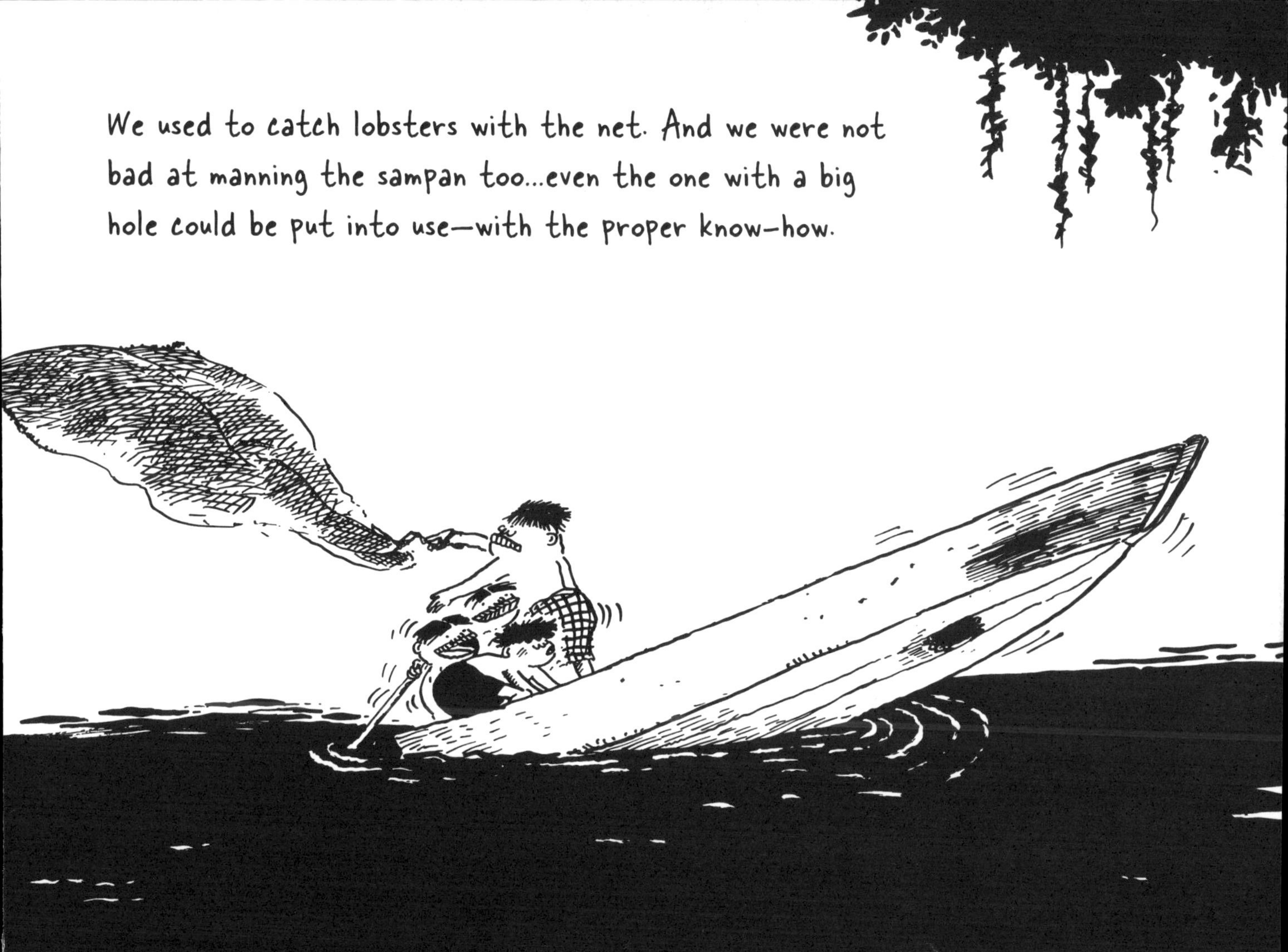

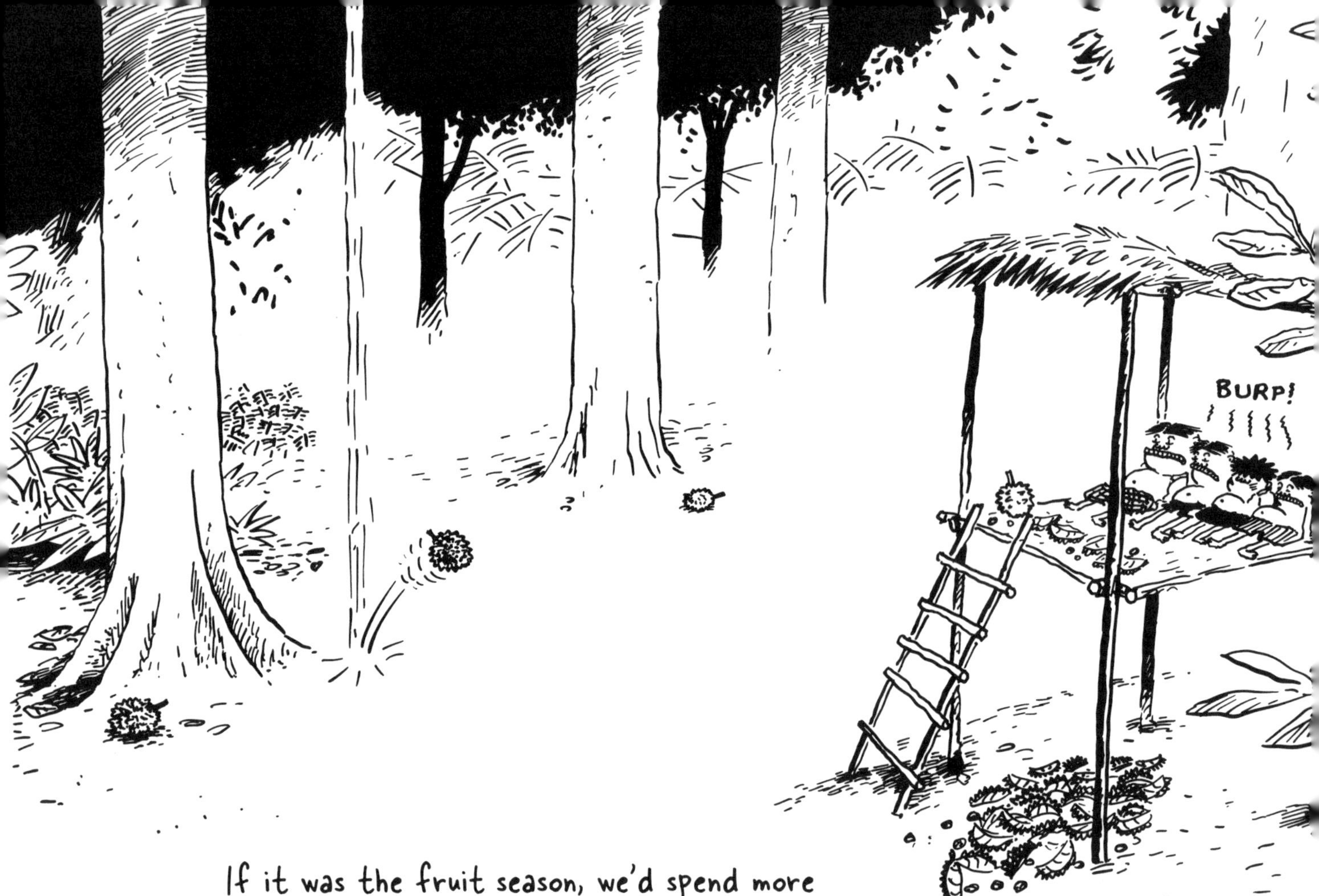
BURP!

If it was the fruit season, we'd spend more time guarding Meor Yusoff's durian trees.

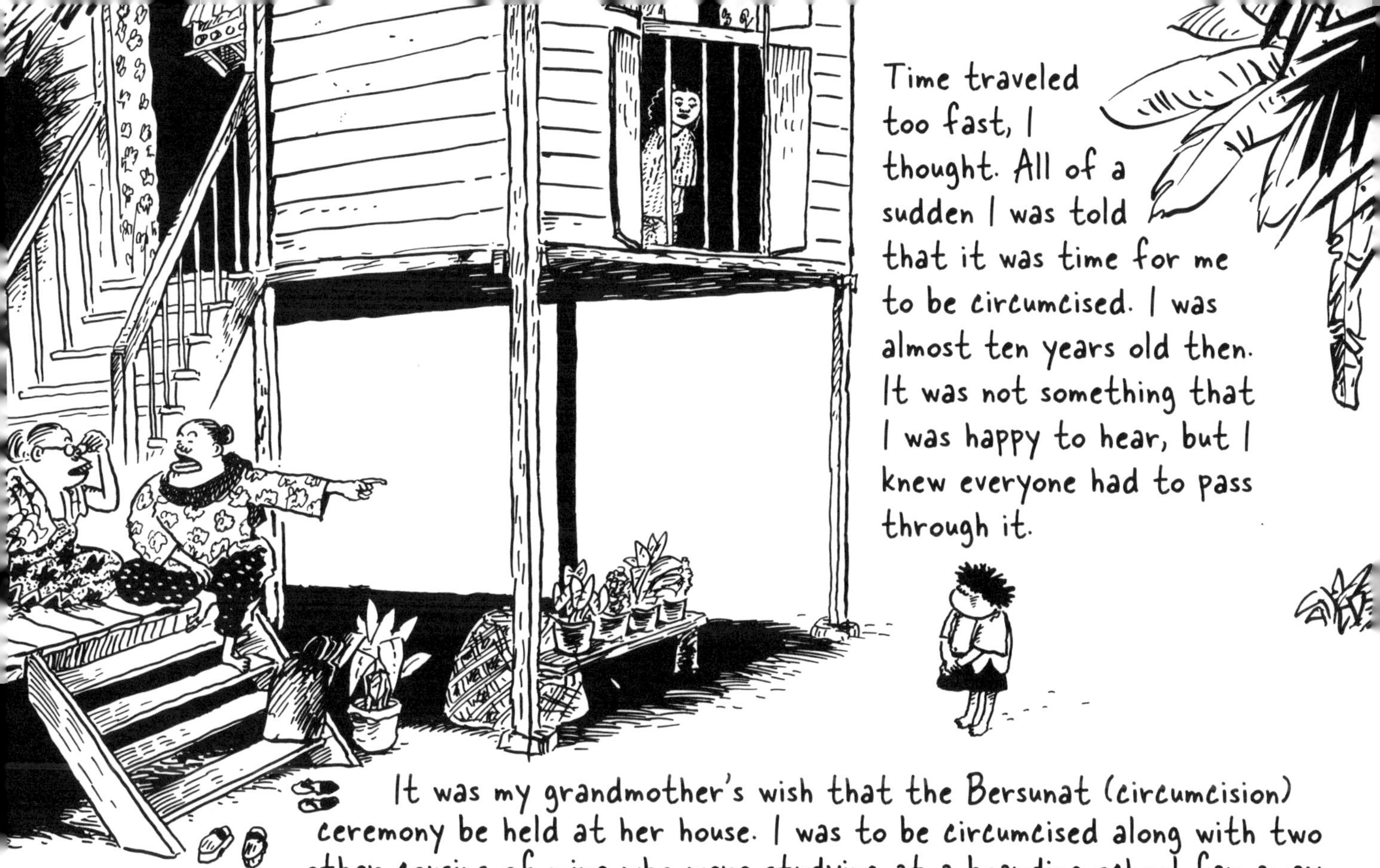

Time traveled too fast, I thought. All of a sudden I was told that it was time for me to be circumcised. I was almost ten years old then. It was not something that I was happy to hear, but I knew everyone had to pass through it.

It was my grandmother's wish that the Bersunat (circumcision) ceremony be held at her house. I was to be circumcised along with two other cousins of mine who were studying at a boarding school far away.

Grandma asked me to come along when she went around house to house inviting neighbors to the occasion.

"Yes, that's the fellow," she'd say to her would-be guests.

And so the big day came...there was a big feast attended by a large crowd of relatives and friends (in other words, the whole kampung).

The three of us were splendidly dressed in the traditional costume. All the good food was placed before us. But we didn't feel like eating.

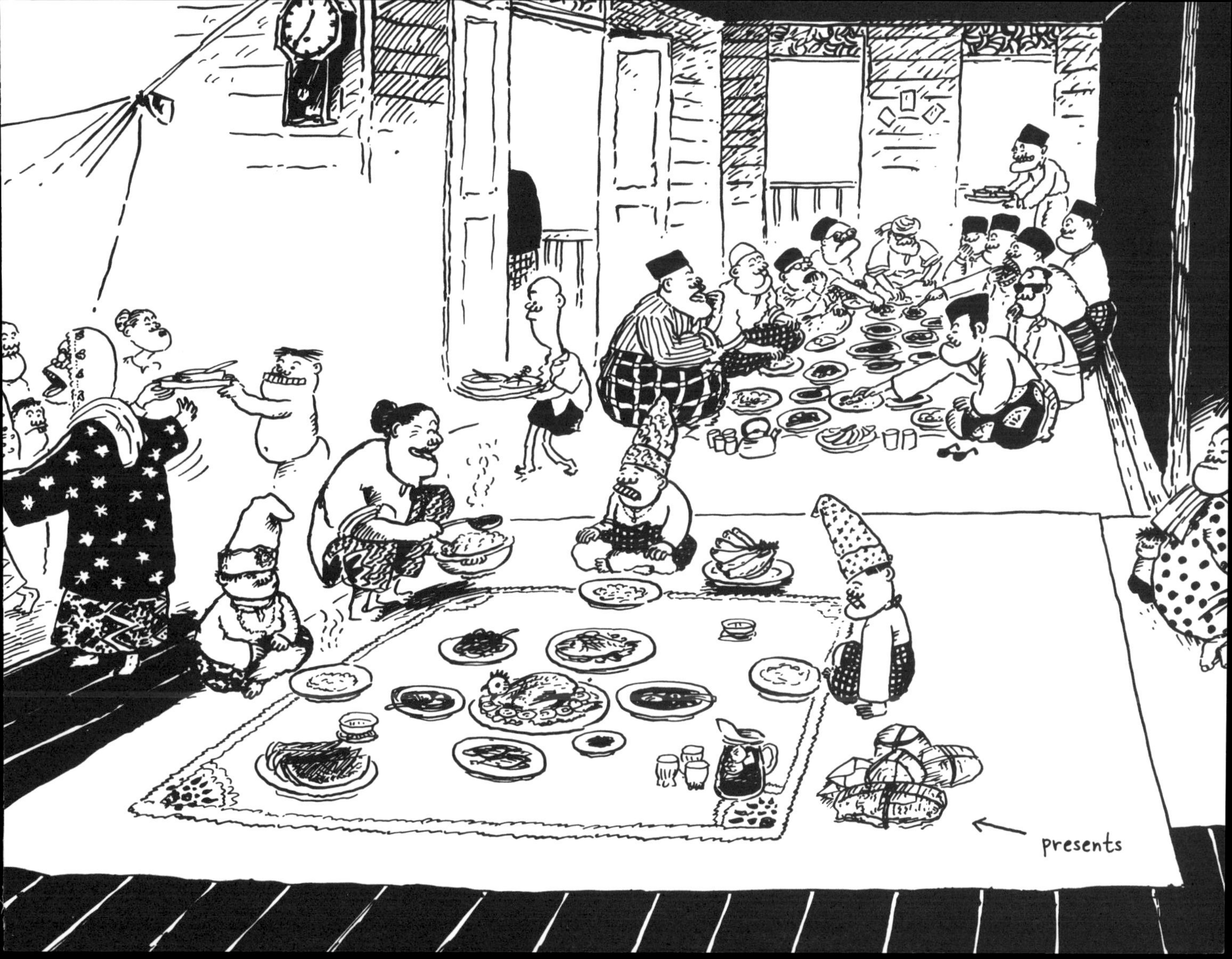
presents

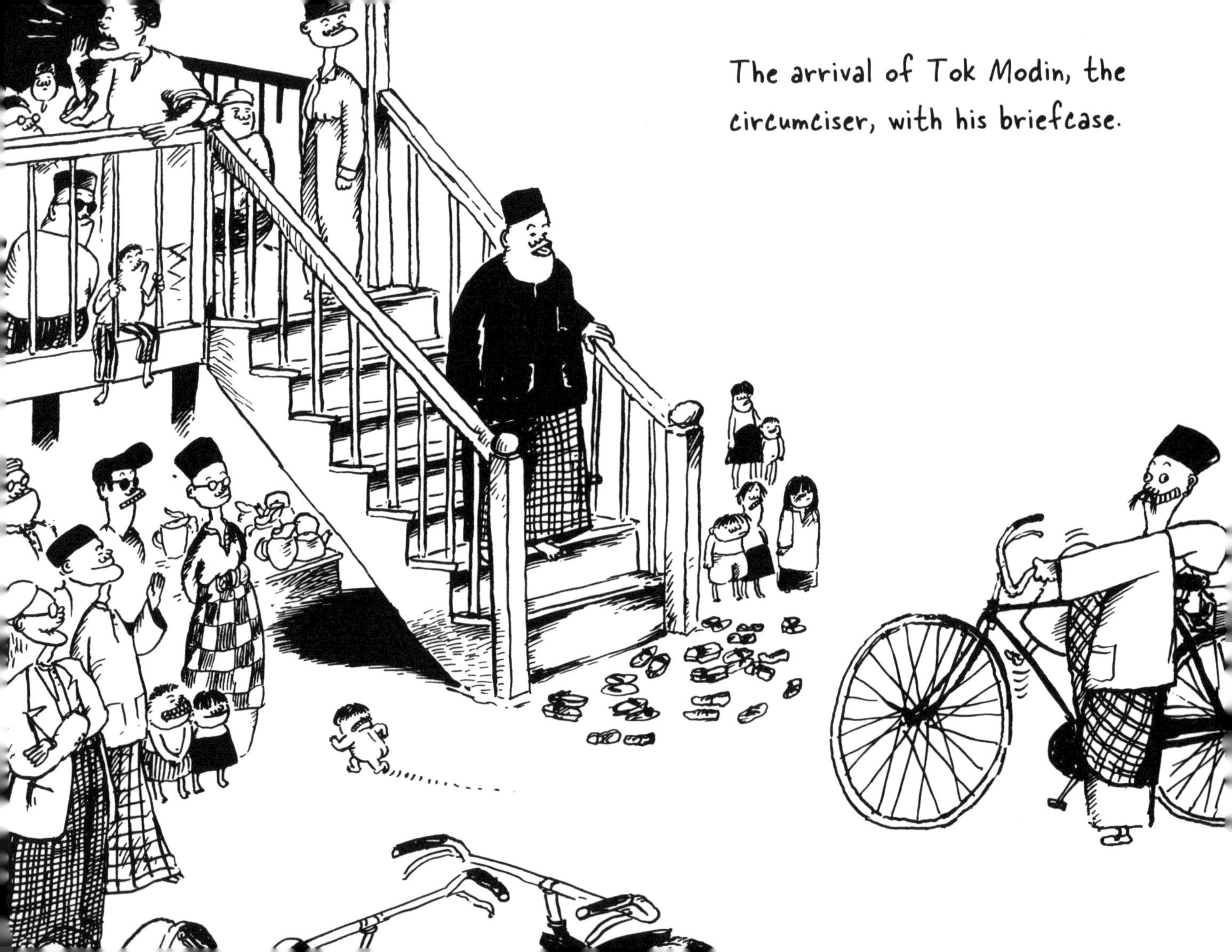

The arrival of Tok Modin, the circumciser, with his briefcase.

The Tok Modin was quite a funny fellow, as we discovered after being introduced to him. We had a brief conversation when he asked us about ourselves, our studies, and our favorite pastimes.

"Have some chocolates," he said later and offered us some "chocolates," which were actually betel leaves and areca nuts.

(Earlier, he had uttered a magical incantation over the "chocolates" so that after chewing them we could undergo circumcision painlessly.)

99

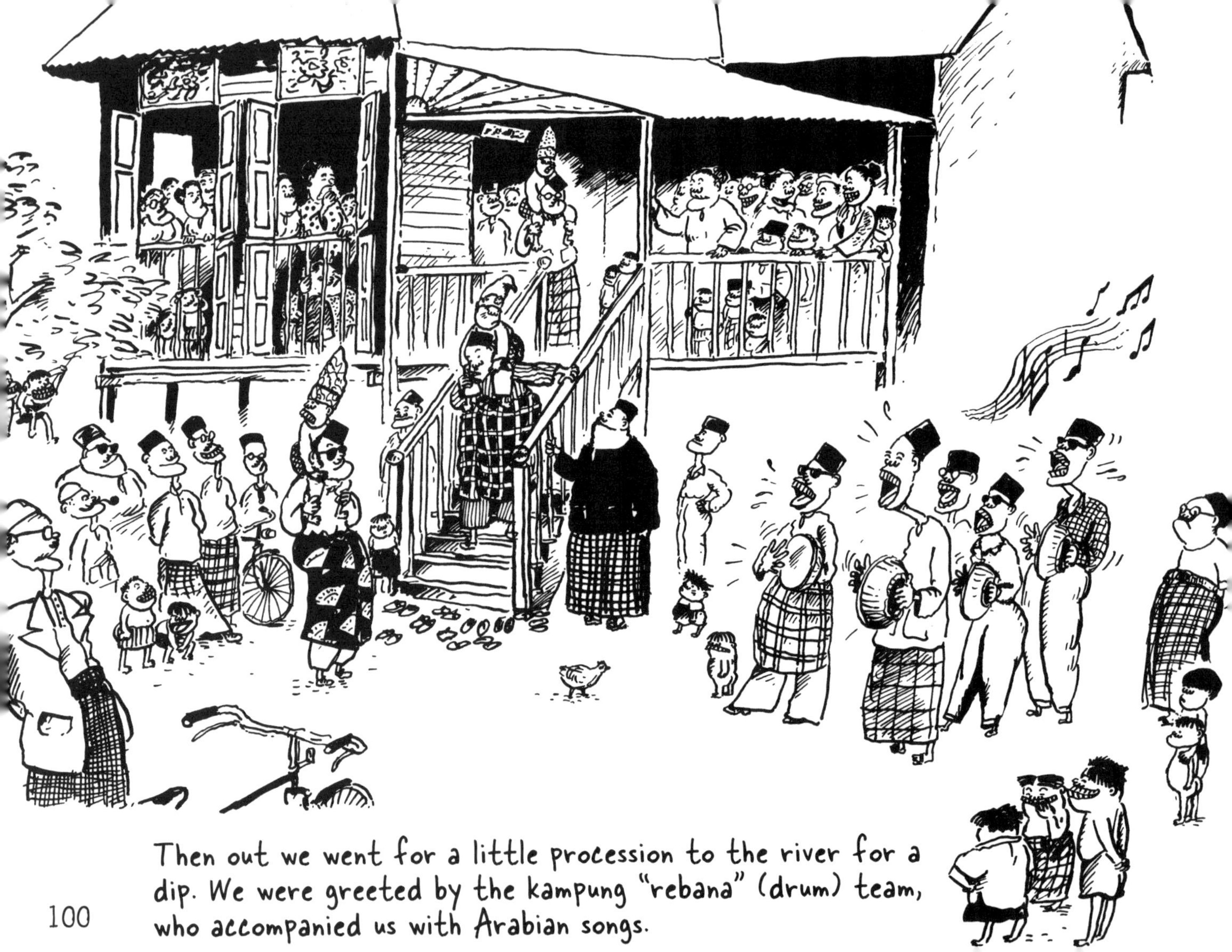

Then out we went for a little procession to the river for a dip. We were greeted by the kampung "rebana" (drum) team, who accompanied us with Arabian songs.

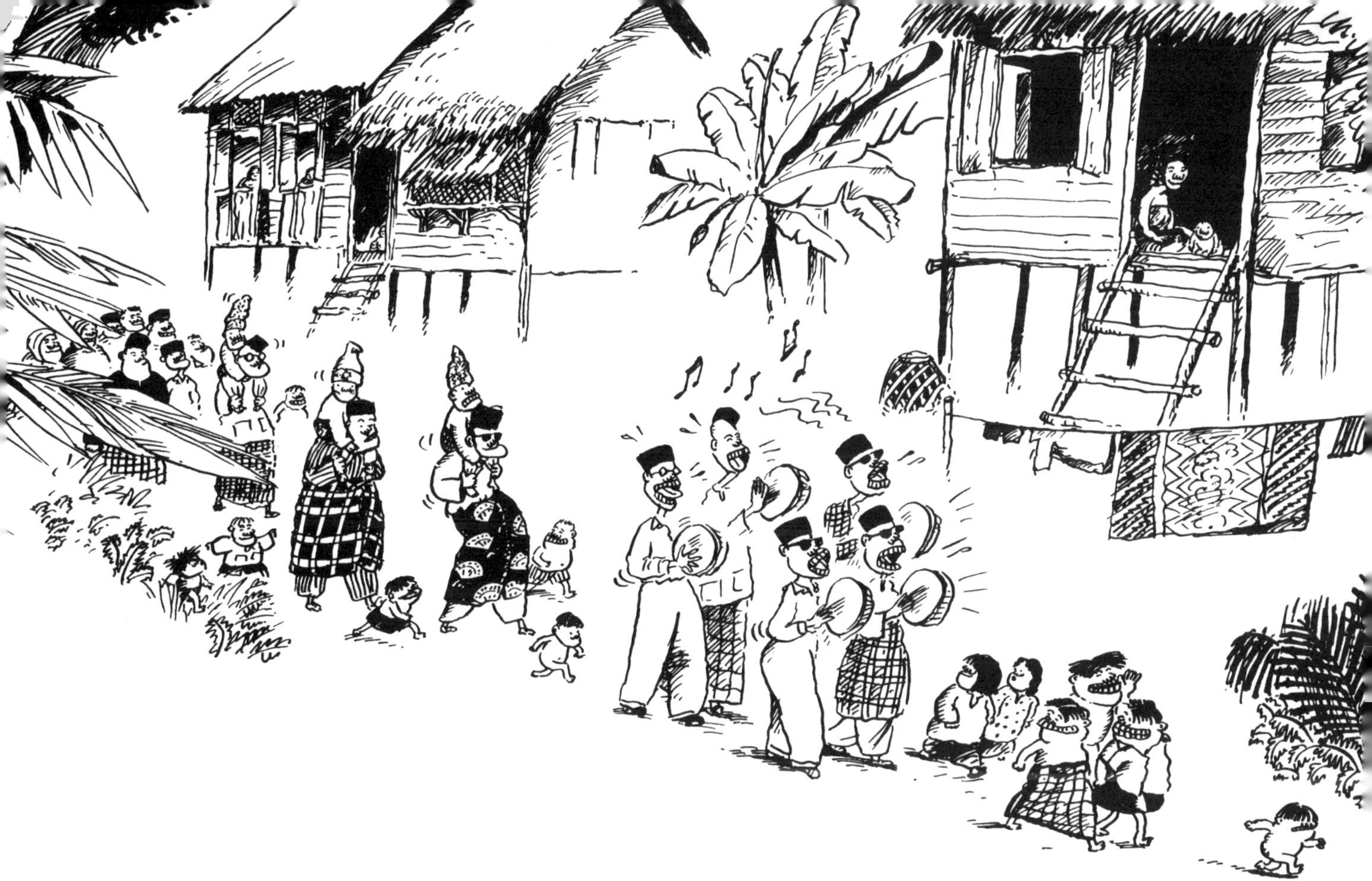

I didn't know what the purpose of this short bath was. Whatever it was, I knew we were very special people that day. Even for this simple dip the guests—including women and girls—followed and watched us.

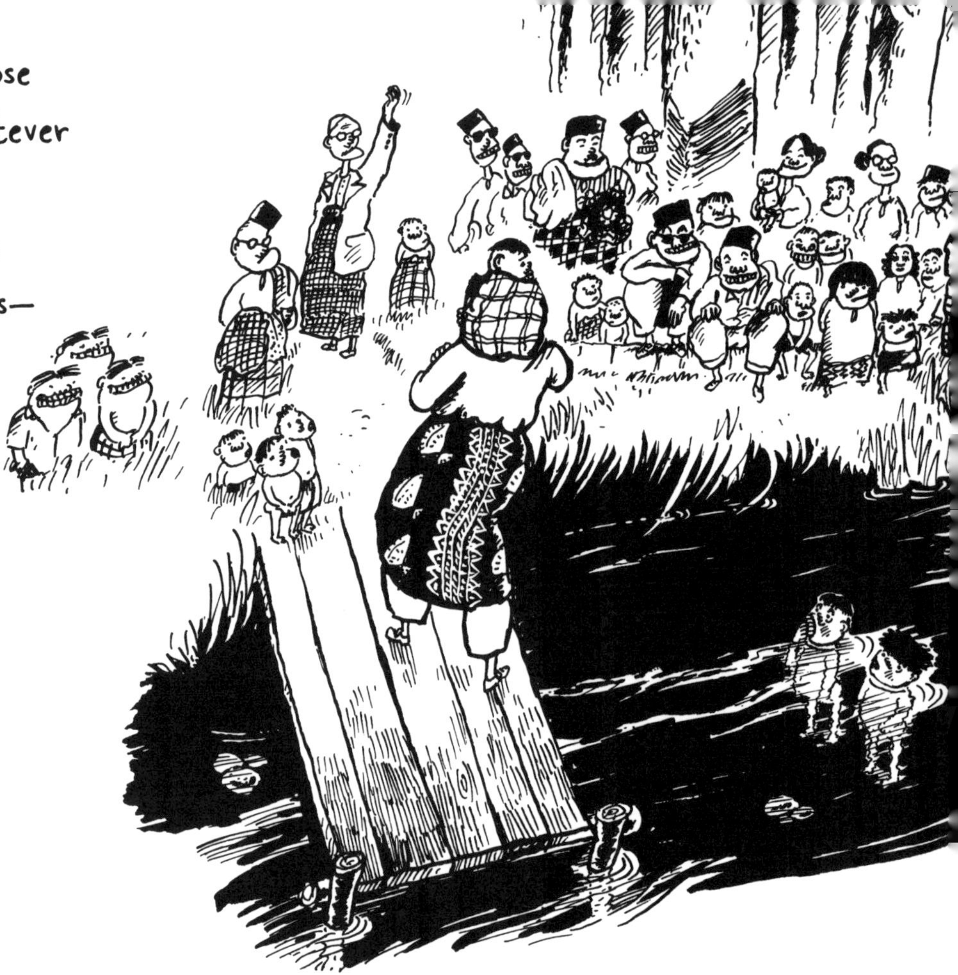

Then the moment came...the first boy (the eldest) was off to see Tok Modin. Good luck to him.

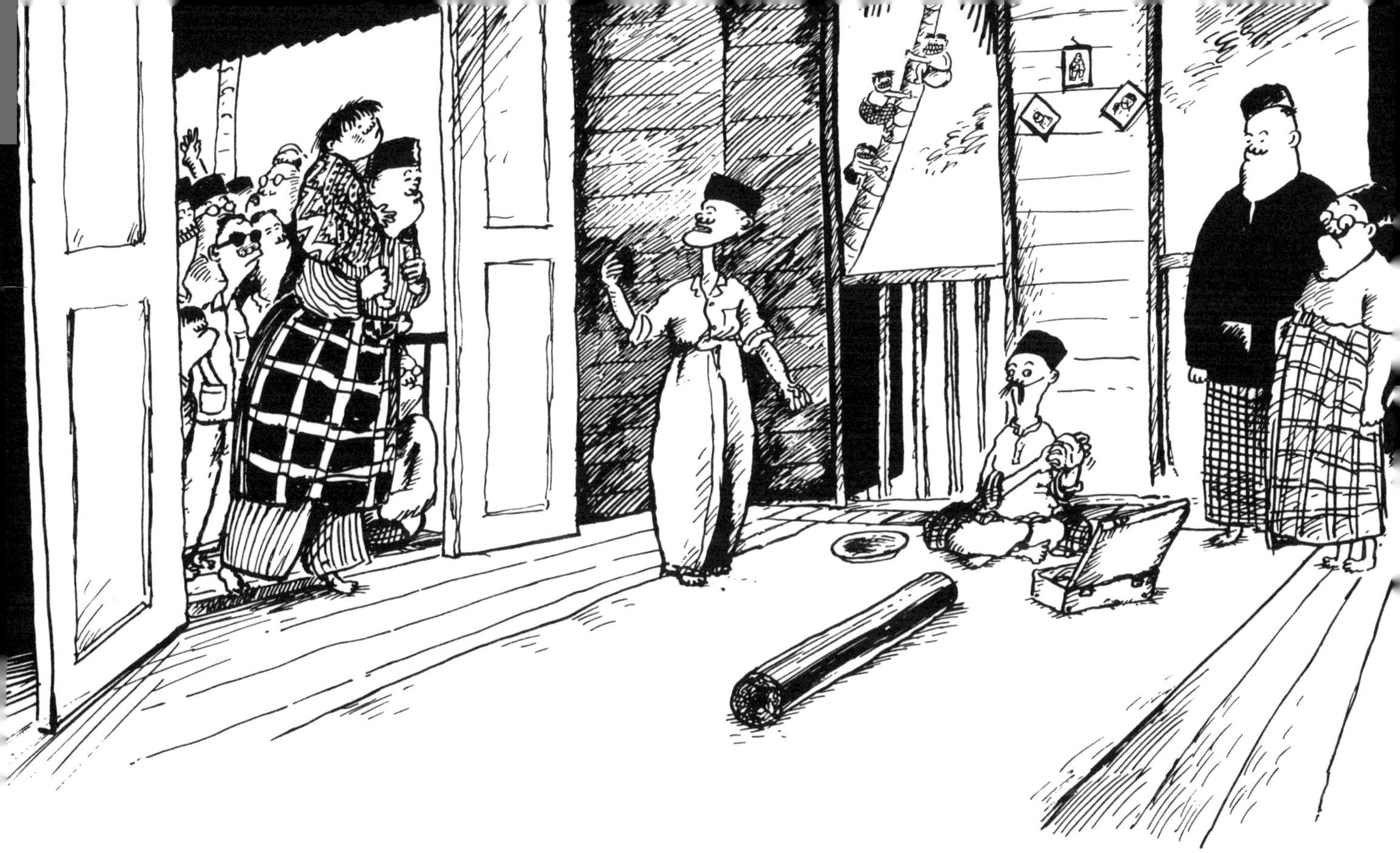

Then it was my turn...

It took place on a banana trunk.

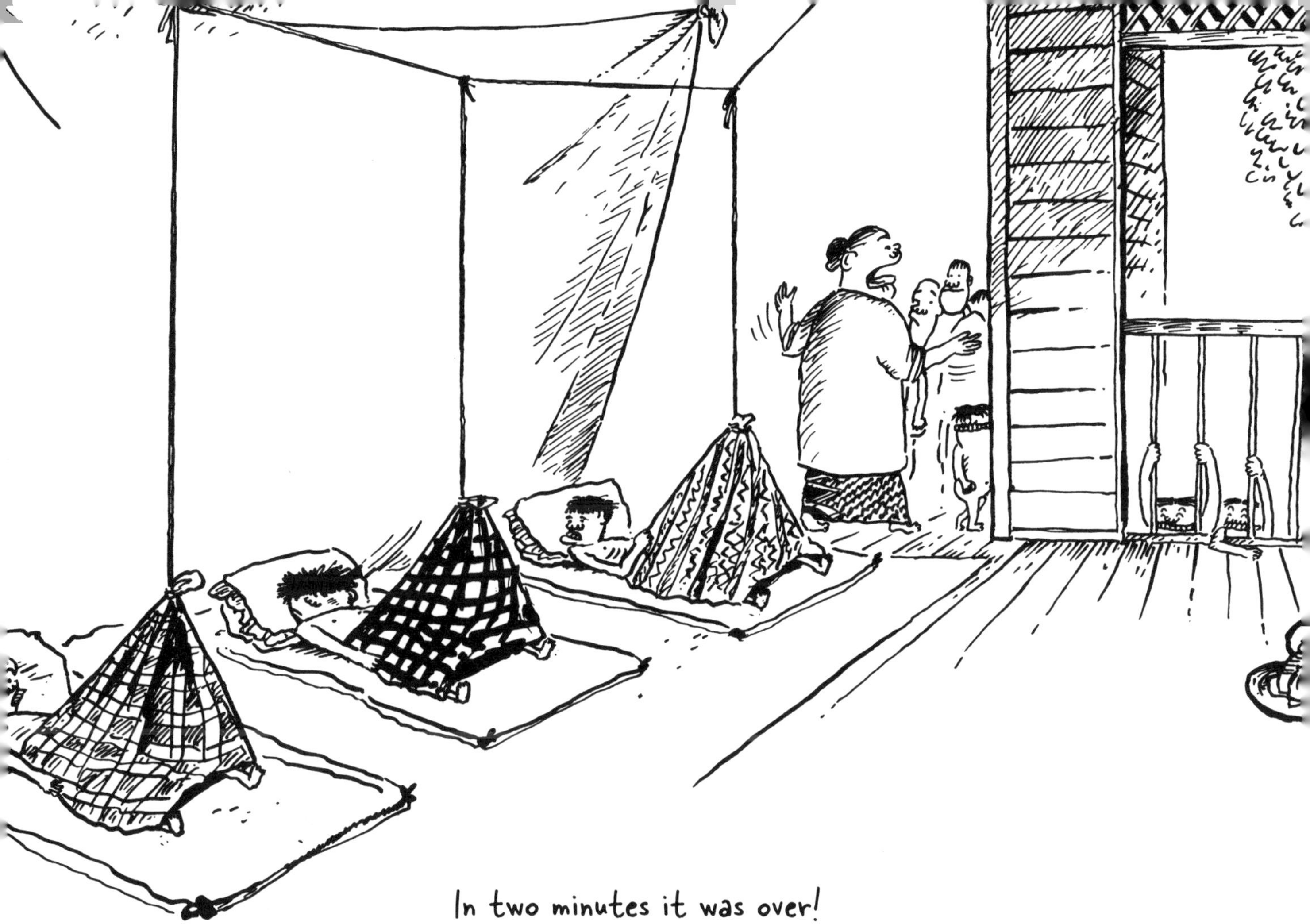

In two minutes it was over!

It was not very painful. Just like an ant bite!

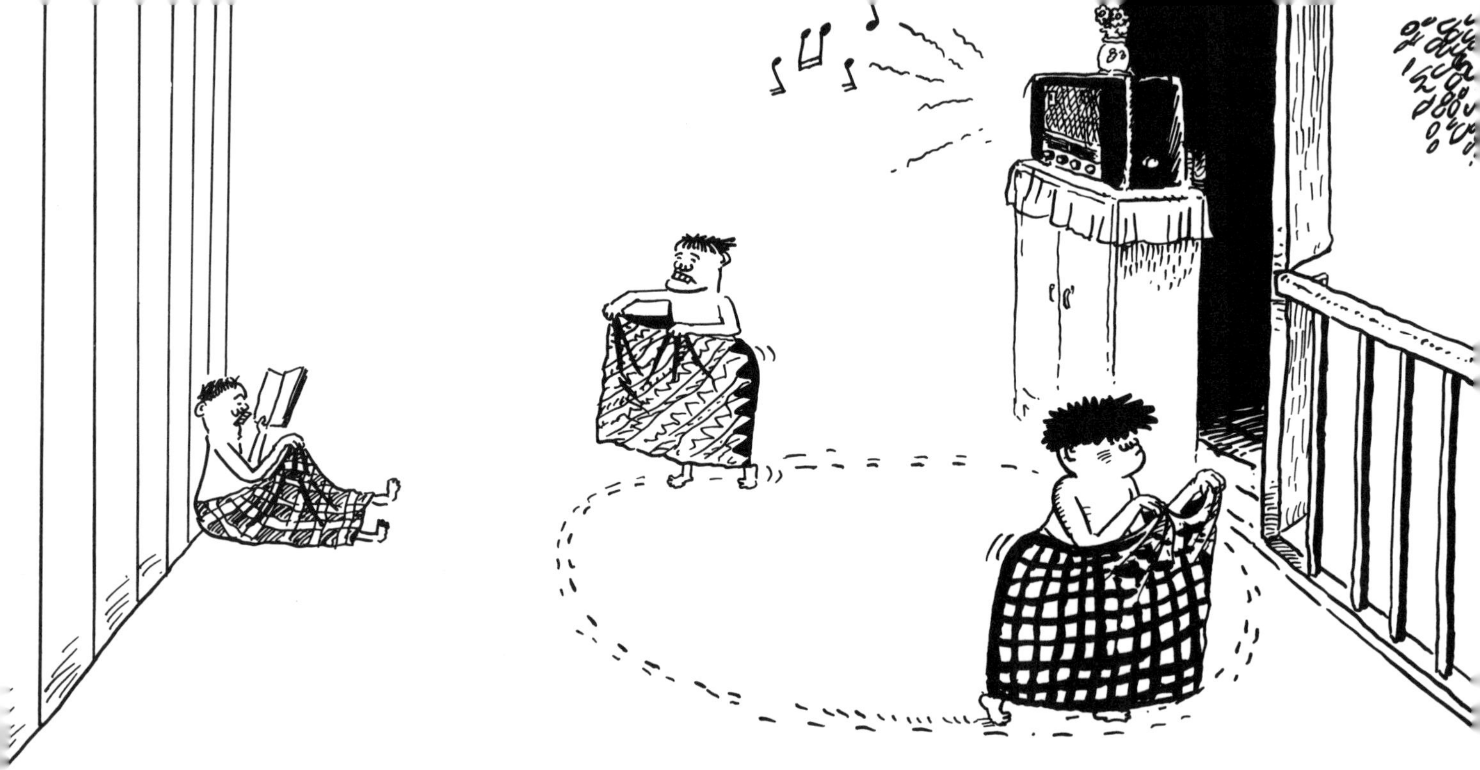

The next two weeks were quite boring. We were not allowed to leave the house, because Grandma was very strict. And what was worse, she only let us eat rice and salt fish...and drink boiled water.

However, after we had become well again, Grandma treated us to a movie in Batu Gajah. My family came along too, and Dad bought the tickets.

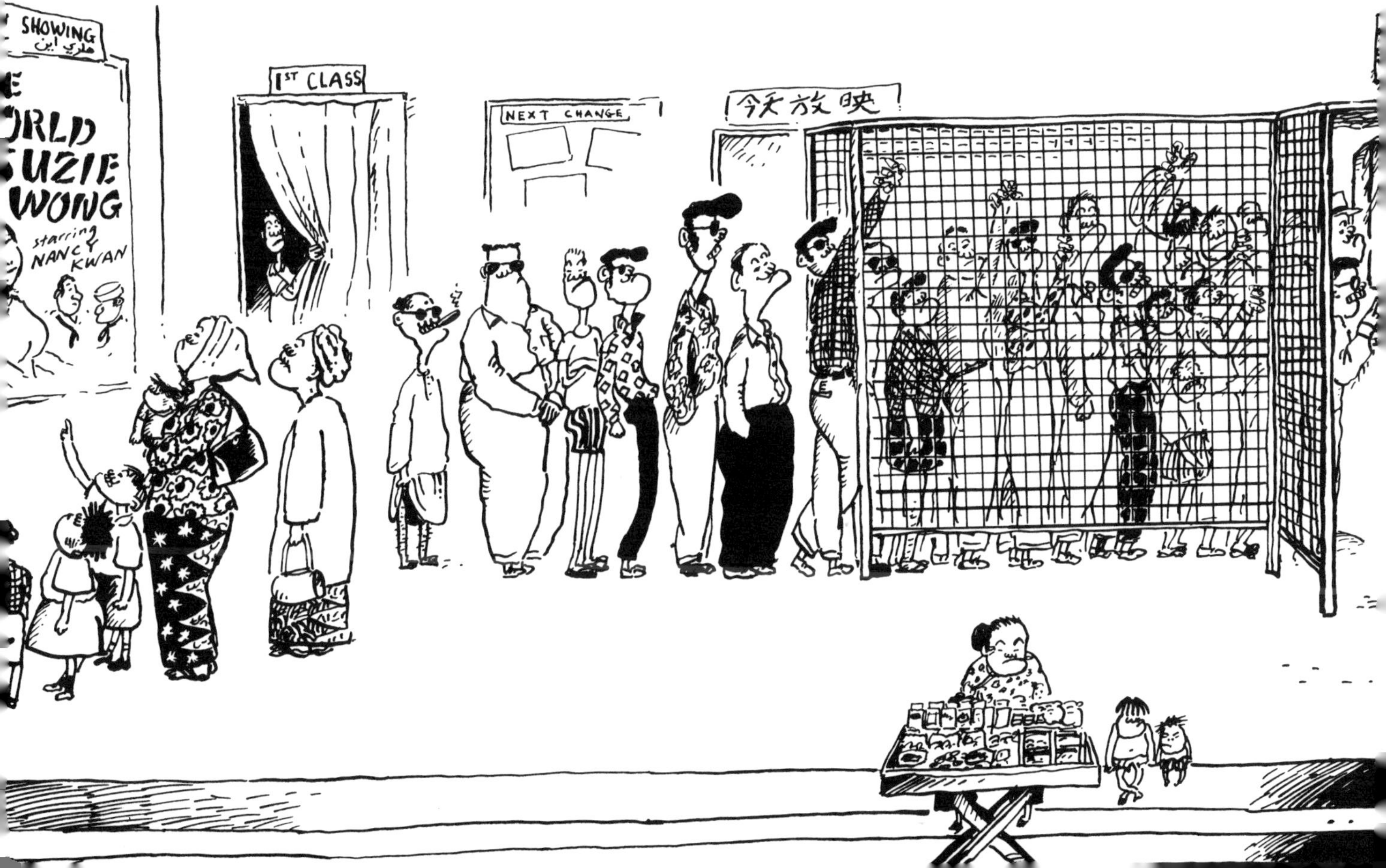

SHOWING
SUZIE
WONG
starring
NANCY KWAN
1ST CLASS
NEXT CHANGE
今天放映

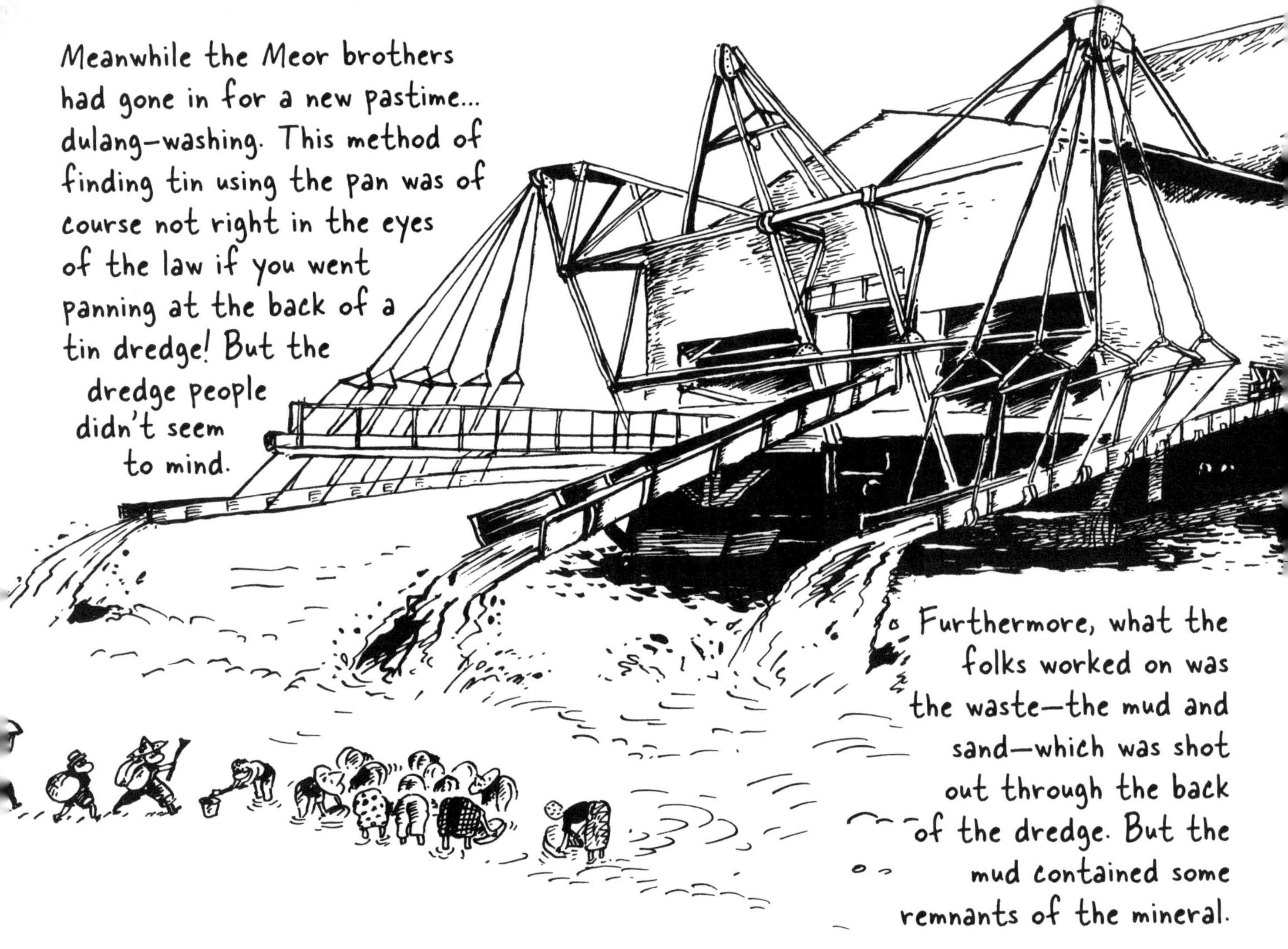
Meanwhile the Meor brothers had gone in for a new pastime... dulang-washing. This method of finding tin using the pan was of course not right in the eyes of the law if you went panning at the back of a tin dredge! But the dredge people didn't seem to mind.
Furthermore, what the folks worked on was the waste—the mud and sand—which was shot out through the back of the dredge. But the mud contained some remnants of the mineral.

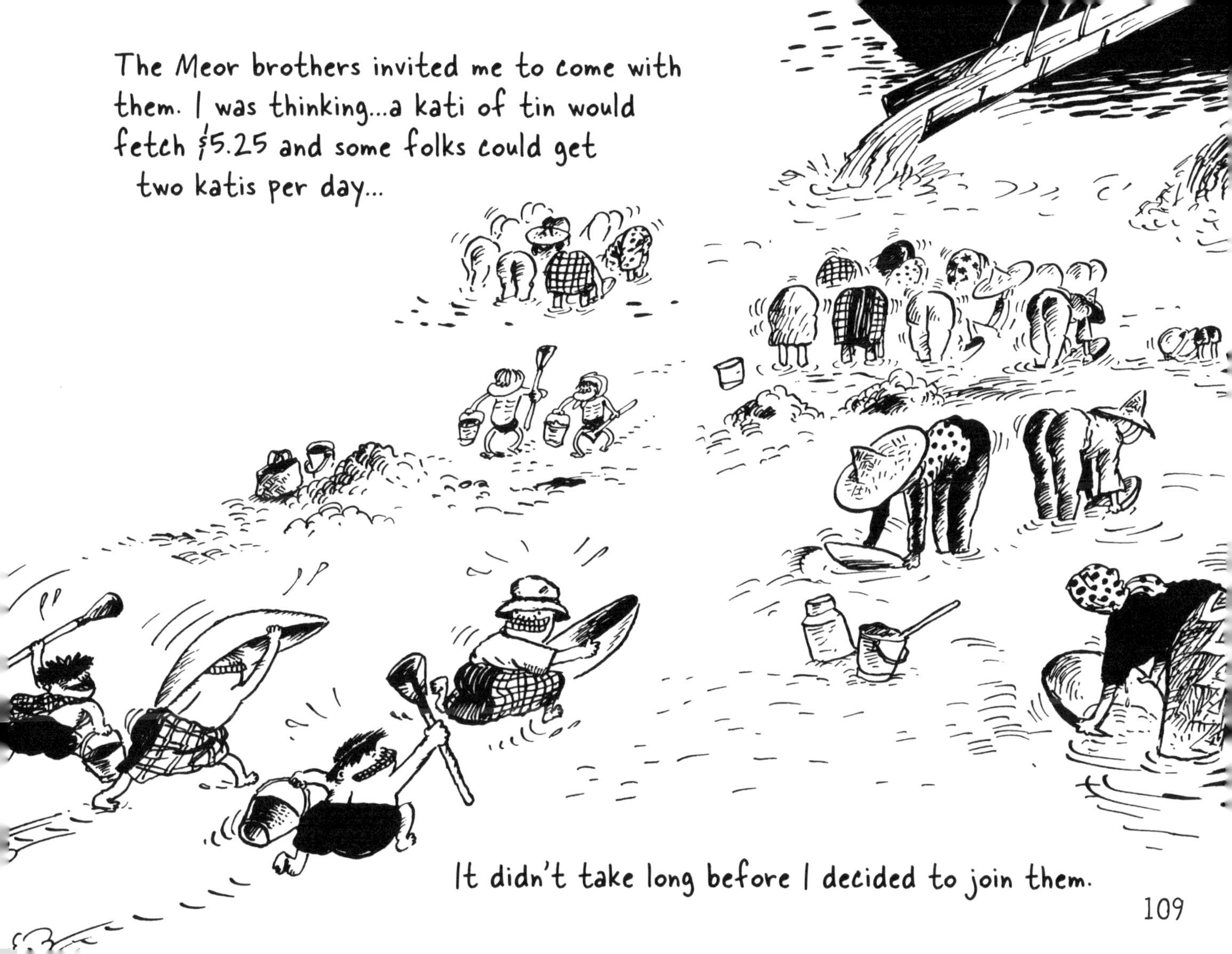
The Meor brothers invited me to come with them. I was thinking...a kati of tin would fetch $5.25 and some folks could get two katis per day...
It didn't take long before I decided to join them.

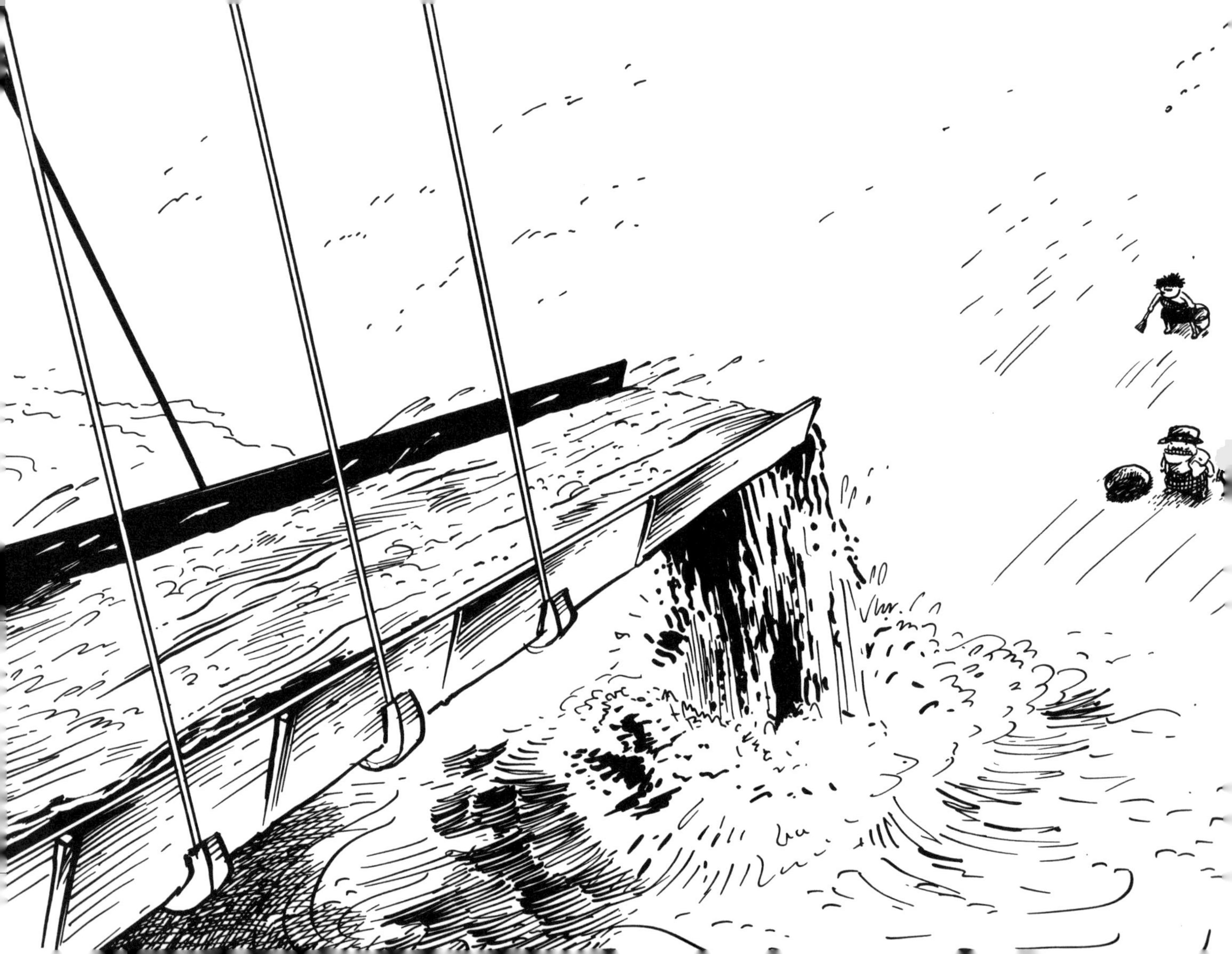

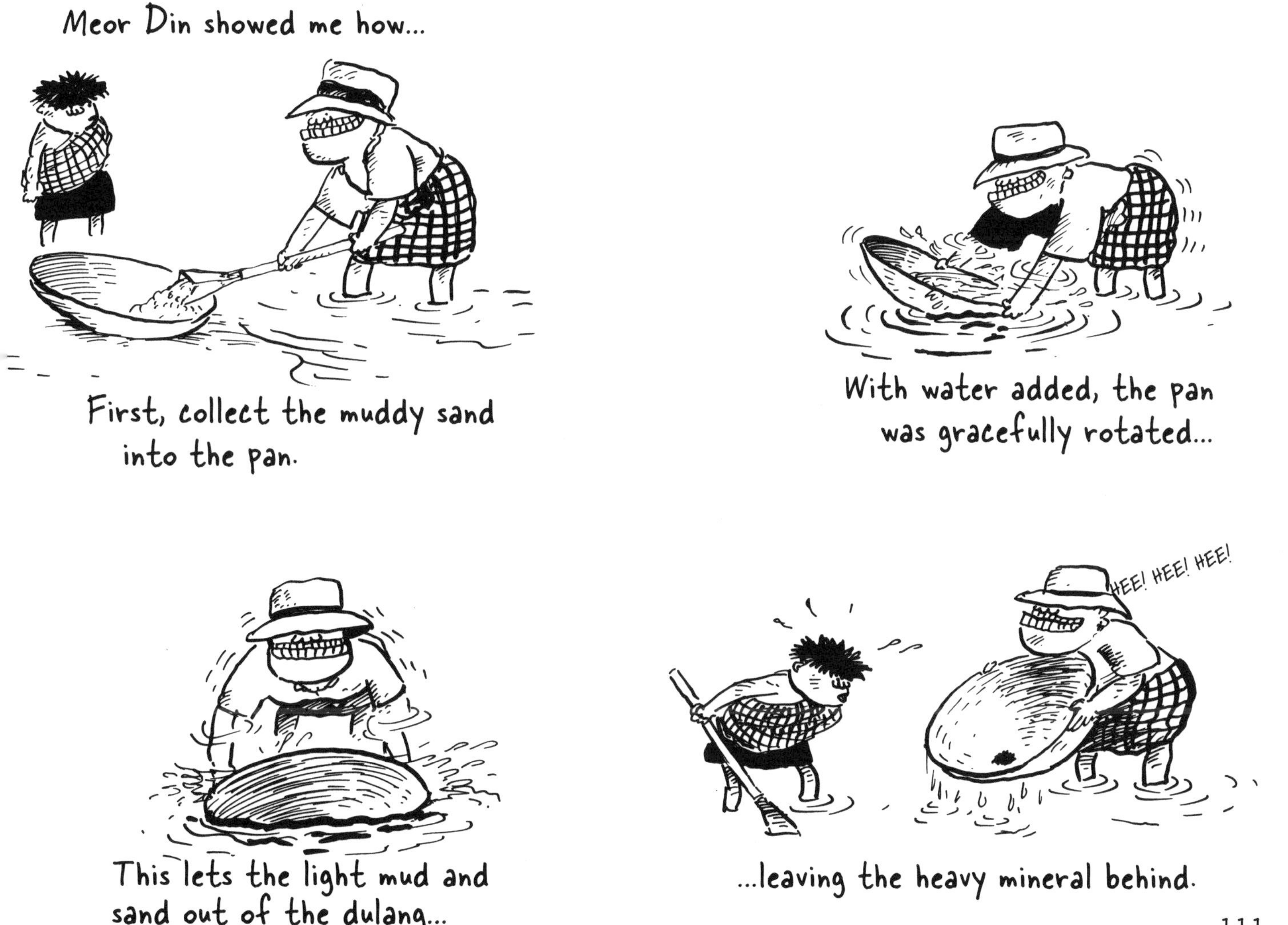
Meor Din showed me how...
First, collect the muddy sand into the pan.
With water added, the pan was gracefully rotated...
This lets the light mud and sand out of the dulang...
...leaving the heavy mineral behind.
HEE! HEE! HEE!

I learned fast.

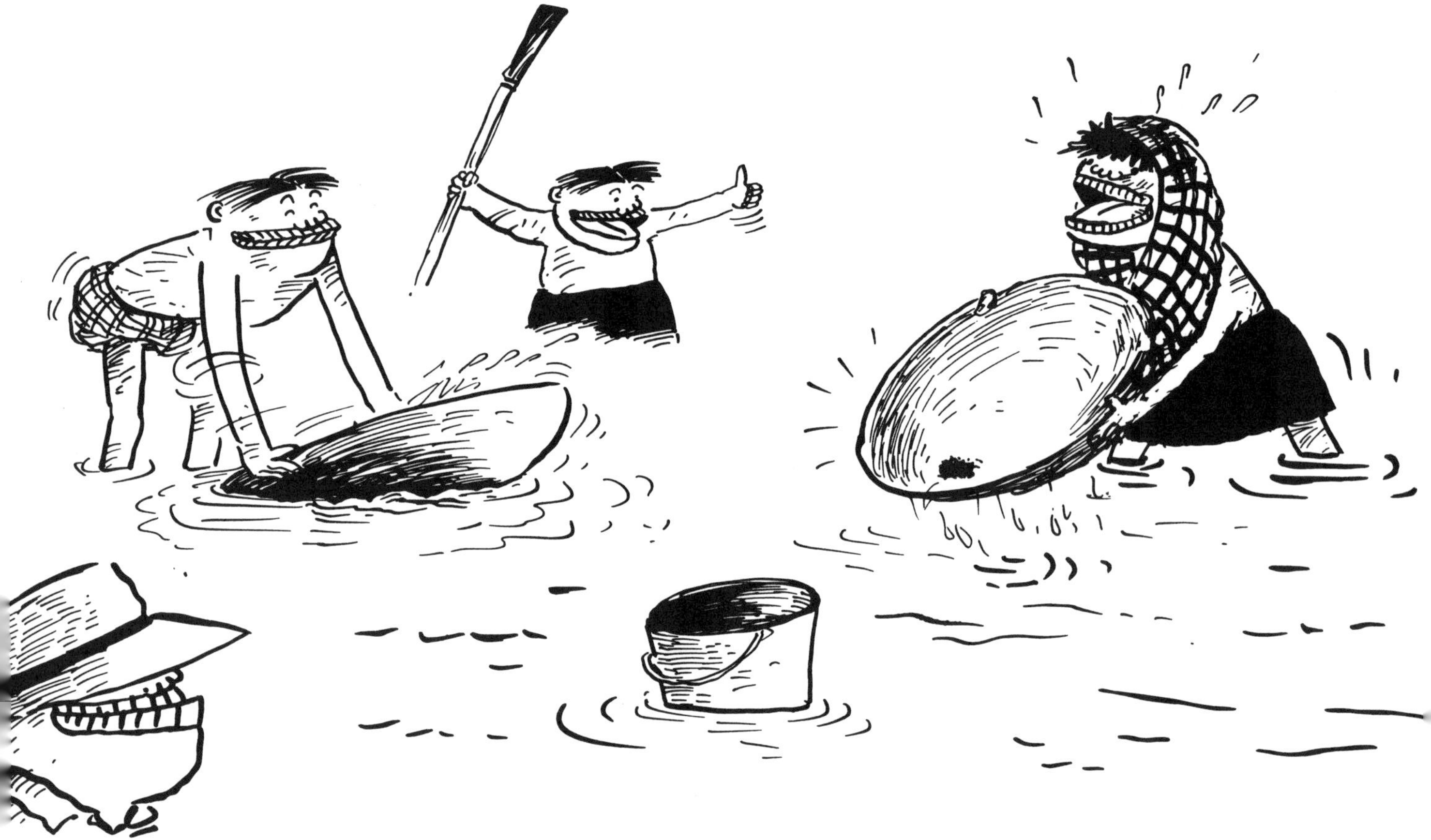

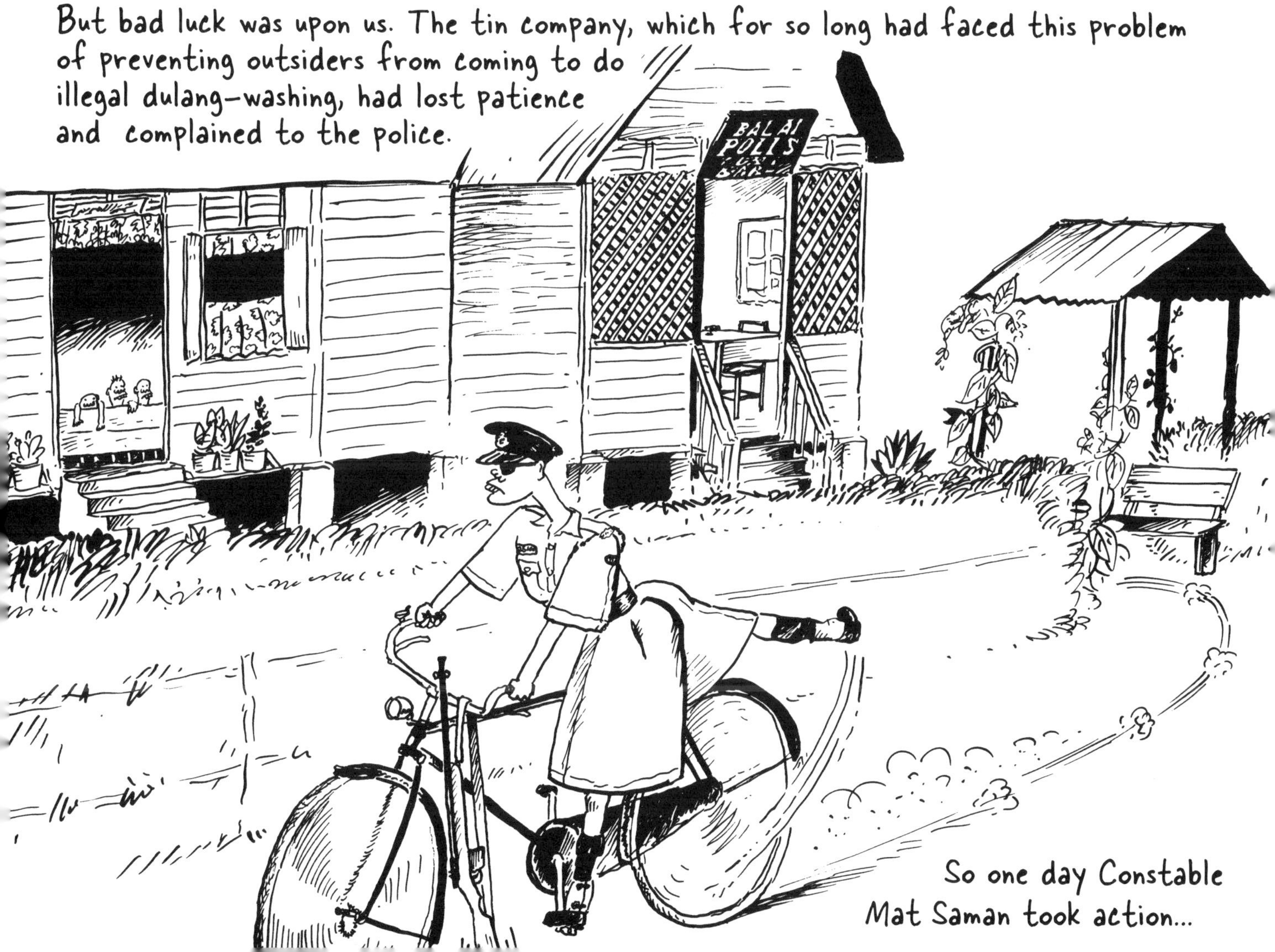
But bad luck was upon us. The tin company, which for so long had faced this problem of preventing outsiders from coming to do illegal dulang-washing, had lost patience and complained to the police.
BALAI POLIS
So one day Constable Mat Saman took action...

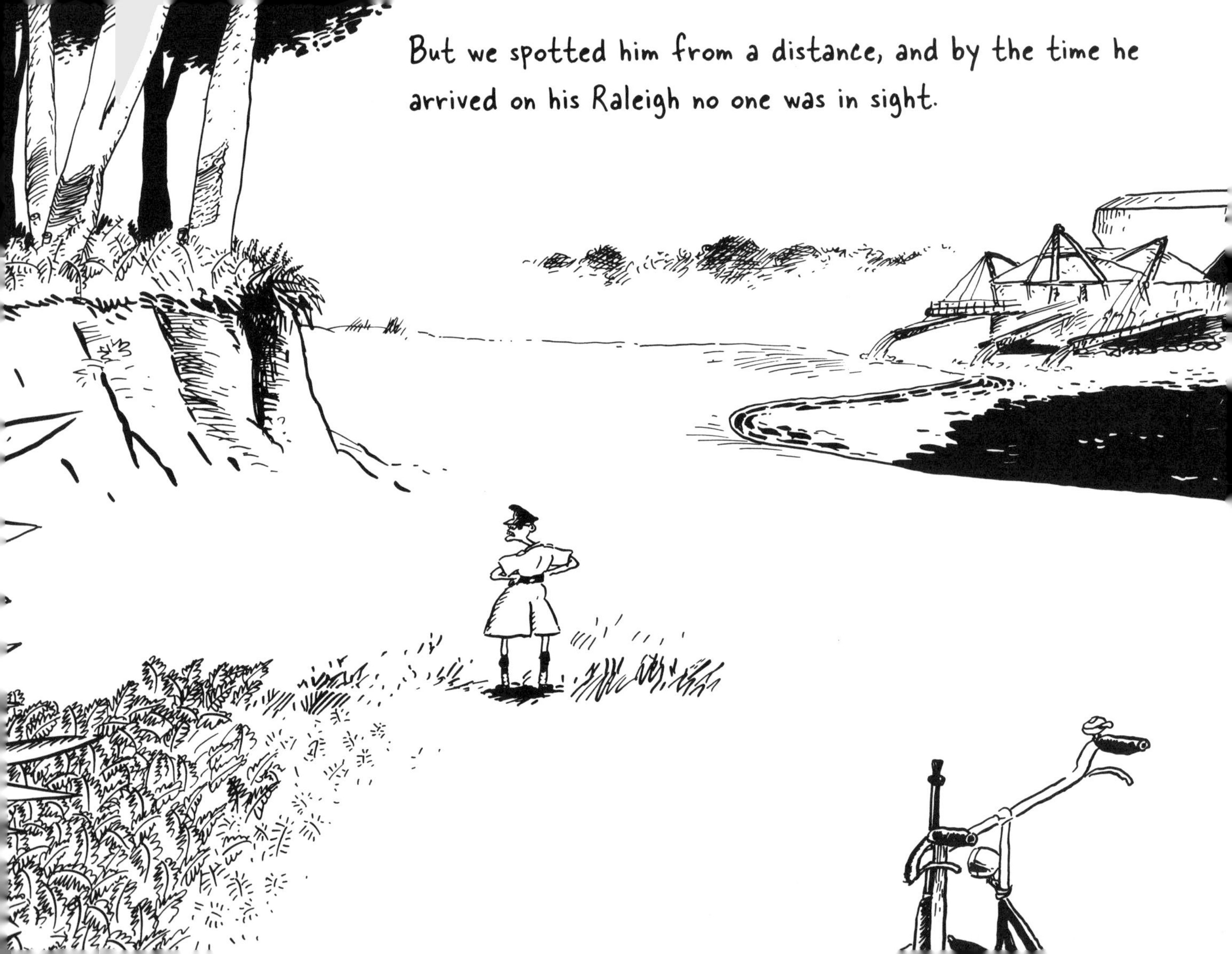
But we spotted him from a distance, and by the time he arrived on his Raleigh no one was in sight.

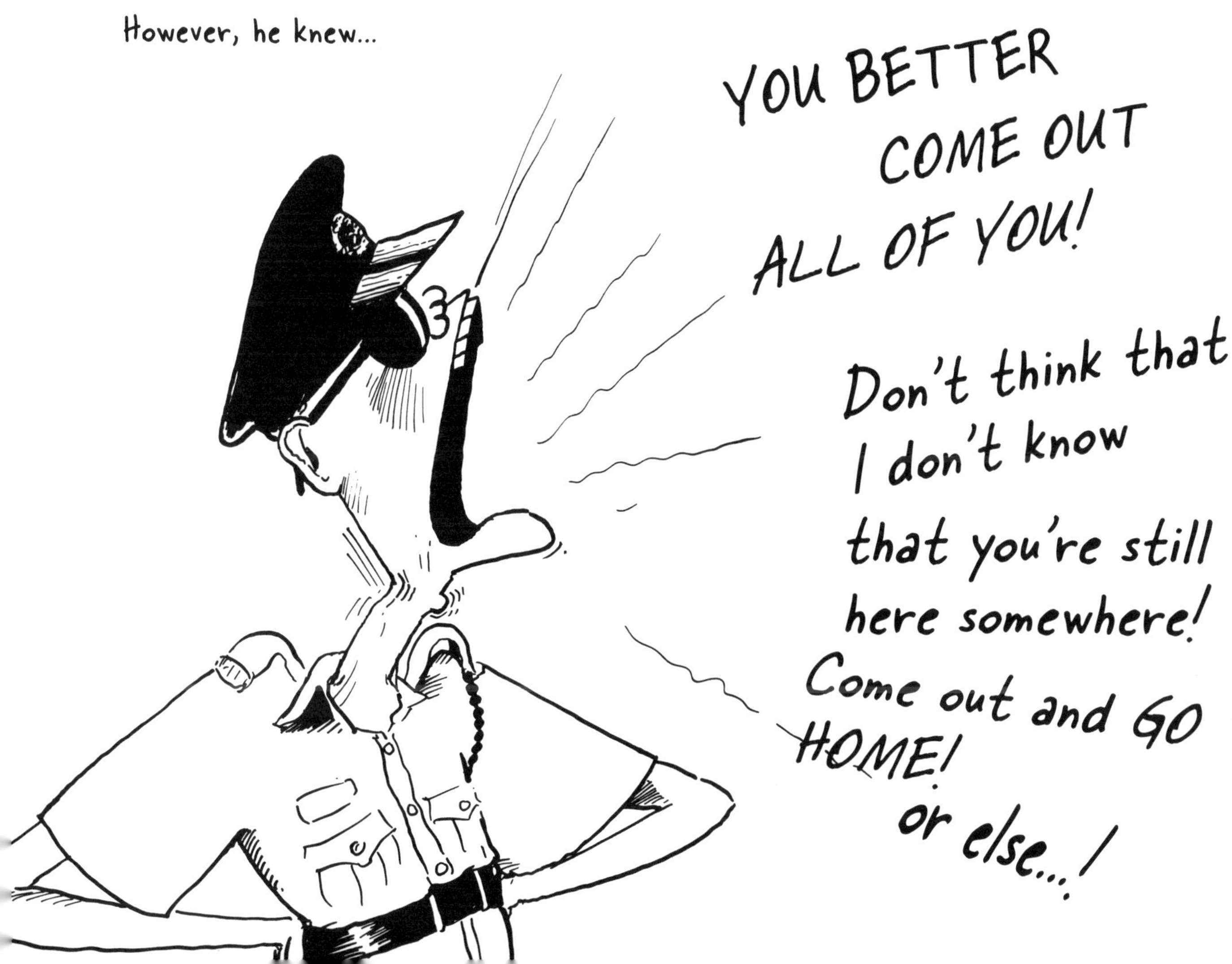
However, he knew...
YOU BETTER COME OUT ALL OF YOU!
Don't think that I don't know that you're still here somewhere! Come out and GO HOME! or else...!

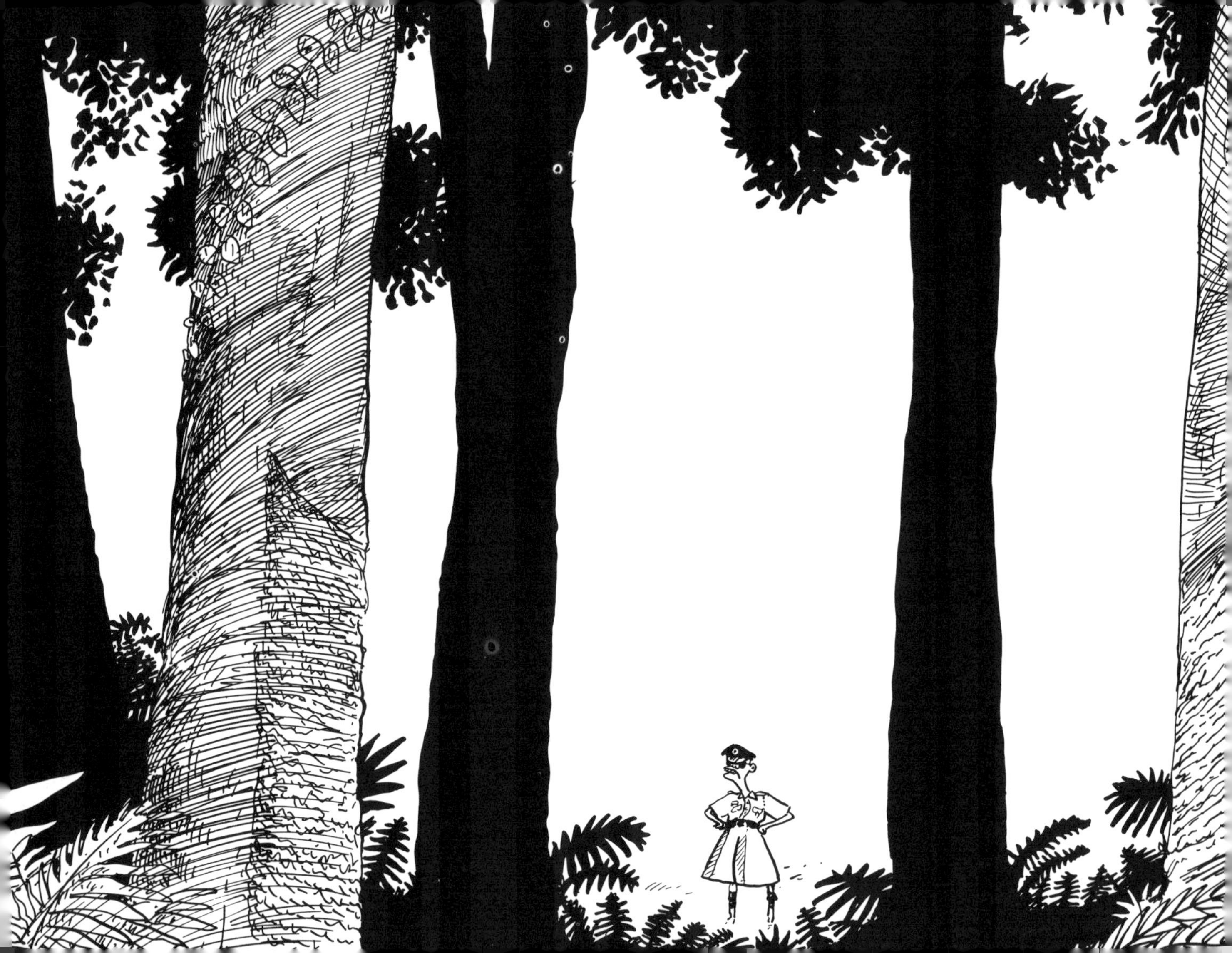

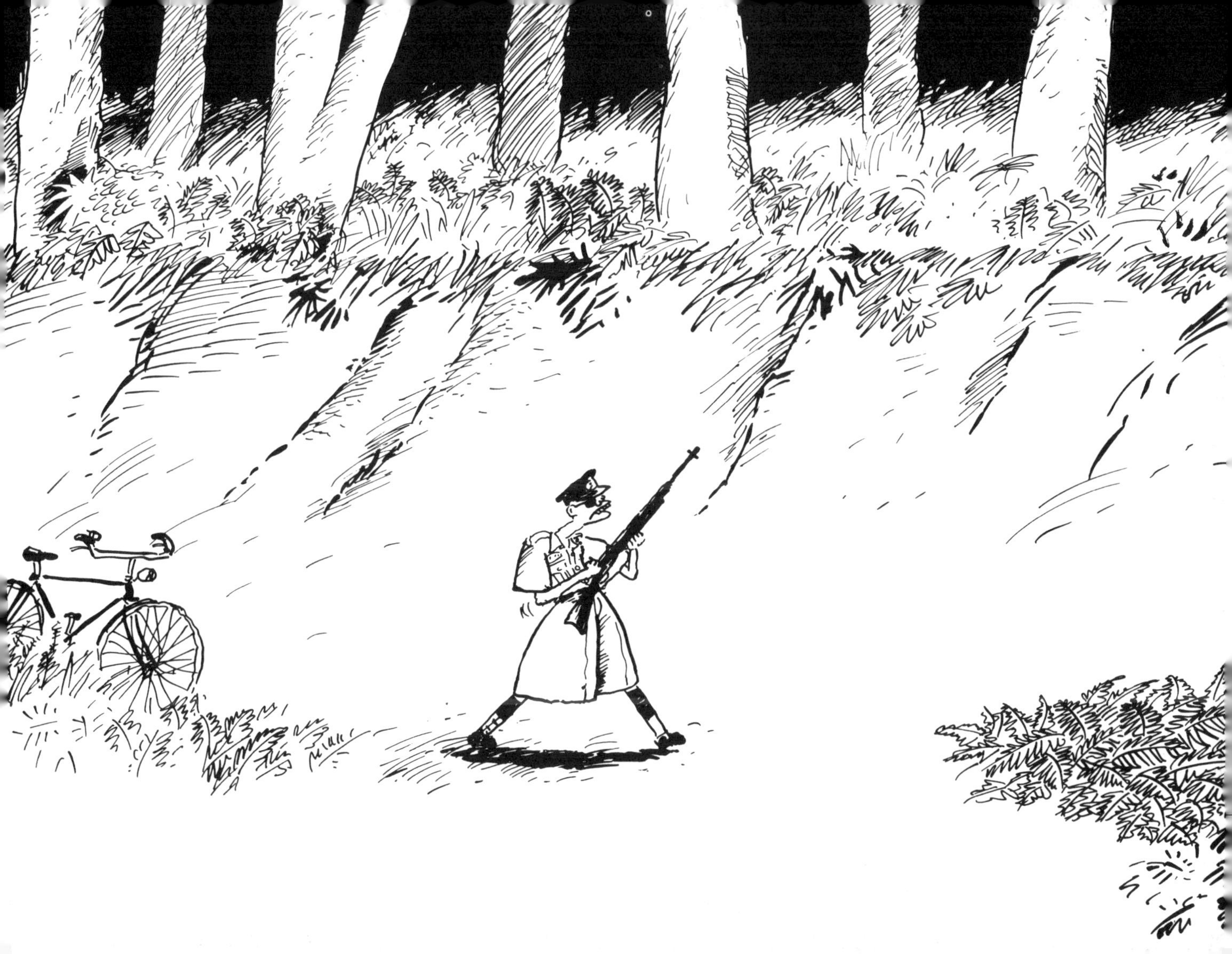

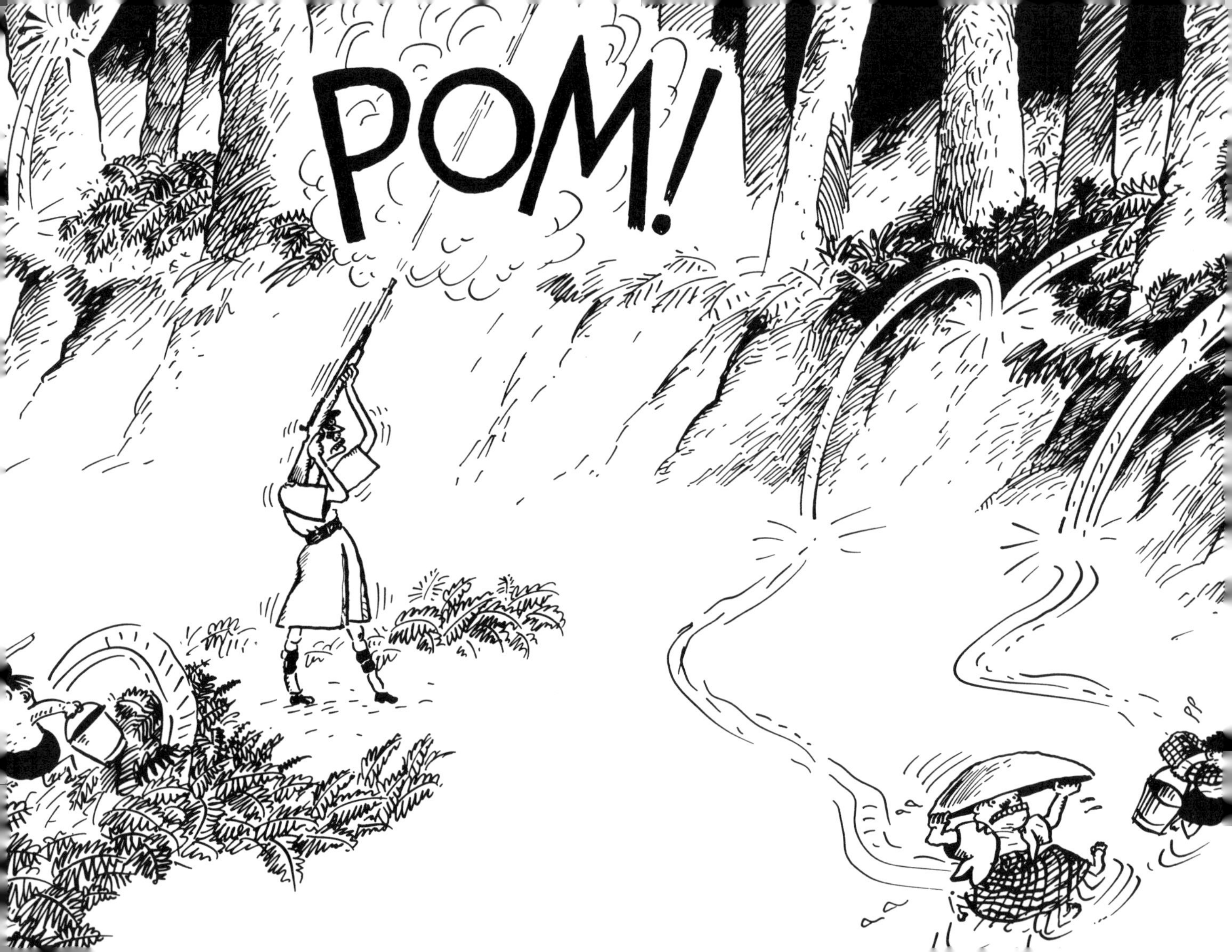
POM!

We went back straight away without looking behind and I didn't think I'd return there again! Dad was home and I couldn't wait to show him what I had collected...

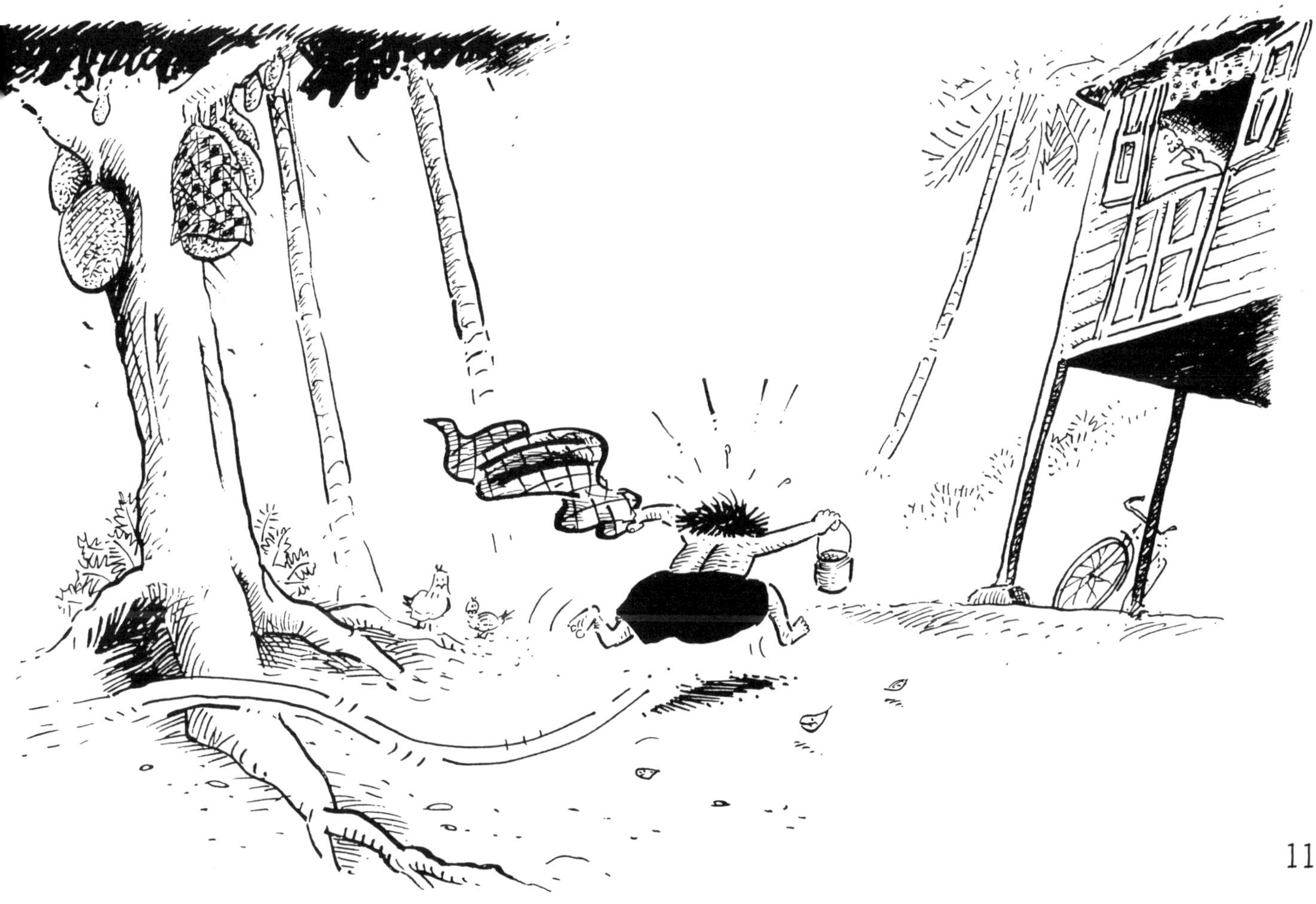

Well...he wasn't impressed.

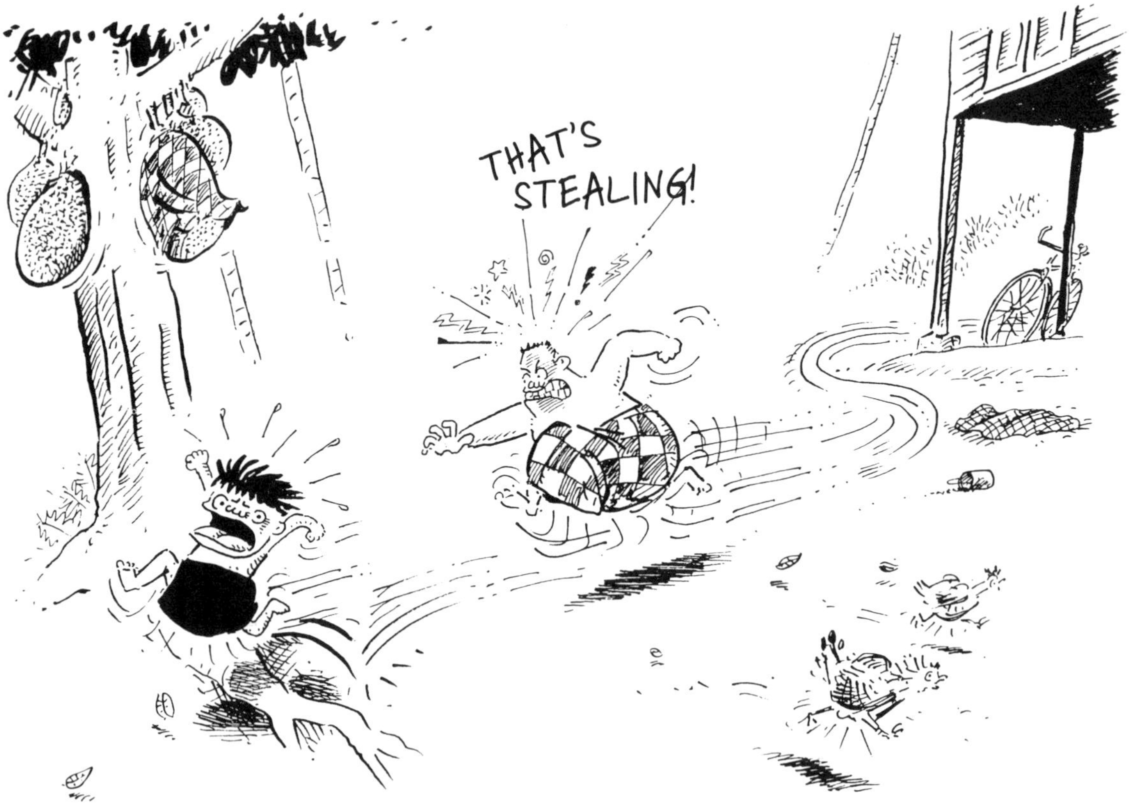
THAT'S STEALING!

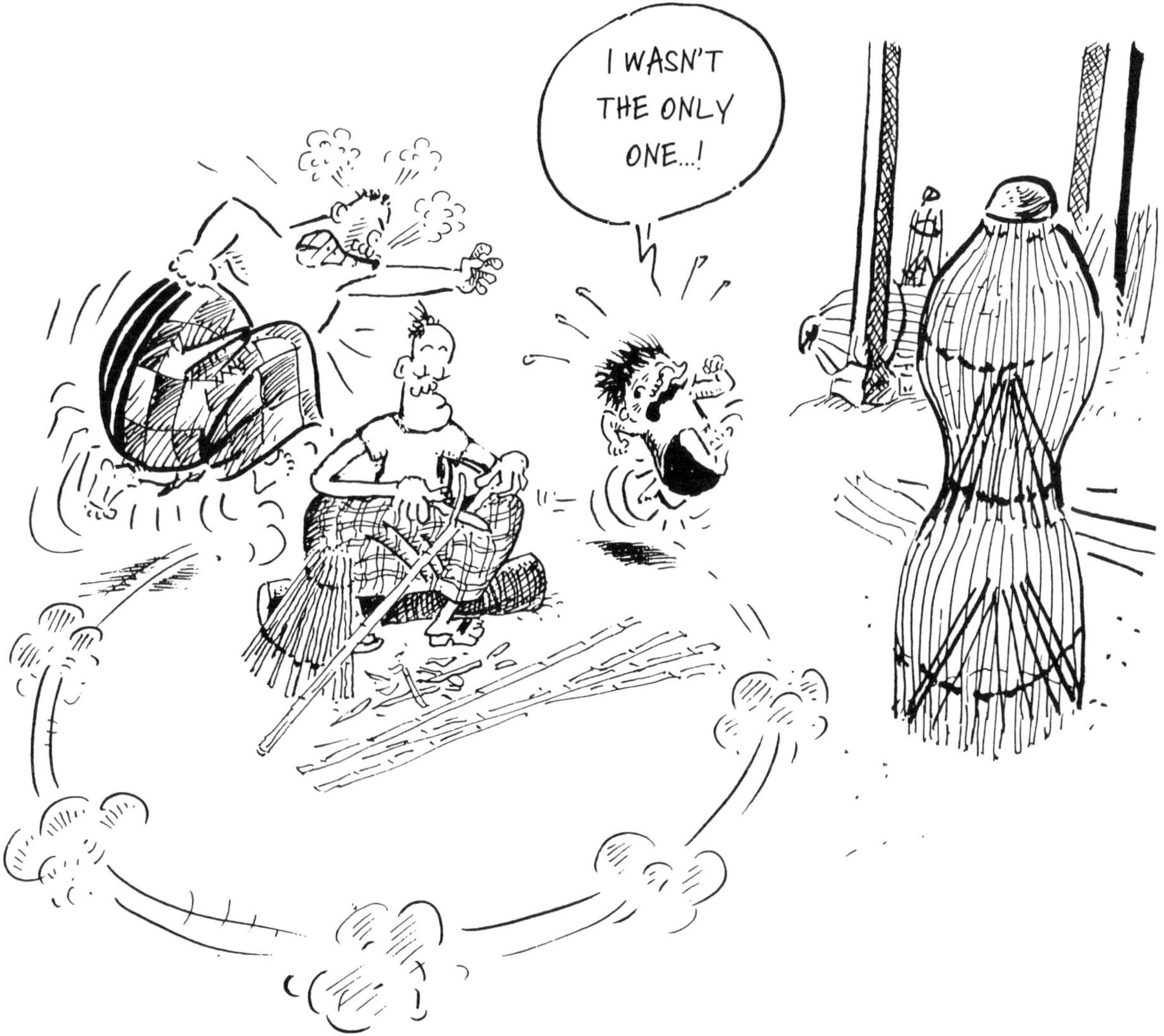
I WASN'T THE ONLY ONE...!

I was caught of course...and it certainly was a good thrashing Dad gave me. He kept on asking why I wasn't thinking seriously about my future ...

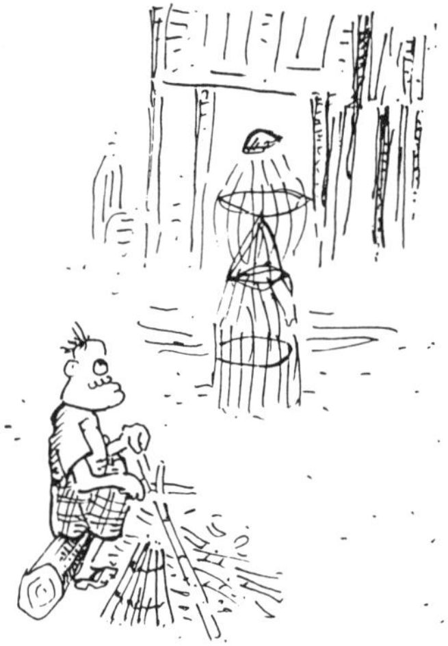

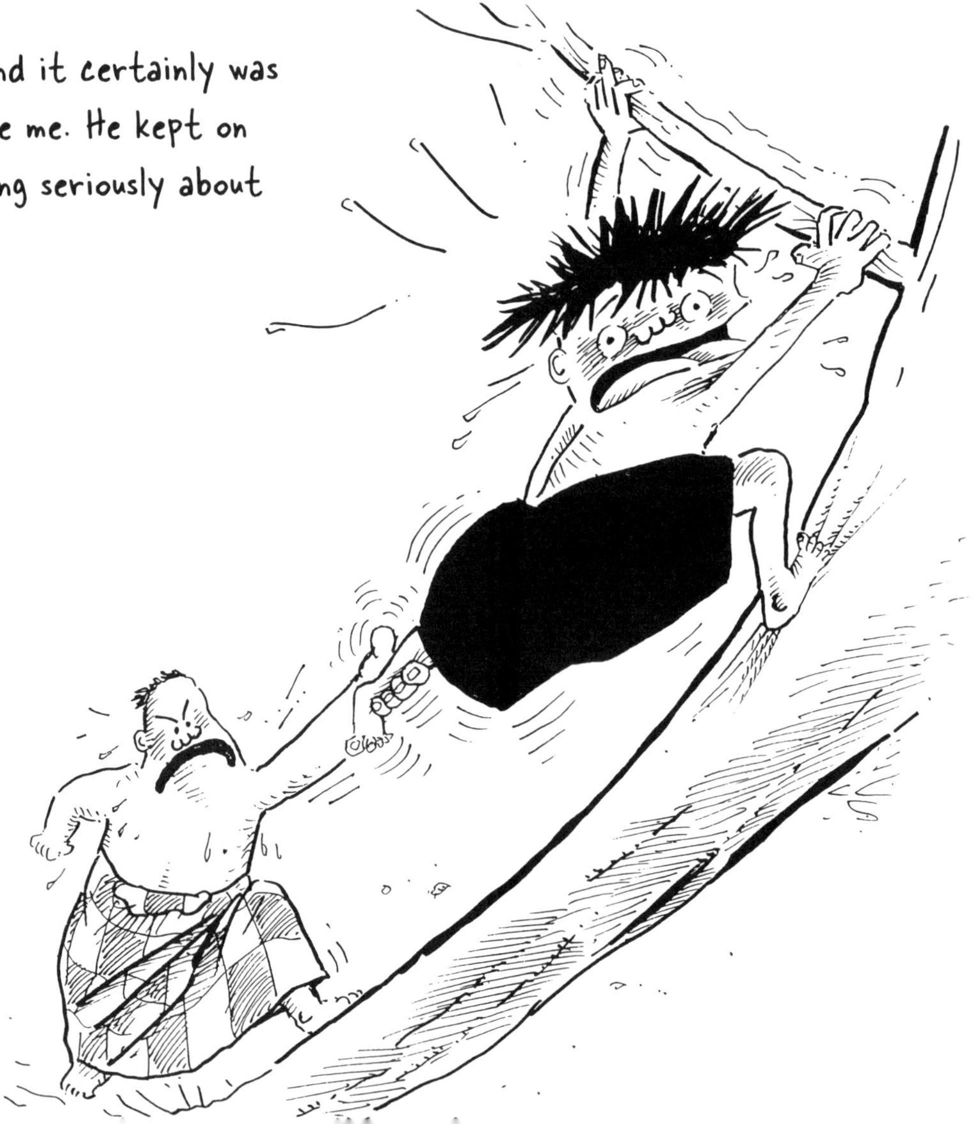

I retired early that night. My eyes were swollen because of the beating and my excessive weeping. And I once again became the subject of discussion between my parents. This time my mother complained that Father's punishment was too harsh.

"He was just trying to show you that he is capable like the rest of the boys," she said.

"He should do well in his studies," said Dad, "instead of stealing tin! His special examination is coming soon and he must pass in order to be admitted to the boarding school in Ipoh."

123

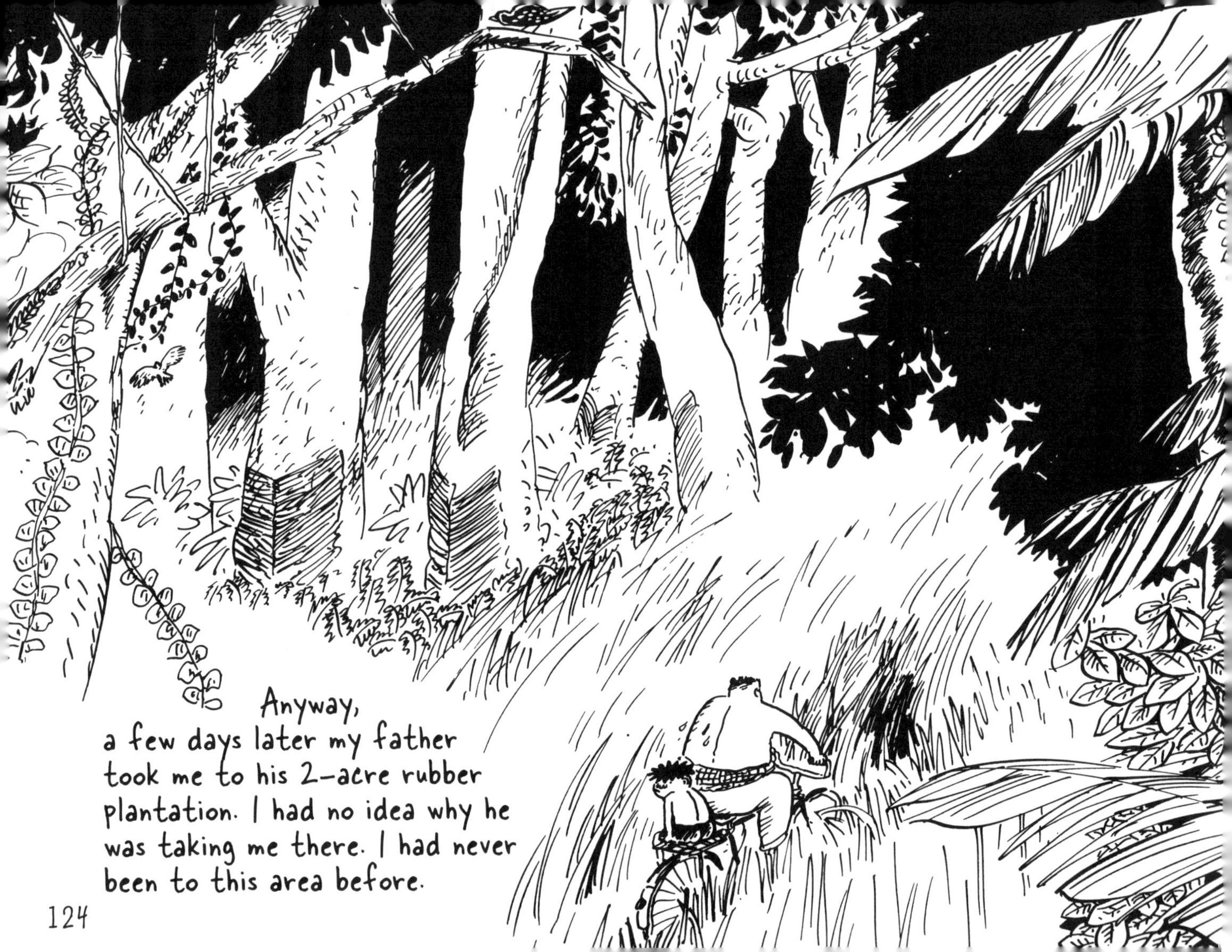
Anyway,
a few days later my father took me to his 2-acre rubber plantation. I had no idea why he was taking me there. I had never been to this area before.

“You should know about this plantation,” he said after the long ride. My father’s huge rubber trees were very old and the whole area was thick with undergrowth. All I knew about his plantation was that a kampung fellow was hired to tap the trees.

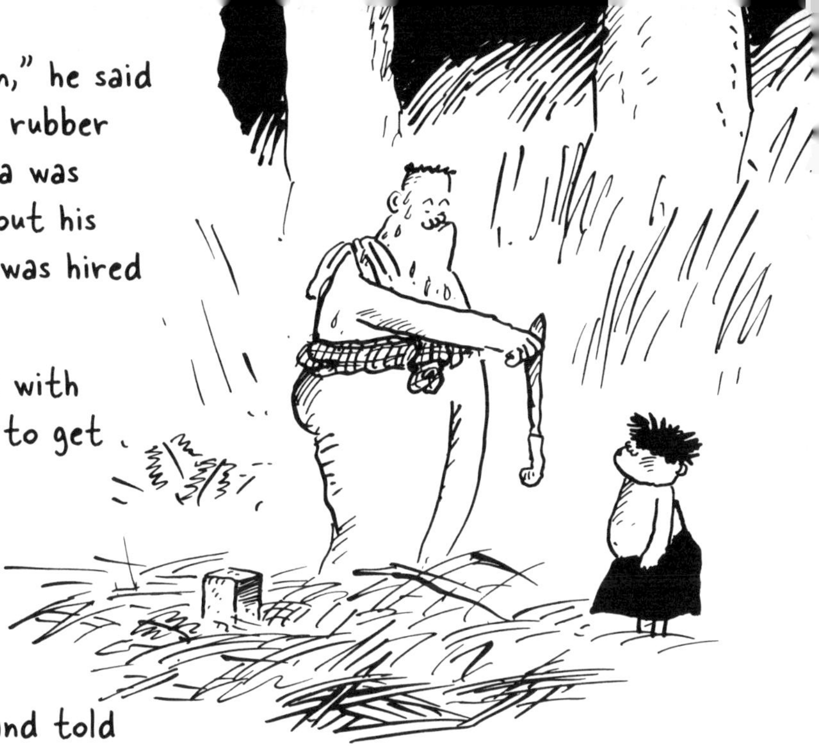

“Soon I’m planning to replant this land with high-yielding rubber. But first I have to get some people to clear it,” he said.

Dad took out his parang and started cutting through shrubs in a particular spot, which revealed a border stone.

He indicated the borders of his land and told me who the neighboring lands belonged to.

“All right,” he handed me the parang, “now you clear the shrubs around the border stones so that we know our borders.”

But I hesitated and said: “But father...why not let the man who looks after this plantation take care of that?”

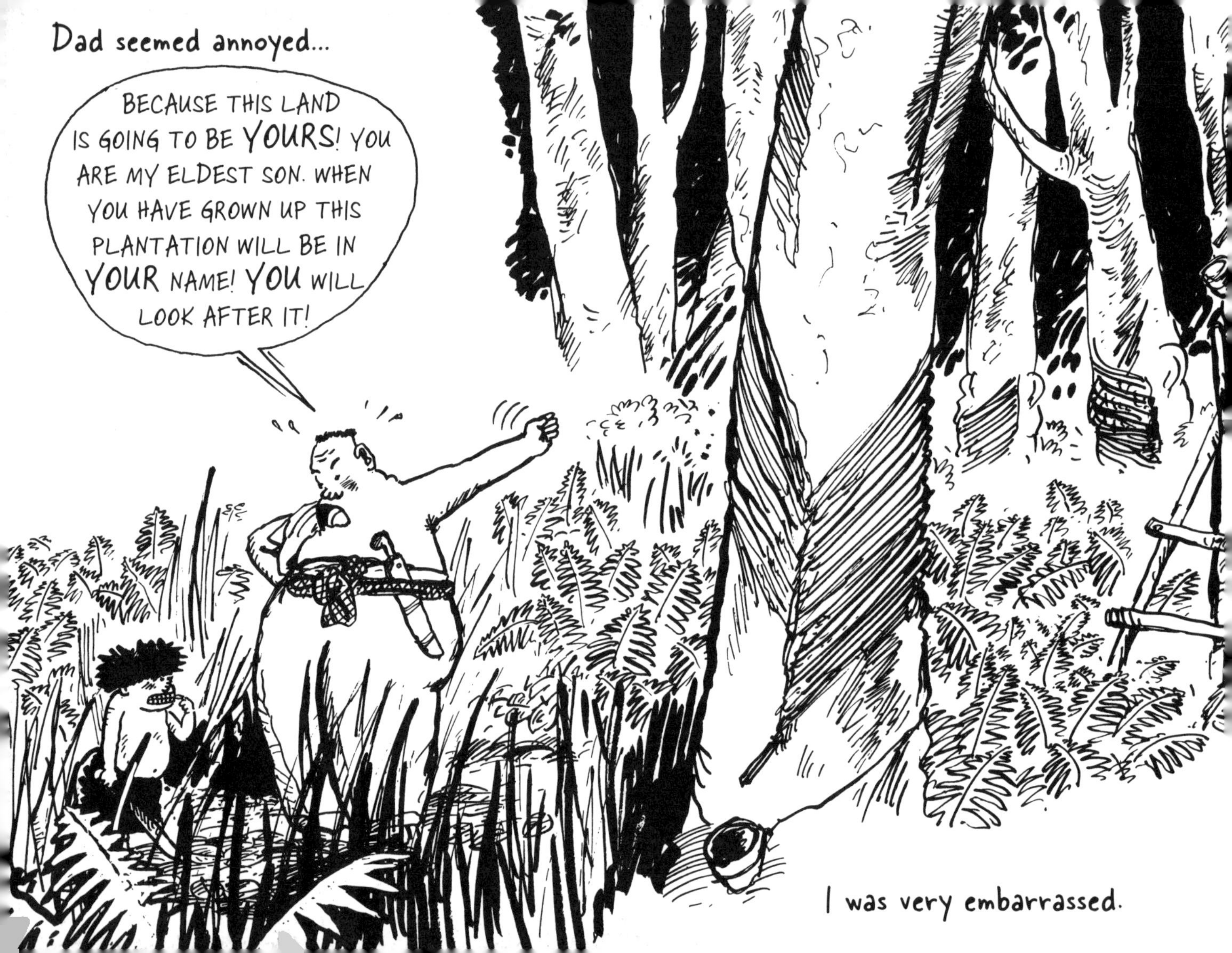
Dad seemed annoyed...
BECAUSE THIS LAND IS GOING TO BE YOURS! YOU ARE MY ELDEST SON. WHEN YOU HAVE GROWN UP THIS PLANTATION WILL BE IN YOUR NAME! YOU WILL LOOK AFTER IT!
I was very embarrassed.

With my face turning red, I started clearing the undergrowth. I was confused, too. Never had I thought my father would announce my inheritance so soon!

Obviously he was trying to make amends after that outburst of temper at the doorstep.

Dad added: "All this is of course on condition that you study well and pass your examination."

"All right, Father."

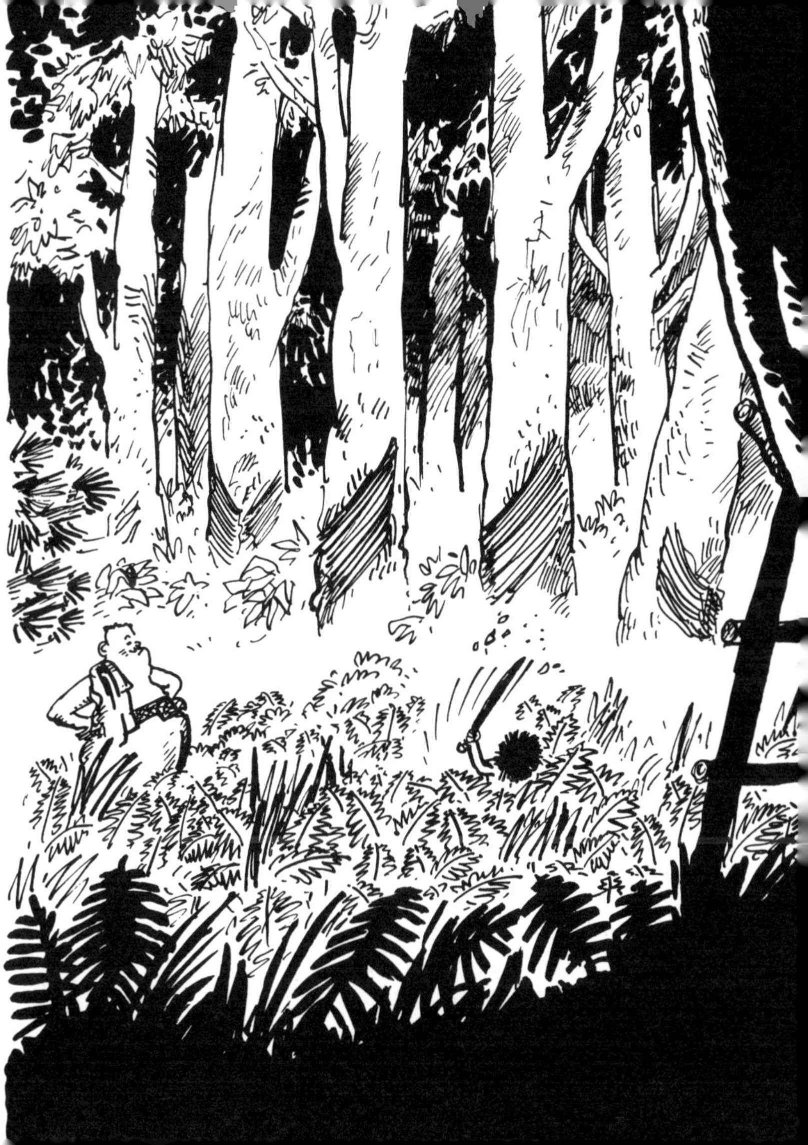

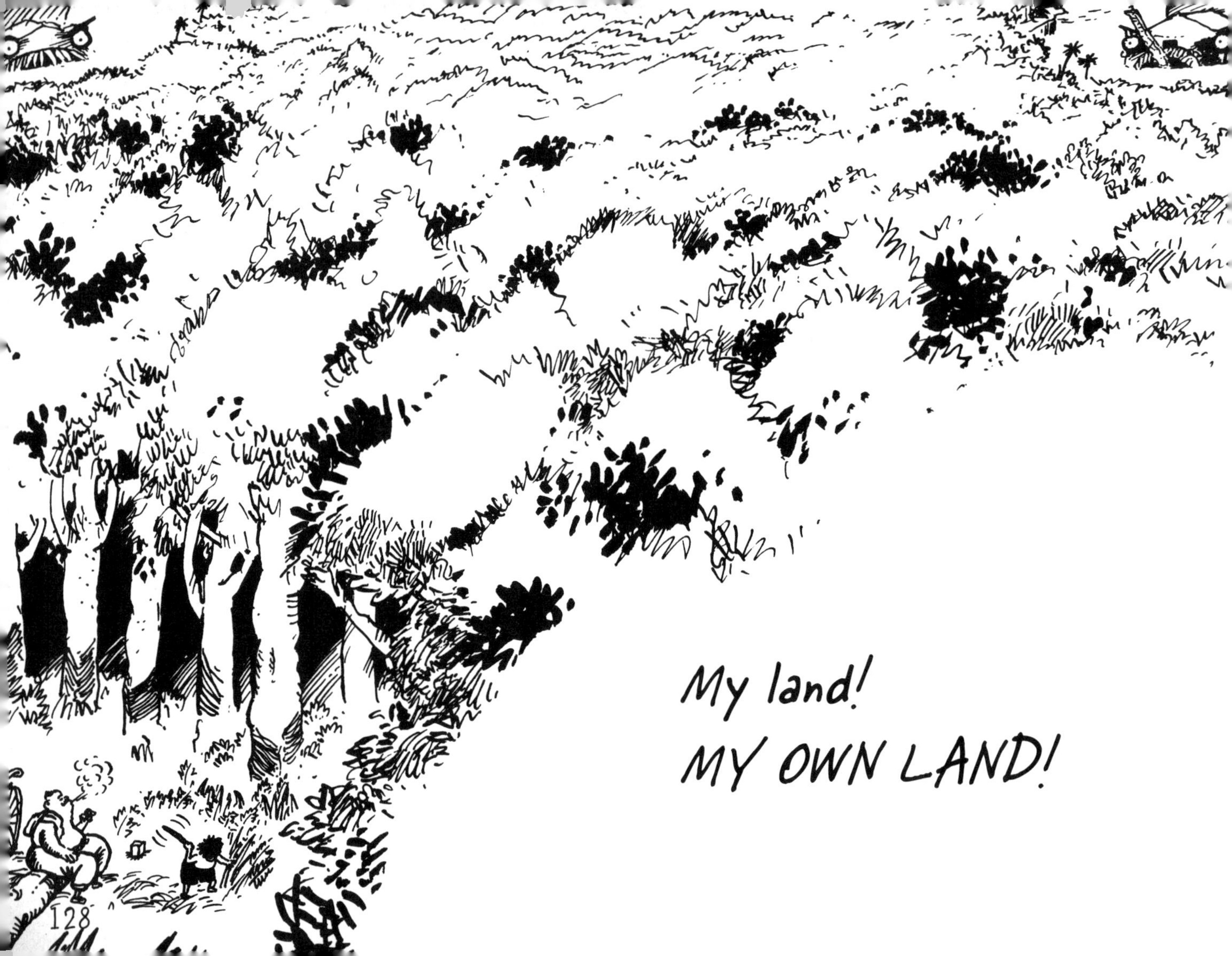
My land!
MY OWN LAND!

The special examination that was approaching was for standard four pupils and several, including myself, were advised by our teacher to take it.

If I could pass I would be admitted to an exclusive boarding school in the big town of Ipoh. I would really be a somebody!

And so...no more hanging around with the Meor brothers. I had to pass!

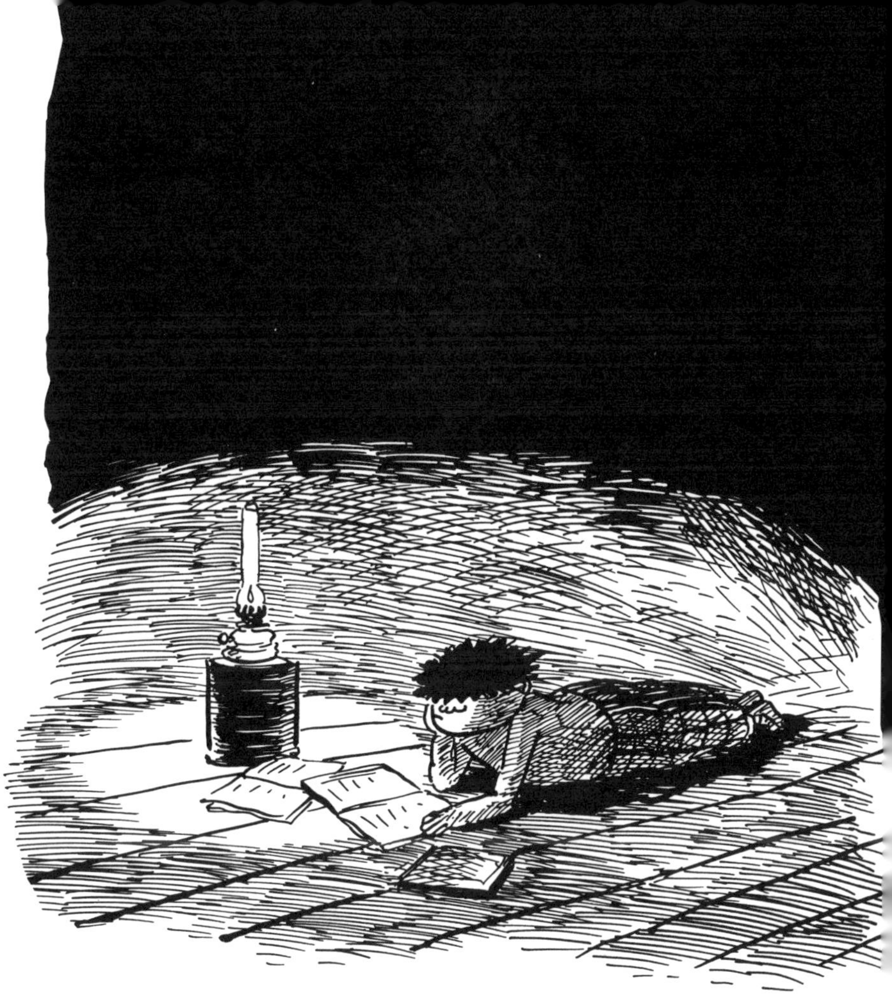

I passed.

It was hard to believe at first.

Our headmaster, who was responsible for taking us to the examination at a big school in Kampar, broke the news to me one afternoon in front of his house.

"Along with three other fellows, you've passed."

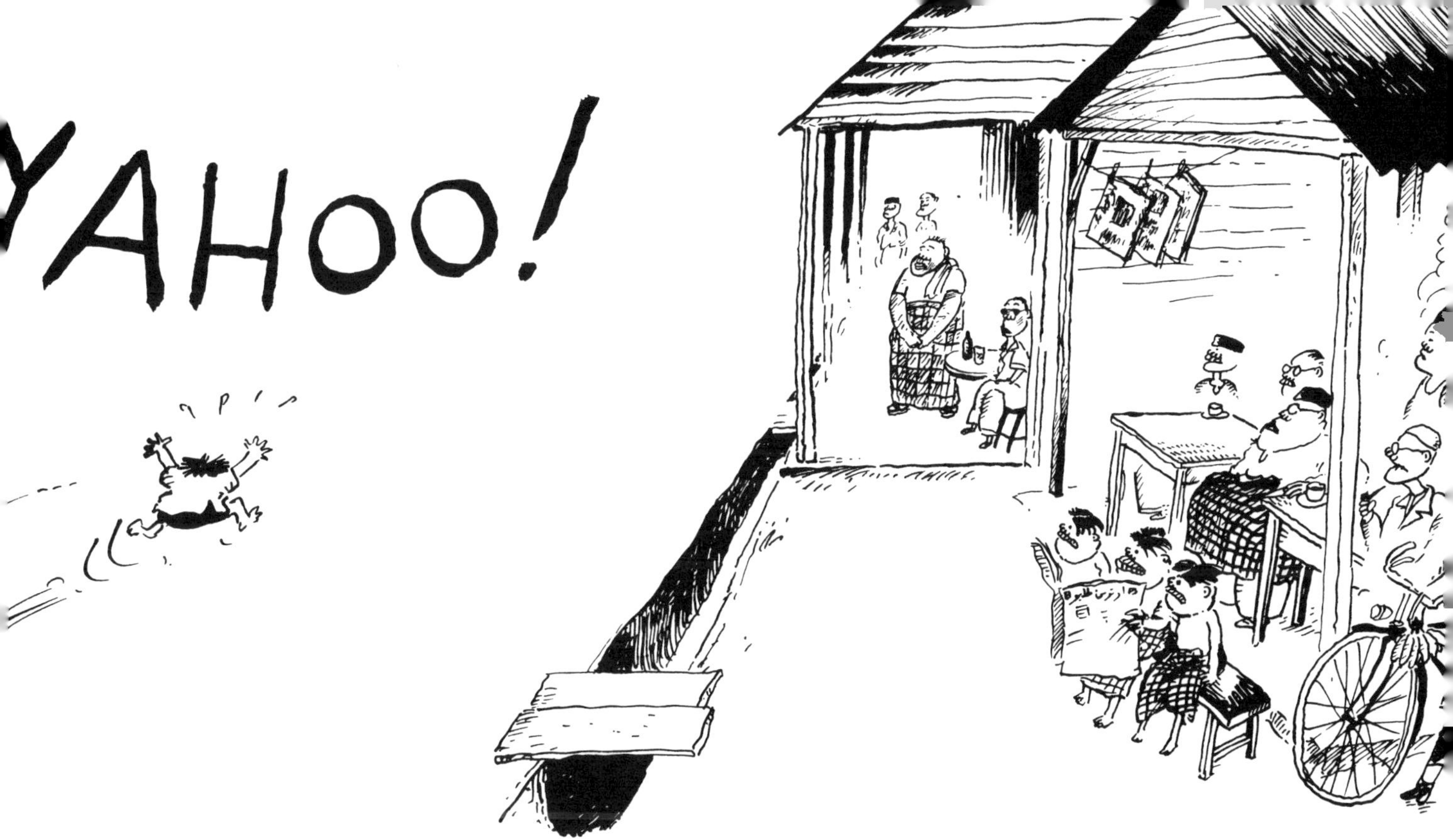
YAHOO!

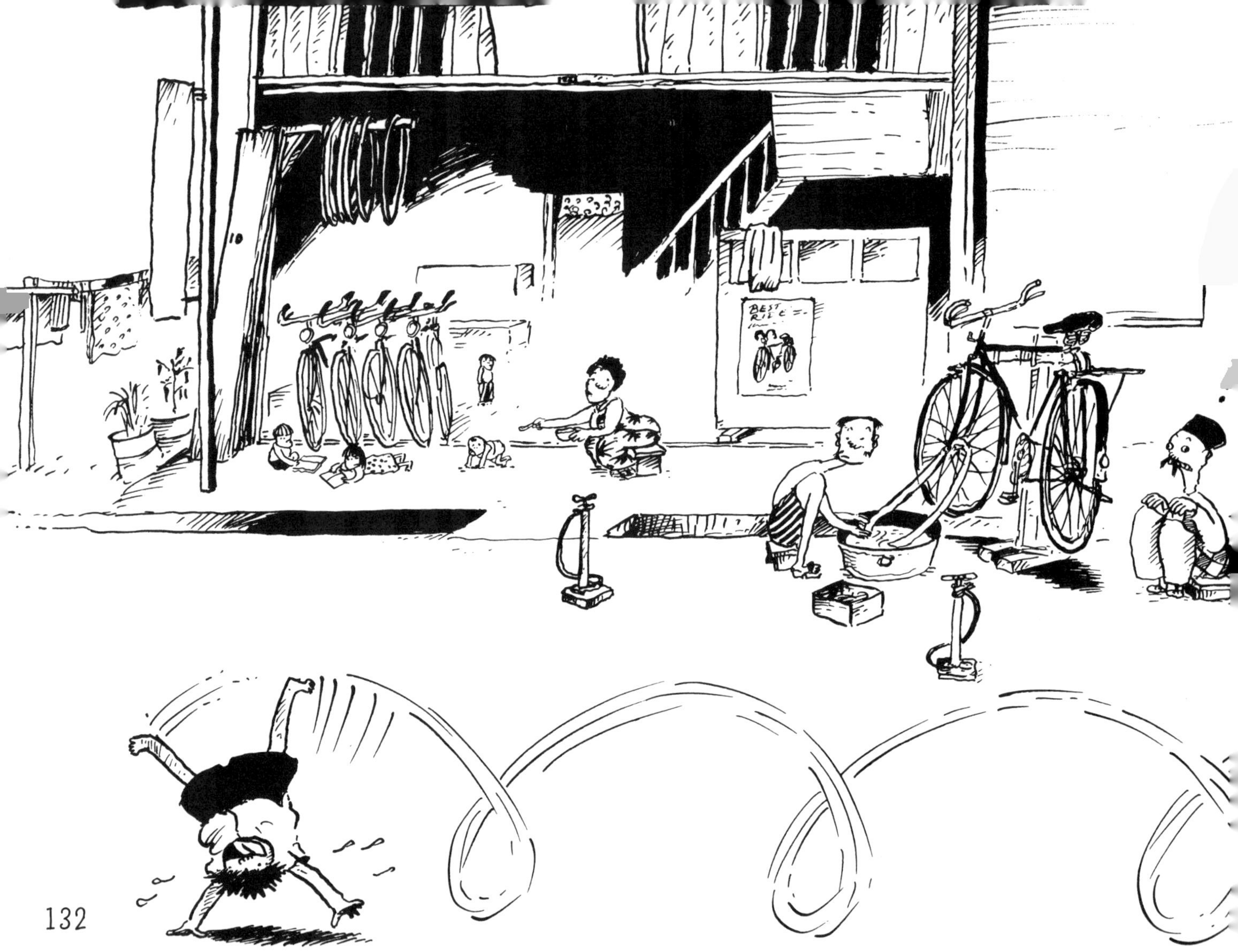
BEST

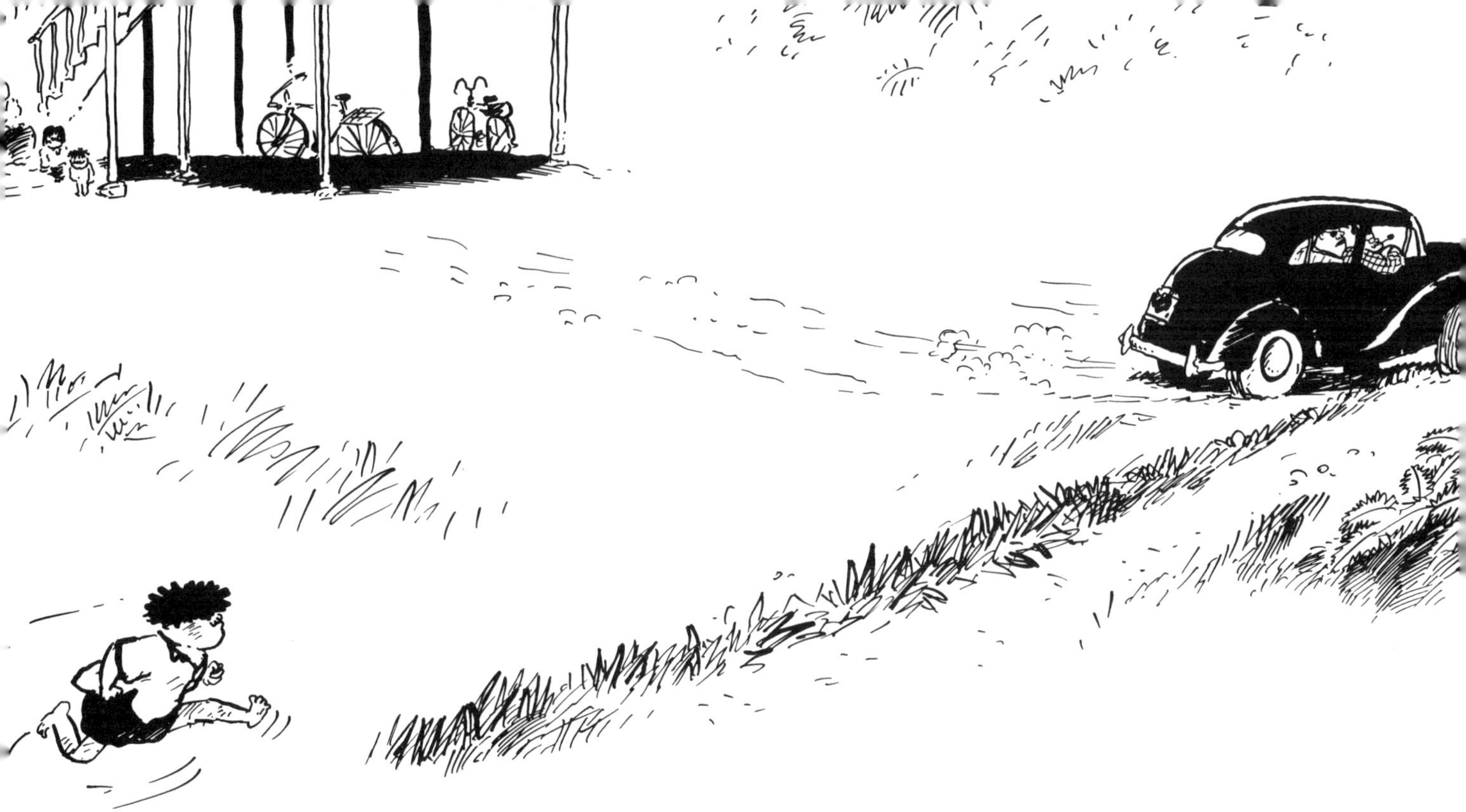

I couldn't wait to tell everyone at home. Especially Father.
But when I got back I saw him leaving in the land broker's motor-car.

Mother said she had known all along I would pass. When I asked where Father had gone with the land broker, she said: "They've gone to his plantation. It seems the tin company people are coming to inspect whether there's tin in the area. Many say there's a lot of tin here and if they buy the land it'll be quite a big sum.

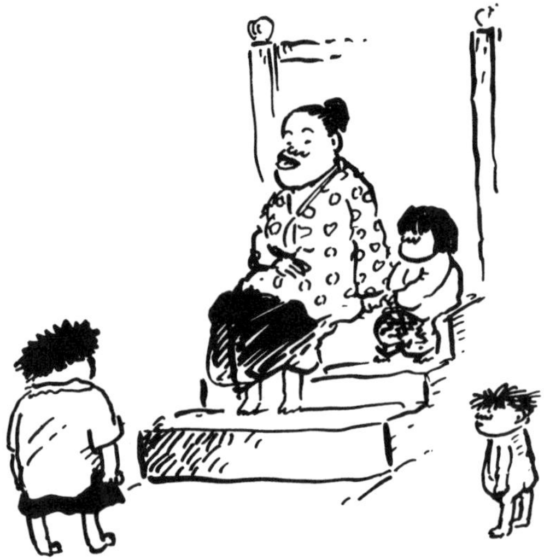

"If they do buy your father's land, we can use the money to get a home in the cheap housing development in Ipoh. Many local folks are thinking the same.

"The tin company people are going to tell us whether there's tin around here, too," she said.

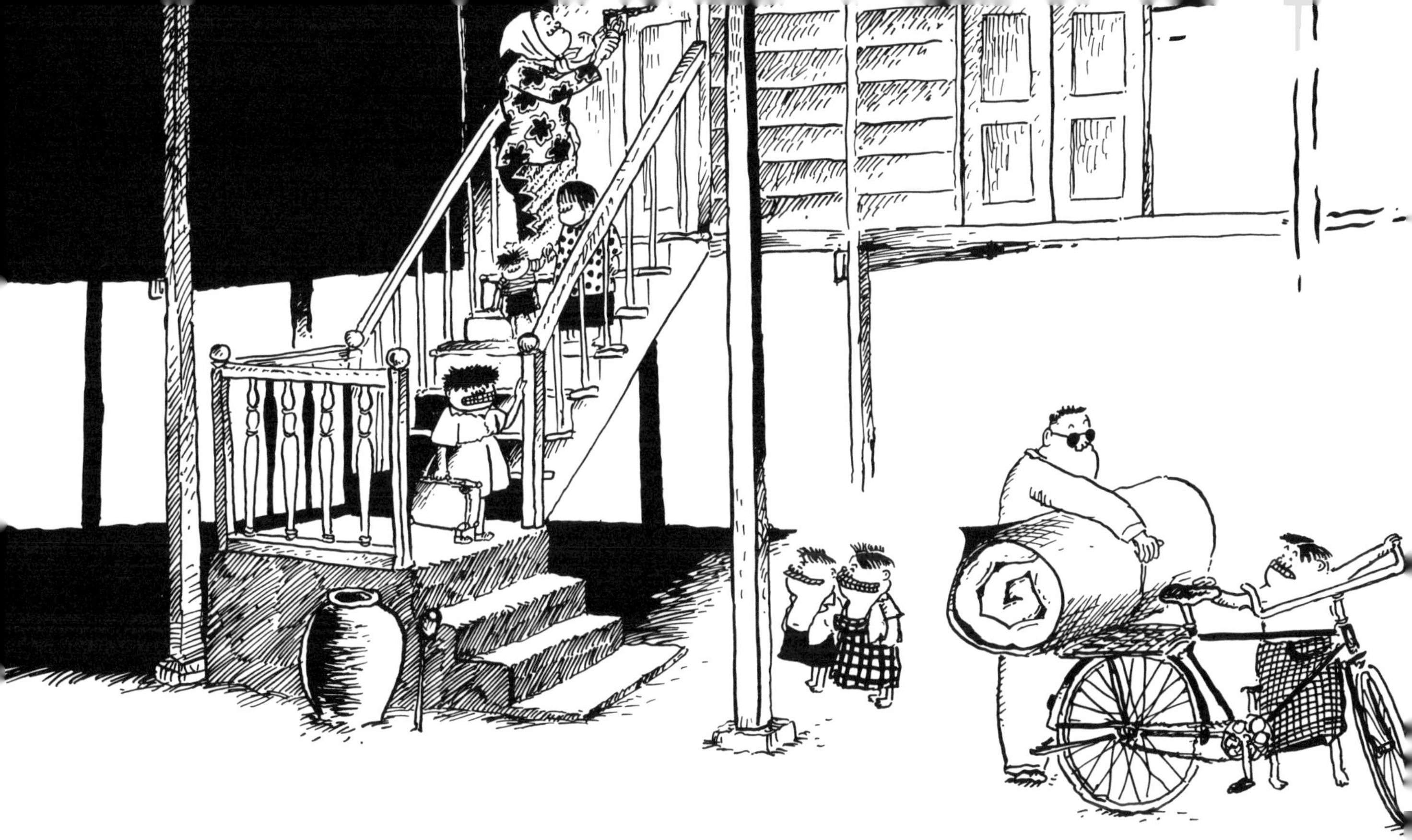

Weeks later, it was time for me to leave for the big school far away. The Meor brothers came to send me off that morning. Dad brought along a mattress (the hostel didn't supply mattresses).

I was looking forward to my new life...

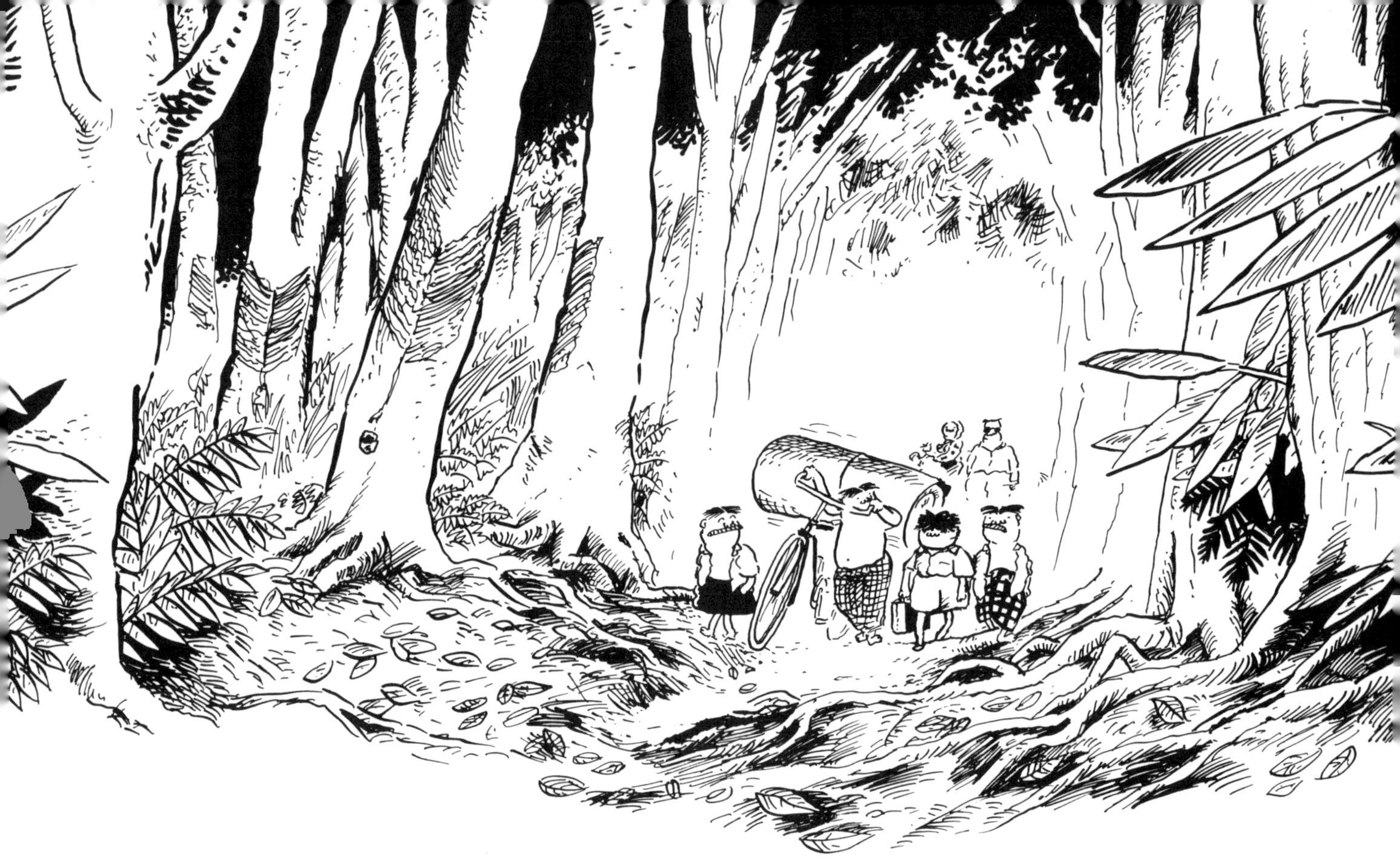

But it was about this time that I suddenly discovered emotions I never knew I felt.

I felt sad...

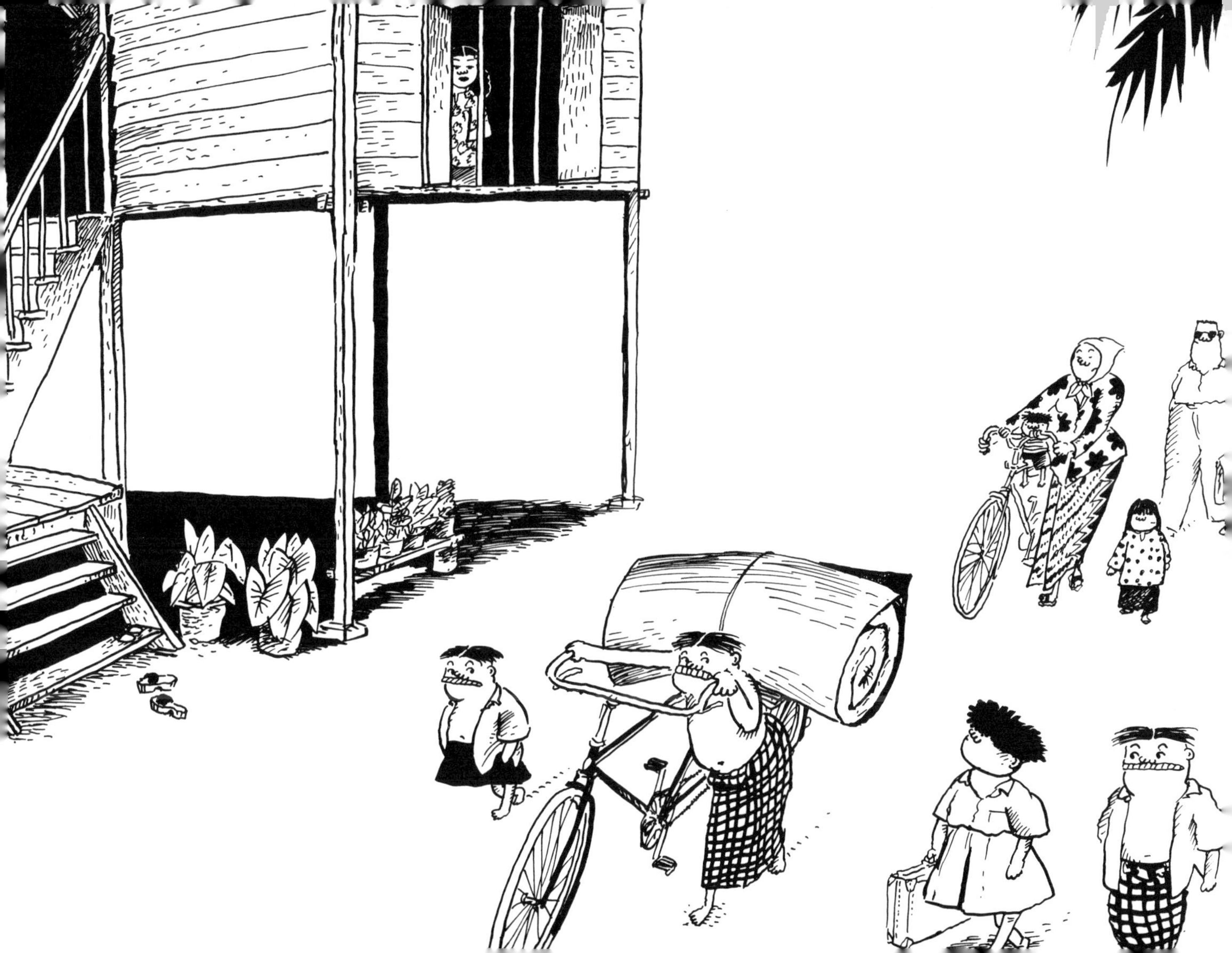

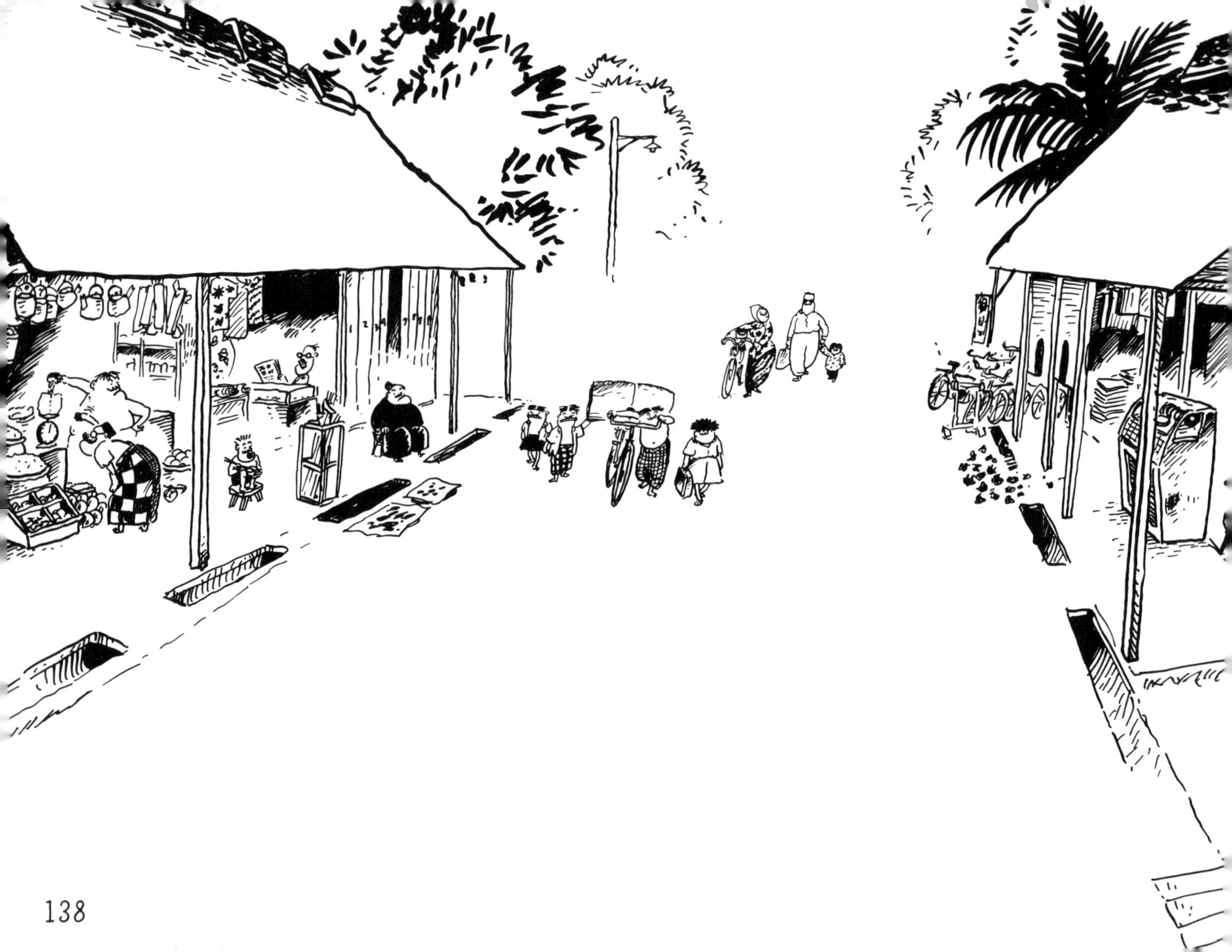

I still remember what my grandmother said while we waited for the bus: "Listen...don't be arrogant there. Be humble because we are humble people. Always remember God and don't forget about us back here in the kampung."

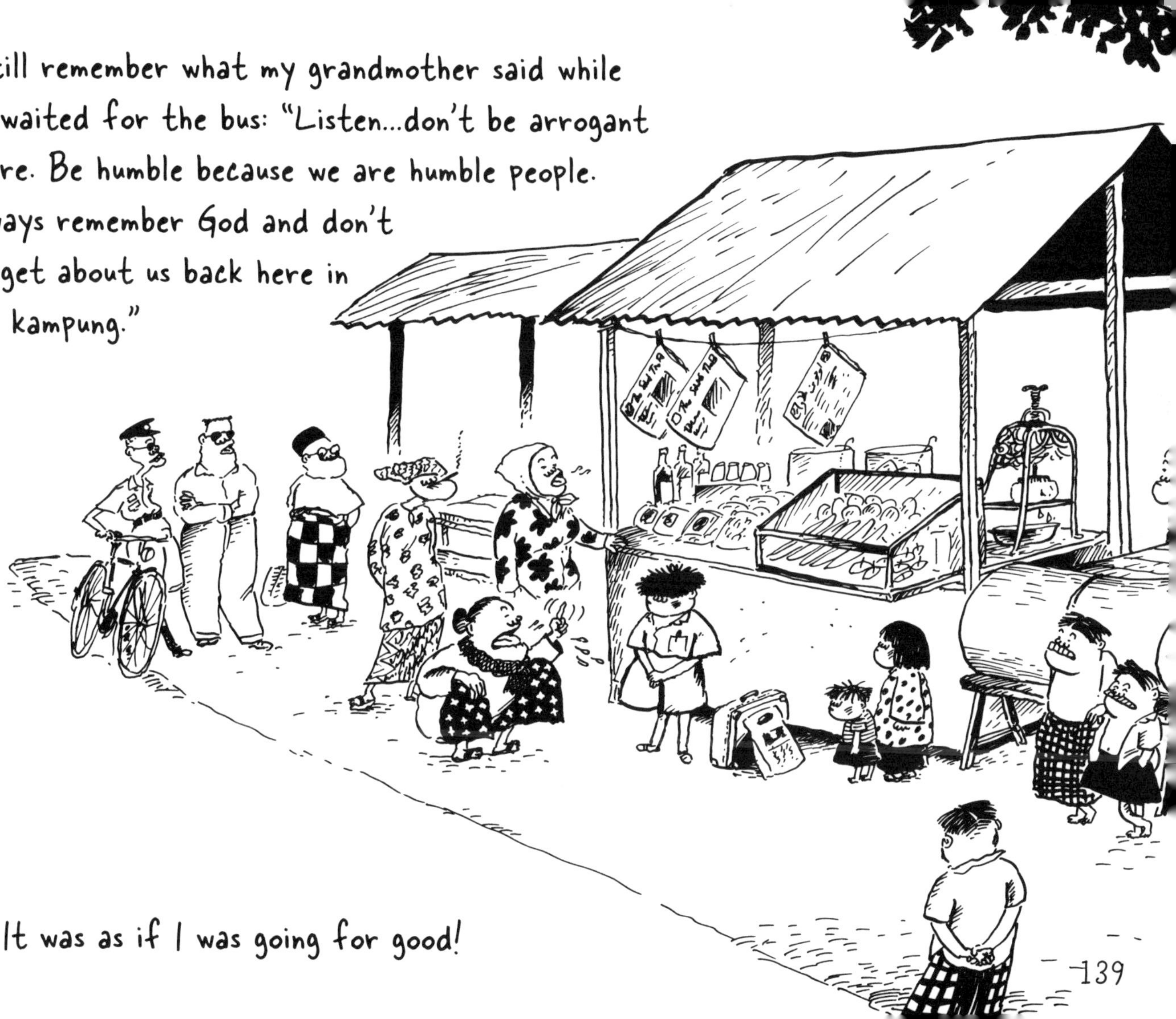

It was as if I was going for good!

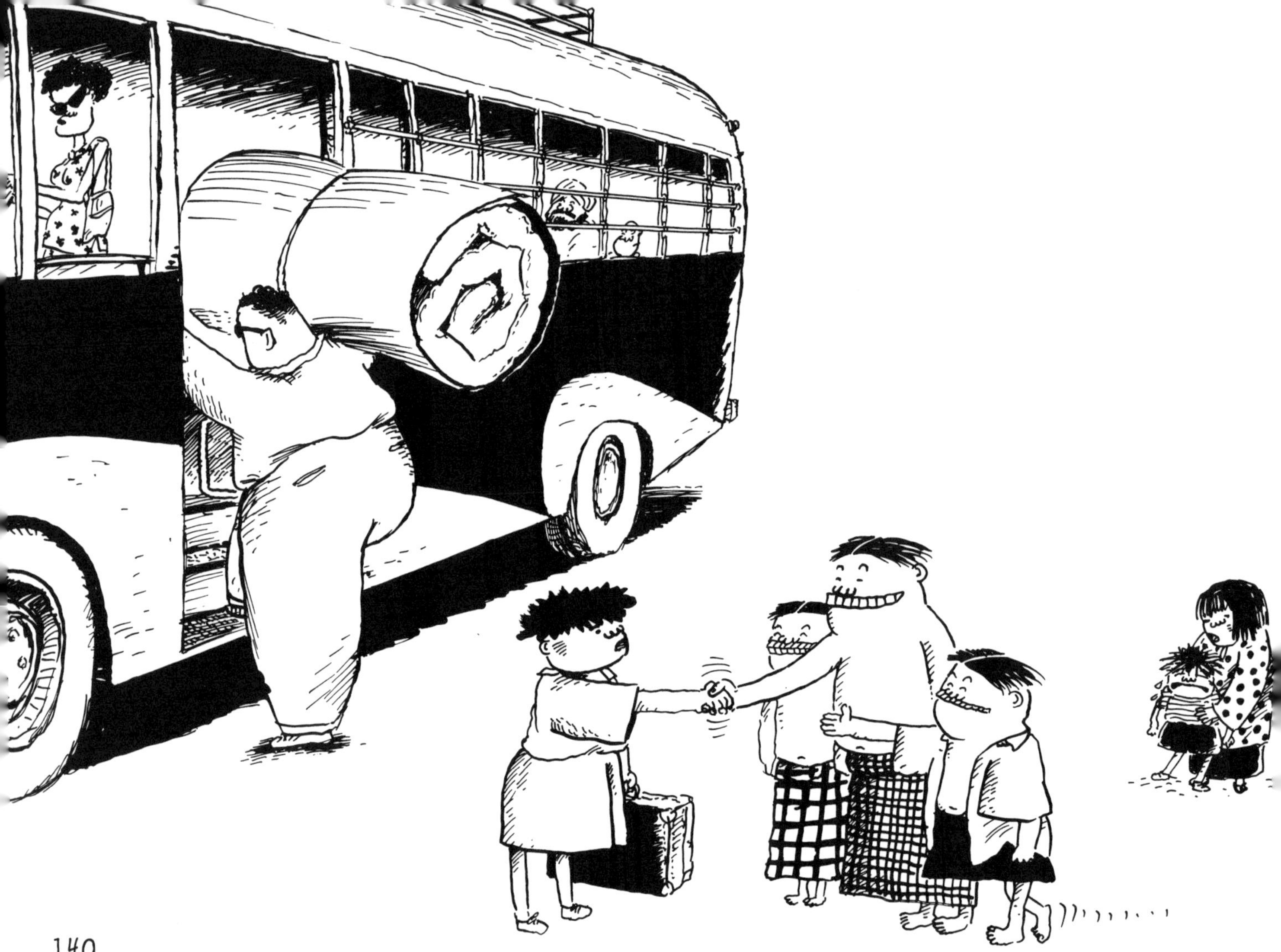

I couldn't describe my feelings as the bus took Dad and me away. I couldn't tell for sure whether the town folks I was going to meet would know my kampung when I mentioned its name...it was so small...people were so few. But I loved it so much...its river, its trees, the quiet houses, and my friends.

And I suddenly hoped they wouldn't find tin there because more than anything, I wanted my kampung to go back to.

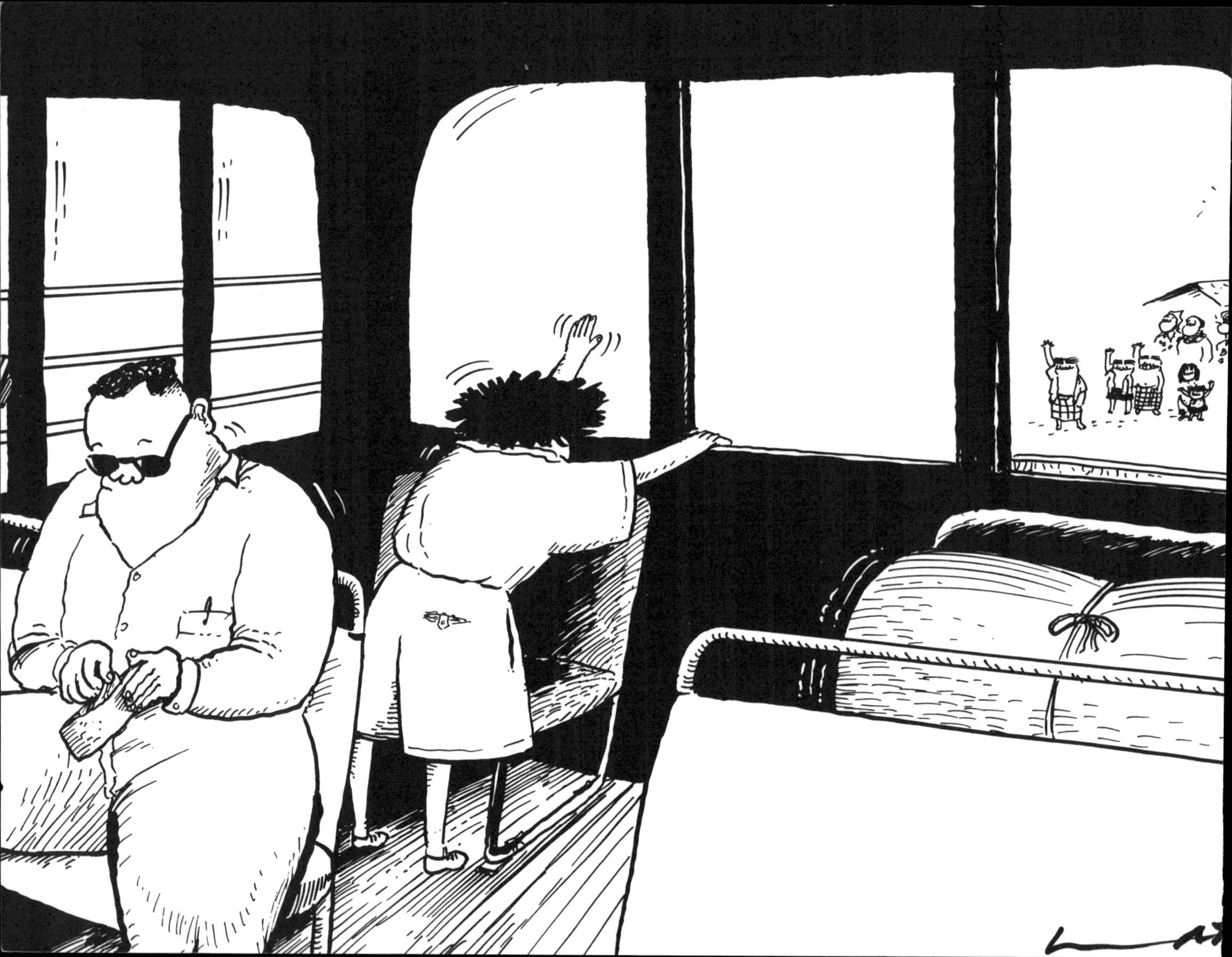

First Second
New York & London

Copyright © 1979 by Lat
Revised edition copyright © 2006 by First Second

Published by First Second
First Second is an imprint of Roaring Brook Press, a division of Holtzbrinck Publishing Holdings Limited Partnership
175 Fifth Avenue, New York, NY 10010

Distributed in Canada by H. B. Fenn and Company Ltd.
Distributed in the United Kingdom by Macmillan Children's Books, a division of Pan Macmillan.
Originally published in Malaysia in 1979 under the title *The Kampung Boy* by Berita Publishing Sdn. Bhd., Kuala Lumpur.

Design by Danica Novgorodoff

Library of Congress Cataloging-in-Publication Data

Lat.
[Lat, the kampung boy]
Kampung boy / by Lat. -- 1st American ed.
p. cm.
First published in Malaysia in 1979 under the title, Lat, the kampung boy, by Berita Publishing.
Summary: Relates the life experiences, from birth to beginning boarding school, of a boy growing up on a rubber plantation in rural Malaysia.
ISBN-13: 978-1-59643-121-8
ISBN-10: 1-59643-121-0

[1. Family life--Malaysia--Fiction. 2. Muslims--Fiction. 3. Countrylife--Malaysia--Fiction. 4. Malaysia--History--20th century--Fiction.]
I. Title.
PZ7.L3298Lat 2006
[Fic]--dc22
2005034135

First Second books are available for special promotions and premiums.
For details, contact: Director of Special Markets, Holtzbrinck Publishers.

First American Edition September 2006
Printed in China

5 7 9 10 8 6 4